W9-CIB-238

THE PERMANENT PLAN

THE PERMANENT PLAN

A Novel

By

Craig Bieber

CNC Alaska   Anchorage, Alaska

This is a work of fiction. Names, characters, places, and incidents either are the product of the author's imagination or are used fictitiously. Any resemblance to actual events or persons, living or dead, is entirely coincidental.

Copyright © 2010 by Craig Bieber

All rights reserved. No part of this book may be reproduced or transmitted in any form or by any means, electronic or mechanical, including photocopying, recording, or by any information storage and retrieval system, without permission in writing from the author.

This edition was prepared for printing by
Ghost River Images
5350 East Fourth Street
Tucson, Arizona 85711
ghostriverimages.com

Cover illustration by: Terri VandeVegte

ISBN 978-0-9801869-1-8

Library of Congress Control Number: 2010903354

View the website at craigbieber.com to Buy His Books,
or buy them at Amazon Books.

Printed in the United States of America

April, 2010

10 9 8 7 6 5 4 3 2 1

Contents

Acknowledgements

Many thanks to the people who supported me as I worked on *The Permanent Plan*, and to the readers who supported the original book about the Saylor Family, Saylor's Triangle. Thanks again to copy editor, Erin Wilcox, graphic designer, Terri Vande Vegte for the book covers and the proofread, and Michael White of Ghost River Images for preparing the book for publication. A special thank you goes to Richard E. Kelly, author of Growing Up In Mama's Club, for reading the manuscript and making suggestions that made The Permanent Plan a better book.

As always, I owe thanks to my family and close friends for their support. Also, I want to express my appreciation to Fred Longcoor for his continuing contributions.

The Author

Prologue

The Alaska Permanent Fund is the tenth-largest sovereign wealth fund in the world. Funds that are larger than Alaska's Permanent Fund belong to countries—not states. The fund is larger than any endowment, private foundation, or union pension trust in the United States. At the end of the 2006 fiscal year, its value was thirty-five billion dollars. The Permanent Fund was established in 1976 by a voter-approved amendment to the Constitution of the State of Alaska declaring that 25 percent of every dollar of revenue the state receives from in-state natural-resource development shall go into a dedicated rainy-day fund. A governor-appointed fund manager and a governor-appointed six-member board of trustees, and their staffs, manage the Alaska Permanent Fund.

Every man, woman, and child in Alaska shares in the Permanent Fund directly by participating in the Permanent Fund Dividend program, whereby residents who have filed a proper and timely dividend application receive a check from the State of Alaska every year. Yearly check values have ranged from one to two thousand dollars for each person. The only requirements are that applicants maintain a permanent residence in Alaska and that they remain physically present in the most beautiful, most remote, and most intimidating state in the country for at least six months out of each year. Most residents are unaware how significant their indirect benefit from the fund is. They blissfully accept their good fortune, living in a state with no income tax and very little sales tax, and blindly protest all types of natural-resource-development projects.

An over thirty-five billion–dollar fund that is invested in publicly traded stocks, private equities, bonds, real estate, and alternative assets in various places around the world makes Alaska the wealthiest state in the United States. Alaska rarely wrestles with budget deficits, and often deals with budget surpluses. Fluctuations in the state's budget are primarily the result of the vagaries of market prices for oil and gas. Through it all, the Permanent Fund remains as a golden parachute for Alaska in times of need. It is not apparent that it has ever been viewed as a thirty-five billion–dollar golden egg for the taking by unscrupulous moneymen . . ..

Greed brings out the worst in mankind. It is not specific to gender, race, or religion, and the limits of the means to the larcenous end are generally proportionate to the size of the prize.
— Fred Longcoor

Fred Longcoor continues his association with the author by contributing incisive and appropriate comments at the completion of each chapter. Many of his comments are drawn from the pages of his unpublished work, Fred Longcoor's Book on Life.

Chapter 1

The Permanent Seed

I can make you rich . . . rich beyond your wildest dreams. You just have to be willing to put a year or two into this.

The words echoed in Stan Faro's mind as the Learjet approached the paved, private runway on the Peet Ranch in southwest Montana. He had barely paid attention a few minutes earlier when the pilot pointed out the fact that they were flying over Ted Turner's Flying D Ranch . . . all 113,600 acres of it!

Stan was tired after the red-eye flight from Anchorage to Salt Lake City and the short flight in Billy Peet's private jet. Tired, and anxious. He thought about the conversation he'd had a week earlier that led to his being in a luxurious private jet, landing in a place he had never imagined he'd find himself.

"Stan my boy, what have you been up to? Have you achieved all the success you and I talked about having in college all those years ago? Are you a rich man? Do you have a trophy wife, a private jet, homes in Montana, Cabo, and San Diego, and a big-ass garage with a couple dozen expensive cars in it?"

As Stan looked around his plain office in downtown Anchorage, he sighed to himself, and grudgingly replied to Billy's loaded question, "No Billy, I ain't got none of that shit. I have a fat ex-wife who left with half of what little I had, a rented apartment, a beat-up old pickup, and I couldn't make a down payment on an ice bucket for a private jet."

9

Stan knew something was coming, but he bit anyway. "And why do you ask?"

"Well, Stanley, because I have all that. I am talking to you from my den in my fourteen-thousand-square-foot ranch house, on my two-thousand-acre ranch in Montana. I just flew back here in my private Learjet from my three-million-dollar house on the beach near Cabo. My beautiful blonde wife . . . my very young, beautiful blonde wife, is taking a little nap to recover from all the fucking we did while we were in Mexico."

There was a pause as Billy let this diatribe sink in.

"Billy, I—"

Ignoring Stan, Billy continued. "Do you know how I got all of this, Stan? Do you have a clue how I got this disgustingly rich?" Billy laughed a wicked, coarse laugh, and continued. "I fucked a lot of people out of their money."

Now he laughed even louder.

Stan was glad to hear from his old college friend, but he couldn't bring himself to join in the merriment. "Well, Billy, I always knew you had larceny in your soul. It sounds like it worked for you."

Billy laughed into the phone again. "You hit it right on the fucking head, Stan my boy. It's worked *very well*."

"Okay, Billy. I think I get it, but what does it have to do with me?"

Billy quickly took on a serious tone. "Because I can do the same thing for *you*. I can make you rich . . . rich beyond your wildest dreams."

"Me? Why me? We haven't even talked to each other in at least ten years. What the hell can I do for you?"

"Well, Stan my boy, you just happen to be in the right place at the right time. You are the man I need."

Stan was confused, but definitely curious. "For what?"

"I've done a little checking. You've had some success in Anchorage. You're sort of a man about town . . . civically involved, kind of well known. You've been connected to a lot of things around there."

"I'm not sure what . . . What do you mean you've checked on me?" Stan tried to sound indignant, even though he didn't want to piss Billy off until he found out what the unexpected call was all about.

"Well, I know you have a degree, 'cause you and I were in college together . . . even though I didn't finish. And, I know you were on the board of directors for the Save the Inlet Wetlands Committee, director of the Denali League, and community advisor for the McKinley Oil Company. You've umpired Little League games for years, you've even been junior pastor at your church—and you sell real estate."

"I don't know what you're getting at, Billy, but none of that means shit. I really haven't done much of anything important."

"I think you underestimate yourself. Those little things look good on a resume, and they impact a lot of people. You've done enough to interest me. If I've said enough to interest you, I want you to fly down here and talk about it."

"Billy, I don't have any idea what you're up to, but I just couldn't do that . . . not right now. I . . . I just couldn't afford it."

After another laugh, Billy said, "You didn't think I'd ask you to pay for it, did you? I'll buy your ticket, first class, and then I'll have my Lear pick you up in Salt Lake. Now, when can you get down here?"

The wheels on the jet screeched as they touched the runway, and jolted Stan back into the present. He looked out the window at the endless rolling prairie passing the plane as it slowed. The wheat-colored grass looked crisp as it gently swayed in the cool November air. He turned his gaze back to admire the luxurious interior of the Learjet. He rubbed the leather seats once more, took in the flat-screen televisions fore and aft, and smiled as he looked at the fully stocked bar. Silently, he wondered to himself, *what the hell am I doing here?*

The jet eased to a full stop in front of a spacious-looking steel building with a large overhead door. The building appeared to be an aircraft hangar that was way too big for the Learjet. After the door to the jet was opened, the huge overhead door to the building began to open slowly. A shiny black Hummer pulled out as soon as there was enough room for it to clear the bottom of the door. Stan wasn't sure what to expect, and he was surprised when the older, but familiar, figure of Billy Peet climbed out of the driver's side.

Billy was still portly, and his hair had thinned, but he still looked like the same guy Stan knew in college—a big happy-looking guy who immediately knew everybody, no matter where he went. He still marveled at how many attractive coeds Billy had bedded when they were in college. He was far from being a good-looking man.

Billy had his arms out and a big smile on his face as he approached Stan. "How are you, my old friend?"

Stan fell into Billy's bear hug uncomfortably and murmured into his huge chest, "I'm fine, Billy, I'm fine. How are you?"

"I'm great, Stan. . . . I'm rich, and I'm great. And, my old friend Stan has come to visit me. What more could I want?"

After getting in the Hummer, they drove along a well-maintained gravel road for a half mile, and then the ranch house came into view.

It was set in a low area near a medium-sized stream. The backdrop of mature cottonwood trees that ran along both sides of the stream made a beautiful frame for the sprawling single-story brick home. Stan tried to imagine how it would look when everything was in full bloom in the summer.

A short distance from the back of the house sat another huge steel building that looked like it was meant to store equipment, and next to it was a large, classically shaped red barn with white trim. Everything reminded Stan of his impression of Billy when they were in college: a big personal slob of a man, who was fastidious about his surroundings.

"Beautiful home, Billy," Stan remarked sincerely.

"Just wait, Stan my boy. Just wait to see the inside . . . and what's *in* the inside." Billy laughed his coarse laugh again.

Billy parked the Hummer in front of the house, and Stan followed him along the stone pathway, which wound through a perfectly landscaped and manicured yard. Billy opened the right side of the huge double front doors, and they walked into a spacious entryway that led to a massive living room. Everything in every part of the house Stan could see looked large and expensive, from the heavy leather chairs and couches in the living room to the grand art pieces on the walls and on pedestals throughout the rooms.

"Billy, you've obviously done something right. This is spectacular. Everything I've seen so far is spectacular. I've read about people who live like this, but wow. . . ."

"Yeah, Stan my boy, and you can have a little taste of this. . . . Actually, you can have a big taste of this. I'm not saying you can be as rich as me . . . at least not right away, but you *can* be living the high life."

"Okay, there you go again. I mean, I'm tired, but when are we going to get down to what this is all about?"

"Relax, Stan my boy. Let's get reacquainted. You still drink that rotgut shit you drank in college . . . what was it, rum and coke, or would you prefer a real man's drink? I've got some of the finest single-malt scotches in the world in my bar. Let's have a scotch."

Stan hadn't developed a taste for scotch, but he said, "Sure, let's have a scotch. You pick one." *I don't care which one, because it's going to taste like shit to me anyway,* he thought.

Billy whistled happily to himself as he poured two large glasses of scotch that cost more than Stan's food bill for a week. He brought them back and set them on the enormous glass-topped coffee table between two of the overstuffed chairs.

Stan lifted his glass toward Billy, and said, "Thank you, and thank you for the first-class ride down here."

"You're welcome, Stan my boy . . . and welcome to my humble abode."

Stan was already thinking that if he heard *Stan my boy* one more time, he was going to puke, but he humored Billy. "This is far from humble. Exactly how did you get this fucking rich, I mean, how many people did you have to kill to get this rich?"

Billy let out a belly laugh, and said, "Thank God. I thought the Stan I used to know had dried up and blown away. That sounded like the old Stan, the one who didn't give a shit what he said. The one who always got right to the point."

"Well, I was kidding, but I'm sure you understand how this whole thing would make someone very curious."

Billy struggled to move his big body forward so he could sit on the front edge of the puffy chair, and put a serious look on his face as he said, "I do understand. You and I haven't talked for years, but when this deal came about, I told my business associates that I thought I had just the man to pull it off in Alaska."

"Pull it off? That sounds . . . I don't know, it sounds . . . illegal."

"That's the beauty of it, Stan my boy. It's not illegal. It's beautifully legal. It *is* involved, and if *you* want to be involved, you just have to be willing to put a year or two into it. A year or two that will set you up for life . . . this life." Billy swung his right hand around the room to designate his surroundings.

"Okay, Billy. How could I not be interested? I barely have a pot to piss in after working my ass off all of my adult life. You've surrounded me with more luxury in the last twelve hours than I've had in a lifetime. But I'm not a criminal. . . . You need to know that. I have no idea what it is you want me for, but I'm just not a criminal."

Billy ignored Stan's final comment, and struggled to pull himself out of the big chair. "I need another scotch, Stan my boy. How about you?"

Stan looked at his almost-full glass and replied, "No, Billy. I'm good. It's too early in the day for me, and I've had a long night."

Billy headed toward the bar, telling Stan as he went, "You need to man up. If you want to play with the big dogs, you need to man up."

Stan was becoming impatient to get to the bottom of whatever it was Billy had up his sleeve when one of the most gorgeous women he had ever seen walked out of the hallway and into the living room. She was tall and blonde, and she wore nothing more than a Denver Broncos tee shirt and a pair of brief white panties.

Stan was so taken, he barely heard Billy greet her. "Hey, baby. How was your little nap?"

The beautiful woman didn't react to Stan's presence, even though it was obvious she had to have seen him in the room. In a deeply accented, sugary voice, she replied, "I slept like a tree."

"Log, baby, you slept like a log." Billy was walking toward her as he corrected her. "Anna, this is my friend Stan, Stan Faro, from Alaska . . . you know, sled dogs, oil."

Stan couldn't move as the scantily clad woman walked toward him. He started to put his hand out, but she pushed her way into him and gave him a big hug. Her face was inches away from him, and he noticed that she smelled like honey as she said, "Hello, Mr. Stan. It's nice to meet you."

Stan was thinking how much he would like for her to stay where she was forever as he replied. "Uh . . . hello. It's nice to meet you as well."

As she let Stan go, and backed up, Billy came up next to her and put his arm around her. "What do you think about this import, Stan? Anna is Russian. Not only is she beautiful, she is smart, and she can cook . . . although she doesn't have to, because I've got people to do that . . . *and, she can suck your dick dry.*"

Billy laughed joyously, Stan's face turned ashen, and Anna's face took on a demure look that was a little too practiced.

"Alright. We've got business to talk about. Let's walk out to the garage. Bring your drink with you. Anna, you probably should get dressed."

Billy led Stan across the large paved area in the back of the ranch house to the steel building. He entered a code on the electronic keypad of an industrial sized door-lock on a small side door, and they entered the building. The interior was slightly illuminated with several dim lights, and Billy flicked on a row of light switches at the side of the doorway. Bright lights illuminated a colorful scene that looked like a metallic candy store. Rows of all makes, models, and colors of showroom-ready classic cars were angle-parked along the building's outside walls, and two rows of angle-parked cars that were butted up to each other sat in a line down the middle of the building.

"Holy shit," were the only words Stan could utter, as he thought to himself, *I don't know what all of these are, but there must be a million dollars' worth of cars in here!*

"Stan my boy, feast your eyes on over two million dollars' worth of cars. It's not the biggest collection in the world, but it's one of the finest."

Billy had barely finished his proud pronouncement about the car collection, when a deep voice no more than two feet behind Stan made him jump.

"Yeah, and I make sure it stays that way."

Stan turned and looked squarely up into the face of one of the largest American Indians he had ever seen. He was dressed in a camouflage uniform and had a handgun holstered at his belt. A two-way radio receiver was fastened to his shirt on the front of his left shoulder. "Stan my boy, this is Jeremiah Standing Tall. He is the head of my security detail. The ranch and the outbuildings . . . especially *this* building, are watched over twenty-four–seven by a detail of eight men who work in shifts. There are always at least two men on duty right around the ranch complex."

"Okay, well you scared the crap out of me, so you must be good at what you do."

It was obvious Jeremiah did not see the humor in Stan's comment, and he said, "That's my job. Nice to meet you." With that, Jeremiah walked away toward the back of the building.

"Man of few words," Stan mumbled.

"Jeremiah has a job to do, and he's serious about it. Enough about that shit. What do you think about my little pile of cars?" Billy started down the rows of cars in the middle of the building, "'34 Ford Roadster, '69 Camaro, '71 GTX—as you can see, I love the muscle cars—'57 Chevy, '69 Boss 429 Mustang, and look at this beautiful '66 GTO. I paid fifty thousand bucks for it. Stole it."

Stan was enjoying the show, but his anxiety level was growing. *What the hell is this all about? What kind of character has Billy become? What am I getting myself into?*

Stan finally blurted it out. "Billy, what the hell am I doing here? I mean, this is a beautiful and impressive car collection. You have a beautiful home, a beautiful wife, a lovely airplane . . . but what the hell does it have to do with me?"

Billy's reaction was to stand and look at Stan with a big grin on his face, not to get angry, as Stan feared he might. "You are right, Stan. Let's get to the heart of this. Come to the back of the garage. I have a little place there I call my man-room where we can talk."

Billy's spacious man-room looked more like a den than a room in a garage. The heavy-leather look that prevailed in the ranch house spilled over into the man-room. All the requisite man-room fittings were there . . . pool table, wet bar, flat-screen TVs everywhere, and a beautiful mahogany poker table with padded leather chairs sitting in one corner. The considerable inventory of furniture was large and comfortable, and all of it rested on a polished dark hardwood floor that Stan guessed was made from some high-dollar wood that nobody else would dream of putting in a garage.

"Let's sit, Stan. Are you ready for another scotch?"

Stan realized that he had finished his first drink, and suddenly, another sounded like a good idea. He decided he may need it . . . and it hadn't tasted too bad at all. "Yeah . . . bring it on."

"That's my boy."

Well, that's better than Stan my boy, thought Stan.

Billy returned with two large glasses of scotch and set them on the table next to Stan. He eased his big body into the chair across from him again and began to talk.

"Well, my old buddy, me and my associates . . . and by the way, these are guys who I have made lots of money with over the years. Anyway, we stumbled upon an idea a while back, and we have been working on it for a couple of years now." Billy paused for a moment and took a big sip out of his glass.

Billy sat back, and continued. "We are at the point now, where we need somebody else to be involved . . . an Alaskan, an established Alaskan. Somebody like you."

Stan began to stammer. "But . . . but I—"

"Let me finish, Stan. Whoever we find to do this job, whether it is you or somebody else, is going to make a lot of money. We are proposing a salary of one hundred thousand dollars a year, probably for two years, and an unlimited expense account . . . because you will be doing a lot of wining and dining. And here's the kicker. You . . . or somebody, will get a five percent share of everything we make."

"Holy shi—"

"Hear me out, Stan. You . . . or somebody, will be soaring with the eagles. I thought of you because we were buddies in college, and because I knew you lived in Alaska. When I did a little research on you, I knew you were perfect."

The scotch was making Stan bolder, and he said, "Perfect for what, Billy? What the fuck are you talking about? I mean, if you want me to kill somebody, that's just not my style."

Stan's comment was tongue-in-cheek, but Billy was serious as he said, "I don't want you to kill anybody. I can find experienced people to do that." A chill ran down Stan's back as Billy continued, "At this point, I can't divulge what we need you to do. All I can tell you is that it isn't illegal, it isn't dangerous, and it will be a life-changing experience for you. We need to build you into more of a community leader and an important businessman . . . in Anchorage, and in Alaska. A *respected* community leader and a *respected* businessman. We—"

"Wait a minute," Stan blurted out. "You flew me down here to tell me you're going to pay me one hundred thousand dollars a year to do something . . . and you're not going to tell me what it is? This is fucking crazy."

Billy wasn't used to being interrupted, but he hid his irritation and replied to Stan as calmly as he could. "Stan, nobody pays somebody one hundred thousand dollars a year without having a real good reason for doing that . . . not even people as rich as me. And if an old friend tells you that it is not illegal and you won't get hurt, it is up to you to decide whether or not you are willing to gamble on that."

Billy struggled forward in the big chair again, and said, "Don't you get it? You just *happen* to be the lucky fucker who *happens* to know me. I . . . we, need somebody . . . you, to get ready to move into a position in Alaska in a year or so where you can help us. Not illegally, but by using your relationships and your experience . . . relationships and experience you are going to build on over the next year or so, by using your big fat salary, your big fat expense account, and some surprising opportunities that are going to come your way."

The tortured look that came over Billy's face as he tried to hide his inner frustration was lost on Stan, who was too much into his own evaluation of what this was all about to understand the nuances of Billy Peet's demeanor.

Take it easy, Billy said to himself, *you knew he wasn't going to just roll over for this.*

Billy hesitated for a moment before he spoke again. He knew he could find somebody other than Stan for this job, but it wouldn't be easy. He knew he had to handle him with kid gloves. "Well buddy, you know, you've been up all night, and you've got to be tired and jet-lagged. How about getting a little rest, and then we'll have a nice dinner and talk more tonight."

Stan needed time to think. "Sounds good," he said. "I'm really tired."

They headed back to the ranch house, and Billy led Stan to a large guest bedroom. The king-sized bed looked inviting. Stan was tired, and he didn't care where he slept. As Billy was closing the door to leave the room, he turned and said, "Okay, I'm not going to bother you until six o'clock, but if you're not up by then, I'm coming to get you. The bathroom . . . excuse me, your private bathroom, is through that door."

Stan was vaguely aware of voices and laughter in the main part of the house, but it didn't bother him, and he was asleep within minutes. The two glasses of scotch were all the sleep medicine he needed.

In Billy's large den, which also functioned as his office, he was talking on the phone, occasionally laughing or making a reply. The den was a long way from the bedroom Stan was sleeping in, and Billy had his door closed, so he wasn't worried about talking out loud to the caller.

"Yeah, he's here. . . . No, well, maybe a little bit. I mean, in some ways, he's the same old Stan, but he's also . . . a little more conservative than he was in college."

Again, Billy listened intently, and replied, "I think he'll be fine. I still believe he's our guy. Like I said, I saw flashes of the old Stan. He's tired, you know, been up all night flying from Anchorage, and I poured two scotches down him. Let me see how he is tonight."

After listening for several minutes, Billy spoke again. "I know how careful we have to be. I also know that we have to get moving. Making a schmuck . . . even though he's a likeable schmuck, into a golden political prince in a year is not the easiest thing in the world to do. I mean, Stan's right when he says he's a nobody. We're going to have to call in some really big chits."

The caller made a closing comment, and Billy laughed his devious laugh. "He'll do it. I haven't come close to laying the trump card on him, and I won't until I've worked him a lot more than I did this morning."

At fifteen minutes to six, Billy heard the guest bathroom being used. When Stan walked into the living room twenty minutes later, he was showered and shaved, and he looked like a new man.

"Stan my boy, you look rested. How'd you sleep?"

"Uh . . . fine. That's a comfortable bed, and it's quiet out here."

"Yeah. No ambulances, commercial jets, trains . . . nothing but the birds and rabbits."

Stan noticed the drink in Billy's hand, and wondered if he had been drinking the whole time he was sleeping. "I think I'd like one of those," Stan said, nodding toward Billy's hand.

"Alright. . . . Stanley is coming around. Too bad we're not back in college. We could run around town, get drunk, and go home without getting laid again." Billy laughed at himself as he headed to the bar.

"We're not in college anymore Billy," Stan said, thinking how it seemed a little like saying, *We're not in Kansas anymore.*

"That's no shit, Stan my boy. We're in the big time . . . at least I am. What about you? You want to be in the big time, Stan, or do you want to scramble for every dime for the rest of your life?" Billy handed Stan his scotch on the rocks as he challenged him.

Stan felt a little more together than he had when he arrived at Billy's ranch in the morning. He had lain in the bed for a while after he awoke from his nap, trying to rationalize his feelings. He still wasn't convinced that he wanted anything to do with Billy's plan . . . but he *was* interested in hearing more about it. "I guess I'm ready to listen to the master," he said.

There was a hint of sarcasm in Stan's voice, and Billy was not sure about his intention, so he replied with his typical bravado. "That's my boy.

Let's talk about bringing you into Billy's world. What do you think about what I told you this morning? Are you interested, or at least interested enough to listen to me a little longer?"

"I . . . I'm . . . I'm interested. I mean, I'm . . . curious."

"Good, Stanley. Let's sit and talk." Stan was trying to figure out why Billy had switched from calling him *Stan my boy*, to calling him *Stanley*, as he was being led into the living room. "I know you're an honorable man, Stanley. I guess I knew that in college. You don't have to break the law to participate in our . . . *plan*. You can move into an income bracket you've never been in before right away, and you can become comfortably well-to-do in a year or two. And, you don't have to break the law. Eventually, you will need to provide a little inside information, a little inside guidance, and maybe, some inside influence."

Stan was listening to Billy intently when Anna walked out of the hallway and into the kitchen. His mind went blank at the sight of her. Her flowing black evening gown was sheer, and it clearly revealed that she was not wearing a bra, and that she had the tiniest pair of black panties on under it. Billy glanced at her nonchalantly as she walked passed them and said, "Hi babe."

"Hi Billy. Do we have any champagne? Since we have a guest tonight, I think I want some champagne."

Billy hurriedly pulled his big body out of his chair, and headed toward the bar like a manservant intent on pleasing the lady of the house. "Yes babe, we've got champagne . . . the best."

With the welcome addition of Anna to Billy and Stan's party of collusion, an evening of drinking and eating began. Chef Bryan, a young man who seemed to be too worldly, too handsome, and too talented to be working at a ranch in the middle of Montana, appeared out of nowhere, and served a spectacular parade of hors d' oeuvres that was followed by a wonderful fresh lobster and Kobe Beef dinner. Billy became more and more animated as he described the virtues of being very rich and making Stan very rich, and Anna happily paraded around the ranch house in her seductive evening wear. Even though the scotch was getting to Stan, the entire scenario was still unbelievable to him.

It was almost midnight when Stan told Billy that he wanted to be part of his plan. Emboldened by the whiskey, he said, "You can't ask me to do anything illegal. I won't do it."

Billy's affirmative reply would be lost in the foggy memory of the evening. Shortly after that, Stan made a slobbery apology about needing to go to bed, and staggered down the hallway.

Sometime later, Stan heard his bedroom door opening. He was intoxicated enough that he wasn't sure if he was dreaming, or if someone was really entering the room. He couldn't move. Then it hit him. Even in his alcohol-induced state, the smell of honey permeated his senses. *Oh my God, Anna's in my room,* he thought. *Billy's going to kill me!*

Stan felt light pressure as Anna sat on the side of the bed. He felt her hand softly touching the covers on his right thigh. She left her hand there for what seemed like an eternity. He felt the beginnings of an erection, and wished she would move her hand higher . . . followed quickly by fear that she would. Then, Anna got up from the side of the bed and stood silently for a moment.

Stan's eyes were adjusting to the small amount of light coming into the room through the partially open bedroom door when he saw Anna begin to remove her filmy evening dress.

Shit, he thought, *Billy really is going to kill me!*

Anna pulled the sheer garment off over her head, revealing the most perfect set of breasts he had ever seen. Stan broke into an instant sweat.

In what seemed like the best slow-motion scene he had ever witnessed, she elegantly pulled her tiny pair of black bikini panties down to her feet and then slowly pulled one foot and then the other out of them. In the semidarkness, Stan could see a neatly trimmed triangle of downy blonde hair. He was too afraid to move or speak, so he did neither. After what seemed like an eternity, Anna bent over Stan and kissed him lightly on the cheek. The smell of honey emanating from the beautiful naked woman engulfed him. Then, as quietly and as gracefully as she had entered the room, Anna picked up her evening dress and left.

Stan quickly succumbed to the effects of the alcohol once more, and he fell back asleep. In the morning, he awoke to the hangover dilemma of whether or not he had been dreaming about Anna coming into his room . . . until he got out of bed and saw the tiny pair of black panties lying on the floor.

Shit! he thought. *What if Billy had walked in here?*

Behold the magic of a beautiful woman. She can make a poor man feel rich, and she can make a rich man poor. She can make the meekest man perform fearless feats, and she can reduce the strongest man to a quivering blob. She can start wars, and end campaigns. She'll break your heart, and break your balls . . . and you'll be back for more tomorrow, if she says she's sorry.

—From *Fred Longcoor's Book on Life*

Chapter 2

The Scarlet Avenger

Thousands of miles away from Montana, on the same Thursday evening Billy Peet was courting Stan Faro, the private line was ringing in the penthouse of the Saylor Building in Anchorage. Beth's elegant manicured hand reached for the receiver and picked it up casually. She knew very few people had access to the line. The caller ID showed that it was her brother, Nick, calling from Hawaii. She was in a perfect mood for one of their frequent conversations as she answered the call. "Good evening, big brother. How are things in paradise?"

"Things are wonderful here. How are you, and how are things at Saylor Industries?"

"Life is good, I am good, and the company is doing very well."

As she frequently did when she talked to Nick, Beth began moving around the penthouse slowly, listening intently. It was a sibling habit that mirrored Nick's behavior when he was the occupant of the penthouse. An occasional "Yeah," or "Sure," punctuated the quiet on her end of the conversation.

After almost two years, Beth was just now getting comfortable in the place that had been Nick's beloved bachelor digs when he was president of the company. The private penthouse, one floor above the executive offices in the Saylor Building, was now *her* sanctuary . . . *her* place to live the life of privilege she had earned as one of two principal owners of one of the largest corporations in Alaska. Years earlier, she and Nick had taken over the small trucking company their father had started when he first came to Alaska and force-fed it into the monstrous business it was today.

"Beth, since you moved back to Alaska from Seattle two years ago, you have done amazing things. Your foresight was right on and you've grown the business tremendously. Your presence was needed there, not in Seattle."

Beth was thoughtful. It had been her conviction that she needed to run the business from Alaska, rather than continuing to try to run it from Seattle that led her to convince Nick that she needed to move back to Anchorage. "You know that I like this job, Nick . . . and I *am* more comfortable managing it here than I was in Seattle. I love Seattle, and I hated to leave there, but our core business is here. You and I both know we created a position for me in Seattle for all the wrong reasons. I wasn't sure I was right for this job . . . you know, before . . . particularly after what happened in Seattle that April, but I know I am now. Plus, you are an intimidating act to follow. Now, I truly understand the responsibility. Honestly, I am humbled by the responsibility . . . but I love it."

"Well, you headed in the right direction, and you had lots of choices." Nick thought about the speech he had made to Beth over two years earlier. *You're an icon. . . . Hell, you're an icon to just about everybody in America, not just to people in Washington and Alaska. You could probably become president. You could have taken advantage of your celebrity, and you didn't.* "Sometimes the few have to make a sacrifice for the good of the many . . . or something like that. Anyway, as far as I'm concerned, your heart was . . . is, in the right place."

"I retired the Scarlet Avenger as quickly as I could. I was a businesswoman before and I'm a businesswoman now, nothing more. I happened to end up in the most unimaginable situation ever because I unknowingly picked a crazy to be my man."

For a moment, Beth thought about the bizarre day in Seattle almost three years before when she stopped her deranged boyfriend from detonating a bomb at KingCo Field with thousands of baseball fans sitting in harm's way. By running after him and tackling him in the outfield before he could detonate the bomb, she had become an instant heroine to millions of Americans. The fact that she did it on national television wearing high heels and an elegant red evening gown with a long slit up one leg made her an instant legend. The Scarlet Avenger, whether she liked the name or not, had been born that day. "Okay," Nick said, "can we move on to something else?"

"Of course."

"Saylor Industries has never been stronger. It's a better company now than it was when I retired and left for Hawaii. With Donnie's superb performance in Seattle complementing your overall job performance, the company has done very well."

Beth visualized the mostly retired CEO of Saylor Industries on his deck in Maui with a cool afternoon cocktail in hand. "Thanks, I hope—"

Nick was in mid-thought, and continued. "I've been thinking about something a lot lately. You know I look over the financials regularly. I know you are aware of this too, and we've even touched on it in some of our past conversations, but we are growing a huge cash position . . . and I don't see any expansion in our future right now."

"You're right, Nick. I have been thinking about talking to you about that very fact for several months. I guess I got buried in the everyday business and just didn't do it. It's easy to get complacent when you are piling up lots of cash. I think we should look seriously at making some investments, and I think we should look at real estate."

The phone was silent for a few moments while Beth waited for Nick's reaction.

Nick was deliberate and serious as he responded. "Sometimes, it's scary. I mean, the way you and I think alike. We do have a lot of cash sitting around doing nothing . . . over twenty-five million dollars as of today. That's enough cash to leverage something significant. Real estate is not work-intensive. We could make an investment, or investments, that we can handle pretty easily. Just put the cash to work. And, it's hard to screw up a real estate deal, if you put a little research into it."

"Sounds like a challenge to me . . . for both of us. Something new to get the juices flowing again."

"Alright, I'll get on it. I know you can't actively participate because you've got a company to run, but you can keep your ears open, and nose around as time permits. And by the way, we don't have to restrict ourselves to Anchorage, or even Alaska."

"I agree. Let's stay in close touch on this."

Changing gears, Nick said, "You should see what a beautiful afternoon it is in Maui. I'm going to stay right here on my deck and wait for the sunset."

"Oh, nice. Winter is coming here. No snow yet, but it's freezing cold. By the way, how is Nani? Any special news yet?"

Nick knew exactly what Beth was referring to. "No news. We're not sure we are ready for kids. We've only been married a year. . . . And, we've got that age difference thing to think about. Truthfully, I was a bachelor for a long time, and I don't know if having kids is right for me. Nani's serious about her charity work. She works hard at the Saylor Foundation, and she's making a real difference for a lot of the local children. She has developed some great programs. I don't think she is ready either."

23

Sensing some melancholy in Nick's voice, Beth asked, "How are you doing? Sometimes I get concerned about you . . . you know, staying on top of your game in your old age."

"Don't give me that old-age crap. I'm happier than ever, and I've got my golf handicap to a single-digit. Besides, you and Donnie have done such a wonderful job with the company, I'm not needed." There was no regret in Nick's statement. There *was* a little hesitation as he continued. "Also, I'm sort of getting involved in local . . . uh, politics, and this potential real estate venture we're talking about gets me kind of excited."

Beth's reaction was immediate and shot right past the mention of the potential real estate venture. "What? You . . . politics? What the—"

"Easy, Beth. It's just the county council. Like the city council in Anchorage. Not a big deal. I'm running in the next election. A few local folks talked me into running. I think it'll be interesting . . . if I get elected. We do have a residency issue to sort out. But Maui has problems, just like every other place."

"I never would have believed this. You told me you hate politics."

"This is small-time politics, Beth. It could be fun . . . just a minor diversion."

"Okay, enough of that, but I'm very surprised. How's your friend . . . our friend, George Jong?"

"George is great. He and I are very close. We golf together at least a couple of times every week." Nick's tone softened, and he continued. "I do worry about him. I think he has some health issues, but he won't talk about it. He won't talk to Nani about it either. He just seems to have slowed down a lot, and he has become very reflective about life . . . everything, actually. I think he'll talk to me soon . . . at least I think he wants to. He's the one who encouraged me to run for the council. In fact, I will be running for the seat he is vacating . . . says he is just tired of the bullshit. Anyway, he's throwing me right into the middle of it."

The unspoken truth about George Jong was that both Beth and Nick, and Saylor Industries, owed him a great deal. It was his ominous vision of happenings at the Saylor family business almost three years earlier that alerted them to a festering disaster within the company and allowed them to react in time to avert a tragedy. George was a Hawaiian kapuna, whose visions and dreams had impacted many lives in a positive way over the years. He was also retired and rich, and loved to play golf, which made him a perfect buddy for Nick. Maybe most important of all, he was Nani's father.

"Sure, and now it's your turn."

Suspiciously, Beth said, "What do you mean?"

"I mean, do *you* have anything to report . . . you know, on the social front?"

Beth's brief laugh registered something between defensiveness and disappointment. "About the only thing new for me is the fact that I finally hit the old-age wall. . . . I just got my first pair of glasses. Everyone tells me I look like the governor now. If you want to know if I have found a man . . . the right man, hell, any man, the answer is no. But, I'm not really looking hard. And you, of all people, should understand my lack of faith in men. Besides, Nick, my job makes me fairly intimidating to most men."

"Glasses? I'll have to see that. I guess I do understand your situation, Beth, but I just feel . . . I just think . . . I think you are at a point in your life when you need somebody." Nick sounded melancholy as he finished his thought. "I think you need someone to complete your life . . . someone like I found."

"Shit, Nick, you were in your middle fifties when you met Nani. I'm a lot younger than you are."

Defensively, Nick replied, "That was almost three years ago. You're not much younger than I was then."

Beth rarely got angry with Nick, but she suddenly felt violated by what he was saying. "I don't think my current love life . . . or lack of, is really any of your fucking business." She was surprised by her own reaction, and wished she could retract what she had said.

Nick was surprised. "Whoa. And I'm not trying to get into your love life. I just care about you, and I—"

"I'm sorry," Beth interrupted. "That wasn't called for. Can we discuss something else . . . besides my love life?"

Nick changed gears again without hesitating. "Sure, how's Mr. Clayton doing?"

"Donnie's a rock, Nick. I can't help but think about all the trouble we would have avoided a few years ago if we had made him the Alaska manager then, and not . . . Devon." Beth's voice took on a disgusted tone whenever she mentioned her ex-husband's name. Years earlier, when Nick left for Maui and Beth became president of Saylor Industries, relocating to Seattle, Devon was promoted to the position of Alaska manager. In a very short amount of time, he had let his personal weaknesses nearly destroy Saylor Industries' business. He ended up dead at the hands of one of his lowlife criminal buddies, but that was little solace to the people who were left to rebuild Saylor Industries' reputation.

"We've had that discussion too many times. I don't want to go there again. It's all in our past and done. Let's move on by seeing what we can come up with on the real estate front. I'm kind of fired up to do something with all this money you and Donnie have made for the company."

"You started it all, Nick. . . . It's all there because of what you built."

"We, sis. We."

"Okay . . . let's get on it. I'll talk to you soon. Tell Nani hello for me."

"I will . . . and anytime you want me to make a trip back there . . . for any reason, let me know. I *know* I'm going to be needed there around Christmas time."

Beth laughed. "You don't *need* to come back, Nick. Sit back and enjoy the fruits of your labor. We all love to see you . . . just come back when you *want* to."

Beth put the phone back in its cradle and stood still for a moment. As she looked around her amazing surroundings, she thought to herself, *I still can't believe this.*

Beth walked to the window and looked out over the city. As she looked at the lights scattered on the distant hillside of the Chugach Mountains, she remembered how dark and foreboding Anchorage looked when she saw it the first time. *I am truly blessed . . . maybe a little lonely, but blessed.*

The day after Beth and Nick's conversation, and the day after he had arrived in Montana, Stan Faro left Billy Peet's ranch house. To a struggling, smalltime real estate agent it had been a mind-boggling thirty hours. He barely noticed the southwest-Montana landscape under them as the Learjet soared toward Salt Lake City. He was deep in thought, trying to absorb everything Billy had rushed into his brain. Following the boozing and schmoozing last night, Billy had been all business this morning.

"You're going to have to hit the ground running, Stanley. Lots to do. In the next couple of days, you'll be contacted by a man named Henry Kuban. . . . You've probably heard of him. He's the president of Arctic North Bank, and he's going to have an offer for you. It's an offer you *will* accept."

"I know who Henry is, I—"

Ignoring Stan, Billy continued. "We're going to be paying you a lot of money, and I'm going to send you home with a little bonus . . . a check for twenty-five grand. Use it to spruce up your image a little. Buy some nice clothes, get a decent car and a nice place to live, and rent some respectable office space. We'll pay the monthly expenses for the office. Send the invoices to me. We'll have some specific instructions for you in a few days, after you start getting yourself settled into your new image."

This was one of those fuzzy day-after mornings like Stan hadn't had in a long time. Adding confusion to the mix of physical and emotional feelings Stan was having created a nauseating brew . . . and he was ready to puke. *I don't like this,* he thought. *I'm not the right guy for this. I'm really not strong enough for this . . . or maybe, I'm just not tough enough. I may not be smart enough, either. I would like to be rich, though. Shit, I've got a twenty-five-thousand-dollar check in my pocket right now, and I'm going to be making one hundred grand a year! I can't believe it!*

Stan tried to rationalize his willingness to be part of Billy's scheme, but quickly came to the realization that his motivation was greed, pure and simple. Financial success was a powerful stimulus. What had Billy always said in college? It isn't money that makes the world go round, it's pussy. Guys want more money so they can get more pussy. The more money they have, the more pussy they get. *That certainly has been a missing ingredient in my life lately,* Stan thought.

For the entire trip back to Anchorage, Stan's thoughts were intermittently invaded by visions of Anna, and the memory of her standing naked next to his bed in the dim light.

I wasn't dreaming. I could smell her. She left her panties there. Why did she do that? he wondered.

Stan had no idea how big the unholy network was that he had just joined. At the same time he was flying back to Anchorage, Billy Peet was having an animated telephone conversation with Henry Kuban, the president of Arctic North Bank in Anchorage.

"Henry, don't go soft on me now. We need to get Stan some quality experience, and some additional public exposure. We need to beef up his resume, and a position as a board member for Arctic North Bank can do that. Why are you waffling now?"

"Billy, I want to help you, but I just can't imagine the reaction I'll get when the board members of the bank see me trying to ram Stan Faro down their throats. They're just not going to get it . . . and I'm going to have a hell of a time explaining it to them." Sitting in his opulent surroundings at the headquarters building of the Arctic North Bank, Henry should have looked like a poster child for power, but it was obvious from the tone of his voice that he was afraid of Billy Peet.

"You're the fucking president and majority owner of the bank, Henry. You can do anything you want to. You've got one board member now whose primary qualification is that he owns a goddamn Chinese restaurant. What did he do? Blow you?"

Henry briefly flared up. "None of that crap, Billy. We have a deal."

"Which you are now trying to back out of. Remember the photos,

Henry. I still have the photos. The ones with the little—"

"Don't say it. I don't want to hear it. That was . . . it was . . . a . . . a bad time in my life. That's over. I'm a happily married man. I have a young son, a ballplayer. I'm a community leader. I live an honorable life . . . *now*." The *now* sounded meek and contrite.

"You've got it, and that's exactly why I want Stan Faro on your board. So, I want you to call him within the next day or two and invite him to be on the board. Use the information from the resume I sent you last week, and sell it to the board members. Stan's a good guy, and he has quite a bit of community work on his resume. He'll be a good addition to your board." Billy hesitated for a moment, and then added, "You wouldn't want me to withdraw that hundred grand I put in your fucking bank last month, would you Henry? It's just sitting there, and you're making money off of it."

"No, Billy, but why? Why do you want Stan on my board? I know a little about him, and he seems to be an alright guy, but he certainly isn't a guy I'd be looking for to bring on at Arctic North. Shit, we just had a board meeting last week. . . . I'll have to call for a special meeting. Why are you doing this?"

Billy's tone changed now, and he sounded almost defensive. "Well, I just can't say right now, other than to tell you I'm just trying to build up his resume a little . . . for the future. A year from now, you'll be glad he's on your board. And that's the end of that. Don't go more than a day or two without contacting him." With that admonition, Billy ended the phone conversation.

Henry Kuban put his phone down, and quietly said to himself, "I have a feeling I am going to regret this for a long time."

Billy Peet hung up his phone and immediately dialed Budge Brown's cell number in Anchorage.

"Hey." Budge recognized Billy's number.

"Hey yourself. What the hell are you up to today?"

"Not much . . . attended my first meeting. Got something for me?"

"Yeah. Email me some comments about the meeting. Stan Faro just left the ranch on his way back to Alaska. As we discussed, I need you to keep an eye on him. I don't mean tail him, I just mean keep track of what he's up to. I gave him money to spruce up his image, and to rent some decent office space. Let me know what you think about what he does . . . you know, what the office looks like, what he looks like, that kind of shit."

"I can handle that."

"For what I'm paying you, you'd better be able to handle it. All you've had to do so far is sit around and play with yourself . . . and go and sit in a meeting."

28

Budge was a little angry and a little defensive as he said, "A two-day meeting! And, it's not my fault that I've been sitting around. You haven't given me a fucking thing to do until now . . . *and,* I've only been here three weeks."

"Don't get uppity with me. You've got something to do now. Stay with it, and keep me informed." Billy hung up without closure to remind Budge who the boss was. Even though they had been friends in high school, their relationship now was strictly business.

Budge was slightly pissed at Billy's attitude toward him, and the rude way he had ended their conversation, but that was a natural reaction for a guy who had a temper like his. Actually, he was sort of glad Billy had ended their phone call the way he had because he was about ready to say something he would have regretted . . . and he had too good a deal to blow in anger.

It was the right time for him to have a new adventure when Billy called him and asked him to relocate to Anchorage for a while. Seattle was a great city, and he liked it there, but he was ready to do something different, to see something different. Being an old buddy of Billy's, he had been kept busy with small jobs in the Seattle area for several years. Check out so-and-so; open a small office and furnish it, and then close it up quickly in a couple of months; put together ads for the newspaper; enlist phony investors to make phony testimonials for new clients; and on and on.

Budge was proud of his jack-of-all trades abilities. He felt like he could pull just about anything together quickly and make it look legitimate, and he had the kind of personality that allowed him to fit easily into any situation. Being a six-foot-four former minor-league baseball player and a multisport star athlete in high school had filled him with confidence, and his almost comical good looks made him accepted in any setting. After baseball, ten years working in the oil fields in West Texas and New Mexico had developed him into the cocky, tough guy he was now, particularly when he was fueling on Jack Daniel's.

Budge had a full head of thick, wavy black hair that somehow managed to look perfectly combed at all times, and the recent addition of touches of silver at his temples gave him a slightly distinguished look. He also liked to dress with a little flash, and somehow his colorful, almost over-the-top wardrobe always fit the occasion. And the name—"Where did you get a name like Budge?" people always asked him.

"Well," he would say, "when my momma was bringing me into the world, the doctor was struggling with me. . . . I was a large baby, and he said that I just wouldn't budge. I've been Budge ever since."

Billy Peet paid Budge well for everything he did for him, and almost everything he did was fun to him. Mostly, he just spent Billy's money, and he certainly had fun during his downtime. In fact, he had way too much fun to ever be a family man. The women in the Pacific Northwest who had seen the *carpe diem* tattooed on his butt in red, white, and blue numbered in the dozens . . . and they all knew he was a true patriot who really did believe in seizing the day!

Billy told Budge that he would be needed in Anchorage for a couple years, and that it would be slow at first, but that it would get pretty hectic in the second year. Billy told him to set himself up in a nice, but not luxurious apartment, and to tell anybody who was curious about him that he was an investor who was living off money that had been willed to him by his rich grandfather before he died. He told Budge to tell anyone who asked him that he had always wanted to come to Alaska. Always wanting to come to Alaska was a common mantra that most Alaskans had heard many times before from newcomers.

There is a separate dimension to Alaska for those people whose soul is in lockstep with its mystery and magnificence. It is a dimension that anchors firmly in your mind if you are brave enough or lucky enough to get away from the civilized parts of Alaska and venture into the heart of the land. If you are a hunter lying in a sleeping bag on the side of a mountain in the Brooks Range, watching the northern sky light up in bright oranges, reds, and yellows like it is on fire, you make a connection. If you are a roughneck who walks into a cold, clear October night on the North Slope and sees the full moon on the horizon, when it looks like it is so close you could step off of the earth onto it, you make a connection. If you have ever been captured by the eerie sight of daylight at midnight, or the early-morning silence of a misty hidden lake that is disturbed only by mysterious splashes and unknown, muted sounds, you are a soul-mate with The Great Land.

To Alaskans who cherish the lifestyle, it is the best-kept secret in America. For those who have been spoiled by the amenities of life in the Lower Forty-eight, living in Alaska is still a challenge. In the fall of 2006, particularly for Beth Saylor, Alaska continued to be a place of destiny. For Budge Brown, it was a place for an adventure that would be nothing like any other adventure he'd ever had.

Have you ever ended up in a place or a circumstance that you never expected . . . and then struggled with the shock of how quickly you got there . . . or how you got there? If it's not life-threatening, go with it . . . because it's usually a bad idea to try to change it.
— From *Fred Longcoor's Book on Life*

Chapter 3

The Trustees

On Friday afternoon in the Turnagain Room at the Susitna Hotel in Anchorage, Jerry Holter and Ron Minty were discussing what to do with money—Alaska's money. At the conclusion of all Alaska Permanent Fund Corporation Board of Trustees meetings, Jerry and Ron always found a watering spot where they could unwind and discuss what had transpired during the two-day meeting. Alternating meetings were held in Juneau, Fairbanks, and Anchorage every couple of months. As members of the board of trustees, they, the executive director, and the other four trustees rarely failed to attend regular meetings. Managing a thirty-five-billion-dollar fund was not a responsibility to be taken lightly.

"That was intense," Ron said. "I'm going to have a martini."

Jerry chuckled and said, "The meetings are always intense . . . and you always have a martini after they are over . . . or three."

"I'm a creature of habit. Damn, I hope that new server is here. She's something else." Ron was scouting the busy lounge as he spoke.

Jerry's mind was still on business, and he ignored Ron's comment. "Does the enormity of what we are doing ever strike you? I mean, do you ever think about the huge amount of money we are responsible for . . . and the obligation we have to the six hundred thousand people in this state?"

Ron became serious for a moment. "Yeah, I think about it, but I don't wake up in the middle of the night in a sweat about it. I mean, we have the best financial advisors in the world at our disposal, and we . . . oh fuck. She *is* here, and she's coming to our table."

Buffy spotted the two well-dressed men sitting toward the back of the lounge and recognized them as occasional patrons who seemed to have plenty of money, and a willingness to spend it. She also recognized the hungry look she was getting from one of them as she walked up to their table. All signs pointed to a good tip.

"Good afternoon, gentlemen."

Ron said, "Uh . . . hi . . . uh, uh, how are you?" *Jesus,* he thought, *you sound like a dork, not a successful attorney who is on the Alaska Permanent Fund Board of Trustees.*

Ever the professional, Buffy said, "I'm fine. What can I get for you?"

As Buffy was walking away after getting their drink orders, Jerry put his tongue behind his upper teeth, and said, "Thay, you really imprethed her," then laughed.

"Fuck you."

"Okay, can we talk seriously for a little bit? I want to know what you think about Mary Brunser. I mean, that is one smart broad. I've heard more good ideas come out of her mouth in the four months she's been on the board than I've heard from everybody else in the last year. She knows more about national and international finance than anybody I've ever met."

"You're a finance guy. You love that shit. I'm a lawyer."

Forcefully, Jerry said, "You are on the Board of Trustees of the Alaska Permanent Fund Corporation. We have more money to manage than lots of countries. Everybody knows you got there because the ex-governor liked you, but we have serious work to do. We need people like Mary Brunser."

"Implying that I'm not needed?"

"I didn't say that, and you have way too big an ego to let that get through your thick skin. I withdraw the question, but I'm telling you, Mary is a very good thing for the board. She can lift us all up. She can help the fund in lots of ways."

Ron was almost mumbling under his breath as he said, "There's a lot of money there alright, and we should all make something from it."

Jerry was wondering to himself what that comment was supposed to mean when Buffy returned to the table with their drinks.

"Here you are, gentlemen. Enjoy, and let me know if you want anything else."

As she walked away, Ron said, "Did you hear that? She wants me."

Jerry scoffed and said, "You're an idiot. That's what they say. That's their job. You are a fucking idiot . . . with an oversupply of testosterone. And what the hell did you mean by that comment about all of us making some money from the fund?"

Ron sat up straighter in his chair and looked Jerry squarely in the eyes. "There are over thirty billion dollars in the fund. It's invested all over the place, in real estate, stocks, bonds, everything you can think of. Now, we're looking for *alternative investments*. You and I are insiders . . . decision makers. We're sending money by the millions—shit, hundreds of millions—everywhere now. Hotels, apartment buildings, land, and who in hell knows what alternative investments are going to mean a year from now? Why shouldn't some of that money go to investments that *we* can make some money from?"

"Shit, Ron . . . you're a lawyer, and you want me to answer that? That's a conflict. . . . That's as big a conflict as we can have. We work for the people of Alaska . . . with their money."

"Oh fuck, let me stand up and put my hand over my heart. There are rich people all over this state who have made truckloads of money off of the fund." As Ron said that, he realized he needed to back off. He didn't want Jerry to think he was serious . . . at least not yet. "Enough of that. I need another martini, and I want another close look at the cute butt on the little lady bringing the drinks."

Jerry wasn't going to let Ron's last fund comment get away. "I don't know who you're referring to, but there are all kinds of safeguards to keep the fund safe, and to make sure it is invested responsibly, but when it comes right down to it, our honesty is within our own control. I'll be the first to admit that the investment options have changed, but that was needed. Remember, there was a time when our only investments were income-producing securities, most of which were government-issue bonds. In those days, the fund didn't have the kinds of returns it has now, so we've moved in the right direction."

"Yeah, yeah. I know about that. I know all of the fund-thumping rhetoric . . . *a model for sovereign funds everywhere.* The truth is, the one thing that did more for the fund managers than anything else was the Permanent Fund Dividend. Alaskans don't give a shit what the fund managers do, as long as they get their check every year . . . and the bigger the check is, the more they don't give a shit. It's just human nature."

Jerry was quiet for a moment. *He's right. It's sad, but he's right,* he thought. "Well, unfortunately, you are right. And nothing either one of us has said changes our responsibility. We are obligated to the people of the State of Alaska to manage the fund by following the *prudent-investor rule.* I think our biggest job right now is going to be to adhere to that in the face of our pursuit of alternative investments."

"There's more of your financial bullshit. What about the prudent-butt rule? That server has the most prudent butt I've seen in a while."

"It's a good thing you're a lawyer and not an English teacher. Do you know what prudent means? There is nothing about the meaning of prudent that would have anything to do with a butt . . . hers or anybody else's! Except that it wouldn't be prudent for you to attempt to make any kind of effort to get near it . . . or even talk to her about it. You are a piece of work. And I thought we could have a meaningful conversation about the two-day meeting we just finished . . . while it's fresh in our minds."

Jerry's words trailed off, but they contained enough emotion for Ron to realize he should change his tune. Ron attempted a recovery. "I thought we had a good meeting. And, I agree about Mary Brunser, even though I'm personally not too crazy about her. She's smart." *Almost too smart,* Ron thought.

Feeling like he had to demonstrate a sincere interest in talking about the meeting, Ron continued. "I know one thing I'm tired of. I mean, it's a good thing to allow public access to the meetings, because it increases public trust of what we're doing, but it takes all the patience I have to sit there at the beginning of these meetings and listen to every whacko in Alaska tell us what we should and shouldn't do with the fund's money. You know, we don't have to do that. The fund's policy for a long time has been not to pander to special interests. That includes the whackos."

"You mean you want us to invest in companies doing business in Darfur?"

Jerry's comment reminded Ron of the parade of righteous housewives and college students who marched in with *Save Darfur* signs and actual Darfur refugees in tow. They were taking advantage of the public option that allowed them time to speak at the beginning of the first day of the two-day meeting, and they were first on the agenda. They pleaded with the trustees to avoid investments in corporations or equity funds with interests in Darfur, and the boring dogma had almost put him to sleep before the real meeting ever began.

Ron replied to Jerry's sarcasm with uncharacteristic sincerity. "We need to look for prudent investments that are right for the fund, without trying to assuage the backers of every do-gooder cause who stumble into our meetings. I don't agree with the things that are happening in Darfur . . . what little I know about them. I know it is complicated, and I know it all starts with the corrupt Sudanese government, but there are probably a jillion things happening in the world that I don't like. We can't look out for all of them. Our responsibility is to the fund . . . period."

At the meeting the first morning, all of the trustees had patiently sat through the Darfur Initiative, as Ron had labeled it afterwards, and Chairman Fred Feck had politely informed the group that the trustees would take their request under advisement. He had done the same for the man who had pleaded with the trustees to consider investing in his plan to ship fresh water to the Lower Forty-eight in oceangoing tankers. Recalling former governor Walter Hickel's idea to build a fresh-water pipeline to the Lower Forty-eight years earlier, one of the trustees commented after the meeting that Mr. Hickel's idea didn't sound so crazy now.

"I like the guy who wants the fund to buy the Seattle Mariners, and move them to Anchorage," Trustee Daniel Oaken said. "I love baseball, and the Mariners aren't very good right now, so maybe their owners would be ready to sell. It would be really nice to have the team here. I could save a couple thousand dollars by not having to fly to Seattle for the weekend once or twice a year." Everyone had laughed at the tongue-in-cheek statement from Oaken.

After another hour of drinking and watching Ron's increasingly pathetic attempts to gain Buffy's attention, Jerry stated that he needed to go home. Ron reluctantly agreed that he needed to leave also, and then made a big deal out of paying the bill and leaving Buffy a much-too-generous tip. Buffy happily took the tip, her experience telling her that Ron would feel silly about it the next morning as he sat across the table from his wife having his morning coffee, and that would be the end of the story.

One thing the two men didn't discuss about their board meeting, because it didn't mean anything to them, was the obscure man who had been in attendance both days.

Budge Brown had attended the meeting of the board of trustees in the Foraker Room in the Susitna Hotel in Anchorage, disguised as a much older man. His phony beard and disheveled brown suit made him appropriately nondescript. It was his intention, and his assignment, to attend every meeting for at least the next year, no matter where it was held. After all of the attendees who were pleading their special interests left the room, there were only a half dozen people left in the public section of the meeting room, and for a while, Budge felt like all the board members were sizing him up. He soon came to the realization that nobody cared he was there.

Scholarly pursuits were not exactly Budge's thing, but he had diligently followed Billy's orders by taking several pages of notes, particularly on anything he perceived as information that Billy would want. It quickly became apparent to him that the board of trustees was like any other politically appointed board, and he wrote down his observations of the executive director and each trustee. Using the biographies provided for observers as they entered, and his own rough-hewn opinions, Budge provided a recap for Billy.

Billy:

Okay, this is the two most boring fucking two days I have spent in a while. When does the exciting part start?

Executive Director Richard Cally is a very personable, educated, and immediately likeable man who appears to have been everywhere, knows everybody, and has done it all. He understands the inner workings of the fund very well. He takes his job very seriously.

Chairman Fred Feck is businesslike, and appears to do everything by the numbers. His background is not as strong as Cally's. He has been involved in tourism, mining, and insurance in Alaska. I feel like he can't believe he is where he is, and for that reason he's going to bust his butt to do everything right.

Vice Chairman Jerry Holter is a former state senator, and has held numerous positions in the banking industry. He seems very competent, and very tuned in to board activities and the fund's performance.

Trustee Ron Minty, like trustee Oaken, was appointed by the former governor. He seems a little like the black sheep of the board. He has only been in Alaska for five years. He is a lawyer. . . . I mean, I think he is a slimy lawyer.

Trustee Daniel Oaken is another lawyer who has specialized in Alaska Native issues, and worked for several Alaska Native corporations. He is the current commissioner of revenue, and is required by law to be on the board of trustees. He didn't say much, and I can't get a good read on him.

Trustee Mary Brunser is very smart. She has a PhD in finance from Harvard. She has had several jobs with large international banks, and reluctantly relocated to Alaska when her husband, John, transferred to Alaska to coach the college hockey team in 2004. She was appointed by the current governor. She had an opinion about everything, and every time she talked, several of the trustees rolled their eyes! I don't ever want to see her naked!

Trustee Amak Tonner is a well-known Alaskan Native who was a close friend of the former governor Jay Hammond. Hammond is called the Father of the Permanent Fund. He started it. Tonner probably didn't say fifty words during the two-day meeting.

Billy, it's obvious there are buddies on the board . . . Probably Holter and Minty, and Oaken and Feck. I don't think anybody likes Brunser, but I think they all are intimidated by her. Minty seems like a loose cannon. Cally seems aloof to all of them, and Tonner appears to be a token. There is an undercurrent, but they are not going to really show that side in public. I know that sounds vague, but it is hard to explain. You know, whispered conversations, little laughs, muted comments you can't hear . . . that kind of shit.

—Budge

Budge had gone back to his condo after the meeting ended on Thursday, painstakingly pounded out the message to Billy, one finger at a time, and sent it to him. He wasn't comfortable with a computer, and sending and receiving emails was about the extent of his use of the laptop that Billy had insisted he buy.

Figuring he had put in two grueling days doing something he hated to do, Budge decided he needed to unwind. He found The Mud Flats bar and restaurant shortly after he got to Anchorage, and he liked the atmosphere at the place, located near the port and close to the downtown area. It was not far from his downtown condo, and it was close to many other downtown bars and restaurants. The mix of dockworkers, businessmen, and the assortment of females who ran with them suited his simple social requirements.

Budge ignored the restaurant side of The Mud Flats as he walked through the double doors and headed straight to the large U-shaped bar. His favorite bartender was working. In his first three weeks in Anchorage, he had developed an across-the-bar friendship with the plus-forty buxom blonde bartender. Her looks were a little hardened. Budge guessed she had been very attractive when she was younger. He didn't care. . . . She had a nice body, and he wanted to lay her, not marry her. He had targeted her right away, and he was a little disappointed that he hadn't gotten any obvious reaction from her. She was as friendly with every man in the bar as she was with him. He had quickly figured out that she carried the social baggage that comes with being a local icon in the bar-and-restaurant scene.

"Vicki, you beautiful woman, how are you?"

"Budge, you are too sweet, and I am great. The usual?"

"Yep. On ice, with water on the side."

As Budge took his seat at the busy bar, he looked around the room. *Nice crowd,* he thought. *Looks like a few unattached women.*

Vicki brought Budge's drink to him and said, "So, what brings you in here today?"

"You, you gorgeous woman."

"You're full of it today. I should have asked you what you're up to, but then I remembered that you don't do anything." Vicki's words were intended to be a lighthearted jab at Budge, and he knew it.

"My days are full, baby. I mean, I have just been in a two-day meeting." As quickly as he said it, Budge realized that he probably shouldn't have, but he made an instant recovery. "My financial advisors . . . you know, telling me where I should put my money."

Budge had been in The Mud Flats enough times for Vicki to know that he was independently well off. He hadn't told her where his money came from, but he had made it obvious that he didn't have to work. "Nice problem to have. I'd sit in meetings for two months, if I had any money to talk about."

Budge laughed politely at Vicki's self-deprecation. "You've got the world by the ass, Vicki. Half the people in Alaska are your friends. All the men in this bar want to get in your pants."

I don't know her that well. That might have been a little too much, Budge thought as he waited for Vicki's reaction.

"You are a nasty man, Mr. Brown, but you're just like all the rest. Half of the men in every bar in the world with a female bartender in it want to get into her pants . . . and it doesn't make any difference what she looks like. For some reason, just being behind the bar makes her more desirable. It's like a jungle law for bars. Men love beer and pussy, and the combination of the two is just too much for them. All of you undergo a metamorphosis when you walk through the front door. We all expect it, so it loses something."

Budge felt like he had been slapped down. "I guess you put me in my place."

In Vicki's peripheral view of the bar, she caught the universal sign of a drinker in need—an upraised glass. "I'm needed elsewhere. To be continued," she said, as she moved away.

Although encouraged by her parting words, Budge was slightly confused by Vicki's reaction to his statement, but he wasn't going to worry about it. Truth was, Budge rarely worried much about what any woman said, and that had been a major contributing factor to his many short relationships. Tonight, he decided he would just continue his quest to get the feel for the ebb and flow of the world he preferred . . . the world of the people who made Anchorage buzz after dark.

In Maui, Nick had slept restlessly and then got up to play a scheduled golf game with George Jong that his mind was not focused on. He was excited about spearheading the search for an investment for Saylor Industries, and he was anxious to get moving. Saylor Industries was still his company, but he relished the idea of having something real to do for it. Selfishly, he was happy that Beth's job running the company prevented her from being actively involved in the pursuit of a real estate deal right now. It would be fun to run with this project. He could do all the research he needed to on the Internet, contact former associates and acquaintances who might have ideas, and then fly to wherever he needed to in The Bird when it was time to get an actual look at whatever they were interested in.

The Saylor Industries corporate jet had spent a lot more time parked at the Executive Air Jet Center in Maui than it had when Beth was living and working in Seattle. . . . And Nick no longer felt guilty about having a forty-million-dollar Gulfstream G550 and two pilots at his disposal. He was fabulously rich, and finally enjoying it the way he should.

It was the middle of the afternoon when Nick returned from his golf game and walked into the main living area of his oceanfront home in Lahaina. Nani, the beautiful woman he had met in Maui and married two years later, was scurrying about the kitchen area as she prepared a special dish she had learned from her Hawaiian-Chinese mother, Keona. Islanders knew Keona only as Mama, and she owned a famous little local restaurant called Mama's A'u House. Her specialty was preparing the prized local fish, A'u, and anybody who ate it once came back for more whenever they could. When Nani married Nick, Mama had given her a crash course in cooking specialty dishes. Mama liked Nick, and she wanted to do anything she could to make sure he was happy with Nani.

"Hey, you gorgeous woman, what are you up to?" Nick said as he entered the kitchen in the huge house.

"I'm trying to keep you slim and trim with one of Mama's special recipes. How's Papa?"

Nick patted his stomach with both hands and declared, "Your papa is fine. He played pretty well today . . . and I *am* slim and trim."

"I know. . . . I just want to keep you that way, so I can show you off."

"Oh yeah . . . to who?"

"To . . . " Nani hesitated. "To *almost* everybody."

Her wicked little smile told Nick exactly what she meant. Everybody but some local hottie. "Competition anxiety doesn't become you. You are the woman of my dreams . . . and you always will be. And I know you know that."

Nani responded by coming around the kitchen island to give Nick a hug. Her tall, lean body filled her brief shorts and halter top beautifully, and Nick got a familiar tingle in his insides as she held him tightly.

"I do know that . . . and I am grateful for it. I love my life with you," she said.

Sensing the time was right, Nick said, "I do have something that just came up that I need to tell you. You know, I talked with Beth last night, and we both feel that we have to do something with the large amount of cash that Saylor is holding right now. We are going to look at a real estate investment."

Nani backed away from Nick with a quizzical look on her face. "Why is that so important that you need to tell me about it? You do business every day that you *don't* tell me about . . . on the phone."

"There's the difference. I'll have to do some traveling. . . . And I'm not even sure where yet. I'll be spending time on the phone and on the computer in the beginning, but eventually I'll have to look at the potential investment candidates. They could be in Alaska, or anywhere in the United States." As an afterthought, Nick added, "They could even be in Hawaii."

Nani's mind was racing. "What about the foundation? If Saylor Industries has extra cash, why not put it in the foundation?"

Because of Nani's dedication to the Saylor Foundation, Nick was ready for the question. "Nani, we are putting tremendous amounts of money into the foundation now. Beth and I are viewing this as an opportunity to gain additional capital, and one of the things we could eventually do is exactly what you are talking about."

Nick was comfortable that he was not lying to Nani, just stating a partial truth. He had *thought* about it, but he had not talked to Beth about it.

"Oh," was all Nani said as she headed back to the food she was preparing, leaving Nick to wonder what she was really thinking.

Nick turned and headed to his home office. He knew that he would spend many hours there, so when he had his home designed, he made sure that the room was spacious, and, maybe most importantly, that it faced the ocean. Built-in teak library shelves lined both sides of the room, and the ocean side was all windows. A large, beautiful teak desk sat in front of the windows. The area under the windows was wall-to-wall teak cabinets, with a computer desk in the middle. When Nick was turned in his black leather chair facing his computer, it was framed by the beauty and serenity of West Maui's rocky beach and softly undulating ocean waves.

When Nick sat down at his computer, he immediately Googled *Commercial Real Estate Listings*. Not surprisingly, almost ten million listings came up. Ever the pragmatist, he clicked on the first one. Following the prompts, he put in Seattle, WA, as the area he was interested in. *Let's see if we can keep it kind of close,* Nick thought.

After an hour of entering various specs, frustration with the number of responses stating, *0 Listing(s) found, please enter another search criteria,* got the best of Nick. He pushed his chair back and sat quietly for a few moments as he tried to wrap himself around what he was trying to do.

This is crazy, he thought. *You're flying blind. You're trying to get information for a potential multimillion dollar investment, and you don't have a clue what you're doing. That's not the way you do your business, Nick. You need some help.*

After thumbing through his battered business card file and finding the card he was looking for, Nick dialed an Anchorage telephone number. The speakerphone was answered before the second ring. "Flacker here."

41

Jimmy Flack had answered his phone the same way since Nick first met him twenty years earlier.

"Jimmy, this is Nick Saylor calling from—"

"Holy shit . . . Nick? I can't believe it. I wasn't even sure you were still alive. I'm sorry, I mean I heard you went to Maui, but that was a couple of years ago. You still in Maui? I heard you're married."

Nick waited for Jimmy to get it all out, and then replied. "I'm still in Maui, Jimmy. I'm married to a beautiful woman, and I'm still very much alive."

"Wow . . . that's good, I mean, that's all good. Shit, great to hear from you though. What's up?"

Without disclosing anything about Saylor's cash position, Nick told Jimmy what he was trying to do. Jimmy had handled commercial real estate in Alaska for years, and he was recognized for his knowledge and expertise. Nick wanted to expand his search beyond Alaska, but he thought Jimmy would be a good resource to start with.

"I know a lot more about commercial real estate in Alaska than I do anywhere else, but I do have Outside contacts and some insider information that you wouldn't be able to find on the Internet. Depending on how much of an investment you want to make, you probably will have to go Outside." Jimmy was fishing, and Nick knew it.

"You find me investments that look solid . . . and by that I mean clean, new or fairly new, no encumbrances, no pending litigation, and an opportunity for positive cash flow, and I'll look at everything. And, positive cash flow doesn't have to mean right now, but there has to be an opportunity there that we can create or enhance by tweaking a few things. And simple . . . I'm too old to want to manage another business. Something I can hire a manager for, and forget. You know, office buildings, warehouses, that kind of thing. Let's just say that I have enough cash to handle a very large investment. You'll get the idea as we go along. As I eliminate them, I'll tell you if they aren't as significant as I would like." After a brief hesitation, Nick added, "Or if they're *too* big."

Jimmy's mind was racing. *Jesus, I think I've hit the mother lode. Nick's got the money. Everybody knows that.* Almost breathlessly, he said, "Okay . . . okay Nick. I think I get the picture. I'll get right on it. What's your email address? I've got your phone number here on caller ID."

Nick gave Jimmy the information he needed, and they talked long enough to catch up on their respective lives before hanging up.

An hour and a half after he sat down at his desk, Nick got up and went back into the kitchen, where Nani was still at work on his mystery dinner. He felt good. He was satisfied that he had done the right thing to get the ball rolling on Saylor's new investment venture. He felt that old familiar buzz that ran through him when he was stirring the business pot.

"Hey baby, something smells really good. I think a scotch or two on the lanai to get me ready for dinner will be just right. Can I pour you a glass of wine?"

Henry Kuban was at his office in the main branch of the Arctic North Bank early the morning after his conversation with Billy Peet. He did not relish the calls he would have to make today to ask board members to come in for a special board meeting, a week after their last board meeting. He needed time at his desk to think, to map out his presentation of Stan Faro as a new board member. His only saving grace was the fact that a longtime board member had died early in the year, and they had never filled his position. Even though Henry really liked old Hank, his death was going to help him now. At least he could show a genuine need for a new board member.

Privately, Henry was disgusted with the position he was in. In spite of his tremendous success, and the wealth that came with it, his checkered past continued to haunt him.

Years earlier, at a time when his first marriage had just failed, he'd slid to the dark side very quickly. The deeply rooted emotions that a divorce brings to the surface and an overwhelming sense of failure were the catalysts for his quick fall. He began by drinking heavily and making a regular habit of paying a small fortune for prostitutes . . . all types of prostitutes. Slipping further and further into a world of self-destruction, he was willing to try anything his money would buy and his depraved sexual partners suggested. A threesome with a prostitute and another man turned into his first of several homosexual experiences. Drugs began to replace alcohol, and he sank deeper and deeper into a foggy, disgusting, seamy pot of sexual stew . . . eventually resulting in a sexual encounter with a young boy.

That was when he hit bottom, and in a way, it was Billy Peet who rescued him. One of Billy's contacts ran in some of the same circles Henry was running in, and he accidentally stumbled onto a handful of pictures of the last act of Henry's tumble from grace. He knew enough about Billy to know that he would pay him handsomely for the pictures. Billy saved Henry . . . but he also got what he wanted. Henry Kuban was his forever.

To his credit, Henry cleaned himself up and became a respectable member of the business community in Anchorage again. He was now a bespectacled, slightly balding, slightly overweight man, just over fifty . . .

but still wealthy. He'd found a new woman, and a year after they were married, they'd had a son. The guilt, as well as worry about the discovery of his past, haunted him, but with the exception of a few small favors on loans for Billy, he'd felt like his past was long gone—until Billy called him about Stan Faro.

Henry still had no idea how he was going to sell this to the board. He began to call the board members one at a time. All of their responses were nearly the same. "What do you mean? We just had a meeting last week. Is something wrong?"

Henry tried to calm them down, assuring them nothing was wrong. He told them that he had some important business he needed to bring to the board. Thinking on his feet at one point, he stated that he had been informed by bank regulators in Alaska that Arctic North was required to fill their empty board seat by the middle of November. He hung the phone up hoping that nobody would have the curiosity or the presence of mind to check it out.

At 4:00 that afternoon, a quorum of Arctic North Bank board members were gathered in the plush boardroom. They laughed, talked, and complained in voices that held an anticipatory edge: "What did Henry fuck up now?" "I wonder what else the regulators found." "Who's going to get the axe today?" "I was supposed to be getting a massage this afternoon."

Henry walked into the room and sat at the head of the table. Respectfully, the banter ended. Most of the board members were there because they had a good relationship with Henry.

"Gentlemen, thank you for being here on such short notice. I know we just had a meeting last week, but we have some business that needs our attention. As I told most of you when I called, we need to fill the board seat that was vacated by the death of Hank, and we need to fill it soon . . . actually, by the fifteenth."

"When did they contact you, Henry? I didn't know bank regulators worried about things like the number of board members on the bank board." Max Ort, an old friend of Henry's, and the owner of a local insurance company, was always the first to question everything.

"Uh . . . just yesterday afternoon, actually. I guess I really didn't realize that either, but frankly, when a bank regulator calls and all he wants to do is remind me to fill a vacant board seat, I'm tickled to death."

There were relieved chuckles around the room, and Henry continued. He went from his casual swagger to looking a little uncomfortable, and many of his old friends on the board noticed it. "I have a candidate . . . someone I have been considering for some time. He's been actively involved in the community, been on several other boards and committees, and I think he would make a fine addition to the board. I know some of you know him. His name is Stan Faro."

The assortment of utterances, followed by a palpable quiet in the room, told Henry this was not going to be easy.

Again, Max spoke up. "Stan Faro? I know who Stan is, and I . . . well I guess I just assumed we would eventually fill Hank's spot with someone who is a little more of a heavyweight than Stan Faro. I don't know much about him, and I think he's an okay guy, but—"

At that point, almost everybody in the room tried to make themselves heard at the same time, and the arguments, both for and against Stan Faro, continued for a half hour. As the meeting progressed, Henry realized two important things. There was an element of protectiveness in the current board membership. They didn't like the invasion of their privileged good old boys' club by someone they didn't really know, no matter how qualified he was. And, no matter what was said that day, Henry was the guy with the fuzzy balls, and all the money, and they would all agree with him eventually. Sensing that, and privately wondering why he hadn't realized it before, Henry brought the meeting to a conclusion.

"Okay, gentlemen, I haven't heard anything here that is a deal killer. I believe Stan Faro will make a worthy addition to our board, even if some of you are not entirely convinced of that. We have enough members here for a quorum, so let's put this to a vote. All in favor of making Stan Faro a new member of the Board of Directors of the Arctic North Bank, signify agreement by raising your right hand and saying aye."

One at a time, every right hand in the room went up, and the aye's were all sounded.

"Thank you, gentlemen. It is unanimous. Stan will be at our next regular board meeting in December. If you run into him anywhere in town before then, please congratulate him, and make him feel welcome."

With the completion of their business, the board members filtered out of the room fairly quickly, with one exception.

Max approached Henry when all the other board members were gone. "What the fuck, Henry? Stan Faro? What hat did you pull that out of . . . or did you pull it out of your ass?"

Max and Henry were old friends, so the full frontal attack didn't bother Henry. . . . In fact, he considered it good-natured jabbing more than anything. "He's alright, Max. He comes well recommended. He has a clean reputation. Shit, he's a junior pastor at his church, or at least he was at some time. He has some powerful friends . . . rich friends who can help our bank."

"Now you're getting down to it. Somebody leaned on you. Somebody's got you by the balls for some reason."

Henry did his best impression of indignation as he said, "Don't piss me off, Max. We're friends, and I'll take some ribbing from you, but I won't take those kinds of accusations. Whatever I do here, I do in the bank's best interest. I will concede that a good customer . . . a very good customer, did contact me on behalf of Stan. That's all, and I am happy that we have made this very good customer happy. I hate the term, but it truly is a win-win. Stan will be fine on the board. Trust me."

Max knew better than to push Henry any farther, and that ended the discussion . . . for the time being.

The well-worn cliché, "It is not what you know but who you know that matters," should be put into a special category of clichés labeled, Clichés to Live or Die By.
—From *Fred Longcoor's Book on Life*

Chapter 4

Monkey Man

Yeren is a legendary, mythical creature that allegedly lives in the remote, mountainous Hubei province of China. Although various descriptions exist, the creature is generally accepted as being covered in reddish-brown hair. When its long beard is covered in frost in mid-winter, the creature takes on an oddly Santa-like appearance. Theories abound concerning the Yeren, including the hypothesis that it is a new species of orangutan. The Hubei province is rich with superstitions and myths, and there have been several hundred "sightings" of the elusive creature over the years. Chinese Wildman, Yeh Ren, and Man-Monkey are just a few of the names tagged on the Yeren during that time.

Johnny Bosco had it all. After a stellar run as a not-big-enough-for-the-pros college linebacker and four years serving his country in the Marines, he spent a few years working in the oilfields in Texas, then moved to Las Vegas and began working in the booming construction industry. A quick study and a hard worker, he branched off to start a small construction business that quickly grew with the burgeoning economy in the Entertainment Capital of the World. Before it all came apart for him, he gathered a million-dollar home, several expensive vehicles, and a beautiful former Vegas showgirl as a wife. At his peak, his biggest problem had been keeping up with his wife's voracious appetite for social events and expensive trips. Money was not a problem.

Johnny was blindsided by the events that ended his glorious run. He knew his wife was a high-maintenance woman. He didn't know that she was a larcenous, soulless, evil woman. She was sexually accommodating at all times and professed to him that he was the love of her life. Children were not in her plans yet, she proclaimed in the early days of their marriage . . . but maybe later. It would be much later when he would reflect on how quickly they had met and married, and how he really didn't know her at all.

Johnny had made a four-day business trip to Los Angeles the week after Christmas in 2005. Curiously, he hadn't been able to get hold of Dottie on the phone for the last two days he was in L.A. As he thought about it on the plane ride from L.A. back to Las Vegas on Monday morning, he realized how strange she had sounded when he talked with her the first two days he was gone, particularly the last time he talked with her on Friday afternoon.

Johnny knew something was wrong when the cabdriver pulled into his driveway. . . . He could feel it. When he walked through the front door, it hit him like a punch in the gut. The house was cleaned out. Nothing remained. No furniture, nothing. Shocked, he walked through each room, marveling at how completely empty they were. He opened the refrigerator, and the only thing remaining was a six-pack of his favorite beer . . . a slap in the face. . . . *Here,* it said, *this is all you've got left.*

He had to call for another cab to take him to his office. His expensive cars were all gone. As he rode to his office in the back of the taxi, he tried to imagine the frenetic scene that must have played out over the last four days as everything he owned was removed from the property. When he arrived at the office of his construction business, his foreman and several of his crew were milling around outside.

"Boss . . . boy, am I glad to see you. What the fuck is going on here?" Tim, Johnny's foreman, moved toward him anxiously.

"I don't know, Tim, but I'm going to find out," Johnny said as he hurried past him and entered the office. Judy, his office manager, was sitting behind her desk in bewilderment. She looked up hopefully when she saw him.

"Mr. Bosco, what's going on?" she blurted out. "I tried to pay some bills online this morning, and . . . and there's no money in the company account."

"Shit," was all Johnny could manage as he sat down in one of the chairs in the foyer. He sat there for a minute, trying to sort it out. Before long, he admitted to himself what had happened. "She cleaned me out . . . everything. She fucking cleaned me out."

The reality of what his wife had done to him sank in over the next few days. She had moved everything out of the house, sold or moved the vehicles, and emptied out their personal accounts and his business account. She had to have some dubious accomplices. . . . The vehicles were obviously stolen, to be sold on the black market without the titles. The neighbors told him that the household goods were moved in a large unmarked trailer van, and the bank accounts were closed at 5:30 on Friday night . . . half an hour after the construction office closed. Johnny cursed himself at his decision to add Dottie as a signer on his business account.

Over the next week, Johnny realized how thoroughly he had been wiped out. He made a futile attempt to determine where Dottie and his money had gone, but she had vanished into thin air. He contacted local authorities, and they made a halfhearted attempt to help him. They told him that the woman he married didn't even exist.

Now, over one hundred thousand dollars' worth of operating capital for his business was gone. As bad luck would have it, his company was between projects, with no revenue coming in. He reluctantly laid his employees off and let his heavily leveraged equipment go back to the suppliers. By selling a couple of pickups and some miscellaneous small equipment the company owned outright, he was able to put enough money in his pocket to get by for a while. He let the leased office space and his equipment yard go back to the landlord. He used part of the cash he had to pay his attorney to begin filing bankruptcy and divorce papers.

Two weeks after the quick and dramatic change in his life, Johnny had called an old acquaintance with Taylor Drilling Company.

A gruff voice answered the phone. Taylor drilling manager Bobby Woods's bark was worse than his bite, but only people who had been around him for a while knew that. "Bobby Woods, what can I do for you?"

"Bobby, this is Johnny Bosco. How are you?"

Bobby hesitated for a moment of recognition, then said, "Little Johnny Bosco, former derrick hand, and now construction-company mogul . . . or so I've heard?"

"That's me, Bobby, but I ain't no mogul, at least not anymore." Johnny gave Bobby a quick recap of what his wife had done to him over the last couple of weeks.

"Shit . . . that's about the worst fucking-over-by-a-wife story I've ever heard. I'm really sorry to hear that, but what can I do for you?"

"I need to do something to recover, Bobby. I heard you have some rigs working in Alaska . . . on the North Slope. I heard the money's good. You know I'm a good hand. I'll work the floor, I'll work anything. Hell, I'll even roustabout. And I don't care what the schedule is, I'll work over." Johnny rushed his words out, hoping he didn't sound as desperate as he was.

Bobby was quiet for a moment. "Johnny," he said thoughtfully, "you were a damn good worker when you worked for us. I hated to lose you when you went off to Vegas. I'd hire you in a heartbeat . . . if I thought you were going to stay with us. In spite of what you've been through, I don't want to send guys all the way to the North Slope of Alaska and have them work a couple of hitches and leave."

"Bobby, I'm a man of honor, I think you know that. If you can put me to work . . . I'll . . . I'll guarantee you I'll stay at least a ye . . . two years."

"If you'll promise me to work at least two years, I think I might have something for you. You've got a little luck on your side. The way things are now in the patch, we can't find experienced men fast enough."

"I promise you, Bobby. I'll make you a hell of a hand."Arrangements were made for Johnny to leave in a week, pending his passing a physical and a drug test, and completing a couple of days of training in Taylor's office in Bakersfield, which was the closest office they had to Las Vegas. Ten days later, Johnny stepped off of a chartered 737 at the Deadhorse Airport, with a duffel bag stuffed full of work clothes, arctic gear, and paperbacks.

The first night Johnny Bosco climbed down out of the derrick on Taylor Rig No. 96 in January of 2006, it was almost fifty degrees below zero on the North Slope of Alaska. His long reddish beard was white with frost, and his toolpusher, Bill "Hurricane" Hamilton, immediately named him Monkey Man.

Bill used many of the countless hours he spent alone in his room in the small drilling-rig camp reading about strange things from around the world. Because of what he had read about the Chinese Yeren, he decided that Monkey Man was a perfect name for Johnny... he spent long hours working ninety feet up in the derrick of Rig No. 96 in all conditions, racking heavy ninety-foot stands of drill pipe between the fingers of the monkey board. When the steam rising off of the rig heaters and his own heavy breath as he worked in the cold covered his beard with frost, the picture was too perfect for his toolpusher to ignore, and he gave Johnny the nickname that stuck with him.

Three months later, it was *only* thirty-five below zero as Johnny came down out of the derrick. His uncut beard was now much longer. "Hey Monkey Man, is it cold up there?" Bill Hamilton's question was followed by a big man's hearty laugh. He knew the answer, having spent many hours working in derricks and on rig floors all over West Texas and Alaska before becoming a toolpusher.

"Fuck you, Hurricane. Have you been nice and warm sitting on your ass in the doghouse?" Jimmy had been working for Hurricane for three months, and knew him well enough by now to be irreverent.

"Yeah, it's nice in there. Got hot coffee and doughnuts too." *In there* referred to the small steel structure near the rig floor where the assorted drilling equipment that measured ongoing drilling parameters was located. All rigs had doghouses, and most doghouses had benches where workers could take short breaks and have coffee and refreshments. Depending on the current rig operation, the toolpusher and the driller could sometimes spend up to twelve hours in the doghouse.

"You must feel good, then. Want to finish my tour for me?" Johnny's rig language made tour come out sounding like tower.

Hurricane laughed again. "Couldn't do that, 'cause you'd have to finish my tour for me, and you'd fuck something up."

Johnny brushed frost from his beard. "You mean, like forget to turn the coffee pot on . . . or knock the doughnut bag on the floor?"

Hurricane liked Johnny, but he quickly had a moment of realization, and he turned serious as he said, "What the fuck are you doing down here? We've still got half our string in the hole!"

"I've got to piss captain, I—"

"Piss . . . *piss*? Where's your fuckin' piss jug? You've got this whole operation shut down to come down here and piss?"

"It's full. I forgot to bring it down and dump it." Recognizing that Hurricane was about to live up to his nickname, Johnny said, "I'll hurry."

Johnny was being a little looser than usual because when they finished this midnight-to-noon tour, he and his crew were heading home for a month off. He had pulled three hitches in a row, and after ninety straight days working his ass off in the darkness and the cold of Prudhoe Bay, he was getting a little randy. He knew that Hurricane would be a little easier on him today. Hurricane wanted him back, and not everybody came back.

Johnny thought about today for many long hours as he lay in his bunk over the last three months. He was a man betrayed, but now, a man on a mission. His former wife's actions had taken a toll on him . . . not just financially, but psychologically. About a month into his time working on the rig, he admitted to himself that he had nothing, and just as importantly, he had no place to go. He decided to find a place in Alaska. A small, remote place where he could sort his life out.

A little later, Johnny and his crew lined up for the security check before boarding the chartered jet that was headed to Anchorage. They were an eclectic lot—big burly guys headed back to Anchorage or Outside to Texas, Louisiana, or dozens of other places in the Lower Forty-eight; wiry, muscular guys like Johnny; bespectacled engineer types; and wizened veterans of the oilfields, all headed away from the frozen land at the end of the earth for some much-anticipated R&R.

One of Johnny's crewmates spoke to him from behind him in the line. "You stopping in Anchorage, Monkey Man?"

Johnny wasn't crazy about his nickname, especially when he was away from the rig, but he made a three-quarter turn and simply said, "Yeah."

"What the hell are you going to do there? You don't have anybody there. There's some nice hookers there. You *can* get laid. I bet you need to get laid. I need to get laid. I been here for a month. Shit, you been here for three months. You need to get laid. My wife even looks good when I been up here for a month."

The roughneck kept up his incessant chatter after he passed through the X-ray machine. "Got some great strip clubs, too. You ever been to the Wild Alaska "Beaver, Damn"? Great place, hot babes. They come to Alaska from everywhere, including Las . . . ." The roughneck stop talking for a minute as he remembered Johnny's situation, but he soon started again. "Lots of good bars. Winter, though . . . it's still winter. I want to get my ass someplace where it's warm." Johnny was beginning to wonder if the roughneck was going to keep talking all the way to Anchorage. He was thankful when he discovered that his seat was not near any of the guys who were part of his crew. He needed time to think.

The first stop Johnny made when he got to Anchorage was the Taylor Drilling Company office. He collected the stack of paychecks for his three months of work that they held for him. With over twenty-five thousand dollars' worth of checks in hand, he had the taxi driver take him to a midtown branch of the Arctic North Bank, where he opened a checking account and savings account, using the Taylor office address as his home address. He pocketed five hundred dollars in cash.

From the bank, Johnny had the taxi driver take him to the Backwoods Realty office. Their advertisement declared that *Remote Cabins and Homes* were their specialty. Their office was close to Taylor Drilling's in a small log cabin on Fireweed Lane. Johnny paid the cabdriver and walked in the front door. A small, attractive blonde woman greeted him like she had been waiting for him.

"Good afternoon. Welcome to Backwoods Realty. My name is Carmen, Carmen Sandy. How can I help you today?"

Johnny immediately felt comfortable with the woman and said, "I'm looking for a cabin . . . something remote, but not too far from Anchorage."

Carmen made a quick appraisal of Johnny as well: Alaska-man look, beard a little too scruffy, but probably handsome under all the hair, well proportioned and muscular looking. "Well, that's what I do, that's my specialty. Big cabin, little cabin, rustic, very rustic, what?"

"I want something small and rustic. I'm pretty handy, and I can fix it up. I work on the Slope, so I don't need anything fancy . . . just someplace to go on my time off. I'm looking for privacy and quiet. Oh, and I don't have a lot of money right now . . . maybe ten thousand to put down."

"Ten thousand dollars will get you into a lot of cabins, if you can qualify for a loan."

Johnny flushed as he said, "I just filed for bankruptcy . . . in Vegas." He sounded bitter as he continued, "My company went broke. I'm making good money now, but it'll take me a little time to recover."

Carmen was quiet for a moment. "Okay, well, that makes it a little more difficult, but not impossible." Her quick mind was sorting through the possibilities. As the owner and sole employee of Backwoods Realty, she had an intimate knowledge of the properties listed with her small company. One property came to mind immediately when Johnny described his financial situation.

More at ease, Johnny said, "Let's see what you've got."

Carmen sat down behind a large antique wood desk and invited Johnny to take one of the cushioned wood chairs in front of it. She began leafing through a large book. "Something comes to mind, and I think it may be perfect for you. An elderly couple from Alaska who retired to New Mexico. . . . They have a small log cabin for sale in Indian Valley . . . that's about a twenty-, thirty-minute drive from south Anchorage . . . maybe forty minutes to the cabin. That means it's within a little more than half an hour of shopping, but about as remote as it sounds like you'd like it to be."

Johnny was sitting on the front of his chair. "That sounds interesting. Do you have pictures?"

"Yes . . . here," Carmen said as she turned the big book toward him.

There were three exterior photos of the cabin from three different angles, and two photos of the interior. The exterior photos showed a beautiful small, clean log structure surrounded by a birch-and-spruce forest. The shot from the rear of the cabin afforded a glimpse of a small boulder-strewn stream about twenty-five yards in front of the cabin. The overall impression was exactly what Johnny was looking for. The two interior photos showed a tidy space with a living room and kitchen combined, plus a small bedroom and bathroom. It was all very basic, but with the rock fireplace, it had a warm, cozy look to it.

Johnny was struck by the idea that it was all too perfect. After what he had been through in the last few months, he wasn't expecting anything to work out well. "It looks very nice. How much property is there, and how much do they want?"

"Well." Carmen stiffened up and moved into her professional real estate saleswoman mode. "It is sitting on a one-acre lot that runs down to the stream. The owners want eighty-five thousand for it." Carmen waited for a moment for Johnny's reaction, and then continued. "I know the owners pretty well, and I know this market pretty well. There's no appraisal on the property, but I believe it is worth what they are asking."

Johnny moved into his own business mode, one that Carmen wasn't expecting from a rough-looking laborer. She didn't know about his past as a successful owner of a construction business. "That doesn't sound too bad, but what about the negatives. . . . There are always negatives. It looks like it's on a gravel country road. What's the situation on road maintenance, especially in the winter? How about power? Does it have electricity to it? And water—does it have a well? I'm assuming the toilet is an outhouse."

"Ah, good questions." Carmen was a little hesitant as she continued, knowing that what she was about to tell Johnny would run most buyers off. "There is no road maintenance, so snow removal in winter is your problem. No electricity and no well either, although there is a large fresh-water storage tank out back. You can get potable water delivered from a trucker who operates out of Indian. The tank's plumbed to run into the kitchen and the bathroom. The toilet *is* an outhouse, a very nice outhouse, but there is enough room in the bathroom to put a chemical toilet in. As I said, it is rustic." Carmen sat back in her chair, waiting for the inevitable, and planning her counter-effort.

Johnny was matter-of-fact as he replied. "I'm going to find an old pickup in Anchorage. I'll bet I can find a cheap used plow, too. I know I can get a five-KW generator for seven or eight hundred dollars . . . five KW should provide me all the power I need. Eventually, I could have a well drilled. . . . I'm in the drilling business, so I understand wells. I don't care about the outhouse. I've used 'em before. In a way, it's kind of peaceful."

Surprised, Carmen erased the last mental picture from her mind. "Well, I—"

"Excuse me, Carmen, but I wasn't finished. All of the things I just described will cost me about ten thousand dollars. Will your client take seventy-five thousand dollars, and will they consider carrying the loan? I can give them a twenty thousand–dollar balloon payment in six months, and pay it off in two years."

Carmen already knew that her clients would accept seventy-five thousand dollars, and they were willing to carry a note, but she had to continue to play the game. "I don't know. I'll have to check with them."

Never a man to hesitate when he thought the time was right, Johnny said, "I'd like to see the place. Do you think the road is passable enough now to get out there? I don't have wheels yet, but I plan to get something as soon as I can."

Carmen surprised herself with her quick response. "I can take you out there. I have an SUV with studded tires. I'm sure we can get there in it."

"What about your office?"

Carmen laughed. "I own it. I'll just put a sign on the door. Let's go." *I've done more than this to make a sale before,* she thought.

As they were driving south on the New Seward Highway, Carmen pointed out the Huffman Road exit and told Johnny that he could do his shopping there and be at the cabin in about thirty minutes, depending on the weather.

"Do they have a liquor store there?" Johnny said. "I haven't had a cold beer in three months."

After a quick stop, they were back on their way down the highway, which hugged the mountains next to Turnagain Arm. The sight of the inlet surrounded by snow-covered mountains was breathtaking. "This is beautiful," Johnny said quietly as he sipped a cold beer.

"It is . . . and it's like this all the way to Seward. Beautiful ocean, beautiful mountains, beautiful lakes and streams."

Johnny continued to drink his beer, and for the first time noticed how far Carmen's skirt had slid up her legs as she drove the huge SUV. *She's a very attractive woman,* he thought, *and she has great legs!*

The road up into Indian Valley was muddy, but the snow was mostly melted. Johnny took the surroundings in as they drove and felt a kind of instant connection with the valley. They passed several nice homes that were tucked back in the trees. The farther up the road they drove, the fewer signs of activity they saw. The homes became more run-down, and the road narrowed, looking less traveled. The forest became very dense. The birch trees crowded the large spruce trees for space, and they in turn were crowded by ferns and bushes. Finally, at a point where there were no recent tracks in the road, Johnny spotted a small log structure he recognized from the photos Carmen had shown him.

The cabin sat in an area that was more open than the thick forest they had just driven through. Whether it was naturally that way or cleared by the owners, it created a postcard setting.

"Here it is," Carmen said, waiting for Johnny's initial reaction before she said more. This was the point where she had lost the last client who showed some interest in the property. He wanted rustic, just not this rustic.

"I like what I see so far."

Relieved, Carmen said, "Yeah, it's neat isn't it?"

The cabin sat uphill from the road. Carmen eased the SUV up the short driveway and parked near the front door.

Johnny couldn't wait to get a look around, and he jumped out of Carmen's vehicle before she could shut the engine off. He made a quick trip around the outside of the cabin and then another trip around it while Carmen unlocked the front door.

They entered the cabin, and Johnny's first impression was that the owners had been fastidious in their organization and upkeep of the small interior. Even though it was now late in the afternoon, and the March temperature had fallen below 50 degrees, the interior had a warm feel to it. Carmen sat in a comfortable chair in the living room area of the main room while Johnny looked everything over slowly and thoughtfully.

"What about the furnishings?"

"The owners have taken everything they want out of here. It will all be yours if you buy it."

Johnny opened a cabinet and found an unopened bottle of Glenmorangie single malt scotch. "Somebody has good taste."

Carmen laughed. "James, he's the owner. He put that there intentionally. He said he wanted the new owner to have it, because anybody who's stupid enough to live out here needs a little snort every night before bed." After Johnny laughed, she cautiously added, "Doesn't it bother you . . . you know, the idea of being out here by yourself?"

Johnny sat down at the hand-hewn table and looked her in the eyes confidently. "Who's going to bother me? Monsters? Bad guys? Ghosts? The second thing I'm going to buy after I buy a pickup is a .357. I was in Desert Storm. . . . I won't hesitate to use it. And, I'm guessing I'll sleep like a baby out here . . . me an' my buddy, Glenmorangie."

"You're an interesting guy, Johnny. So, what do you think?"

"I'd like to buy it. What do you think about what I asked you, you know, the price reduction and the note?"

Carmen decided to drop the saleswoman bullshit. "I'm virtually positive they will take it, particularly if you will sign the note as you suggested, with the balloon payment, and the payoff in two years."

Johnny stood up. "Great, let's have a drink to celebrate. Do you drink scotch?"

Without hesitation, Carmen said, "Does a big bear shit in the woods?"

An hour later, it was almost dark, and they were both feeling good. Carmen suggested they should think about getting back to town, and Johnny countered with the idea that he would like to build a fire in the fireplace. He dug around and found a kerosene lamp and matches. Soon, they had light in the cabin. There was dry wood and kindling stacked up next to the fireplace, and he had a roaring fire going within a few minutes. Without really intending to do so, he had created a rather romantic atmosphere, and the scotch heightened their respective moods.

"I think you're a good woman, Carmen." Johnny was stretched out on a honey-colored brown bear rug in front of the fireplace, sipping his scotch. Carmen left the chair she had been glued to for an hour and moved over to sit cross-legged on the rug near him.

"As I said earlier, Johnny, you're an interesting man. I think you are a good man, too. I also see a handsome man under all that hair. I see a man's man in you. I was never quite sure what my dad meant when he was talking about a man's man, but I think I know now. I . . . I'm curious. I know you have a story. Would you mind telling it to me?"

Johnny had been reluctant to tell the guys at the rig about what had happened to him, other than some vague details. He suddenly wanted to tell somebody his story. . . . He wanted to tell Carmen his story.

Carmen sat transfixed as Johnny told her what Dottie had done to him. When he finished, all she could say was, "Shit."

Both of them were silent for a few moments, and then Carmen spoke up. "Nobody deserves that. No man deserves that. What are you going to do?"

Johnny smiled. "I'm doing it. I can work rigs on the North Slope for a few years, and put a few hundred thousand dollars away if I live like this." He indicated living in the cabin by swinging his head from side to side and looking around the room. "It won't cost much to live here, and it doesn't cost me anything when I'm at work. I'll save my money and start another construction business. I was pretty good at it."

"I've got a feeling you were." Suddenly, feeling warm, slightly inebriated, and benevolent, Carmen blurted out, "When was the last time you were with a woman . . . I mean, you know, *with* a woman. Oh shit, how long's it been since you got laid?"

"You real estate people are blunt," Johnny said with a slightly evil smile on his face. "It's been, I guess . . . the last time I was with Dottie. A little over four months ago."

Carmen looked downright wicked as she stood up and said, "Four months is long enough. Especially for someone who has been fucked over by a woman."

"Carmen, you are a beautiful woman, but I don't want a mercy fuck."

"Oh, this is not going to be a mercy fuck. In fact, I've got a feeling this will be much better for me than it will be for you."

There was an ethereal quality to the mutual removal of clothing that was taking place in the small fire-lit cabin. They still hadn't touched by the time they stood naked in front of each other. Johnny marveled at Carmen's taut little body and the way her ample breasts defied gravity. Her blonde triangle of hair looked golden in the light from the fireplace.

Carmen was having her own moment of revelation. Out of his workingman's clothes, Johnny was indeed the sinewy hunk of man she'd thought he would be. She could see enough of his tight muscular buttocks to wet herself with anticipation. He was already erect, and in fact, his excited state had made it a struggle for him to remove his underwear.

They made love on the bear rug for hours. Carmen couldn't remember a single session with a lover when she had been in so many positions. Johnny was inexhaustible and very physical, and when he gently put her legs over his shoulders and entered her, he held her easily and made love to her until she sobbed with pleasure. In the middle of the night, the fire was still hot from the mound of simmering embers, and they made love again. They both laughed when Carmen's head ended up next to the bear's head, and soon they fell back asleep.

There was some awkwardness to the morning, but not much. The type of mutual gratification they had shared trumped morning-after embarrassment. Johnny slowly awoke like a hungry bear waking after a long and satisfying winter sleep. He was covered with a warm blanket, obviously compliments of his bedmate at some time during the night. He heard her rustling around in the kitchen.

Johnny rolled over on his side. He couldn't see Carmen, but he could see her naked legs by looking under the kitchen table. She was opening cabinets, and mumbling to herself . . . "No fucking coffee anywhere . . . no water anyway."

His good-morning greeting surprised her. "Good morning," she replied. "How are you? I'm trying to find some coffee, but I'm not having any luck. Whenever you are ready to go, there is a nice little restaurant at Indian where we can have some breakfast. I don't know about you, but I'm hungry as hell." Carmen walked around the kitchen table, and came toward Johnny. He was instantly aroused as her neatly trimmed triangle of downy hair presented itself a foot away, just a little above his eye level.

"You shouldn't do that to me in the morning."

Coyly, Carmen said, "Do what, Mr. Monkey Man?"

"Shit, I did tell you about that, didn't I? I hate that name. . . . I don't want to hear that name when I'm away from the guys on the rig."

"Well, it's kind of appropriate. I've heard about *wild-ass monkey love*, and now I know what it is."

"Put that beautiful thing of yours down here," Johnny said as he patted the bear rug.

They made love again, passionately, and quickly. When they were lying on their backs, it hit both of them that they had things they needed to get done. "Okay," Johnny said, "now I am really starving, and that restaurant you mentioned sounds very good."

"Yeah, and I have a business to run, and some paperwork to get done for you."

"I've got lots to get done too. How long before I'll be able to move in here? I don't have much yet. That duffel bag I threw in the back of your Expedition is about it right now."

"This cabin has everything you need to get started. I'll get hold of the owners. If you want to put the ten thousand up right away, I think there is no reason why you can't move in right away."

Bore Tide Bill's was like everything else around the immediate area. A cozy log-cabin restaurant with a menu that would make any truck driver happy. Huge portions, great coffee, and a killer view of the water boiling in Turnagain Arm. Carmen and Johnny talked while they ate.

"Johnny, last night was . . . I'm not sure what the right word is. Exciting, sexy, wonderful?" After a hesitation, Carmen added, almost apologetically, "Maybe, needed. Whatever it was, I want you to know that I don't do that with all my clients. I don't do that with many men the first time I'm with them, either. You've probably heard this before, but I wanted to say it."

Johnny was sincere in his reply. "Carmen, you didn't need to say that. I can tell what kind of woman you are. And, it was exciting and needed for me as well. You are quite a woman."

"Ditto . . . I mean, man, of course. Okay, if you're done eating, let's get on the road. We can talk more in the car."

Carmen agreed to drop Johnny at a used-car dealership where she knew and trusted the owner. She gave him suggestions on places where he could buy some of the basics he needed. As he started to get out of her vehicle at the car dealership, she had one more thing to say that she had been thinking about.

"You've had a lot hit you in the last few months. I just met you, and I like you, but I doubt that you are looking for a relationship right now. I guess I'm sort of trying to . . . to offer myself. I know that sounds cheap, and I've never even used this term before, but if you would like to have a casual relationship . . . that is, someone who would like to be with you . . . oh shit, a booty call, then I'm available."

Johnny knew that what Carmen had said was difficult for her, and that she was embarrassed, so he answered her gently and sincerely. "Carmen, that is one of the nicest things any woman has ever said to me . . . and I would definitely love to be your, uh, booty-mate." They both laughed, and Johnny agreed to meet Carmen at her office in the afternoon to finalize the details of his purchase of the cabin.

As Carmen drove away, she thought, *That was probably sleazy on my part, but I want to keep that man in my life . . . at least until I get to know him better.*

Carmen introduced Johnny to the big friendly man who owned Lester's Used Cars, Tommy Lester, and he patiently waited for the two of them to finish their conversation. Johnny quickly found an eight-year-old faded red four-wheel drive F150 with a long bed, and agreed to buy it for four thousand dollars after an easy negotiating session with Tommy. Tommy drove Johnny to his new bank, where he withdrew seven thousand dollars in cash. He paid four thousand dollars to Tommy for the pickup and was headed off to the hardware store within an hour.

Johnny felt empowered as he circled through the aisles in Lowe's. He bought a five-KW portable generator, extension cords, a few simple porcelain light fixtures plus some electrical supplies to hook them up, a small assortment of hand tools, gas cans, assorted nails and screws, two flashlights, batteries, and a chain saw. When he reached that point in his shopping, he smiled to himself and thought, *this is like getting ready for a camping trip.*

Johnny's next stop was the local Fred Meyer store, where he bought a good sleeping bag, blankets and towels, lantern fuel, some toiletries, and enough food staples to last him at least a week. He also bought a case of beer, and another bottle of Glenmorangie, thinking, *it brought me good fortune last night. I think I'll stick with it for a while.*

The last stop Johnny made before he drove to Carmen's office was a local sporting-goods store. A knowledgeable clerk led him to a Smith & Wesson .357 revolver, which he paid eight hundred dollars for. He filled out the paperwork and was told he could pick it up as soon as they completed his background check. He was grateful to be in a state where handgun owners didn't need a permit or a license, and where they didn't have to register their handguns.

It was almost four o'clock when Johnny parked in front of Backwoods Realty. When he walked in the front door, Carmen was talking on the telephone, and she gestured for him to have a seat in one of the chairs in front of her desk.

"Yes, he's a very nice man. In fact, he just walked in the door. Would you like to talk to him?" Carmen threw a questioning look toward Johnny, and he nodded.

Johnny took the phone from Carmen. "Good afternoon, Mr. Young . . . or maybe good evening for you."

The happy voice on the phone obviously belonged to an older man. "Hello, youngster. Buying my cabin, huh? You'll love it out there. Me and the missus started fucking every time we got out there . . . even in the last few years we owned it when we didn't do much fucking. Something about being out there, you know, nature, fresh air. It was only a few miles from our home in Anchorage, but we loved to go out there. You gotta watch out for the bears though. Big fuckers. That's why I built that shitter so stout. Don't want to be sittin' in there and have a bear waiting outside for you. Check that creek out too . . . got some nice rainbows in it. Hardly anybody comes up there to fish. So, you gonna buy it?"

Johnny was chuckling to himself. "Yes sir, it's just what I want. And don't worry about the payments. I'm good for it."

"Well, sonny, that's what Carmen says, and she wouldn't bullshit me. Gotta go. Metamucil's kicking in. Let me talk to Carmen. Good luck."

Johnny handed the telephone to Carmen. The grin on his face didn't surprise her.

"Okay, James. You are more than welcome. We'll be talking. Well, yes he is, and we'll see about that. Goodbye."

"So, what do you think about Mr. Young?"

"He's a character, but he sounds like someone I'd like."

"You would. I've known him and Ethel for years. They are fun people. They're the kind of people you hate to see grow old. They love life, and they've made the most of it. He's a handful, though." Changing gears, she continued, "Well, we have a deal . . . unless you've changed your mind."

"Not now. I've bought thousands of dollars' worth of stuff for the place, and I'm anxious to get out there before dark. What now? You need a check, right, and I have to sign some papers?"

"Yes." Carmen was disappointed that Johnny made no mention of them doing something together. She had tucked that hope in the back of her mind.

They completed their business. Carmen had Johnny's cashier's check from the bank for ten thousand dollars in her hand when he said he needed to go because he had to stop by the sporting-goods store to pick up his new gun. They hugged and shared their mutual appreciation for the deal that was done. Johnny was headed out the door when he turned and said, "I've got things to get done, but I'd like to take you out for a nice dinner one of these days."

Carmen's heart jumped a little, and she said simply, "I'd love that."

61

Johnny felt a little contentment for the first time in months. It was March of 2006, only six months after his wife had taken everything from him, and he had something to start his new life with.

A few hours of pleasure can be a life-changing experience . . . and sometimes, it's just a lot of fun.
—From *Fred Longcoor's Book on Life*

Chapter 5

Reverend Raymond

Everybody at Billy Peet's ranch knew they were not supposed to answer calls to his private line. When it continued to ring like it was doing at the moment, the entire staff became nervous. Billy would be pissed if they answered it, and he would be very pissed if he missed a call because nobody answered it. It was a catch-22 mandated by a rich, self-absorbed tyrant.

The incessant ring of the overhead bell in the vehicle-storage building was particularly nerve-wracking to all who could hear it. Jeremiah was about to answer it and suffer the consequences when he heard Billy come out of the restroom in his man-room.

Billy was pulling his pants up as he hurried to the portable phone on the bar. He answered the phone with his right hand while holding his pants up with his left. "Billy," he said a little impatiently, and then quickly changed his temperament. "Yes sir. How are you?"

"Okay," the deep, stern voice of Mario Delaney replied tiredly. It was the voice of a man with a powerful past who now lived in the shadow of what he had been. "I think Benny found something . . . something for you. Seattle—Seattle, Washington. Some rich old bastard kicked it. Old man had a few billion dollars. Now there's a rich old widow broad with billions of dollars. According to what Benny picked up in the newspaper, she's been something of a philanthropist in the past . . . and she's a religious nut. Anyway, her old man just completed building a new warehouse complex in the Kent Valley. Supposed to be a hundred-million-dollar warehouse complex. He finished it, and died. Hadn't done anything with it yet. Rich old fart built it on spec. Benny thinks this is an opportunity for Reverend Raymond to do something."

Benny was Mario's right-hand man, and his research specialist. He spent hours and hours poring over newspaper and Internet stories looking for opportunities for his boss and his partners. When he'd spotted the article about Seattle computer billionaire, Del Brooksher, dying of a heart attack at the relatively young age of sixty-seven and leaving all of his wealth to his wife, Betsy, he immediately thought he had something. When the news reports subsequently suggested that Betsy was a little odd, and that she and Del had no children, Benny was convinced he had hit the jackpot.

The Reverend Raymond Mario referred to was another story. He was a complicated man who carried on like the Southern gentleman he was not. His mature, handsome features, neatly trimmed silver beard, and full head of silver hair made him look exactly like what he loved to pretend he was: a righteous, caring, and powerful Southern preacher. His façade hid the real man. More than once, Reverend Raymond had helped Billy, Mario, and their cohorts extort money from unsuspecting and generally needy widows.

Billy took it all in and said, "I'm not sure where Raymond is. I haven't heard from him in a while, but I have a cell number for him . . . if he still has the phone."

"Benny can find him if you can't. Can you put Budge on this from your end?"

"I sent Budge to Anchorage several weeks ago . . . and you know what that's for."

"Shit, I forgot about him going up there. You got anybody else who can get to Seattle and see what this is all about? I'm thinking about that big-ass warehouse sitting there, and some goofy old broad not having a clue what to do with it. And, you know, there are unscrupulous people out there who are probably going to try to take advantage of her." With that, Mario laughed a deep laugh.

"Well, you're right about that, so we need to get moving. This may be something with lots of promise. I'll try to find someone, or send Budge back down there for a few days. I'll try to find the Reverend."

Billy hit the off button, then quickly hit the talk button and dialed Budge's number in Anchorage.

"Wow, another call this week."

"Don't be a fucking smart ass. I need you to do something. You need to jump on the first plane you can catch going back to Seattle. In case you've already met the Eskimo woman of your dreams, you can tell her that you'll only be gone a few days, so the igloo shouldn't melt by then."

Budge ignored Billy's lame attempt at sarcastic humor. "What . . .

Seattle? I'm just getting settled here, you know, starting to take care of business here . . .your business. What the fuck is this all about?"

"Benny stumbled onto something. Mario wants you to check it out, set it up for Reverend Raymond. Sounds like a big deal. There'll be a bonus in it for you."

"How much of a bonus?"

Shit, I don't know. Trust me. Haven't I always treated you right? Probably, say, a couple grand . . . if it's taken care of right."

"Back at you. Don't I always take care of things right? Have I ever let you down?" Budge was rapidly running some past incidents through his mind, hoping Billy didn't remember them.

"I'm not going back through all that bullshit. Just take care of it right."

Billy spent the next fifteen minutes giving Budge all the details about Mr. Brooksher and his widow, as well as instructions on how everything should be handled.

"Get down there as fast as you can. Dig up everything you can about Mrs. Brooksher. Lay the groundwork for the Reverend. Try to get close enough to find out how many other wolves there are at the door. If there is somebody we need to get rid of, talk to me first. Don't talk to Mrs. Brooksher. If you think you need to for some reason, call me. I don't know what the probate laws are in Washington . . . in fact, find out something about that, but we want to be prepared to act before anybody else does. Take your computer with you, and I'll have Benny email you everything he can find out before you get there.

Budge was pissed when Billy first told him what he wanted, but as he thought about it, he realized that an all-expense-paid road trip back to familiar stomping grounds for a few days should be fun . . . with a cash bonus to boot.

Billy would soon find out that Reverend Raymond was holed up in a rundown motel along I-10 in Casa Grande, Arizona. Raymond's current circumstance would not surprise Billy, since his standard of living was always directly proportional to his immediate supply of cash. Saving money for a day when he wouldn't have income was never something that entered Raymond's thought process. When he hit on something big, he lived big. He spent it all on booze and women, and he lived in expensive digs for as long as he could afford it. Finding a regular job had never interested him. He tried that a few times in his life, and he just couldn't stay with any job he found. Getting up early, taking orders from some idiot who wasn't as smart as he was, and doing the same old crap day after day was not Raymond's style.

It had been several months since he was part of a successful scam. When the money ran out, and a private investigator began sniffing around, he moved out of his expensive rental in Phoenix and landed fifty miles down the highway in the middle of the desert in a roach- and scorpion-infested dump of a motel. He had been in the motel long enough that he was close to being thrown out for not paying his bill. Raymond Smith was currently registered at the sixty-year-old Don's Desert Oasis motel as Jim Smith.

An impatient sounding knock on his motel-room door brought Raymond out of his sweaty sleep. The beat-up old window air conditioner barely cooled his room on the unusually hot November morning. From his bed, he answered, "What. . . . What do you want?" Reverend Raymond had already intimidated the motel manager when he had knocked on the door two days earlier, and his response now sounded more apologetic than forceful.

"Sir . . . Mr. Smith? This is the motel manager. You . . . uh, you are a week behind on paying your bill. If we don't receive a payment today, you are going to have to . . . to leave. Did you get the money you said you were going to get yesterday?"

Raymond got out of the bed slowly, and walked toward the door. He knew that his six-foot-three-inch frame and righteous demeanor would intimidate the motel manager enough to get him another couple of days. He morphed from a sloppy unshaven con man into Reverend Raymond in the short walk from the bed to the door. Raymond pulled the door open forcefully, and the motel manager jumped back a foot.

"You, sir, are going to hassle me about that again today? I told you I have money coming. I thought I would get it yesterday, but that didn't happen. I called my benefactors this morning, and they apologized and told me that a courier would deliver the money within two days . . . at the most. I am a religious man, a man of God. Do you actually think I would cheat you out of your money?" Pulling himself to his full height, Raymond pronounced, "'Be ye angry and sin not: let not the sun go down upon your wrath.' Ephesians 4:26."

The nervous motel manager, who was way over his head being the manager of anything larger than a lemonade stand, timidly said, "I am sorry sir. I . . . I just have a job to do. I . . . I, *we*, will give you two more days. If you do not . . . I mean cannot pay us by then, you will have to—" With that, the rattled motel manager turned and hurried back to the motel office.

Raymond closed the door and laughed to himself, thinking, *You don't fuck with Reverend Raymond!*

Among the three things Reverend Raymond always kept with him, no matter how far down and out he got, were his cell phone and his white three-piece suit. Actually, Billy paid the bill for the cell phone so he could contact the Reverend when he needed him, and it was a lifeline they both had needed more than once. The white suit was the Reverend's work uniform, and when he wasn't working, it was carefully covered in plastic and hung in the closet. The suit was the defining stamp on his identity when he was Reverend Raymond.

The curious thing about Raymond Smith was that he really believed he was blessed . . . that he had somehow been anointed for bigger things in life. He was convinced that some supreme being had taken him under his wing to perpetually protect him . . . in spite of what happened to him when he was young. He even believed it when he was sweating up a stink in a musty bed in the squalor of a long-forgotten motel along Interstate 10 in the Arizona desert. His faith did waver now and then . . . as it was doing now. He knew how to survive when he reached the point he was at now, but he didn't like it. He could steal enough to get by, but he became restless. That's when his demons came alive.

Raymond blamed his protector when his demons took over. *You are letting me down*, he thought. *Where is my salvation? I have no strength to fight them without proper sustenance.*

When Raymond's demons came alive, he became a much different character than he was when he was Reverend Raymond. He became the antithesis of anything pious. He became an evil man.

In the recesses of his soul, Raymond had finally confronted the events that were the likely cause for his relapses into periods of depravity. It was convenient for him to blame an imaginary protector, but in rare moments of self-admission, he would let his mind wander back to the time and place where his life was been impacted in a way that would affect him forever. It was an embarrassing and deeply hurtful time for a very young boy.

Raymond's deeply religious mother had insisted that he become an altar boy in the local church. He protested to his father, but he was too weak to fight the issue with his domineering wife. Raymond didn't mind weekly visits to the church for services on Sunday mornings, but that was as far as he wanted to go. In fact, he actually liked Sunday mornings because he enjoyed seeing all the pretty young girls decked out in their Sunday-best dresses, and the family always went out to a restaurant for a nice breakfast after the service.

The minister was a jovial man who welcomed Raymond as an altar boy with obvious joy. Raymond was often fawned over by the ladies at the church for his apple-cheeked good looks, and the minister's first words to him were, "Welcome, Raymond. We are very happy to have a handsome young man like you join the other altar boys here in God's house." The minister had a hand on each shoulder as he welcomed Raymond, and he put his face close enough to Raymond for his sickeningly sweet breath to engulf him. *Train a child in the way he should go, and when he is old he will not turn from it. Proverbs 22:6*

Raymond heard whisperings about the minister from the other altar boys over the next several months, but he didn't understand what they meant. The minister was attentive to him, and often touched his arm or his shoulder as he talked to him, but Raymond never sensed that there was anything irregular about that. He didn't realize that the minister was playing a mind game on him, either. It built gradually: "Raymond, do you understand that I am God's messenger?" "Raymond, do you understand that I am here to be your protector?" "Raymond, I am here to comfort you when you need comforting." "Raymond, you must always trust me. . . . I will sometimes ask you to do things that you don't understand, but you must always trust me." *Satan himself masquerades as an angel of light. II Corinthians 11:14*

By the time Raymond had been an altar boy for over half a year, he liked the minister, and he trusted him. In fact, he felt a strange closeness to him that he didn't fully understand. An experienced, patient pedophile, the minister decided it was the right time to approach Raymond late one Saturday afternoon when all the other boys had left the church, and they were alone. After making sure all the doors were locked, he approached Raymond in the basement, where he was sweeping up after the day's events.

The minister was excited, but he knew he had to hide his feelings as he approached the boy. "Raymond, you have worked hard. . . . It is time to relax. I have a special treat for you. It is God's reward for your hard work."

There were many things about that afternoon that Raymond remembered in hazy details, but he would always have a vivid memory of the chalice that the minister handed him. It was gold, and it looked magical to his young eyes. The drink was sweet and cold, and tasted wonderful to him after the long day. The flavors were all new to him, and that made the drink even more special.

Very soon after Raymond started drinking the cold liquid, he began to feel warm and sleepy. As he tried to stay awake, he listened to the minister's soothing words.

"You are a very handsome young man, Raymond. I would like to see all of you. . . . I would like to worship you, your entire body." Raymond was almost lifeless as the minister undressed him. *Let the little children come to me, and do not hinder them, for the kingdom of God belongs to such as these. Mark 10:14*

When Raymond staggered out of the church an hour later, his body and soul were permanently soiled. He didn't understand the sick things the minister had done to him, but he felt the pain. The minister's guilt-ridden pleas for Raymond to keep the afternoon's events between them were wasted on him. . . . There was no possibility he was going to tell anyone about the humiliating things that had happened to him in the church basement. *Unto the pure all things are pure: but unto them that are defiled and unbelieving is nothing pure; but even their mind and conscience is defiled. Titus 1:15*

Raymond gradually dismissed that afternoon from his everyday thoughts, and his resolve to get revenge on the minister was buried with it. He hated the minister, but in a curious juxtaposition of blame, he came to hate religion and the Church more. His refusal to return to the Church earned him beatings and long periods of being grounded by his parents, but he was so steadfast in his refusal that they finally gave up.

Raymond's own fall from grace took several years. Every time he reached a low point, either financially or emotionally, his actions became more depraved. The fact that he had been molested by a minister as a child was buried in his memory, but not hidden from his subconscious. His eventual *discovery* of his demons was more a means to explain his increasing awareness of his perverse desires than anything else. He both hated what had happened to him and desired to find a way to make the religious establishment pay for it.

The third thing Reverend Raymond always had with him was a set of black clothes with a black jacket and a large black Stetson. It was his work uniform when times were bleak . . . at times when he had to steal food to survive, or steal whiskey when he needed it to numb his existence. It was his work uniform when he couldn't exact revenge on organized religion by being Reverend Raymond.

It was late in the afternoon when Raymond pulled the stolen bottle of Gentleman Jack Daniel's out of the drawer in his dingy motel room. He believed that if you were going to steal a bottle of whiskey, you should steal a bottle of good whiskey. He sat on the edge of the bed in his long-sleeved black shirt and his underwear and unceremoniously removed the cap from the bottle. Holding it up in front of him at arm's length, he toasted himself and took a leisurely swig from it.

Two long swigs later, as Raymond was beginning to feel the effects of the whiskey, he was also beginning to use his righteous indignation to justify a night of revenge. Raymond took another drink from the bottle and looked with satisfaction at the one-gallon gas can sitting in the corner of the room. That was when the cell phone in his duffel bag rang.

"Fuck. Who can that be?" he said out loud. "There's only a couple people who even know I have a phone. Must be a wrong number."

The phone continued to ring, and he decided to ignore it. When it became quiet, he took another long pull on the bottle. A minute later, it rang again. This time, Raymond looked at the number on the caller ID.

Shit, he thought. *It's Billy.*

Trying desperately to sound as together as his whiskey-tainted brain would allow, Raymond said, "Hello. . . . This is Reverend Raymond."

Billy was relieved when Raymond answered the phone, and his words rushed out. "Raymond, this is Billy. How are you? Where are you?"

"Billy? I . . . I'm fine. I'm in Arizona. What's up?"

"Arizona! What the fu . . . never mind. I think I've got a job for you. Could be a really big one. It's in the Seattle area . . . Kent, actually. Can you do it?"

Raymond's mind was cloudy, and he was flustered at his inability to respond coherently. "Uh . . . well, I'm kind of busy. I'm working a little deal here in the desert. I . . . I . . . what do you have going?"

"It's a rich widow . . . a fucking billionaire's rich widow. Benny found out about her. I think she might be really vulnerable, but we need to act fast. Budge . . . you remember him, don't you? Budge is going down there right away. He's going to check everything out, and set it up for you . . . if you're interested."

Raymond recognized Billy's ability to fall into big opportunities. He had made lots of money from his past dealings with him. "Well," he said, "I may be able to move some things around. When do you need me?"

"As quickly as you can get your righteous ass to Seattle. How soon can you get to the airport in Phoenix?"

Raymond's foggy mind was racing. *I don't think I want to risk going back to Phoenix. Time for a little fib.* "Uh . . . actually, I'm closer to Tucson. I think I could be there tomorrow."

"Phoenix, Tucson, I don't give a shit. I'm going to order you a ticket to Seattle from Tucson for tomorrow. I'll try to find something in the afternoon to give you time to get there. I'll call you back and give you the flight information . . . and I'll do an electronic ticket so you can just check in at the counter. When you find a place to stay in Seattle, let me know where you are."

"An advance. . . . I'll need some cash. I . . . I'm a little short right now."

"I'll get back to you, after I figure out how to get it to you."

Raymond closed his cell phone, and sat silently on the bed for a few moments. *Well*, he thought, *I'm back in the money!* He stared at the gas can, and wondered, *Should I still go ahead? I can score two for the boys if I do.*

Early the next morning as Raymond crawled into the cab of the big Peterbilt tractor headed to Tucson from the truck stop in Casa Grande, smoke still billowed from the remains of the First Southwestern Church in the distance.

"Thanks, man, I really appreciate this," Raymond said to the driver as he threw his duffel bag into the sleeper.

"No problem. Nice morning . . . except for that little happening over there. Looks like a church got smoked. I hope nobody got hurt."

"Yeah . . . that's too bad. Somebody must have lit a few too many candles. I'm sure nobody got hurt . . . I mean, if it started in the middle of the night."

When it was early morning in the Arizona desert in November, it was an hour earlier in Seattle and two hours earlier in Anchorage. Jimmy Flack had been trying without success to get hold of his contact for commercial real estate in the Seattle area, Doug Faithsen, since 7:00. The two were not close friends, but they had made a couple of successful long-distance real estate deals together over the years. Jimmy did know that Doug was not someone who made it a practice to be at his one-man office early in the morning, so he decided to just keep calling him until he answered.

The two men had never met face-to-face, so Jimmy had no mental picture that would give him an idea about the cluttered, dank office Doug was sitting in when he finally answered the phone at almost 9:00.

"Doug here. Can I help you?" The voice was almost squeaky, and was not something that immediately instilled confidence in callers.

"Doug . . . Flacker here. Jimmy Flack . . . in Anchorage. How are you?"

Doug hesitated for a moment to let his whiskey-addled memory catch up, then said, "Flacker, how are you? How are things at the end of the world?"

"It's top of the world, and it's frozen, and getting more frozen by the day."

"I'll bet. So, what's on your mind? You got a deal working?"

"Well . . . I certainly have something I'm working on that has some potential. I have a wealthy client who has an interest in buying something commercial. I don't think I'm going to find anything in Alaska that meets his requirements."

Doug was immediately interested, *wealthy* and *client* being the salient words. "Great," he said, "give me some details." Jimmy started talking, and the only time he was interrupted was when he mentioned Saylor Industries.

"Kent, the Kent Valley," Doug blurted out. "I know about Saylor Industries. They have a huge distribution facility there, and they have service stations all around the area."

Jimmy continued. "Yeah, that's them. Nick Saylor and Beth Saylor. Nick's mostly retired, but he's still the big dog. Beth is his sister, and she's the company president now that Nick spends most of his time in Maui. I'm a little unsure about who's making the investment . . . whether it's Nick or the company. It doesn't make any difference, though. He's one of the richest guys in Alaska, and Saylor Industries is one of the largest companies in Alaska."

As he listened, Doug was thinking, *Fuck, I may have just stumbled into the best thing I've seen in a long time, and I need it.* "Well," he said, "as you know, there's lots of properties here, and lots of them are warehouses or high-rises. I can certainly help you. How much of a bite does he want to take?"

"Well, he was purposely vague about that. Sort of gave me the surprise-me approach and said it would become clear to me after we talked about a few places. My gut says that he's ready to spend a lot of money, and he wants something that he doesn't have to worry over. He just wants . . . maybe, needs, to spend a lot of money."

How fucking perfect is that? thought Doug. *I can handle that!* "Damn," he said, "don't you hate clients like that? Do you think he has gone to other brokers?"

"I really don't. Nick and I have known each other for a long time." Jimmy was running a little bit of a bluff, but he was fairly confident that Nick hadn't gone to someone else.

The two of them talked over details, like the potential split on the commission and how soon Doug could come up with something Jimmy could get to Nick, and ended their conversation. In spite of their earlier deals, had Jimmy known the man he was dealing with better, he probably would not have called him back or returned his calls. It wasn't that Doug was crooked, it was that he was weak and slovenly. He drank too much, and he frequently did business when he was drinking. He was a balding, bespectacled, chubby little man, and those facts combined with his less-than-manly voice made him an unpleasant package in person. In truth, an anonymous relationship like the one he had with Jimmy Flack was perfect for Doug. He did know real estate, and he knew the commercial real estate business in the Seattle area very well.

Jimmy Flack was beginning to wonder if Doug was doing anything when he called him back late one afternoon a week later. Doug wasn't a morning person, but he could make things happen later in the day.

"I found a few things that might interest your client." Doug made a sipping noise as he finished the sentence, and Jimmy assumed he was drinking coffee. Doug set an empty glass down on his desk and poured more cheap whiskey into it as he continued. "I've got stuff from five million to a hundred million. Condominium complexes, high-rises, warehouses. I've got a dozen properties we can talk about."

"Wow, you've been busy. Sounds like an impressive portfolio. Can you give me some details?"

Doug spent the next thirty minutes giving Jimmy information about the properties . . . locations, individual prices, conditions, pluses, and minuses.

Jimmy absorbed it all, made notes, and then said to Doug, "My gut tells me that five million is way under what Nick is looking for, although I have a feeling that more than one property would interest him if they were the right properties. I'm not sure that a hundred million–dollar property is out of the question, but I know Nick well enough to know that it would really have to be right to interest him. I mean, low maintenance, positive cash flow, relatively new, no apparent problems."

Doug was finishing another sip of whiskey, and he half choked and half laughed as he put the glass down. "That's what everyone wants."

Jimmy tried to sound serious as he said, "Not everyone can afford to buy a hundred million–dollar property."

"Sorry, you're right. How about the stuff in the middle. Anything there interest you?" *Damn,* thought Doug, *don't shit in your own mess kit. This could be a huge deal.*

"Yeah. Let's try to narrow it down a little, and then I'll get hold of Nick and give him the information about what we've found."

After another long discussion, they decided to go with a high-end condominium building and three distribution warehouses. Jimmy ended the phone conversation wondering about Doug's remarkable personality change over the hour they had talked. He seemed almost giddy. Jimmy dismissed it as excitement over the potential of the deal they were discussing.

Early the following morning, Beth Saylor was entering the elevator in the penthouse of the Saylor Building for the quick ride down one floor to the executive offices of Saylor Industries. She was always there by 6:00 in the morning, and she relished the time alone in the offices. It was a time that touched her senses. She loved the silent morning views of the spectacular Alaska skyline and the smell of the fresh coffee brewing. It was a heady time for her, and in some ways it was the most empowering time of the day. There was not an arrogant bone in Beth's body, but she had reached the point where she was brimming with satisfaction and confidence, and she felt those feelings particularly strongly when she was alone in the corporate headquarters building in the early morning.

There had certainly been some challenges when Beth moved back to Alaska. Saylor's growth in the Pacific Northwest had been spectacular, but Alaska was still the heart of their business activities. Donnie Clayton was now doing a wonderful job of taking care of their operations in Washington and Oregon.

The night watchman had put the morning edition of the *Last Frontier News* in the mailbox by her door and turned the coffeemaker on for her, as he always did. Beth poured a cup of coffee and sat at her desk to read the paper. She didn't have to justify it to anyone, but she considered reading the paper to be part of her job. She rarely read it without picking up on something that could impact their business in some way.

Peter Schiff of Euro Pacific Capital continues to predict a serious recession in 2008, caused in large part by tremendous debt-financed consumption. North Slope gas producers can't agree on a gas pipeline plan. Water carriers to increase fuel surcharges. Commercial construction in Alaska at an all-time high. Several new retailers on the Anchorage horizon for 2007.

Beth absorbed the assorted news stories with a practiced eye. They were often contradictory, and it fell to her to make solid judgments about the direction Saylor Industries would take by sorting out the truth from the BS ... or more appropriately, by separating the most likely scenarios from the wild speculation and self-serving dogma. It was generally her common sense, much as it had been for Nick when he was actively running the company, that kept Saylor Industries in the right places at the right times.

Beth finished reading the paper just before 7:00, and that was when her phone rang for the first time. *Probably Donnie,* she thought, since it was 8:00 in Seattle, and he checked in with her many mornings.

"This is Beth," she said, without looking at the caller ID display.

"Good morning, you beautiful woman. Is it crispy in Anchorage today? It's already seventy degrees in Maui."

Ignoring Nick's envy-inducing weather report, Beth said, "Nick ... what a pleasant surprise. What's got you going so early in the day?"

"Business, sis, real estate business. I'm thinking about making a trip to Seattle. Flacker ... Jimmy Flack, you remember him, right? Well, he has some connections in Seattle, a guy there who has a few properties he'd like me ... us, to look at. I'd love for you to meet me there. You know the area way better than I do."

"Wow, that was kind of fast. Uh, what kinds of properties?"

"A small luxury high-rise condominium building, and three warehouses. Distribution kinds of warehouses. Staying close to something we know interests me. I'm not sure the high-rise does, but I told Jimmy I'd look at it. So, what do you think?"

Beth ran her immediate schedule through her head and realized there wasn't anything on her plate that couldn't be postponed or cancelled. "I'm in. When do you want to go?"

They agreed to fly to Seattle the next day. Nick would take The Bird, and Beth would fly from Anchorage commercially. When they concluded their business there, Nick and Beth would fly back to Anchorage in The Bird. After a short stay in Alaska, Nick would fly back to Maui commercially so the company would have access to the plane in Alaska for corporate business.

Beth was excited about seeing her brother and visiting Seattle, a city she had grown fond of . . . in spite of that one bad memory. And then there was the pending flight in The Bird. Flying all over the western United States in a forty million–dollar private jet that belonged to the company she co-owned with her brother had not grown old yet.

"Okay Nick, I'll see you in Seattle tomorrow . . . uh, are you going to bring Nani?"

"No. She's really busy with the foundation right now. I think she's a little worried about George, too. He's not feeling well, although we just played golf, and he played as well as I've seen him play in a while. I'll see you tomorrow."

Sometimes, adversity brings out surprising strengths in us. Sometimes, it is an unexplained burst before the end . . . and sometimes it is a rebirth.
—From *Fred Longcoor's Book on Life*

Chapter 6

Making Stan

After the board of directors of his bank had approved Stan Faro as their newest member, Henry Kuban called Stan. Thinking how much like putting the cart before the horse the entire deal was, he dialed Stan's number soon after the last board member left the bank.

"Faro-Way Properties, this is Stan Faro," Stan answered.

"Mr. Faro, this is Henry Kuban . . . with Arctic North Bank. How are you today?"

Respectfully, because Henry Kuban was known to everyone in Anchorage, Stan replied, "Mr. Kuban, I am fine, thank you. To what do I owe the honor of this call?"

Choking back his doubts, Henry said, "Well, Mr. Faro. I have what may be a surprising offer for you. I would like for you to join our bank as a member of the board of directors."

Stan was so surprised he was momentarily speechless.

"Mr. Faro, are you still there?"

"Yes . . . yes, excuse me. I'm, I guess I'm just really surprised. Why? I mean, why me?"

"Well, we have had an opening on the board for several months. One of our board members died, and we just have not replaced him. We began a quiet search a few weeks ago with input from some of our more important clients, and your name surfaced. Frankly, while I had heard of you, I didn't know much about you. Our search committee did some checking and liked what they found. Have I said enough to interest you?"

"Well, certainly, Mr. Kuban. I am very flattered. How about the—"

"Compensation? Well, the retainer is ten thousand dollars a year, and the board fee is five hundred dollars per meeting. There are committee fees as well, if you end up on a bank committee. Does that sound appropriate to you?"

"I'm still a little shocked sir, but yes, that sounds fair."

"Fine. I'm available all of today if you could manage to come by the main branch office and discuss it with me . . . maybe meet some of our people."

Stan was driving to the meeting when something Billy had said to him during his mind-numbing visit to Montana hit him. *You are going to hear from Henry Kuban. He's going to have an offer for you. It's an offer you will accept.* That conversation with Billy had been lost in his foggy memory of everything Billy said during his whirlwind trip to the ranch. The remembrance took some of the glow off of his impending meeting with the bank president. The thought of adding ten thousand dollars plus meeting fees to his one hundred thousand–dollar salary over the next year restored the glow. The unknown baggage all of this carried with it was slipping out of his consciousness. Stan met with Henry Kuban later that day, and the deal was sealed.

In the period since then, Stan had been busy. Following Billy's instructions, he had secured the new office space and put some attractive, reasonably priced furniture in it. He moved into an upscale condominium building between his new office and the downtown area. He also leased a new Lexus, and, most awkwardly of all, made a trip to a men's store for some new clothes. Stan had never been much of a clothes guy. He usually wore Dockers and white shirts. He now had new suits, new sport coats, a nice topcoat and a closet stocked with new shirts, dress slacks, ties, and shoes.

With everything that was happening, there was one thing that Stan couldn't get out of his mind. He daydreamed, and had real night dreams, about Anna coming into his bedroom. He could still smell the honey scent of her and feel her small hand gently resting on the covers over his naked body. The sight of her naked form standing next to his bed was burned into his memory. And the question wouldn't go away: why was she there?

Stan was slowly beginning to feel like somebody. A nice office, a nice condo, a nice automobile, and new clothes certainly were a big part of it, but mostly, it was the money. All of a sudden, he was making more money than he had ever made in his life. He was busy, so he really couldn't even spend it. As he gradually got out and about in Anchorage, he frequented all the best places . . . all the places he couldn't afford before. People he knew who saw him out just assumed that his real estate business had taken an upturn . . . an upturn that now did not seem unusual for someone like Stan. He often thought about how amazing it was that his new look of success had changed people's impression of him so quickly.

Manny Zito, the owner of Mr. Z's, was talking with one of his servers when Stan entered his upscale restaurant. Manny was quick to notice anybody who seemed to have money and came into his restaurant more than once. Stan liked being recognized by someone like Manny. Manny's restaurant catered to many of the big spenders in Anchorage, and being recognized was a big part of what Billy Peet wanted from him.

Manny quickly noticed Stan. He had only been in the restaurant twice in the last few weeks, but he looked familiar. He knew he had been around Anchorage for many years and had been in occasionally in the past. Manny also knew Stan had ordered some expensive wines both times he had been in the restaurant recently. He quickly left the server he was talking to and approached Stan.

"Mr. Faro. It is nice to see you again."

"Thank you, Mr. Zito. It's nice to see you."

Stan loved the pretend closeness with Manny, even though he knew it was a show that most customers were part of.

"Is someone joining you, or are you going to sit at the bar?" Manny was pretty sure Stan would be by himself, and that he would be sitting at the bar as he had the last two times he was there.

"Bar, Manny. I'm a bar guy . . . best place in the house."

"Okay, I agree. You know the way. Enjoy yourself, and I'll come by and chat with you in a little while."

"Thank you." Stan knew Manny's reputation, and he knew he would come by, particularly if Stan ordered a nice bottle of wine. It was not something that offended Stan, or anybody else. Manny was a first-class guy who ran a first-class restaurant, and his guests always offered him a glass of their wine.

Stan moved to an area toward the middle of the bar that had become his favorite spot. He liked Mr. Z's, and he particularly liked the fact that he could eat at the bar. He would have felt silly sitting at a table by himself in a restaurant, and especially sitting by himself at a table in a nice restaurant where many of the city's luminaries ate.

Like Manny, the bartender recognized Stan. Stan remembered seeing him behind the bar for many years. Unlike Manny, he didn't remember his name.

"Good evening, sir. Mr., uh . . . I'm sorry, I've forgotten your name."

"Faro, Stan Faro." Stan's face registered disappointment at the bartender's failing, while the bartender privately promised himself he would remember this man's name in the future.

"Yes, Mr. Faro. What can I get for you? Do you need a menu?"

"You know, I do need a menu, but not just yet. I think I feel like having a martini, up, and just sitting for a little while. How about Three Olives?"

"We've got it. Coming right up."

Stan watched the early-evening dinner crowd beginning to enter the restaurant and recognized several of the customers. A few people even came over to the bar to greet him, and he was feeling very much the man about town.

Not bad, Stan, he thought to himself. *You are becoming someone to be reckoned with in Anchorage.* Stan sipped his martini and continued to feel good about himself until his cell phone rang. When he looked at it, he saw Billy Peet's number on the caller ID.

Trying to sound businesslike, he answered, "Billy, how are you?"

"Well, I'm fine. Are you having fun spending my money?"

Stan knew Billy pretty well, but he couldn't make a judgment on what his tone meant. "I'm fine. I guess I am enjoying spending your money. I like to think I'm spending it the way you want me to."

Billy laughed. "Don't be so sensitive. . . . I'm fucking with you. I pay you enough money to entitle me to fuck with you. I talked with Henry. Sounds like that went okay. You've got your first board meeting coming up, right?"

A little more at ease, Stan replied, "Yeah, in a few days. I've met most of the board members. Some are kind of standoffish, some are okay, and several of them act like they don't give a shit."

Billy laughed a short laugh again. "They *don't* give a shit. In case you haven't figured it out, that board thing is a free ride . . . a nice little bonus check, some prestige, and very little to do. I'm sure there are guys all over Anchorage who are pissed that you got on that gravy train instead of them." Billy's tone turned somber. "Just remember what you are there for. Learn, be recognized, use it."

"I know. I'm not sure what to use it for right now, though."

"Get off your ass. Don't wait for me to hand everything to you on a silver platter. There are some very influential men on the board. Find out ways to use them. Shit, some of them have boards of their own. Try to get on their boards. Find out what kinds of things they support, and get involved. I'm not paying you all this money just to sit in bars and suck down martinis."

Stan looked up, half expecting to see Billy somewhere in the restaurant. "I . . . I don't just sit around in bars sucking down martinis."

Billy ignored Stan's reply. "Get out there, Stan. Put that college-educated brain of yours into gear. Find ways to become more visible and more known around Anchorage."

Stan was getting pissed, and he made an out-of-character, condescending reply. "Sure Billy, I'll get on it."

"Don't talk shit to me, Stan. I'm paying you enough to demand whatever I want from you. Get off of your ass and do more than just cash my checks." With that, Billy ended the conversation.

"Billy, I—"

The phone connection was gone. He gritted his teeth and talked into the silent receiver with just his lips moving. "Fuck you, Billy. I'm going to sit around this bar and drink martinis." And that's exactly what Stan did, until he became more intoxicated than he had been since he was at Billy's ranch. After Stan slobbered his way through an expensive dinner that he would never remember, Manny had to call a cab for him, and he staggered into his condo and passed out on his bed with his clothes on.

When Stan was waking up with a huge hangover the next morning, Beth was settling into her first-class seat on an Alaska Airlines Boeing 737-900 bound for Seattle. She was excited about her trip and her joint effort with her brother to find an investment for Saylor Industries. It was always fun being around Nick. She knew that good food and good wine would be included in their activities, and she relished the idea of squiring her brother around turf that was way more familiar to her than it was to him.

It was very satisfying to know that she had been a big part of creating and managing the business success that had allowed Saylor Industries to build its huge cash reserves. *Spending some of this cash should be fun,* she thought.

Beth always thought of herself as a keen observer, and she noticed the tall and strangely good-looking man sitting across the aisle from her when she took her seat. She thought his silky blue suit was a little bit much, but he looked interesting . . . and he *was* riding in first class. She had no idea that Budge Brown was on a mission similar to hers. He was also looking to help set up a real estate deal, but he was expecting to facilitate one much more lucrative than Beth and Nick's.

The tired-looking old lady sitting by the window next to Beth was sleeping shortly after the plane left the ground, so she concentrated on a magazine and kept one ear tuned to what the man across the aisle was saying. She wasn't nosy; she preferred to think she was curious. Anyway, the man was just loud enough for her to hear almost everything he said.

The flight attendant approached Budge, and before she could ask him what he would like, he said, "Good morning, pretty lady. What can I help *you* with?"

The not-so-pretty woman put a practiced smile on her worn face and said, "Well, I think you took my line. What can I help *you* with?"

"Well missy, I think I'd like to buy you dinner in Seattle tonight. The finest place you know."

Having heard every come-on imaginable from thousands of ego-bloated first-class customers, and having passed being a missy many years before, she added a touch of sarcasm to her reply. "Well, thank you, sir. That's a sweet offer, but I'll be dining with George Clooney in Los Angeles tonight, which is where my final destination is. In the meantime, would you like something to drink? We have—"

"Yeah, I know what you have," was Budge's sharp reply. "I'll have a Bloody Mary . . . extra olives."

Beth caught the entire exchange, and within thirty minutes of having an ever-so-slight interest in Budge, she decided he was an obnoxious dick. With little else to do, she continued to entertain an angry fascination with him and tried to listen to his conversation with the man in the seat next to him.

"I'm going to Seattle to make a big real estate deal," Beth heard him brag in response to the man's question about what he did. "It's going to be a hundred million–dollar deal," Budge gloated.

Bullshit, Beth thought. It was then that she realized the man was talking as loud as he was in a vain attempt to impress her. She didn't bite, and she didn't respond to his attempts to establish a conversation with her by throwing more of his lame lines out:

"Say pretty lady, could I borrow some of that newspaper in the seat pouch in front of you?"

She soon bored of the exercise of having anything to do with the arrogant man, and fell asleep.

Nick had arranged for a limo to pick Beth up when she exited the Alaska Airlines baggage area in Seattle. A crisp-looking middle-aged driver was waiting near a white limo with a sign in hand that read *Beth Saylor*. He had prematurely gray hair and a full, neatly trimmed gray mustache that gave him a safe and friendly look.

As Beth approached the limo driver, he said, "Ms. Saylor?"

"That's me," was Beth's jaunty reply.

"Welcome, Ms. Saylor—"

"Beth . . . I'm Beth." Her interruption came out more bluntly than she had intended.

"Okay . . . Beth. Welcome to Seattle. I am supposed to tell you that

Mr. Saylor's plane is due at Boeing Field in about half an hour, and he wants me to take you there to meet him. My name is Eddy."

"Okay Eddy," Beth said as he opened the door and she crawled into the back of the limo. "Sounds good to me."

It only took them fifteen minutes to get from Seattle-Tacoma International Airport to Boeing Field, and through a chain-link fence Beth saw The Bird taxiing up to King's Row Executive Service as they pulled into the parking area. Eddy parked the limo and hustled around to open Beth's door.

"Is that Mr. Saylor's plane?"

"Yes, Eddy. Nice timing. My brother has a thing about being on time, and it looks like you do, too."

Eddy laughed. "Just luck," he said, privately wondering what Beth and her brother did to have the wealth they apparently had.

Beth left the limo and went through the front door of King's Row Executive Service, headed toward the waiting area. A familiar-looking woman who had either done her research or remembered her from previous trips she had made through the center greeted her as she entered the room.

"Welcome, Ms. Saylor. It looks like you arrived just in time to meet your brother."

"Yes. Great timing by all parties," Beth said as she noticed her brother exiting the G550 and coming down the air-stairs. Her first reaction was one of surprise as she perceived that Nick had aged dramatically since the last time she saw him. As Nick got closer to the building, familiarity took over, and she realized that he was the same man he had been for as long as she could remember. *We are getting older though,* she thought.

Broad smiles and a warm hug followed Nick's entry into the waiting area. Nick stepped back proudly and said as he held Beth at arm's length, "Beth, you are as beautiful as ever. It is great to see you. I know it's only been a couple of months, but it seems longer."

"It's because seeing each other is important, Nick. We don't have a big family, and it's a diminishing family. . . . ." Beth's voice trailed off, and Nick knew she was thinking about their mother, Brenda, who had passed away just six months earlier.

Nick put on his big-brother persona and pulled Beth close. "Life goes on, sis. I miss Mom too, but you and I and Chris have a lot of life left in us . . . good life, and hopefully, Dad has some good years left in him, too."

Nate Saylor, founding father of the company and family patriarch, had retired in Fairbanks years earlier and now lived a quiet life socializing and occasionally traveling with some of his old buddies from the trucking industry. Nick and Beth made sure he had everything he needed or wanted, but he was happiest living a fairly modest life among the people he had worked with to pioneer the trucking business in the forty-ninth state. The death of his life-mate had taken a toll on him, and Beth and Nick both worried about him daily.

"Let's get going, sis," Nick said. "We'll get settled into the hotel, and then we should have enough time to look at one property before the end of the day. Flacker . . . Jimmy Flack, flew down here from Anchorage yesterday, and he and his local contact are waiting to hear from us."

"I'm ready, Nick. I'm rested. I sat across the aisle from some blowhard who put me to sleep."

Nick laughed, and said to Eddy as they got into the back of the limo. "Eddy, take us to the Executive Plaza Hotel, next to the airport." Turning to Beth, he explained, "I wanted to be close to the Kent Valley. The Executive is close to our office, and close to all but one of the properties we are going to look at."

"You're the boss, big brother. I've stayed there several times. Great restaurants, nice rooftop bar. Let's go."

"We've got Eddy as long as we want him. I told the limo service we may be here two or three days."

"Good. He seems nice."

Nick called Jimmy Flack and told him they would meet him in the lobby of the Executive Plaza Hotel in an hour. Jimmy was excited, and hoped he didn't sound that way to Nick. He wanted to sound businesslike.

Jimmy had just met Doug Faithsen a couple of hours earlier, and he was feeling more than a little concerned about his liaison with the strange little man. After Doug briefed him in detail about the properties he found, Jimmy's fears were eased a little, but he wondered how the man had ever sold anything to anybody. He figured it had to be his knowledge about the business, because it was certainly not his refined appearance or bubbly personality.

When Nick and Beth walked into the lobby of the hotel an hour later, Jimmy was immediately struck by what a stunning woman the mature Beth had become. He hadn't seen her for several years. He thought Doug's eyes were going to pop out of his head.

They exchanged greetings all around, which were made awkward by Doug's tongue-tied inability to acknowledge Beth: "Nice to see . . . ah, meet you Madam, uh Miss . . . or Mrs. Saylor."

Jimmy looked down at Doug's crotch, half expecting to see that he had wet his pants.

They all piled into the limo. Doug regained his composure a little when Jimmy asked him to give Nick and Beth information about the property they were going to look at. As Doug reeled off market information and statistics about the building they were going to look at, it quickly became obvious he knew his business well.

The first property was a vacated furniture distribution warehouse near the Southcenter Mall in Tukwila. It was central to the airport, downtown, and the Port of Tacoma, and right next to all the stores in the mall. Doug had code access to the empty warehouse. They opened an overhead door and drove the limo into the warehouse.

Nick always considered himself a gut-feeling kind of businessman. Not that he wasn't pragmatic, because he definitely was, but there was something about the building that immediately made him feel uncomfortable. They all got out of the limo and followed Doug around as he laid out a litany of reasons why the building represented a great opportunity.

Nick listened carefully as they examined the warehouse and the enclosed suite of offices. It was obvious that the building had been subjected to hard use, and that provided Nick with a justified opening.

"How old is this building?"

Doug immediately transformed into the stammering lump of human flesh he became the first time he saw Beth. "Ah . . . it's ah . . . let me look at my, ah, let me find my pap . . . oh, now I rememb . . . it's, it's thirty-two years old."

Jimmy jumped in to try to make a save. "It looks like it's in good condition Nick—"

"Good condition? Come on, Jimmy. Have you really looked around? The floor is worn to the point that it would need to be resurfaced. I'll bet the electrical is all out of code. The offices are dingy. There is damage everywhere. This is not the kind of crap we want to look at, Jimmy. Just out of curiosity, how much do they want for this dump?"

Doug spoke up. "They want five million for it . . . but I think they'd negotiate."

Nick snickered. "I would hope so."

Everyone, including Beth, was taken aback by Nick's brief outburst. They all were silent for a moment. Beth spoke first. "Nick, can you and I talk for a minute?" She turned and walked away, and Nick followed her.

"Nick, I know you very well, and you changed the minute we got in here. I know you don't like this place, and I don't like it either. I think it's creepy. That's all we need. Let's get out of here. Now, go make nice with those guys, and let's hope the next one is better."

When Nick approached the three men waiting by the limo, with Beth trailing him, he tried to sound a little contrite. "Look Jimmy, this is not what we're looking for. We want to see something newer. We would consider something that requires a little work, but this needs a lot more than a little work. Do we have time to see something else today?"

Jimmy turned to Doug. "Doug, is there something else we can look at today?"

An obviously distressed Doug replied, "The Redoubt Plaza. I think. All of the condos are leased, but I know one tenant who I believe would let us in on short notice."

Jimmy turned back to Nick and Beth. "That's the luxury low-rise condo building. It's not far from here." As an afterthought, he added, "It's pretty new."

After Nick's affirmative, "Let's go," Jimmy said to Doug, "Call 'em."

After an accommodating tenant of the Redoubt Plaza led them through her spotless and luxurious condominium unit, they toured the utility rooms and the underground garage, then gathered back in the limo.

Nick and Beth had not had an opportunity to discuss what they had seen. Nick said, "Jimmy, that is more the quality we are looking for. I'm not sure how Beth feels, but I don't know if we want to be in the condo-leasing business. What's the asking price?"

Doug replied, "Nine million dollars . . . asking. I'm sure we could do better than that. The owners are having some financial problems."

"Okay, let's call it a day. Beth and I can talk over dinner tonight. I want to meet at our hotel at nine o'clock tomorrow morning and go look at the other two properties. Are they . . . more substantial than what we've looked at today?"

Doug opened his mouth to speak, but Jimmy was tuned into Nick's message, and he answered before Doug could. "Yes, we'll be here, and the properties we'll be looking at tomorrow are much more substantial than the two we looked at today."

Beth noticed a flash of surprise in Doug's eyes.

After the group goodbye, Nick and Beth entered the lobby of the Executive Plaza Hotel. They did not see the animated conversation taking place between Jimmy and Doug in the parking lot.

"What the fuck are you doing?" Doug said. "What are you talking about? The two properties we are looking at tomorrow are in the same price range as the low-rise."

"Look, Doug. Didn't you get Nick's message? He's looking for something bigger . . . I think a lot bigger, and newer. You need to get your ass back to your office and find something, or two somethings, that are bigger and better than what we looked at today. Warehouses. He likes warehouses . . . preferably somewhere in the Kent Valley. Twenty million, shit, fifty million. Don't be bashful."

Nick and Beth were having a drink before dinner in the hotel's four-star restaurant when they had their first opportunity to discuss the day's events.

"So, Nick. We didn't like the furniture warehouse in Tukwila. I think the condo building was nice, but I personally don't want to deal with a bunch of spoiled, rich renters."

"Me neither, sis."

Fine wine and fine food followed the fine scotch they were drinking, and Nick and Beth had a leisurely three hours together discussing their investment mission and getting caught up on each other's lives. As always, their mutual passion for Saylor Industries was on the front burner, and that conversation dominated most of the evening.

Beth went up to her room at ten-thirty, more intoxicated than she had been in a while. It had been a nice evening, and she was happy. She knew she had done a great job of managing Saylor Industries, but she loved to have her brother heap praise on her performance. After all, it was Nick's balls and foresight that had moved Saylor Industries from being a modestly successful Alaska trucking company to being a huge full-service freight-handling company, now one of the largest and most successful companies in Alaska and the Pacific Northwest.

Untypically, Beth began to remove her clothes as she entered her suite at the hotel. She threw them all over the room as she headed toward the huge bathroom. She had a strange déjà vu moment as she entered the extensively mirrored bathroom. Her thoughts went back to the night she had viewed her body in her own condominium in downtown Seattle before she dressed and left to have dinner by herself at Ivan's. She felt very good about herself then as she viewed her naked body in the full-length mirrors. That was the night she ran into John Westbrook . . . her former lover from college. It became both an alcohol-fueled sexual reunion with her old friend and the restart of a relationship that almost destroyed her, Saylor Industries, and thousands of people.

As Beth viewed her tall, athletic, naked body in the mirrors, she became melancholy, and the happiness she'd felt after the dinner with Nick faded. Drunkenly, she thought to herself, *I am an attractive woman. I am a successful woman. I am a proud woman, and I'm not an arrogant woman.* Beth spread her feet apart. With her high heels still on, she looked like a sex symbol. She bent her head over, and with both hands she fluffed her long auburn hair. As she lifted her head, she thought, *why do I just attract bad men? What's wrong with me? Why do I just attract crazy men?*

Beth put her hands on her hips and said to herself, "Isn't there some good man out there who wants me . . . who wants all of this?"

Tears were welling in Beth's eyes as she turned and crawled into the huge bed by herself. She was a strong woman, but at times like this she admitted to herself that she was lonely.

Budge Brown would have happily crawled into Beth's bed that night, or any other night. He had stood on the opposite side of the baggage claim conveyor watching clandestinely as she left the baggage area and was led to the white limousine. He was pissed that she hadn't acknowledged his obvious overtures on the airplane. His ego had long ago failed to realize that women like Beth Saylor were not attracted to men like him. He managed to get next to lots of women, but they were all women of a world with fewer rules and more desperation than Beth's. Budge couldn't know that Beth was having a moment of quiet desperation herself right now, but even if he had, it wasn't the kind of desperation that would have allowed him in.

Budge collected his luggage and picked up the rental SUV he had reserved. He drove the short way to the Holiday Inn Express near to the airport. It was not the luxury hotel he would have preferred, but it was comfortable, and he knew Billy would be all over him if he asked to be reimbursed for staying in an expensive hotel.

When he checked in, the young woman behind the counter said, "Good afternoon, Mr. Brown. Welcome to Seattle. You have a message waiting for you."

Budge took the folded note and opened it. The cryptic message read, *At the Executive Plaza Hotel, room 1001, call me. Rev.*

"Fuck," Budge blurted out loud. The clerk behind the desk jerked her head up from where she was entering Budge's credit card into the computer and gave him a steely look.

"I . . . I'm sorry, miss. Some shi . . . some bad news."

Reverend Raymond is staying at the fucking Executive Plaza Hotel, and I'm at the fucking Holiday Inn. Room 1001 is probably a suite too, he thought. Budge had been involved with Reverend Raymond a couple of times on past deals of Billy's, and he didn't care for him. In his opinion, Raymond was one creepy fucker.

Budge looked up the number for the Executive Plaza Hotel and called Raymond as soon as he got into his own room.

"Reverend Raymond." The voice was officious and immediately annoying to Budge.

"This is Budge."

"Well, praise the Lord. Welcome to Seattle."

"Don't give me your holy-roller bullshit, and I don't have anything for you yet. I just got here. I need a day or two to get the lay of the land, and you need to lay low . . . in your high-dollar hotel room. I'll get back to you."

"I pay my own expenses," was all Raymond said, thinking about the fact that he could afford the room he had for about two more days.

"I don't give a shit about that. Just be available when I need you." With that, Budge hung up.

Budge got his laptop out of the carrying case and hooked it up to the Ethernet cable. As soon as he got into his email, he saw the expected message from Benny.

Betsy Brooksher lives in Kent. Big house on the hill, address is 1200 Brooksher Blvd. She reportedly is in deep mourning . . . her and the old man were married for over 40 years. Hasn't been in the news much, other than the standard stuff about what a great guy he was, blah, blah. I have noticed several references to a guy named Marc Madrid (now there's a name for you) who seems to be a family/business accountant, although sometimes he's referred to as an administrator and close friend of the family. Sounds to me like a guy who may be trying to horn in on the action. The company operates out of an office building near the Southcenter Mall (I don't know the address for it, but it's called the Brooksher Building). Let me know if you need anything else. Benny

Budge said to the empty room, "Yeah, what about the probate laws? What about the address for the new warehouse? What am I supposed to do with this Reverend fucker while I try to figure this all out? Maybe I'll schedule a revival."

Budge typed out a short reply to Benny, and hit send: *I need expense money. Five grand. Put it into my account in Anchorage, and I'll use my debit card. I'm guessing you are going to be hearing from the Reverend. He's staying in a high dollar hotel I don't think he can afford. Budge*

The next thing Budge did was pull a small dog-eared green booklet out of his computer bag and look up a telephone number.

"The Finder's Group, how may I help you?" Budge pictured Kitty Finder's receptionist with her pretty little pixie face, short blonde hair, full lips, and generous bosom sitting behind her desk near the front entrance to the small suite of offices.

"Sweet Sandy . . . this is Budge . . . Budge Brown. How are you?"

"Budge, Kitty told me you were in Alaska. Are you calling from Alaska?

"No, I'm in town. I came to town to see you . . . unless you're still married to that big ugly guy."

Sandy snorted her short, annoying laugh and said, "You know he's not ugly, Budge, and I'm still with him."

"Oh, well, in that case, is your boss available, or is she sleuthing around somewhere?"

"She's available." Knowingly, she added, "And I bet she'll be happy to talk to you."

"Great. Thank you. And if you ever—"

"Budge, you are such a bad boy. I'll get Kitty."

"Kitty Finder. How may I help you?"

"Ah . . . good afternoon. I'm looking for a kitty. A cute little brown one. I haven't seen her for a couple of months. I miss touching her."

"Look, this is a private-investigation office. We don't look for kitties . . . you need to . . ." Kitty paused for a moment. "Budge?"

"Gotcha. How's the hottest investigator in King County? And, I've heard you're good at your job, too."

"I'm fine. I thought you were in Alaska . . . are you in Alaska?"

"I'm right here, baby, and I want to see you. Business *and* pleasure, if you can handle it."

"I've always got time for you, Budge, even though you're a bad man, and I don't understand what I see in you."

"Maybe you like what I see in you."

Kitty caught the double entendre. "Yes, you are a bad man."

They both let Kitty's last words hang for a moment, and then Budge said, "Well, I'd like to see you. I have a business need . . . and a personal need, to see you. How about dinner? The Rusty Turtle, about six o'clock?"

Kitty hesitated, then replied, "Well Budge, I have sort of met someone . . . just recently. I mean, nothing serious, but I do like him."

Budge was disappointed, but he needed Kitty professionally more than he needed to have sex with her. "I have a job for you, Kitty. I'm doing some work for Billy Peet."

Kitty ran a legitimate investigation office, but she wasn't afraid to push the envelope, and she recognized Billy's name from past work she had done for Budge—very profitable work. "I guess we could have dinner and talk about it. My friend is going to a ball game tonight, anyway. I'll meet you at The Turtle at six."

You can start in any direction you want to, but that thing is going to

lead you wherever it wants you to go. It fears naught . . . danger, discovery, embarrassment, financial loss. Follow it no more forever!
— From *Fred Longcoor's Book on Life*

Chapter 7

The Pyramid

Ron Minty had the Alaska Permanent Fund on his mind all the time. Granted, being on the Board of Trustees of the Alaska Permanent Fund Corporation required him to think about the fund, but he had become preoccupied with it since the last board meeting. He couldn't get the idea out of his mind that there was a fund worth thirty-five billion dollars sitting there that he was partially responsible for managing, and all he was making from it was a fee that was pitiful in comparison to the value of the fund.

Ron never felt like he was dishonest. In the rare moments when he confronted the reality of his life, he admitted that he had made some choices that would not be acceptable in society . . . or maybe even in the eyes of the law. He certainly did some cheating in law school . . . and even in the way he got into law school, but it was easy for him to rationalize tha. He *did* graduate from law school, and he was in fact *close* to being an honors student. And now, he *was* a valued member of society. He'd all but forgotten the fact that he'd skipped out on almost two hundred thousand dollars' worth of student loans . . . and besides, he knew several former students who hadn't paid their loans back either.

Still, being so close to thirty-five billion dollars was eating at him. Just think, *if I could just make one-tenth of a percent . . . or one-hundredth of a percent off of the fund, it would be a fortune. And it wouldn't be noticed or missed.* Ron had often thought that there should be a way for him to use his position on the board of trustees to take advantage of the fund.

After the early November meeting, he began to formulate a loose plan. He started working on it after he saw a television story about Charles

Ponzi, who ran a famous pyramid scheme in 1920. As he thought about it, he convinced himself that he really wouldn't do something like that, but he continued to refine the details in his mind, and finally committed it all to a private document. When his wife was buried in some smarmy sitcom that he didn't care about, he would head off to his den and research details that he could mold into a plan.

The Plan, by RM

It shall be called PF Investors, Alaska. As a member of the Board of Trustees of the Alaska Permanent Fund Corporation, all correspondence will be directed to me at a post office box designated as PF Investors, Alaska. I'll get a separate telephone number, and return all the calls myself . . . unless I can find someone to work with me. Potential investors will be told that a recently uncovered Alaska State Government fairness statute requires that a total number of investors outside of Alaska equal to 1% of the total number of Alaskans who receive annual Alaska Permanent Fund dividends must be offered the opportunity to profit from the fund. To qualify, they must have blood relatives living in Alaska who receive the annual Permanent Fund Dividend. Potential investors will further be told that they will be guaranteed a minimum of a 25% per annum return on their investments, fueled by the investment success of the Permanent Fund and the new oil money flowing into the fund. Investment minimums will be ten thousand dollars (One Unit), with a maximum investment of twenty thousand dollars (Two Units). Investors will be told that their returns will be paid on a quarterly basis. Since this investment cannot be offered to everyone, investors will also be required to sign a "secrecy" document and provide "proof of relationship" by giving PF Investors, Alaska, the name of their relative in Alaska and providing a copy of their own driver's license. They will be told they will become an approved investor after completion of an investigation that confirms their relationship with the named Alaskan.

Every time Ron read the last line, he chuckled to himself. *You want to send me ten or twenty thousand dollars, the investigation is over. You're in!* The more Ron refined his document, the more he began to believe that it would work. To him, the true beauty of his plan was that he wouldn't actually be stealing from the Permanent Fund. He would just be using it and his position as a board member to take money from people who had enough money to make that kind of investment. *People who can afford to lose it,* he rationalized. *And I will return 25 percent to the initial investors.*

Ron realized there was jeopardy in his plan . . . but he was a lawyer. He knew how to set up dummy accounts and corporations. He also knew he would need to hit and run. If he ran the program for six months, he would be able to capture lots of investors in the second three months by paying off the right investors with 25 percent returns after the first three months.

Sometimes he would lie awake at night and dream about what he would do with the money if he got a hundred or two hundred investors . . . or even more. He wasn't worried about what his wife would think . . . he wouldn't tell her. He would just divorce her when he was rich, and leave the state.

Ron knew he needed an accomplice, but he was at a loss to come up with one. Ideally, it would be someone else on the board of trustees. He had worked his way through the list of trustees many times, and he always came to the same conclusion: there wasn't one person on the board who would fit into his scheme. All of his reasons ignored the one real reason nobody would join him, namely, there wasn't one of them who was stupid enough to think his plan would work.

Undaunted, Ron kept refining his make-believe plan, and it kept looking more doable to him. Without really admitting to himself that he was actually going to attempt to go ahead with his scheme, he decided to launch a search for an accomplice. He had no idea where to begin. With the busy Christmas season approaching, Ron's big plan was going to stay in the drawer for a while.

In Seattle, larceny was also on Budge Brown's mind. He had sex on his mind, too, because he and Kitty had been casual sex partners ever since the first time he contacted her to help him with one of Billy Peet's schemes. Kitty was fun . . . approaching kinky, and her sexual appetite was as big as his. As he showered and prepared to meet Kitty, he thought, *We'll see how committed she is.*

Budge felt good on his first night back in the Seattle area. He was dressed in another of his almost-trashy sport coats, a white shirt, crisp faded blue jeans, and gray cowboy boots when he strolled into the bar at The Rusty Turtle. Like many of the restaurants in the area, it was a comfy blend of rustic and elegant. Budge recognized the hourglass figure and almost boyish brown hair from the back. Kitty was already sitting at the bar.

"Hey gorgeous," he said as he pulled the stool beside her out.

Kitty turned to him, and Budge immediately realized how much he wanted to sleep with her again. Her pretty face lit up as she saw him. His first glance at her large green eyes was followed by a quick glance at her lovely chest, which, in true Kitty fashion, was mostly exposed. "Hello, Budge."

Budge hugged Kitty and was momentarily lost in the familiarity of it . . . the perfume, the taut feel of her body, memories of many steamy nights with her.

"It is wonderful to see you. Thank you for coming."

Kitty quickly became businesslike. "It's good to see you too, Budge. I'm anxious to hear about this professional need you have."

Budge turned the bar stool toward Kitty and sat down. As he started to talk, the bartender approached them. Budge ordered a drink and asked, "Would you like another?" Knowing Kitty could out-drink most men, he was fairly sure of her answer.

"Sure." There was nothing demure about Kitty. She played a man's game in a man's world, and she was good at it.

"Well . . . I need some information on someone. And, I need some general information that you probably already know. Do you know anything about Washington State probate laws?"

"Some. I know Washington State law does not require a probate. What do you mean?"

Budge was shocked, and it showed on his face. "Say that again!"

"Okay, don't take this verbatim, but filing for probate in Washington State is entirely discretionary. It's not required. The most common reason for filing for probate is if the decedent had substantial assets. If the decedent had a will, the law requires that it has to be filed. One of the things that happens when the will is filed is that the State will determine if a probate is required."

"Wow. How long does all this take?"

"Typically . . . if there are no problems, nobody contesting the will, about four months. The State is pretty clear about the fact that a decedent's wishes are to be honored. If the will is clear, it can be pretty simple. What's this all about, Budge?"

Budge was trying to absorb everything Kitty had said, and her question brought him to the uncomfortable part of his quest. "Well . . . I, uh, I need to find out something about someone who died recently."

"Okay, that's probably easy. Who is it . . . a relative?" Kitty took an unladylike drink of her second martini as she finished the question.

"No. It's somebody well known, somebody you've heard of, I'm sure. Del Brooksher. I need to find out some things about Betsy . . . Betsy Brooksher. Del's widow."

Kitty turned and looked Budge directly in his eyes. "Betsy Brooksher? What the fuck are you up to, Budge? Are you trying to scam a poor little old widow?"

Budge snickered. "She's not poor. She's the widow of a billionaire. And I'm just interested in a little part of it. You don't have to be involved, other than just getting me some information . . . some of the stuff you just mentioned. Did he have a will? Is anyone contesting it? Are there any distant relatives? All of that kind of stuff. It will pay well."

"I don't like to fuck with little old ladies, Budge. Even rich ones. Is that all there is to it?"

"Not quite. There's another player involved. A guy named Marc Madrid. He's some kind of accountant, or was a personal assistant to the old man, or both, but I think he's right in the middle of everything."

Budge could see Kitty's professional curiosity going to work. Thoughtfully, she said, "I think I've seen his name in the papers, or heard it on the news. Mr. Brooksher dying is a big deal here. He's been a big deal in this area for a long time."

"I'm sure. Billionaires don't just kick it every day. So, can you help me?"

"It'll cost ya. Double my regular rate. I've got a feeling I'll be fucking with something I don't belong in. And, I need another martini."

That was the point when Budge knew he had scored on two counts. Kitty was good—she would find out everything he needed, plus some things he hadn't thought of. He also knew how she changed when she had a few martinis. He remembered the time in the same bar they were in now when she removed her panties under the table and told him to take his shoe off and put his foot between her legs. She had removed his sock, and proceeded to have a perfectly lovely . . . and rather vocal orgasm by rubbing herself on his big toe. It was a real happening imitating a fake movie moment, and Budge had been glad the evening crowd was well enough into their own moments to miss what was going on.

"You've got it, lady. I aim to please."

"Don't try to shit me, Budge Brown. You are aiming to get in my pants . . . and I'm probably going to let you."

Budge raised his glass in a toast and said, "You have always been a woman of few words, Kitty. Here's to a profitable and enjoyable new venture between us."

When Budge awoke the next morning, he had the strong smell of all-night sex so close to his face, he thought he was still in the middle of the erotic dream he had been having. As the hangover fog lifted, he had to try hard to remember what happened. When he was able to focus, he realized that his favorite part of Kitty's anatomy was inches from his face. It all started coming back to him, and he remembered Kitty falling asleep while they were trying to negotiate a sixty-nine position they were both too tired and drunk to finish.

At the same time Budge was waking up, Beth and Nick were standing in front of the Executive Plaza Hotel waiting for Jimmy and Doug to pick them up. Beth was unassumingly elegant in a cream-colored pantsuit that showed off her athletic body. Nick had noticed Doug's reaction to Beth the day before, and smiled to himself at what was coming.

Ever the businesswoman, Beth said, "I hope they do better than they did yesterday."

"I'm thinking they will. I'm not so sure about this Doug guy, but Flacker is pretty good at what he does. I detected his dissatisfaction with what his guy found, and I'm sure he put some pressure on him. You better be careful, sis. I think this Seattle real estate tycoon has the hots for you."

Beth turned to see what kind of look Nick had on his face and quickly realized he was pulling her leg. "Not funny, Nick. He's . . . he's weird. And he smells."

Eddy pulled the limo into the covered driveway in front of the hotel foyer at about the same time Nick noticed Jimmy and Doug walking toward them from the parking area. "Alright," he said. "Everybody's on time."

Eddy jumped out and hurried toward the back door of the limo. Nick had already opened the door and was helping Beth climb into the back of the huge car. "Good morning, sir. How are you today?"

"I'm fine, Eddy. Is there somewhere you can stop so we can get some coffee . . . maybe a Starbucks?"

"Absolutely. There's one pretty close to here."

Once Nick and Beth were settled, Jimmy Flack crawled into the back of the limo, with morning greetings for both of them. Doug followed, stumbling through the door and falling into a side seat as he mumbled, "'Morning."

Nick had been silent as the bumbling Doug entered the limo. "Good morning to both of you. Eddy is going to find us some coffee somewhere, and then we'll be ready to go to the first property. I hope you have something special picked out." Nick was completely ignoring the fact that they had previously given him a list of properties they were going to look at, the implication being that they had better have found something else.

In familiar fashion, Doug began to speak: "Well, we—" and Jimmy cut him off.

"I think we have a better idea of what you want to see after yesterday, Nick, so Doug and I spent quite a bit of time looking for other properties after we dropped you off. The two we picked are more high-end, and they're both warehouses in the Kent Valley."

The truth that was hidden in Jimmy's statement was that he had told Doug to get his shit together and find what Nick and Beth were looking for or their informal partnership was over. Doug had gone back to his office and spent a couple hours drinking his rotgut whiskey, cursing Jimmy, and somehow managing to find a couple properties that he thought they would like.

After picking up lattes and mochas, they headed toward a warehouse that was only about two miles away from their own Saylor Industries distribution warehouse. The modern-looking warehouse was bustling with activity, and they learned that the tenant had a long-term lease with the building's owner.

Seeing Nick's reaction to the property, Jimmy beamed with confidence as he said, "The tenant is Alaska Sea-Pro Consolidators, and they have eight years left on a ten-year lease. They are a big— "

Nick turned, and was walking back to the limo as he said, "That's one of our competitors, Jimmy. . . . We can't own a building with one of our competitors in it."

Flustered, Jimmy said, "Well . . . you could, I think you could break the lease."

"Too messy, Jimmy," Nick said as he climbed into the back of the limo.

Through all of this, Doug had been mostly silent. He wasn't feeling well after the night before, and all he could think about was the tall, elegant woman who was sitting across from him in the limo. He had fantasized about her since the first moment he saw her, and then he had dreamed about her all night. He felt like he had to do something to prove his value to her.

"I think you will like this next property," Doug said. "It is a large warehouse. It's also in the Kent Valley . . . not far from here. The owner died, and it belongs to his son. He wants to get rid of it. I think he just wants to take the money and run."

Ten minutes later, Eddy pulled the limo up to the gate in front of a huge warehouse and spoke into the call box. The big gate swung open, and they entered the deserted property.

As they exited the limo, a slight-built young man in a cheap-looking black suit emerged from the front door of the office. His tousled hair and bouncy demeanor didn't go with the suit. The look made it obvious he was trying to be somebody he wasn't.

Doug made the introductions. "Ahh, this is um, Sid . . . Sidney, Sidney Black. He's the owner of this property. Sid, this is Nick, and his . . . um, sister, Beth. And this is Jimmy." Satisfied that he had participated in some way, Doug shrunk back out of the spotlight.

Sid was overly ebullient. "Okay. Welcome. It is nice to meet all of you. It's lovely to have you here. Come on in, we've got lots of warehouse to show you." Nick thought it sounded like a game show line.

The warehouse was impressive. It was only five years old, and it covered more than one hundred thousand square feet, with loading doors and ramps down both sides and an overhead crane running down the middle. There were five thousand square feet of tastefully finished office space. Outside, the paved storage area covered five fenced acres.

After their tour, Sid went into the offices and left the four of them standing in one corner of the warehouse. Nick said, "This is impressive. How much do they want for it?"

Hesitantly, Jimmy said, "They're asking seventy-five million for it."

Nick didn't show any signs of emotion as he said, "That's a lot of money."

Doug decided to weigh in. "That's way too high. The kid set the price. He don't know shit, he just wants to be a rich kid. And, he's a stubborn little shit. Says he won't negotiate."

Nick's anger welled up inside, and he could sense that Beth was getting angry too. She couldn't hold it in. "What the hell are we doing here, then? Did you think we were going to overpay for something just because we have money?"

Nick calmed himself enough to ask, "Does he have an appraisal?"

Jimmy looked toward Doug, who said apologetically, "He has an appraisal . . . it's fifty-two million."

Nick was steely-eyed as he took Beth's hand and said, "Okay, let's get out of here." He took a couple of steps, then stopped and dug into his pocket, pulling out a wad of money. He peeled a hundred-dollar bill off, turned, and handed it to Jimmy. "This is enough taxi money to get you wherever you need to go. I'm really disappointed in you. You bring us to a young punk who doesn't know shit, except that he has a warehouse worth fifty-two million dollars that he's not going to sell for less than seventy-five million. Do we look like we just got off the turnip truck?"

"Nick, I'm—"

"Forget it," Nick said as he walked toward Beth. He put his arm around her, and the two of them headed to the limo.

Frustrated and angry, Nick and Beth made a quick trip by the Saylor Industries distribution center, and were in The Bird headed to Anchorage later that afternoon.

Nick reclined the comfortable leather seat, with a glass of eighteen-year-old Chivas Regal on the rocks in his hand. "Well," he said, "that was a bust."

Beth was still pissed. "What a pair. I mean, I know you've done business with Jimmy Flack before, but he did a lousy job of picking a partner. That Doug guy is creepy. He . . . he kept staring at my crotch."

Nick burst out laughing and almost spilled his scotch. "I wondered if you noticed. . . . I think he loves you." With that, Nick continued laughing.

Beth couldn't help but get caught up in Nick's merriment, and she was trying to muffle a laugh as she said, "Not funny, Nick. We both wasted two days with those guys. I could have looked in the classifieds and done better than that."

"It's a lesson learned, sis. We're both naïve if we think we can go off and make a multimillion-dollar investment in a day. This will take some time. I'll get hold of some of my contacts in Seattle and see if they know of a reputable commercial real estate agent who can help us. I feel a little bad for Jimmy. I think he got sucked in by a shyster. He should have been smart enough to realize that." Nick's voice trailed off, and he took a large sip of his scotch as he reflected on the events of the last two days.

Beth suddenly sounded cheery. "Well, big brother. We had a nice dinner and a nice talk last night, and we get to ride in this lovely airplane . . . and drink very fine scotch as we continue our conversation."

Nick raised his glass to Beth and said, "Amen to that."

A moment later, the copilot, Greg, emerged through the door to the cockpit and walked toward Beth with a strange look on his face. "Ms. Saylor, I would have called you on the intercom, but I thought this was important. The governor—of Alaska—is on the phone for you. It's blinking. Line one."

Nick smiled. "Sis has hit the big time."

"Oh, I kind of know her. You know, fundraisers, that kind of thing." Beth was trying to act casual as she picked the phone up and punched the button. "This is Beth Saylor."

"Beth, this is Governor Powers . . . Stacey. Where on earth are you? I've been patched all over the place."

"Governor, I apologize for that. I'm in The Bird . . . I'm sorry, the Saylor Industries company jet. We're, that is Nick and I, are just leaving Seattle and coming back to Anchorage. It is a privilege to hear from you."

"Oh, don't be so formal, Beth. You and I have tipped too many glasses of wine together for that. I do have some serious business to discuss with you, though."

"Okay . . . let's hear it."

"Well, I doubt that you know this, but one of the members of the Alaska Permanent Fund Corporation's Board of Trustees will be at the end of his term in March. Amak Tonner. He's also in ill health, so it's time for him to step down. I'll cut to it. I'd like to appoint you to his spot." The governor hesitated, waiting for a reaction.

"Wow. I'm flattered. I don't know what to say. I mean, am I qualified?"

"Beth, you are the most successful female executive in the state. Because of that little stunt you pulled off in Seattle a few years ago, you're also the most popular woman in the state. . . . I wish to hell I had numbers like yours. Amak is an Alaska Native, and I want to replace him with someone who will be accepted by everybody. You will be."

"Thank you, Governor. I . . . I don't know what to say."

"Say yes."

"Can I think about this? I'd like to sit down and discuss the responsibilities—"

The governor interrupted, "And the pay?"

"I guess I'm not concerned about the pay. I'm just concerned about how much time I'd have to devote to it."

Never a woman to hesitate, the governor said, "How about lunch tomorrow. My office. I'll have something brought in. That way we can keep the gossipmongers at bay. Say, eleven-thirty."

"Yes, Governor. I'll be there. Thank you."

Beth hung up the phone and turned to look at Nick with a stunned expression. "The governor wants me on the Board of Trustees for the Alaska Permanent Fund Corporation."

Nick had a look of satisfaction on his face as he unbuckled his seat belt and came across the aisle to hug Beth and kiss her on the cheek. "I'm very proud of you, Beth . . . and I hope you take the job."

"I don't want to compromise Saylor Industries, Nick."

"From what I know of it, you won't. A few meetings a year. They have a big staff, and lots of consultants doing the day-to-day business of managing the fund. You'll be part of the decision-making team, and you're good at that."

Beth sat back in her luxurious seat and sighed, "Shit."

Back in Seattle, Budge was a very satisfied man. He had a private investigator he trusted gathering the information he needed about the Brookshers. And, he had spent the night with a woman whose sexuality continually amazed him. It was icing on the cake that the investigator and the woman were the same person. He just had one uncomfortable bit of business to take care of this day.

The voice Budge hated answered the telephone again. "This is Reverend Raymond."

Sarcastically, Budge spoke. "Mr. Smith, I presume. This is Budge. I've got an investigator checking out the Brookshers. I'm not sure how long it will take for her to come up with something, but you need to keep lying low. I don't know why the fuck Billy got you here this early, and I don't know why the fuck you are still staying in that high-dollar hotel, but that is between you and Billy."

Grudgingly, Raymond said, "I'm moving. Tomorrow. You can get me on my cell phone if you need me. I'll let you know where I am."

"Good," was all Budge said before he hung up.

Reverend Raymond had been restless for the last two days in his expensive hotel room. He couldn't afford to be there, and he knew it. He had finally called Billy Peet.

"This is Billy."

"Billy, this is Raymond. Budge says it's going to be a while before he has something for me to do. I . . . well, I will need a little more money. I'm kind of short, I—"

"Don't try to shit the shitter, Reverend. You're staying in some expensive-ass hotel, and I'm not going to fund that. I probably sent you up there too soon, and that's my fault, but you need to get your ass out of that hotel and get it into a Super Eight, or something like that. Find a Fast Cash, or someplace close where I can wire you some money. I'll send you a couple grand, and I'm not going to send more until you've done something to earn it. Don't cause any trouble . . . and don't fucking burn anything down!"

Raymond was shocked at Billy's last words. "What makes you think I'd do something like—"

"How fucking stupid do you think I am? Every time you've done something for me, some goddamn church burns down. I'm not sure why you've got a hard-on for religion, but keep it in your pants. This deal has huge potential. I don't want some whacked out, half-assed preacher with a grudge fucking it up."

Timidly, Raymond told Billy that he would call him back with information about where to wire his money, and their conversation was over.

In spite of the financial promise of the pending scam for Billy, Raymond was approaching a black period. He was staying in a fancy room he couldn't afford, and he didn't want to skip out on the bill because he was going to be in the area for a while. He had stolen some booze, but he couldn't afford to pay for a woman, and that was what he wanted. He even considered rape . . . he had done that before, but he had barely escaped without being caught. He also knew he had hurt the woman, and that was not something he really wanted to do.

Hold on for another day, Raymond thought. *Get Billy the information he needs so you can get some money.*

In Anchorage the next morning, Beth was preparing to meet with Governor Powers. Even though she had a fairly comfortable social relationship with the governor, she had never sat down for a serious meeting with her before. She had a little case of pregame butterflies. Nick was staying in the extra bedroom in the penthouse and he wasn't making it easier for Beth before she left.

"Yep. I'll bet she is really going to grill you. Probably want to know everything you know about the Permanent Fund."

"I don't know squat, Nick. I know it's a lot of money . . . money that belongs to the people of Alaska. I know everybody gets a big fat check from the fund every year, and I know how pissed they'll be if it's not big and fat again next year. I mean, do I need this? Does Saylor Industries need this?"

"Okay, little sister, you're taking this way too serious. Go talk with the governor. If it sounds like it's something you don't want to do, say no."

"It's not nice to piss off the governor."

"Maybe not, but what is she going to do if you turn her down . . . run you out of the state? I wouldn't worry about it. You're a great businesswoman. There is no reason to believe you won't be great for the Permanent Fund board. I think you'll want to take the job. Should be kind of fun, and it certainly won't hurt Saylor Industries in any way. Beth Saylor, political juggernaut."

"Okay. That's enough of that. I'm off to see the governor. Wish me luck."

"You won't need it, Beth, but good luck."

Beth decided it would be too much to have Vince drive her to the governor's office in the limo, so she drove herself. She began to get a nervous stir in the pit of her stomach as she drove along Bill Egan Drive, the newly completed tree-lined street that leads to the beautiful new state Capitol complex at the foothills of the Chugach Mountains. The street was decorated with green-and-white lights for the holidays. Her nervousness was overtaken by a shiver of pride as she saw the beautiful white classic colonial-look State Capitol building come into view at the end of the street.

Like many Alaskans, Beth had taken the open house tour when the new Capitol opened. She was among the many Alaskans who cheered when the Governor originally announced the results of the vote that mandated the move out of Juneau. She felt bad for the economic loss that hit the citizens of Juneau, but realized that limited access to the Capitol had been a realistic issue for most Alaskans since the south-central part of the state had become the business hub of Alaska. Now, she was excited about her first visit to the new Capitol on official business.

Beth followed the signs indicating valet parking for visitors and stopped next to a man dressed in a warm-looking winter wool uniform. The uniform was navy with gold trim, and almost had a military look to it. His gloved hand reached for her door as she began to get out of her SUV. "Good morning. Who are you visiting this morning?"

"The governor," Beth said uneasily. She was unsure how to say it without sounding like a name-dropper.

"Ms. Saylor? The governor said you would be arriving about now."

"Oh . . . great. Yes, I'm Beth Saylor. Thank you."

The valet attendant walked Beth to the front entrance of the massive Capitol building, where one of the governor's aides was waiting.

The handsome young aide, who was dressed in a perfectly cut medium gray suit, said, "Ms. Saylor, I presume. My name is Teddy. I'll take you to the governor's office."

"Thank you, Teddy. I'm Beth Saylor."

As they walked, Beth marveled again at the Alaska Native art of all types that adorned the walls and was displayed in the hallways. "You must enjoy working here, Teddy. This is a magnificent building, and the Native art is beautiful."

Beth turned toward the young man as he answered, and was captured by his cherubic face and close-cropped brown hair. "It is a pleasure to work in this building . . . but mostly, I mean honestly, I just love working for the governor."

Beth immediately caught the real meaning of Teddy's answer. She sensed a case of youthful puppy love. Not an uncommon phenomenon in the forty-ninth state, since his employer was an uncommonly attractive governor.

"I'll bet you do. Governor Powers is an amazing person."

As they approached the massive double doors to the governor's office, the receptionist acknowledged Teddy. "A visitor for the governor, Teddy?"

"Yes, Susan. Could you please announce Ms. Beth Saylor to the governor?"

Governor Powers opened one of the big doors shortly after Beth's presence was announced. "Beth. It's wonderful to see you. Come in, please."

While Beth followed the governor into her inner office, she marveled at how attractive she was, and admired the crisp and fashionable business pantsuit she was wearing. An observer would have marveled at the mature beauty of both women.

"Beth, I'm so happy you are here," the governor said as she settled into her chair behind her huge mahogany desk. "I think my offer to you is a stroke of genius . . . and I hope you do, too."

"I'm certainly flattered, Governor, and I—"

"Stacey . . . please call me Stacey . . . at least in a private setting like this."

"Okay . . . Stacey, as I said, I am very flattered. I don't know what the responsibilities are or what your expectations are."

"It's pretty simple, Beth. You are a strong, exceptional business-woman. You are extremely popular, and you are well known and accepted by Alaska Natives because of Saylor's business interests all over the state. Since you will be replacing an Alaska Native board member, I think that is important. All I expect is that you conduct board business the way you conduct your own business . . . with this exception. If I appoint you, I expect you to be on my team. We don't have to march to the same drummer, but we need to be in the same band. Does that make sense to you?"

"Of course. I am registered as an Independent, but I voted for you, and I am more of a Conservative than anything else, if that makes a difference. More than that, I agree with most everything you have done as governor."

"I know all of that, Beth. I obviously had some informal research done on you before I called. As to the details, the board meets six to eight times a year. The meetings are two days long, and they rotate between Anchorage, Fairbanks, and Juneau. The pay is—"

This time, Beth interrupted the governor. "I'm not concerned about the pay. I will probably donate it to a charity."

"Alright, well, that's great. As far as responsibilities go, you can ease your way into that. It's a four-year term. You will learn, and then, the amount of time you devote to it away from the board meetings will be up to you. The board is one big clique, filled with two or three other cliques, and you will have to fit into that as best you can. . . . It will be a lot easier for a beautiful woman. The executive director, Richard Cally, is very good, and very dedicated. He will help you a lot. The chairman, Fred Feck, is good too, and he will also help. If you decide to do this, I think it will be a rewarding experience."

Beth was temporarily embarrassed by the governor's beautiful-woman comment, but quickly put her focus back on the issues. "I think I'm interested . . . Stacey, but how do I make sure we are in synch on the issues? I mean, if we have apparent differences, will I have the ability to discuss it with you?"

Stacey Powers' little laugh suggested collusion. "Beth, there are not many people in my inner circle. I have to protect myself. I think you and I can be friends. I need someone to share a bottle of chardonnay with occasionally, and talk girl talk. People tend to put someone like me on a pedestal, and I'm a woman, just like you. I like jokes women can share, I like sports, I like sex, I like talking about sex—I even like a nice glass of scotch or two now and then. If you decide to take this job, you will have easy access to me."

Beth was taken aback by the honest conversation with the governor, but she understood. In some ways, she was in the same position. She was thoughtful as she said, "Stacey . . . Madam Governor, I think I am interested. I would like to discuss it with my brother, Nick. He's still the CEO of Saylor Industries, and more than that, someone whose opinion I respect. I'm pretty sure I know what he'll say, and I can talk with him later this afternoon, but I do want to do him that courtesy. I can let you know by this afternoon, or tomorrow morning at the latest."

"That is excellent, Beth. If it was later in the day, we could have a toast. We'll celebrate when it's finalized." The governor stood up from behind her desk as she said, "Thank you for coming. I'll wait to hear from you."

Politics creates strange relationships. All politicians have agendas, and very few of those agendas are pure. Even politicians with good intentions eventually stray from the narrow path that leads through the valley of temptation.
—From *Fred Longcoor's Book on Life*

Chapter 8

New Year, New Lives

By the first week of January, Stan Faro's life had changed dramatically. Now firmly ensconced as an up-and-coming man about town in Anchorage, with two Arctic North Bank board meetings under his belt and a real estate business that had strangely become very busy of late, not to mention the huge paychecks he was receiving from Billy Peet, he was feeling very good. Other than the two calls a week from Billy, which were annoying, he really didn't have to answer to anyone.

Stan walked out of his office into the lobby of his small two-room suite and looked proudly at his new office assistant, Polly Hasey. Because of the surprising increase in his real estate business, he decided he needed some help. Billy didn't like it, but Stan convinced him it was all part of his new look, and that he needed her to handle the real estate business. Stan had carefully selected a woman with great qualifications. She came with the added benefit of having an outgoing personality. She was not particularly attractive . . . but she had a spectacularly athletic body, which was not lost on Stan when he interviewed her.

"Polly, good morning . . . anything new today?"

"Good morning, Mr. Faro. Nothing new yet, but I'm expecting a call from the man who called late yesterday about the condo in the McMillan Building. Would you be able to show him the building this morning?"

"Sure, Polly. I've got a lunch appointment, but other than that, I'm okay. I'll be right here. Billy will probably be calling this morning."

Billy had become pretty consistent about calling on Tuesday and Friday mornings. The conversations had become labored for Stan, because

Billy always wanted more than he could give him. He was on the board at the bank, and he was seen around town on a regular basis, such as the Chamber of Commerce's monthly meeting. He joined The Alliance, an oil industry support organization, and attended their meetings regularly, as well as the meetings of the Resource Development Council. He had failed to connect with anybody who could get him on another board, which was something Billy was hung up on.

As expected, Polly buzzed Stan with the message that Billy was on the line an hour later.

"Stan . . . what the hell's going on in the frozen city?"

"Trying to stay warm, Billy. What's going on with you?" Stan spent a great deal of time trying to get Billy on any subject other than what he was doing.

"You doing any good this week, Stan? You got anything new going on that's going to help our cause? You doing anything to justify all the money I'm paying you?"

The tiring questions were always the same, and Stan always replied pretty much the same way. "Nothing new, Billy. I'm all over the place, and I think I'm making some good contacts on the Arctic North board. I can't just force my way onto another board if there isn't an opening. I'm just getting to know these guys."

"I'm paying you a lot of money, Stan. . . . You can't just sit on your ass."

"I'm not sitting on my ass, Billy. I'm working hard. I've come a long way in a couple of months. I know a hell of a lot more important people in this town than I knew a couple of months ago. There's a tight little business community here, and I'm working my way inside . . . and I don't even know what for."

Stan's final statement hung there for a moment before Billy responded. "You know that I'm paying you a lot of fucking money, don't you? You'll know why in due time. I've got a call. I've got to go." Billy ended their conversation in typical Billy fashion.

Stan sat at his desk with the phone in his hand. "Fuck," he said, "what am I doing? How did I get into this?"

Polly came to the doorway. "Is everything alright, Mr. Faro?"

"Stan, Polly. Stan. And yes, everything is okay. Billy is a real . . . well sometimes he can be a real challenge."

"What is his connection to you? He doesn't even live in Alaska. I've seen his number when the calls come in."

"It's a long story, Polly. We have some business dealings outside of Alaska. Billy and I were in college together. He's sort of a . . . partner.

And sometimes, he really pisses me off, but I guess you can tell that."

"Okay, well, I just wanted to make sure everything was alright." Polly turned and went back to her desk.

I kind of like the fact that she's looking out for me already, Stan thought.

Johnny Bosco had been working for Taylor Drilling on the North Slope for over a year by March of 2007. He had become one of the boys months ago. His great work ethic and his rugged yet compassionate traits gave him a real-man personality. Even though the driller on his crew was the official crew leader, Johnny had become the quiet leader the roughnecks came to.

In his time off over the last year, he turned his small cabin into a comfortable, rustic place with many of the conveniences of a suburban home in Anchorage. In the frame of mind Johnny was in when he bought the cabin the previous March, the crude supplies he had outfitted the place with seemed appropriate. As the year moved along, he'd wanted more of the traditional comforts he was used to.

Money was no object. The largest part of Johnny's huge paychecks was still staying in the bank. Through a connection of a drilling buddy, he had a water-well drilled on his property for almost nothing, with him acting as the well driller's helper. He rented equipment and installed his own septic system, reluctantly putting James Young's prized outhouse into semi-retirement after he installed a flush toilet in the remodeled bathroom. The outhouse was still functional, and he used it himself occasionally just to enjoy the solitude.

Since Carmen Sandy was a frequent visitor when he was in town, he also wanted his place to be comfortable for her when she was there. He added a ten-KW generator and made the smaller generator an emergency backup. Then he put in modern kitchen appliances, new lights, and a fuel heater. He rolled the sleeping bag up and put it away, and purchased a new king-sized bed for the newly expanded bedroom.

During the summer of 2006, Carmen had helped him with some minor landscaping outside the cabin. She added flowers while he built a stone walkway. By late summer, they were able to relax on the front deck in the afternoons and enjoy the serene setting. It was during one of those peaceful afternoons on the front deck that he once again focused on the rough path that continued on just past his cabin, where the gravel road ended. The rough path never seemed to completely disappear, like there was some type of continuing traffic on it, but there were never any tire tracks visible, and Johnny never saw anybody on it. The previous March, soon after he had moved into the cabin, he'd occasionally noticed scattered tracks in the snow that followed the path, and he just assumed it was a game trail, with an assortment of animals using it.

Johnny took a sip on his cold beer and said, "I wonder what the hell is at the end of that path."

Carmen was sitting beside him with a glass of wine in hand. "What do you mean?"

"Somebody or something is using that path, but I've never seen anybody on it. I've seen a few moose walking along it this summer, but something is using it summer and winter."

"Monsters."

"Funny, but I'm going to find out what's up there. Let's go for a ride on the four-wheeler tomorrow." Johnny had built a small shed that summer and bought a nice used four-wheeler that he kept in it.

"I'd love to, Johnny, but I've got an office to open tomorrow morning. I could do it Saturday or Sunday."

"Okay, well, I'll see. Maybe I'll just run up there myself tomorrow."

"If you do, be careful . . . monsters."

Johnny laughed. He enjoyed his time with Carmen. He didn't necessarily feel like she was *the one*, but she was intelligent, fun, and attractive. His curiosity about the path was now piqued, and he knew where he would be going the next day.

Carmen left the cabin early the next morning to get to Anchorage in time to open her real estate office. "It's a beautiful morning, Johnny. Have a great ride, and be careful."

"Okay, get out of here, and *you* be careful. The Seward Highway is a much more dangerous place than this valley." Johnny prepared the four-wheeler ready for the trek into the woods. Not knowing how far he would go or what to expect, he put a small lunch and a couple bottles of water into his backpack. He also put his belt and holster on, and placed the loaded .357 in the holster.

Johnny was excited as he steered the four-wheeler along the worn path. He quickly encountered his first surprise of the day. Barely a hundred yards beyond his cabin, he encountered a sign that identified the place he was headed toward as Chugach National Park. Choosing ignorance of the law over turning back, he continued on. He was alert as he drove because he knew the woods were full of moose and bears in the summer. In fact, there were lots of moose, and sometimes they were more frightening and more unpredictable than the bears. He thought about the video he had recently viewed of a moose killing a man in front of one of the buildings on the University of Alaska, Anchorage campus. He knew a large bull moose or a pregnant female wouldn't hesitate to take on a man and a four-wheeler if they felt threatened.

As Johnny slowly motored along the well-defined path, he noticed occasional signs of past human activities. There were the remnants of old fences with rotted fence posts and tangled strands of barbed wire, and there were a couple small caved-in old cabins with sod-covered roofs. Their logs had long ago faded to gray. Here and there, rusty pieces of equipment were strewn haphazardly, and he spotted the pitted remains of a very old pickup truck with huge flattened tires on it.

He began to get an eerie feeling that gave him a chill on the back of his neck. The realization that he was now deep in the woods, and very alone, came to him. Johnny stopped the four-wheeler, and, inexplicably, it quit running. He was immediately engulfed in a total silence like he had never experienced before. Every haunting story from his past of mystical and real dangers in the deep woods flashed through his mind. Absent-mindedly, he touched the handle of the .357.

Johnny sat in the solitude for several minutes, his ears tuned to the sound of nothingness, his eyes scouring the quiet woods. He finally realized there wasn't anything of significance where he was, and he sighed loudly when he turned the key and the four-wheeler started right up. He continued along the old path. The odometer on the four-wheeler told him he was now two miles past his cabin.

Johnny was not only struck by the solitude and beauty of the forest, he was amazed that the path he was following was as well defined now as it was immediately past his cabin. He was also aware that he had been making a gradual climb toward the foothills of the Chugach Mountains, and, as he climbed, the big spruce trees were giving way to smaller birch trees and dense alder bushes. It was equally beautiful, but decidedly different. The thick alders crowded the path, and he continually thought about how quickly a moose or bear could charge out of the brush.

As the birch trees began to thin out, and the alders gave way to shorter bushes, Johnny saw that he was coming to a beautiful plateau at the foothills. The path made a gradual turn to the right, and he followed it. Then he suddenly stopped and turned the four-wheeler off.

What the fuck is that?

He smelled smoke . . . a smoke unlike any he had ever smelled before. His eyes followed his nose to a place at the confluence of the base of the mountain and the edge of the plateau, where a small trail of smoke curled out of the trees. He sat quietly as he tried to decide what to do next. Someone was obviously there. Maybe a hiker.

What the fuck, he thought. *I didn't come all this way to hightail it.*

Johnny started the four-wheeler and followed the path, which headed toward the billowing smoke. As he approached, a subterranean log structure dug deep into the base of the mountainside became partially visible. It was covered in moss and dirt, and draped with animal skins on the two sides he could see. The smoke he had seen and smelled was coming out of an opening in the roof.

As Johnny moved closer, he could see a tidy area that was cleared of brush surrounding the modest structure. For reasons he didn't understand, he felt welcome at the strange homestead, even though he had yet to see a human. Off to the side and the back of the cleared area and the log structure, he saw a good-sized cache mounted about twelve feet up on heavy log stilts. A hand-hewn ladder made of sturdy birch branches rested against two of the log stilts. Near the cache and partially buried in the mountainside were two small doghouses that looked like mini versions of the main log structure. On the back edge of the clearing, to the right of the main structure, stood an octagon-shaped log structure much smaller than the main structure.

Johnny slowed the four-wheeler to a crawl and stopped in front of the clearing. He shut the engine off and was once again engulfed in silence. His mind jumped from thoughts about what a beautiful and surreal place he had stumbled upon to curiosity about why there were signs of habitation, but nobody around . . . and no dogs barking in spite of the fact that there were two doghouses.

"You are the man from the cabin." The voice came from behind him, and it was strong and authoritative.

Startled, Johnny turned to see a dark-skinned man holding what appeared to be a long spear standing about ten yards behind him. He looked about six feet tall, and he was flanked by two patient huskies standing at attention, one on each side of him. He had a weathered, ruggedly handsome face, and he was dressed in clothes made of animal skins. There was a strangely mystical aura about the man, and the perfectly spoken English didn't fit his look.

Unafraid, Johnny said, "Yes. I live at the other end of this road . . . or path. My name is Johnny Bosco. I . . . I apologize for barging into your place, but I have been very curious about where the path led to for months."

"You have lived there for a year."

"Oh . . . sorry. You are right. I have been curious for about a year."

The man stood his ground and said, "My name is Marty Stevens." He indicated first the dog on his left, then the dog on his right. "This is Shesh, and this is Genen. The names mean brown bear and shaman. Shesh is the male . . . he protects me. Genen is the female . . . she warns me."

"Oh, okay. Marty? . . . That is . . . I mean, you look—"

"Native? I am an Athabascan Indian. We come from many places, and many of us have English names. I was educated at the University of Washington, and that is why I speak your language well."

"Well, what are you do—" Once again, the man interrupted Johnny.

"What am I doing here? I tired of the world you live in many years ago. I decided I wanted to live the way my ancestors lived . . . off the land, the ocean, and the rivers. What are you doing here? You are a man with a story, also."

"Oh, well, yeah, I guess I am. I too wanted to escape, but I have not dismissed the modern world. I needed to find a place where I could . . . recover. I needed some solitude, a place to think."

Marty began to move slowly toward Johnny, and the dogs moved with him. As he approached, he extended his hand. The resulting handshake was as much an exploration of each other as men as it was a friendly greeting. Marty's rough strong hand grabbed Johnny's rough strong hand firmly. There was an unspoken mutual appreciation of each other's strength as they released their grips.

"I have some high-bush cranberry tea left from last summer, if you would like to join me in my small kashim."

"Kashim?"

"It is an Athabascan word for a man's house. For my ancestors, it was a place for men to sleep and work, and conduct ceremonies. For me, it is just my house."

"Okay, well, thank you, Marty, I would love to join you in your . . . kashim."

Johnny followed Marty into the small house. The floor was made of split rough-hewn birch logs. In the middle of the cabin, a small pile of burning embers in a rock fire pit buried in the floor were producing the trails of smoke that was drawn out of the opening in the middle of the roof. A crude log table and two chairs sat in one corner of an area that appeared to be the kitchen, and a comfortable-looking log bed covered with animal skins and furs lay on the opposite side of the room.

Jesus, thought Johnny, this is the kind of place you see in a heritage museum. There has to be a good reason for Marty to live like this. He must have killed someone.

Marty scurried around and delivered two steaming cups of tea, using hot water from a pot that hung from a birch-wood tripod that squatted over the fire pit. As Marty put the cups of tea on the rough surface of the table, he said, "And there is."

"Pardon me?"

"A reason why I am living like this."

Surprised, Johnny replied, "No . . . no, I wasn't thinking—" Johnny paused for a moment, feeling guilty about the small fib he was about to tell Marty, and slightly unsettled that Marty knew what he was thinking. "Yes, yes I was."

"Okay. It is reasonable for you to wonder how an educated man ended up living out here . . . living like this. It is a story I have not told anybody, but I feel we have a bit of a connection. We are connected by this valley, this special place, and we are connected by tragedy."

"Well, I really haven't had any trag—"

"A problem with a woman can be almost as much of a tragedy as a . . . a . . . death. A problem with a woman and a death can put you where I am . . . a little farther removed from society than you are . . . a little farther up the valley."

"Why do you think I had a problem with a woman?"

"It is written on you. You are a handsome man, and you enjoy women, yet you live out in the woods like a hermit."

Johnny started to ask Marty how he knew he enjoyed women, and then he thought about Carmen. He has seen Carmen at my cabin. He didn't say anything, and Marty began to tell his story.

"I graduated from the University of Washington fifteen years ago. I had a degree in environmental engineering, and I went to work for a large construction company in Puget Sound. It was a good company . . . a company that cared about environmental responsibility before it was really in vogue. A year after I graduated, I married a woman I met at the university. We had a good life . . . for a little while."

Johnny could see the pain in Marty's eyes as he told his story, and he remained silent.

"Angie, my wife, began to change. She liked to party and she liked the nightlife, and that wasn't my style. She was a beautiful woman, and before long she was having an affair with a man who was more like her than I was. I caught them . . . in bed. I didn't know it, but the guy was a small-time gangster, and he had a gun. He got out of bed and pulled it out of his pants pocket. His pants were on the floor, and I couldn't see what he was doing. I thought he was reaching for his pants so he could leave. I wasn't going to do anything to him. From where I stood, she looked like a willing participant. Do you want some more tea?"

Johnny was engrossed in Marty's story, and his change of direction surprised him. "Yes, that sounds good. I've never had tea like this. It is very good."

Marty filled the two metal cups with tea and continued. "When I saw the gun coming out of his pocket, I lunged at him. We wrestled with the gun, and it went off several times. His finger was locked onto the trigger. Two bullets hit me in the legs . . . superficially. One bullet hit Angie squarely in her left bicep. One bullet hit Mr. Gangster in the middle of his chest. To make a long story a little shorter, I was tried for manslaughter. The prosecution's case was weak. The physical evidence was strong. Mr. Gangster had residue on his gun hand that proved that he had fired all the shots, and then Angie finally broke down and supported my story," Johnny sighed heavily, and took a drink of his tea.

"I lost my job. My company didn't want a killer working for them, even though I was exonerated. They blamed it on a work slowdown, but that was bullshit. That was when I decided to come up here. I had been fascinated by my ancestry for years, and I felt like I didn't want any human contact. I was lucky enough to get this property on a State of Alaska homestead giveaway that was tied to the Alaska Native Claims Settlement, even though it is actually part of Chugach National Forest. The only requirement was that I had to live on the property for five years. I've lived on it twice that long."

Marty lowered his head. He seemed drained at the telling. Johnny wasn't sure if Marty was lamenting the loss of his previous life, or if the reality of his current life had just sunk in. In either case, he could relate to Marty . . . . In everything but the death, their stories were very similar.

"I am sorry for your losses, Marty. My story is something like yours. No death, but still similar." Johnny then told Marty about what had happened to put him in this remote valley in Alaska with him. When Johnny finished his story, they both sat in silence for a few moments. Finally, Marty spoke.

"I am glad you came out here, my friend . . . . May I call you my friend? I haven't called anybody that in a long time."

"I would be honored to have you as a friend, Marty. I am fascinated by you, and how you live out here . . . and what is that smell coming from the smoke?"

Marty laughed. "Candlefish, you know, hooligan. I dry them, and then mash them up for the oil. See that small pot on the grate? That is the oil. My ancestors ate them, but I don't care for them. I eat salmon, trout, and halibut when I can get it. I have a small boat hidden near the shore of Turnagain Arm, and when the weather and the tides permit it in the summer and fall, I fish for halibut."

"Turnagain Arm? How do you get there? That must be seven or eight miles."

"I walk . . . me and Shesh and Genen. I walk there in the morning, fish, and walk back in the evening. I dry the fish. I have a smokehouse . . . the small log house next to this kashim. I also have the cache. When I am gone for long periods hunting and fishing, I have to put my food supplies in a place that animals . . . mostly bears, can't get to."

Johnny was in awe. "You are an amazing guy, Marty. Do you ever go to town? What about medical needs, and important stuff, like beer and scotch?"

Marty laughed again. "I am healthy, and I make some very nice liquor out of berries. I do miss having a cold beer once in a while. I guess a serious illness or an injury would test my resolve, but I have not had that yet. I don't get things like viruses, because I'm never around other people. I've managed to live like my ancestors for over ten years. I don't care about society. I just want to be left alone." Marty stopped speaking for a moment. "I'm sorry. . . . I am glad you came out here. You are different. We may be kindred in some ways. I just hope that you will respect my privacy, and keep it to yourself. You are welcome here. Nobody else." There was a hint of threat to Marty's closing words.

Johnny spent another hour with Marty as he showed him around his small compound. Marty had rigged warning devices, built rain-gathering equipment, made candles out of hooligan oil, built racks for smoking fish and game meat, and sewn clothes with porcupine needles, using leather strips as thread. He even dammed the creek up, and stocked the dam with trout and salmon so he would have a ready supply of fresh fish during the summer.

Curiosity finally got the best of Johnny. "How did you end up ten yards behind me? I never saw any sign of you as I came in."

"Ten years out here makes you animal-like. Your senses sharpen. You become one with the forest. There are Athabascan tribes all over the Pacific Northwest, Canada, and Alaska, and they all live a little differently, but they all believe that all creatures and many objects have spirits . . . and I have found it to be true. Shesh and Genen have spirits . . . I have a spirit. You have a spirit, and you have yet to discover it. A spirit gives you another dimension . . . another sense."

"That is fascinating stuff, Marty. I mean it's intriguing stuff, but it still doesn't explain how you just showed up behind me out of nowhere."

"You will understand one day, my friend."

Johnny and Marty shook hands again and wished each other well. Without any firm commitment, they agreed that they should meet again. Johnny told Marty to stop at his cabin if he ever needed anything, and then he headed the four-wheeler back down the path. For some strange reason, he felt like a changed man. He felt refreshed, and really good about himself.

Only twenty miles over the Chugach Mountains as the crow flies from Marty Stevens' woodsy homestead, Beth was in her luxurious penthouse at the top of the Saylor Building preparing for her second meeting on the Alaska Permanent Fund Corporation Board of Trustees. Amak Tonner's health had deteriorated quickly, and he stepped down in January in time for Beth to make the first board meeting of the year. She had been loudly praised and welcomed to her new position by a cross section of Alaskans after the governor announced her as the new board member. Her first meeting was mostly ceremonial . . . welcomes, introductions, instructions regarding protocol, and quiet observation on her part as they discussed the fund's performance issues.

The first meeting she attended was held in Fairbanks, a small political victory for Beth, since that was where Saylor Trucking had started its operation in the late sixties. It was her home for many years before she and Nick moved to Anchorage. The seats that were reserved for the public were full, and almost all the public attendees were there to tell the board what a great choice Beth was to be a member of the Board of Trustees.

Now, Beth was preparing for their March meeting in Anchorage, one she hoped to use to demonstrate her abilities. She had spent many hours since January studying the history of the Alaska Permanent Fund, and studying the board's recent performance. This morning, she did what she frequently did on important days . . . she called Nick.

"Good morning, sis," Nick said from his oceanfront deck in Maui. He was sitting at the deck table, having coffee and reading the paper. Every once in a while he put the paper down to watch the humpback whales in the ocean in front of his home. It always fascinated him to watch them at this time of year, realizing they would soon be on their way to his other favorite place, Alaska, for the summer. "What's going on in Alaska?"

"Good morning. I'm just getting ready for my next meeting of the Alaska Permanent Fund Corporation's Board of Trustees. I hope I can contribute this time. I was just an observer at the first meeting."

"I wouldn't spend any time worrying about it. You've got four years. You'll be running the damn meetings in six months."

"I'm not that pushy, Nick. I just want to feel like I deserve to be there."

"You do. You'll be fine. I'd rather hear about what's going on at Saylor. Anything new?"

"Business as usual. You have any new information on the real estate front?" Nick and Beth had made one more useless trip to Seattle and one to Portland looking for the right property for Saylor Industries to invest in, while the company's cash reserves continued to build.

"Nothing. I've got to admit that it's a little frustrating . . . I mean trying to spend a few million dollars, and not being able to do it."

Beth laughed. "Nice problem to have though. Is Jimmy still working on it?"

"He is, even though he got his feathers singed pretty badly on that first deal with your Seattle Casanova."

"Seattle letch would be more appropriate. Maybe I can make some contacts from this board experience. You know, the fund makes real estate investments all over the place . . . big investments."

"Keep your eyes and ears open. You never can tell what you may stumble on. I'll keep searching the Internet. I'm becoming an Internet real estate expert, even though I haven't found anything that works for us. I also found a couple of legitimate brokers in the Seattle area, and I laid down some pretty stringent restrictions on what we are interested in. Nothing good from them yet."

After finishing her conversation with Nick, Beth took one last look at herself in the bathroom mirrors, and headed for the elevator and the short walk that would take her to the board meeting at the Susitna Hotel.

There is no such thing as a cosmic game plan for anything . . . or is there? Even for the believers, the individual pieces are unrecognizable in the beginning. As they begin to connect, the roll begins, and it becomes something that won't be denied. When it's over, whether it is good or bad, you have to sit and wonder at it.
—From *Fred Longcoor's Book on Life*

Chapter 9

Hunters and the Hunted

At his ranch in Montana, Billy Peet was still stewing about Beth having been put on the Board of Trustees of the Alaska Permanent Fund Corporation. He had been ranting to Anna since the announcement was made the first week of January. Anna dutifully listened to Billy, thinking, I don't know what he is talking about, and I don't care.

"Fuck, that was our opportunity. If Amak would have retired when he was supposed to, Stan could have gotten that seat."

Mario Delaney was listening to Billy patiently. Finally, he said, "Billy, Amak was scheduled to retire in March. There is no way Stan would have been in a position to get that seat in March. You're barking at phantoms. Remember our plan. We agreed this was going to take a year, maybe two."

Reluctantly, Billy said, "I guess you're probably right. I'm just anxious. You know, I'm not getting any younger. And . . . I am a greedy fucker. . . . I want the money now. Show me the money! And, speaking of that, the Reverend is making progress in Seattle. The information Budge gathered on Mrs. Brooksher is helping, and the unfortunate death of that Madrid fellow has helped." Billy couldn't help but chuckle as he thought about the clever way Budge had disposed of the roadblock to the Brooksher fortune. He had the copy of the newspaper article Benny had obtained for him on his desk.

Seattle News,
Saturday, February 2, 2007
Another Brooksher Tragedy

Marc Madrid was a name many Seattle area people had never heard before the untimely death of billionaire Del Brooksher. He was a broker and money manager for several financial institutions in the Pacific Northwest after graduating from Harvard with a degree in accounting. His star ascended when he was appointed chief financial advisor for Del Brooksher over a year ago.

Marc's star is no longer shining. Authorities reported yesterday afternoon that Mr. Madrid was found dead in his garage, apparently the victim of his own carelessness. According to a police spokesman, he was found under his new Mercedes convertible, which had slipped off of four jack stands and crushed him to death while he was working under it. Authorities speculate that a recently coated slick garage floor and a jump into the front seat of the convertible by his large St. Bernard, Fortune, may have combined to knock the vehicle off the support devices.

Mr. Madrid was unmarried, and has no surviving relatives. Betsy Brooksher tearfully reported that she is devastated, and that she was counting on Mr. Madrid to help her sort through the settlement of Mr. Brooksher's estate. Betsy Brooksher recently put Marc in charge of all of the Brooksher businesses. Authorities are investigating the incident, but stated that they were confident it was an accident.

Marc Madrid's fate was sealed from the moment Budge read Kitty Finder's report on Del Brooksher in January. According to the report, Betsy Brooksher had agreed to provide Marc with several million dollars out of the Brooksher fortune after Del Brooksher's death, and to put him in charge of the company business. Maybe more importantly, there were unsubstantiated allegations in her report that Marc Madrid wormed his way in with Del Brooksher from the beginning, with the intent of arriving at exactly the place in the business where he'd ended up.

Unsubstantiated information would have been ignored by Budge if it came from anybody but Kitty Finder. He knew how good she was, and he knew how reliable she was. Budge called Billy with the information from Kitty's report.

"This is Billy. What's up?"

"I got the report from the investigator I hired in Seattle. Basically, Mrs. Brooksher has already given a huge chunk of money to this Madrid guy . . . out of her own funds that aren't tied up in the settlement of the estate. Kitty thinks it was something over a million bucks. He just bought a new black SL 500 Mercedes convertible, the hundred forty thousand–dollar kind, and he just bought a big fancy house. She also put him in charge of everything, and I mean everything. He basically has control of the entire business. And here's the kicker. . . . Kitty thinks he has been on a mission to do just what he's doing since before the old man hired him."

"I guess you need to make another trip to Seattle. Somebody needs to look out for a guy like that. He could have an accident . . . maybe in his garage in his big fancy new house while he's fussing with that new convertible."

Budge had scheduled a return trip to Seattle right away, and as much as it pained him to stay away from Kitty, he didn't tell her he was going to be there.

Using information from Kitty's report, Budge quickly found the elegant new home that Marc Madrid had purchased in the Meridian Valley. It was obvious that Kitty's assessment was right on. . . . Money had already been flowing his way, even though it would be more than two months before the Brooksher estate was settled. Budge chose Friday afternoon to visit Marc's home, acting on information that Kitty provided that he frequently washed and detailed his new Mercedes before the weekend. Patiently waiting an hour after he saw the black convertible turn into the gated subdivision late in the afternoon, Budge approached the guard gate in his nondescript rental van.

An elderly uniformed man came out of the guard shack as Budge drove up. "Can I help you, sir?"

"Yes sir. Thank you. I have a part I need to get to Mr. Madrid right away. He's working on his car."

"Oh, so Mr. Madrid is expecting you?"

"Yeah . . . he said to tell you to let me right in." Budge chuckled and said, "It's Friday. Maybe he has a hot date tonight."

The guard chuckled also. "He does like to show the ladies around in that fancy car. What is your name . . . for my activity form?"

Without hesitation, Budge said, "Bob, Bob North."

Dutifully, the guard wrote *Bob North* and the time of arrival on the form on his clipboard. Then he reached inside the door and hit the button to open the gate. "Have a good day, Mr. North."

Budge located Marc's house and pulled into his driveway. The garage door was open, and the Mercedes was sitting inside it. A vacuum and assorted rags and bottles were sitting around the Mercedes. Marc Madrid was nowhere in sight. Budge sat in the van for a few moments, and then Marc came out of the interior door leading from the garage to the house carrying a bottle of beer, with a huge St. Bernard following him. When he saw the white van in his driveway, he walked to the open window on the driver's side as the huge dog flopped down on the newly coated garage floor.

"Can I help you?"

Budge was immediately turned off by the sickening amount of cologne that Marc had poured on himself at some time during the day. "Yes, are you Mr. Smithson?"

Impatiently, Marc said, "No, I'm not Mr. Smithson."

Budge made a point of looking down at the paperwork he had in his lap. "Shit. This is the address they gave me. Uh, my damn cell phone is on the fritz. Do you have a phone in your garage I could use?"

"Sure . . . I guess. There's a wall phone right over there," Marc said as he pointed toward a phone near the door he had just come through.

"Thanks," Budge said, and he left the van and walked toward the phone. As he entered the garage, he was rapidly assessing the interior. He quickly noticed that the garage door controller button was right next to the phone. He turned toward Marc, just so he could see where he was and what he was doing. "Love this nice big garage. I wish I had one like it."

Absently, Marc said, "Yeah, it's great," as he picked up a rag and began wiping the chrome on the Mercedes.

Budge knew that Marc wasn't interested in him or in what he was doing, so he reached for the phone and dialed a phony number. He then clicked it off and had an imaginary conversation about his delivery. Budge was standing sideways so he could see Marc. As Marc opened the Mercedes door and bent down to wipe the chrome doorplate, Budge hit the close button on the garage door controller.

"What the fuck! What are you do—"

Budge was on Marc before he could even stand up, grabbing him from behind. With his quickness and his strength, he snapped Marc's neck before he could utter another shocked word. As his body went limp, Budge pulled him around to the front of the Mercedes so he would be out of sight when he opened the garage door.

Budge's actions had been so quick and so quiet, the St. Bernard had barely stirred. He was not even slightly aware of what had just happened to his owner.

Budge quickly went to the garage door controller and hit the open button. He hurried out to his van and removed a floor jack, which he pushed into the garage and ran under the front end of the Mercedes. He then went back for four jack stands. Within a few minutes, with the garage door closed again, he had jacked all four corners of the Mercedes up and installed a jack stand under each.

Budge looked around Marc's workbench and spotted a flashlight. He then dragged the body around to the side of the Mercedes and slid him under the car on the slick garage floor. He threw the flashlight under the car near Marc's right hand. *I hope he's right-handed,* he thought. *Even if people know he's not mechanical, they'll just assume he was looking at something under his new car.*

Budge started to open the garage door and push the floor jack back out of the garage, and realized that someone would question how Marc managed to lift the car onto the jack stands if the floor jack wasn't in the garage. He reluctantly left the floor jack inside the garage, realizing it could be traced to the auto-supply store where he'd purchased it on the way to Marc's home.

Budge walked deliberately to the back of the Mercedes and stood there for a moment. He had a déjà vu moment thinking about the sports car crashing through the glass wall in *Ferris Bueller's Day Off* as he put his foot on the back of the convertible and pushed it off the jack stands. There was a sickening sound as the heavy car dropped on the dead body of Marc Madrid. *You could easily have your neck broken in an accident like that,* Budge thought.

Fortune stood up, and was sniffing at Marc's lifeless feet. That was when Budge had the idea to put the big dog in the convertible. *This big horse jumping into the car would be enough to knock it off the jack stands,* he thought.

When Budge left Marc Madrid's house, he took one of the alternate exits out of the subdivision, thinking the less the guard at the main gate saw of him the better. As he pulled up to the gate, he breathed a sigh of relief as it opened automatically for his exit.

On the way to the airport, Budge called Reverend Raymond.

Raymond was in his preacher mode as he answered. "This is Reverend Raymond, God's messenger. How may I help you?"

"Fuck you, you whacko preacher. This is Budge. I have paved the way for you to proceed without any interference."

"What . . . what does that mean?"

"You are a thick-headed prick. He's gone . . . the troublemaker is gone. I mean . . . really gone."

"I still don't under . . . oh, oh, you mean that Mar—"

"Shut the fuck up," Budge almost shouted. "Yeah, no more problems from the guy . . . her guy."

"Oh, well what happen—"

"We don't talk about that, you fucking idiot. Not on a cell phone. Just go ahead and do whatever it is you do. And stay in touch with me and Billy." With that, Budge abruptly closed his phone.

Budge was on a plane returning to Anchorage less than eighteen hours after he arrived in Seattle.

By March, Reverend Raymond was very restless. He had been hanging around in hotel rooms in Seattle for several months. For a while, doing nothing every day and drinking every night had been fun. His demons had not bothered him, probably because there was the promise of a big payday ahead of him if he kept his cool. Billy kept the money he was sending Raymond kind of tight, but by going for days without eating much, Raymond was able to pay for a hooker every week or so. He just stole the liquor he needed. It was easy for him because of the many liquor stores in the area.

Okay, Raymond thought, *time to get to work. Marc is out of the way. It's time to meet Mrs. Brooksher.*

Raymond had his white suit cleaned and pressed, and he found a barbershop close to his hotel where he had a haircut and a shave. He gambled that Mrs. Brooksher would be at the Brooksher Building, with the recent demise of her right-hand man. The taxi let him out in front, and he walked up to the stately entrance. After entering the first set of doors, a guard opened one of the interior doors for him.

"Good afternoon. May I help you?"

Putting on his best Southern drawl, Raymond said, "Kind sir, I am Reverend Raymond. I am God's messenger, here to help Mrs. Brooksher in her hour of need."

"Oh . . . uh, is she expecting you?"

Moving close to the diminutive doorman so he could impress him with his height and his commanding voice, Raymond said, "No. I have been sent here by friends of Mrs. Brooksher, and by our divine God." *Do not forget to entertain strangers, for by so doing some people have entertained angels without knowing it. Hebrews 13:2*

Reverend Raymond didn't know it, but he had just struck his first piece of luck in his pursuit of Mrs. Brooksher's money. The guard was a deeply religious man . . . and he was more than a little intimidated by Reverend Raymond's presence. "I . . . well, I will escort you to Mrs. Brooksher's office," he said. "You can talk to her receptionist."

When Raymond was fully into his Reverend Raymond character, he felt a personal power and righteousness, and it was then that he knew he could not be denied. He knew he was going to get past the receptionist, and he relished the idea of charming the rich widow. It did not surprise him that the guard helped him with the receptionist.

"Mary, this is Reverend Raymond. He was sent here by friends of Mrs. Brooksher. He is here to help her in this difficult time."

Before Mary could speak, Reverend Raymond said, "Mary, it is my mission to comfort Mrs. Brooksher, and to provide her with guidance in this time of need." *It is more blessed to give than to receive. Acts 20:35*

Mary looked confused. She didn't want to deny a religious man access to Mrs. Brooksher because she was well aware of Betsy's religious activities. At the same time, she wasn't expecting Reverend Raymond, and didn't want to push him into Betsy's office if she didn't want to see him. "I need to ask—"

"God *does* work in mysterious ways, young lady. Mrs. Brooksher will be very happy to see me. If she is not, I will apologize profusely to both of you, and leave. Please allow me to enter alone."

Mary was caught up in Reverend Raymond's holy aura, just as the guard was, and hesitantly, she said, "Well . . . alright. Let me open the door for you . . . so she knows that I know you are coming in."

Mary opened the door and said, "Uh, Mrs. Brooksher . . . someone to see you."

Betsy started to question Mary, and stopped when Reverend Raymond walked through the door. To her aging eyes, he looked like a holy vision in white as he entered her office. All she could say was, "My God."

Raymond made sure to exude all of his power and strength as he walked toward Mrs. Brooksher in the huge office that had been her husband's. She looked small and fragile behind the big oak desk that Del Brooksher had custom-made when they built the Brooksher Building. "Mrs. Brooksher, I am Reverend Raymond, and I am here to counsel and comfort you in your time of need."

Raymond reached across the desk with his big hand. Betsy hesitated for a moment, and then put her tiny hand in his. She felt the warmth of his hand, and was immediately comforted.

Raymond held Betsy's hand for a moment and said, "'Blessed are the pure in heart; for they shall see God.' That is from—"

"Matthew 5:8. I know it well. Now, *who* are you?"

Raymond eased into one of the big chairs in front of the desk. "As I indicated, I am Reverend Raymond. I am God's messenger. I seek to help good people who are having bad times. I know you lost your husband . . . and I am very sorry for your loss. I also know you have lost a trusted employee recently. I saw that on the evening news. I may seem presumptuous, but I am not sure you have anybody to help you through these losses."

"What church do you represent?"

"I am a wandering messenger of God. I had a beautiful parish house in Louisiana, with over two thousand parishioners, but I completed my mission there. God sought me out to travel the country to comfort his

children. I show no favoritism in my ordained quest. I know you are a
wealthy woman, who can pay for any services you need, but I am not
a seeker of fortune. I serve the downtrodden as well. 'He will give his
angels charge of you to guard you in all your ways. On their hands they
will bear you up, lest you dash your foot against a stone.' Psalms 91:11-12.

Reverend Raymond could see the desperation in Betsy's face. In a
tragic and strange way, he knew he was going to comfort her. *Hell,* he
thought, *if I nick her for a hundred million, she'll still have a few billion
left. Maybe I can get more . . . .*

"Mr. Raymond, uh, Reverend, I don't know you. I have just lost the
man I was married to for over forty-five years. A few days ago, I lost the
man I turned the management of all of my husband's businesses over
to . . . a man I liked and trusted. Now, because my husband and I are very
wealthy, every crackpot in the country is trying to get involved in our
business. You seem like a nice man. Whether you are really a nice man
or a nice man without a larcenous agenda is something I don't know. I
know I'm vulnerable right now. I am devastated by my losses . . . but I am
not a stupid woman. In many ways, I am as responsible for our incredible
wealth as my husband was."

Reverend Raymond knew this was a critical juncture in his relationship with Betsy Brooksher, and he responded carefully and deliberately.
"Mrs. Brooksher, I am a man of God. You have already proven to me that
you are a woman who believes in God by your knowledge of the Bible.
I don't want anything *from* you. I am here to give to you . . . at the time
of your choosing. I will pray for you. I will pray with you, if you allow
me to. I will comfort you with words from the Bible when you have low
moments. I will give you a shoulder to lean on when you have doubts
and fears. If you want me to, I will stand beside you in support as you
deal with difficult issues."

As Reverend Raymond was talking, he reached inside his suit pocket
and drew out a business card that was shiny white, with a gold leaf border
around it. In large, elegant letters, it simply said, **Reverend Raymond.**
Below the name was the area code and number of Reverend Raymond's
cell phone. Raymond knew it was a gamble, but he said, "I know you are
a busy woman, so I will leave you alone now. Here is my card. Call me
anytime. I am staying in the area, and I can come to you at any time. God
bless you and keep you in this difficult time."

As Raymond rose up from the chair, Mrs. Brooksher stood also. It
was apparent she was surprised by the Reverend's sudden decision to
depart. "Well . . . I, uh, I appreciate you coming here." She reached her
small hand out to Reverend Raymond again. When he gently took it, she

was once again amazed by how warm it felt.

"Thank you, Mrs. Brooksher. I can tell you are a brave and strong woman, but I will be here for you if you need me."

As Reverend Raymond headed for the door, Betsy followed him. She was again taken in by him as he walked through the big door. He was a white vision of strength and wisdom, and a kind of holiness she had never been that close to. "Reverend . . . thank you very much for coming here," she said as he left, more than a little surprised at her own words.

Reverend Raymond was glowing internally as he exited the Brooksher Building. *I've got her,* he thought. *I've fucking got her!*

"This is going to go very well, Billy," Raymond said after Billy answered his phone. "I made my first contact with her today, and it couldn't have gone better. I didn't push her. In fact I did almost the opposite of that . . . but I got to her."

Ever the skeptic, Billy fired back, "What do you mean, you got to her? How in the fuck do you know that?"

"I just know it, Billy. She was almost gushing as I walked out the door. She's very religious. Shit, everybody who works there is religious. I'm the perfect guy to do this. The ball's in her court now. It's up to her to call me . . . and she will."

"Yeah, and what the fuck are you going to do if she doesn't?"

"She will."

The doorman at the Susitna Hotel recognized Beth as she approached the main door to the lobby. "Good morning, Ms. Saylor. Board meeting today?"

Slightly surprised at the recognition and the awareness of her reason for being there, Beth said, "Yes. Thank you."

"Ms. Saylor, the meeting will not be in the Foraker Room today. It is in the Oosik Conference Room."

"Thank you," Beth said as she entered the hotel and proceeded to the Oosik Room with the same question in her mind that was always there when she entered that particular conference room: *Why would anyone name a conference room after a walrus dick?*

When Beth entered the room that would be her home for the next two days during the March meeting of the Alaska Permanent Fund Corporation Board of Trustees, the usual early gaggle of board members and interested citizens were settling in. Beth looked over the section of the room dedicated to the everyday people who would be allowed to testify at the beginning of the two-day meeting. Unlike the other board members, she was untainted by the public's testimony, having only heard favorable testimony from the public in Fairbanks at her first board meeting. She hadn't thought about the fact that those had been friendlies who were there primarily to support her. She was unprepared for what she would hear in this meeting.

Trustee Ron Minty was standing near the table with coffee, juice, and cookies on it at the back of the room as Beth entered. He had been talking with fellow trustee Jerry Holter, and he immediately stopped his conversation midsentence. "Jesus, look at her," Ron cooed to Jerry. "She's fucking gorgeous. Look at that ass . . . and those long fucking legs. I like our new board member. I'd like to—"

"You're a pig, Minty," Jerry said. "She's a businesswoman, a successful businesswoman, a businesswoman who has the governor's ear. From what I've heard, she'd chew you up and spit you out."

"She can chew on me anytime," Ron said quietly, thinking, *and I'd like to chew on her!*

A few minutes later, the room had filled, and Chairman Fred Feck's call for a quorum confirmed that all board members were present. He then called for public testimony after laying out the ground rules for those who wanted to testify. . . . Public begging was what Trustee Mary Brunser called it when she warned Beth about what would happen at the beginning of the meeting.

Chairman Feck began the process. "Okay, is a . . . Mr. Smith prepared to make a testimony?"

A nervous-looking, slightly balding man with short blond hair and horn-rimmed glasses stood up in the public seating area. "Uh, yes. Yes sir, I . . . I'm ready."

When he was standing, it became apparent how tall and thin he was. His conservative attire was that of an educated and dedicated man who cared more about his mission in life than he did about how he looked. He wore a brown suit with a rumpled white shirt and a too-thin tie. He stumbled his way out of the back row of seats and walked tentatively to the table reserved for people speaking to the board. After sitting down, he put one hand on the microphone, as if to steady it, and began talking. He was obviously nervous. "My name is Zed Smith. I'm a contract economist. I wish to speak about—"

Chairman Feck interrupted Mr. Smith. "I'm sorry, Mr. Smith, but what is a contract economist?"

Again, nervously, Zed said, "Well, I do contract work for city and state governments, the federal government, and private companies. I do all sorts of micro- and macroeconomic analysis for these entities, and make recommendations. That means I do analysis of how entities make decisions to allocate resources, and the impact those decisions have on supply and demand, and eventually, prices. In the case of a macroanalysis, I look at total economic activities, dealing with growth, inflation, and unemployment, and the government's impact on them. I am—"

Again, Chairman Feck interrupted. "Mr. Smith, what qualifies you to do what you do?"

Zed seemed to relax a little, and he answered with reserved pride. "Well sir, I graduated from Stanford University with a dual major in business and economics. I also have an MBA in economics from Stanford, and a PhD in finance from Princeton. I have twenty years of experience as a working economist for various companies and governments."

Feeling like he had been put in his place, Chairman Feck said, "Very impressive. What would you like to discuss today?"

Zed sat up straighter in his chair. "I would like to discuss the Knik Arm Bridge. I have done an analysis of the project. I have charts, and a PowerPoint presentation, but I would like to give you enough information today to pique your interest."

Vice Chairman Jerry Holter spoke up. "Who commissioned you to do this analysis, and what does this have to do with the Permanent Fund Corporation, Mr. Smith?"

Zed did not hesitate in answering. "I did the analysis myself, and I did it for the people of Alaska. I think the bridge should be built with Permanent Fund money, and the Knik Arm Bridge and Toll Authority should operate it. It could be built under a new resolution which relates to infrastructure. I am aware that the Alaska Permanent Fund Corporation Board is looking at adding a resolution to invest a portion of its assets in infrastructure development."

There were a number of reactions from the members of the board. Most were wry smiles, or even low chuckles . . . with the exception of Trustee Mary Brunser, who spoke up.

"Mr. Smith, you are obviously aware of what is on the board's agenda . . . but are you aware of all the information that has been presented about the Knik Arm Bridge? That it is not economically viable? That it is not needed? To say nothing about the Bridge to Nowhere publicity?"

"I am aware of all of that, and it is all . . . crap." While a murmur went through the room, Zed continued. "All of that data is the product of shortsighted antidevelopment thinking. South-central Alaska is a new area in terms of development, compared to virtually every other place in the United States. Fifty years from now, that bridge would be the lifeline to an unlimited amount of land resources that would have made the Cook Inlet Bowl one of the finest metropolitan areas in the United States . . . and it would be paid for."

Every member of the board had removed the idea that Zed Smith was a crackpot from their heads right after he gave them his credentials. Now, as the power of what he said was sinking into their thoughts, they all sat in silence.

Emboldened, Zed continued. "There is almost forty billion dollars in the Permanent Fund. We don't need the US Government. We don't need private investors. We just need to approve it and build it. The idea that has been floated that three dollars for a toll is not enough to support the bridge, and that it's too expensive, is ridiculous. Make it five dollars. Would you rather drive for an hour at the current price of gas . . . which is going to go higher, or would you rather pay five dollars to drive ten minutes? Do a mileage calculation, and figure out how many more accidents and deaths there will be for the driver miles over the highway in the next fifty years, and compare it to the bridge miles. A macro-analysis looks at all of these things, and many more. It's all in my PowerPoint presentation."

Again, the room was silent, and again, Mary Brunser spoke up. "Mr. Chairman, I am fascinated by what Mr. Smith has to present. I recommend that we schedule a time when we can all sit and view his presentation."

For the first time since the meeting started, Executive Director Richard Cally spoke up. "Mary, I agree with you. Let's have a vote."

Richard Cally's endorsement was all it took. The vote was unanimous, and a day and time was scheduled for Zed's presentation.

The meeting went downhill from there. When Chairman Feck called for the next public testimony from a Mickey Muse, the most bizarre exchange the board members had ever heard began.

"Is Mr. Muse in the room?"

A scruffy looking man who looked like a street person who had been cleaned up a little before making his appearance raised his hand. "That's me, Your Honor. I'm Mickey Muse."

"Forgive me, Mr. Muse, but you have an interesting name."

As the man stood up, he looked almost comical. A poorly trimmed beard and the red nose of an alcoholic were completed by an ill-fitting suit that looked like a clown's costume. He shuffled out of the back row of the public section, and when he walked he had a sideways gait. He was sitting down at the speaker's table as Fred spoke to him. "It's given, Your Honor. That's my name."

"Okay. I would prefer to be referred to as Chairman, not Your Honor. I'm not a judge."

"Sorry Your Hon . . . Your Chairmanship. I'm just more familiar with judges."

"I'll bet," said Ron Minty under his breath, but loud enough for several of the trustees to hear him. Richard Cally gave him a stern look, and most of the trustees smiled.

"Okay, Mr. Muse. What do you have for us today?"

"Well . . . uh, I know Alaska's got a lot of money. I know you guys . . . and the two broads there, you spend a lot of it."

Richard Cally spoke up immediately. "Mr. Muse, the two women on this board are highly regarded businesswomen in Alaska, and referring to them as broads is extremely rude."

"I'm sorry, sir. I just . . . well, that is street talk. I apologize. May I continue?"

With an affirmative reply from Richard Cally, Mickey Muse continued. "I don't know if you recognize it, but I am what is referred to as a *street person*."

"No shit," was Ron Minty's whispered reaction, again heard by several of the board members. This time, Fred Feck and Richard Cally both gave him a stern look.

"There are lots of people like me living on the streets in Anchorage . . . and lots of people like me dying on the streets of Anchorage. People are dying in the woods, in cardboard boxes behind liquor stores, in creeks, and all over town. Most of them die in the winter." Mickey waited for his words to sink in.

"I will ask you the same question Mr. Holter asked Mr. Smith. What does this have to do with the Alaska Permanent Fund Corporation?" Chairman Feck moved forward in his chair as he addressed Mickey.

Mickey leaned forward as well as he went to the heart of his testimony. "Well, I think the Permanent Fund should build houses for us homeless people . . . you know, someplace warm and safe."

Ron Minty spoke out loud this time. "You mean someplace we pay for where you could go after wandering the streets all day and getting so drunk you don't know where you are?"

Ron's comment surprised the entire board, but it surprised Mickey the most. "No . . . I mean, maybe . . . if the homeless person happens to have had too much to drink, they would have a place to go, instead of sleeping . . . and dying, in an alley."

By now, every member of the board was churning inside. Ever the voice of reason, it was obvious that Richard Cally was trying to contain his impatience as he responded. "Mr. Muse, this board is challenged with the responsibility of taking care of money that belongs to the people of the State of Alaska. Our mission is to find places where this money can generate a reasonable rate of return and be reasonably safe. We are not charged with being a social-service entity. If the State of Alaska wants a program to build houses for street people, the governor and the legislature will have to decide that. If that is the sum of what you want to discuss here today, then your time is up."

Mickey looked confused . . . and pissed. "You mean you all are sending Alaska's money all over the world, and you won't do anything for people who are suffering right here in Anchorage?"

Feeling the need to make some kind of contribution to the meeting, Beth spoke up. "Mr. Muse, Mr. Cally was trying to make you understand that this is not the place to make a pitch for funding for what amounts to a social-service project . . . a questionable social-service project at best."

Mickey Muse jumped up from the speaker's table and shouted, "Questionable! I know you. You're that rich Saylor cunt. What the fuck do you know about social-service projects. I'll bet your tight little ass has never had to sleep in a cardboard box."

Stunned for only a second or two, every man on the board stood up. Fred spoke the loudest, and there was venom in his voice. "You are out of order, Mr. Muse, and I want you out of this room—now."

"Fuck you. My friend Ready Freddy used to be a lawyer, and he said I have a right to be here."

Jerry Holter said, "You've used your rightful opportunity up. Get out of the room, or we'll have you thrown out."

Mickey started to take his jacket off. "Come and get me. I used to box. I can whip all of you candy asses."

As Mickey started to move toward the board's table, Richard looked at the public section of people who were sitting closest to the door and pleaded for someone to call hotel security.

At that moment, a tall man stood up in the public section. He had a white Fu Manchu mustache that matched the color of the long hair that was visible under his white Bailey Davis straw hat. He was wearing a baby blue sport coat over a navy sport shirt and crisp-looking jeans. His polished black cowboy boots completed the urban-cowboy look.

The cowboy moved around the seats and approached Mickey from behind. Mickey had reached the board's table, and was right in front of Beth. "What do you know about street people, you snooty bitch? Have you ever passed out in a snow bank and been butt-fu—"

When the urban cowboy got to Mickey, he reached around him with both arms. He locked Mickey's arms up tight against his body and lifted him off the floor. As he turned to head Mickey toward the door, only Beth noticed the corner of his Fu Manchu mustache come loose slightly. The big cowboy carried Mickey out the door, issuing an admonishment that nobody in the room could hear well enough to understand. There was not another word out of Mickey, and the man in the baby blue coat did not reenter the room.

Beth was in deep thought about how the tiny glimpse of the cowboy's real face had given her the feeling there was something familiar about him as Chairman Feck was saying, "Who was that man? Somebody find him." Fred sat down and said quietly, "At least *he* had the balls to do something. We owe him."

Beth decided to keep her little secret to herself. *I can't prove it now,* she thought. *I'm not even really sure of what I saw, and if I said anything now, everybody would probably think their new board member is an emotional chick . . . or broad.*

Nobody found the cowboy. Billy Peet was pissed when Budge told him what had happened and admitted he missed most of the first day of the Permanent Fund Corporation Board of Trustees meeting because of it.

"You're not there to be a fucking hero," Billy said. "You're also not supposed to draw attention to yourself. I'm paying you to be there so you can gather information. You'd better find a way to get back in there tomorrow."

Little glimpses change lives . . . because they were missed, because of a fleeting recognition, or because they capture an emotion.
—From *Fred Longcoor's Book on Life*

132

Chapter 10

Putting the Pieces Together

Doug paced around his grungy real estate office in Seattle most of the afternoon. He had stumbled upon something exciting, and he wanted to call Billy Peet about it, but he hated to. Billy loved to talk down to him, and he constantly belittled him. On more than one occasion, Billy threatened him, usually in reference to some real estate scam that didn't go like he wanted it to. The deals he helped Billy with in the past were all smalltime, but this time he smelled something big.

Billy was sitting at his desk in the ranch house in Montana when the phone rang. Recognizing the caller from the caller ID, Billy answered the phone after one ring. "What do you want, you real estate hack?"

Doug was surprised at the quick answer, but not at the remark. "Billy . . . how are you?"

"Too fucking busy for small talk."

"Well, I have something that might interest you. I have a client, a big client . . . from Alaska. He, or they, are interested in something commercial in the Seattle area. They—"

"What do you mean, they?"

"Well, it's a rich guy, and his sister. They own a big company . . . Saylor Industries. They want to make an investment, and they like warehouses and the Kent Valley."

Surprised, Billy said, "Yeah, I've heard that name before. So, what does this have to do with me?"

"Well, there's a rich old broad here. . . . Her husband died recently. Billionaires. Anyway, he built a brand-new warehouse in Kent. Spec.

133

Never used. It's supposedly worth a hundred million, and I think my guy has the horsepower to buy it."

Billy was silent for a moment while his brain spun. *Fuck, everybody has the same idea we have. I can't let on that I know about this. I need to find out everything Jimbo knows.*

"I still don't get it," he said. "What does this have to do with me?"

"I don't have the horsepower to swing a deal. I could connect the potential seller and the potential buyer, but there's got to be more in this if someone else . . . someone like you, bought it and resold it. I know you have . . . uh, ways of making deals that I don't have."

Again, Billy was silent for a few moments. "Well, my grubby little friend, why don't you find out what you can about this? Don't approach the widow, just nose around and find out if it's for sale, what they want for it, that kind of stuff." Playing dumb, he continued. "Find out if it's in probate, when that will be cleared up, you know, that kind of shit."

"Okay. I can do that." Hesitantly, Doug continued. "If you're interested, I mean, if it works out, will I get a finder's fee . . . and a real estate commission?"

"You're a greedy bastard."

"Maybe, but I'm probably the only guy who has connected the two parties."

You've got me there, Billy thought, *and I am really glad to find out the Saylors may be interested.*

"Let's see what happens. If something actually comes out of this, I'll treat you right. All you have right now is a hair-brained idea. Remember, if this does work, I'm the guy who has to put up a pile of money."

Billy ended the phone conversation and immediately dialed Budge in Anchorage.

"What's up, Billy? I'm just typing a recap of yesterday's second day of the board of trustees meeting."

"Oh yeah, well, what happened yest . . . never mind, I've got something important to talk to you about. You remember Doug Faithsen, in Seattle?"

"Yeah, I remember him. Creepy little bastard. Helped us with that Boeing Field property deal."

"That's the guy. Well, he just called. He's stumbled onto the Brooksher warehouse in Kent. More importantly, he also stumbled onto somebody who may be interested in buying it."

"You're shitting me. He doesn't know anything about us, about the Reverend, does he?"

"Shit no. I don't know how in hell he would know about that. I'm not sure how to handle the fact that he's aware of the warehouse, but he may be valuable with the buyer, you know . . . once we've secured the warehouse. Now, are you ready for this?"

"I don't know," was Budge's wary reply.

"The potential buyers are from Alaska . . . the Saylors."

For a moment, Budge was too shocked to respond. Finally, he said, "You mean the snooty bitch whose pretty little ass I saved yesterday?"

"That's the one. Her, and her pretty big brother."

"Fuck. Small world. What do we do now?"

"I'm not sure we do anything. I've got Jimbo on a phony research project . . . trying to find out if the old lady wants to sell, how much it's worth, that kind of shit. We need him until we can figure out if we can drill around him to connect the Saylors with the property. I don't know what we'll do when he finds out we've left him out. Maybe he'll need to take a swim."

"What if he contacts Mrs. Brooksher?"

"I told him not to. If he does, he'll be bottom-fishing with his dick for bait sooner rather than later. So, what about the meeting yesterday?"

"Oh, well, do you want me to just read this, or email it? It's ready. All I've got to do is hit Send."

"Send it. Oh, and call the Reverend and let him know about Doug . . . just to be safe."

Budge closed up his cell phone and looked over his report one last time before he sent it.

Billy:

Okay, other than the excitement yesterday, this was more boring shit. Speaking of shit, that street clown I threw out the door shit his pants when I grabbed a handful of his balls and told him I was going to cut them off if I ever saw him near the board of trustees again. He headed right to the bathroom. I'll bet he won't be making any more board meetings.

There was quite a bit of discussion about what happened yesterday, and there were two security guards at the meeting today. They questioned me about who I was and why I was there, and I had enough bullshit ready for them. It's going to make each meeting a little tougher for me to get into. It sounds like yesterday's little goat-roping pretty much shut that meeting down right after I left, so I didn't really miss much.

Other than a recap of the fund's recent performance, which was good, most of the meeting was about adding a new asset class . . . infrastructure. The smart guy who talked to the board about the Knik Arm Bridge yesterday seems to be in tune with the board's agenda. His proposal to build the

Knik Arm Bridge under an infrastructure investment resolution makes a lot of sense. I don't know if it will pay for itself, but he seems to think it will.

Other than that, it was about a bunch of ticky-tacky little shit. Reports from fund managers, reports on asset classes, responses to questions raised by the public at the last meeting, last meeting's minutes, etc.

The next meeting is in Juneau. Do you want me to go to it? I'm going to need a really good getup if I go.

—Budge

After the second day of the board meeting concluded, Ron Minty and Jerry Holter were preparing to head to the Turnagain Room for their usual few post-meeting drinks when Ron abruptly stopped at the doorway.

Jerry came to a stop as well, and said, "What are you doing?"

Ron turned around and started to walk back into the conference room. "I've just had an epiphany."

Jerry was shocked as he saw Ron walk up to Beth, who was gathering her papers at the board's table.

Beth looked up to see Ron standing over her. "Mr. Minty, what can I do for you?"

Nervously, Ron said, "Well, Jerry and I usually go for a drink after these meetings. I thought . . . since we all don't know you that well yet, that you might be interested in going with us. You know, kind of get acquainted. It's not a big deal . . . just a couple drinks, and some BS about the meeting. We're going to the Turnagain Room."

Surprising herself and Ron Minty, she said, "Sounds good. Go ahead, and I'll be there a couple minutes behind you."

"Great," was all Ron could manage. He turned around and walked toward Jerry with a grin on his face that Jerry would later describe as "shit-eating."

"What the hell was that all about?"

Ron lifted his chin, turned his head slightly, then looked down at his shorter companion in a haute imitation of a noble being who was delivering a defining missive and said, "Beth . . . Ms. Saylor, will be joining us for a drink."

Jerry was almost speechless. "You're shitting me!"

Back to being Ron, he replied, "I'm not shitting you. That gorgeous hunk of woman is going to follow us to the Turnagain Room, and I'm going—"

Jerry said abruptly, "You are not going to do anything fucking stupid, not while I'm around. I'll get up and leave you to dig your own way out."

"Yeah, yeah. I'll be good," was Ron's unconvincing reply.

"I don't know why I'm worried about it. You can just go ahead and fuck up your own life. From what I've gathered, Beth Saylor is a pretty classy woman. You don't treat a woman like that like she's just a piece of ass. In fact, if you just keep your mouth shut, you might even learn something. She's apparently a hell of a businesswoman."

Server Buffy Lantry saw the two familiar men enter the Turnagain Room, and she quickly recognized the big tipper. Just as quickly, she remembered the tiny tip she had gotten the last time they came in. They went to the back of the room to the booth they usually sat in, and she followed.

"Gentlemen, what can I do for you?" She knew her question was faintly suggestive, rather than just asking them what they would like to drink. It was her favorite opening for big tippers, and she wasn't going to give up on that just because of one bad experience.

"Belvedere martini, dry, up, three olives," said Ron.

"Sounds good," Jerry echoed.

Ron and Jerry were just touching glasses in congratulations for the completion of the day and the beginning of their winding-down moment with a special woman when she walked into the room. Beth spotted them and walked toward their table. Both men stood up.

Ron was tongue-tied, but Jerry expected that. "Welcome. Thanks for joining us for our little post-meeting ritual," he said.

"Yeah," was all Ron could muster.

As Beth took a seat, Buffy approached. Unhappy about another change in dynamics and its possible effect on her tip, she was fairly cool to Beth as she said, "Would you like something to drink?"

Beth pointed at Jerry's martini and questioned, "Vodka?"

"Yes."

"Alright, I'll have one of those. Belvedere if you have it."

Jerry laughed. "Bingo," he said as he pointed at his drink.

Ron was taking a large drink of courage and trying to recollect his macho. "It was nice . . . I mean, nice of you to join us."

"Thank you, Ron. I appreciate the invite. I would like to get to know all of the board members a little better. It's uneasy being the rookie. I feel the need to contribute, but I know I have a lot to learn. It's just a little easier if you know everyone, that is, if you are comfortable with everyone."

Jerry smiled. "You're right Beth . . . Ms. Saylor . . ."

"Beth."

"Okay, you are right, Beth, but there's no hurry. You've got four years. You'll be a vet before you know it."

The talking juice was relaxing Ron, and he finally spoke up normally.

"Jerry's right. There's too much there to absorb in two meetings. The one thing you need to remember is that we have a terrific staff working behind the scenes. It's pretty hard for us as individual board members to screw something up without someone catching on pretty quickly. And there are too many bright people on the board for us to screw up as a unit very often. I'm not saying it can't happen . . . it has, but it doesn't happen very often."

"That's good advice, Ron. Thank you. I will try—"

At that moment, Beth's cell phone rang. "I'm sorry," she said. "Excuse me a moment." Beth was looking at her caller ID as she stood up from the table, and the two men heard her say, "Governor, what an unexpected pleasure," as she walked toward the hallway outside the Turnagain Room.

"Is this the rich Saylor cunt, or the snooty bitch?"

"Governor . . . I mean, I'm not sure what to say. You obviously have someone on the inside. And the language. . . ."

"I told you, Beth, I'm not some snooty bitch. I'm a regular woman who just happens to be the governor. In fact, I'm a regular single woman who just happens to be the governor. And yes, I do have my sources. Are you bothered by what happened?"

"No, I understand the man was a street person. They have needs. They just don't understand how the system works, and it sounds like he's been getting bad advice from some former lawyer who also lets his bad habits rule his life."

"Good. I don't want you to get discouraged. The day may come when I really need you."

"What do you mean?"

"I mean, we are both successful, tough women, but we still need to stick together. Being successful single women complicates our issues. Many men can't deal with our success, especially mine, because it is so public. You know, big man egos. Sometimes, though, I think the women are worse than the men. I get these bike-riding, tree-hugging, poster-waving women who are way out of the political mainstream on my butt all the time. Most of them can't rub two nickels together and don't understand real-world political and economic issues. I don't want this to sound egotistical, but I think there is an element of jealousy involved."

"You are being very candid, Governor . . . Stacey. You're also probably right on. I don't have the same kind of problems you have for one simple reason: I own the company, or at least, my brother and I own it."

"You are right, Beth, but I am the figurative owner of Alaska . . . and I can play that card, too."

There was silence for a moment, and then Beth said, "I appreciate the call, Stacey. Is there anything else you need from me?"

"No, Beth. I just wanted to make sure you are handling this bullshit alright. I'll stay in touch . . . and it is alright for you to call me."

Beth thanked the governor, and then stood in the hallway for a moment to think about their conversation. *I like her,* Beth thought. *She is regular . . . but she wants something out of me. I hope I can handle it when it comes.*

Back at their table, Ron was beside himself. "Shit, that was the fucking governor. Does the governor ever call you on your cell phone? She doesn't call me. What the fuck is going on?"

"She knows the governor, Ron. That's how she got on the board. Do you remember how you got on the board? The ex-governor put *you* on the board. These are political positions, no matter how you cut it. I mean, you have to have some credibility and some experience, but let's face it, Alaska is full of people who are more qualified to be on the board than you are . . . but you were favored by the governor."

"Wait a fucking minute. How about you? What makes you better than me?"

"Did I say that? I was appointed by the ex-governor too, but I was a former state senator. I didn't ever say I was better than you." Jerry got a big cheesy grin on his face and added, "But I am."

"Well fu—"

"I'm sorry, gentlemen," Beth said as she came up behind Ron. "I needed to get that." As she sat down, Jerry spoke first, trying to keep Ron from quizzing her about her phone call.

"Well, Beth, you don't seem to be any worse for wear after yesterday's little attack on you and the board. Kind of a tough way to get started. I mean, we've never had a character like that testify before, and we've had some real characters up there."

Beth was still thinking about her conversation with the governor as she replied. "It was no big deal. Remember, I grew up in Fairbanks working around Haul Road truckers. Language doesn't bother me. And he wasn't attacking *me,* I just happened to be the one who spoke up. I also understand a little about the plight of these street people. Most of them are good people who just can't control their wants."

Ron let the phone call from the governor go and decided to enter into the conversation. He wanted to impress Beth. He wanted her to like him. "You're right, Beth. I agree. It's just that it's not the responsibility of the Alaska Permanent Fund Corporation to handle social needs. We need to make money. We need to make the Permanent Fund make money. I may agree emotionally that I would like to see us bail out everybody in the state who has a need, but that is not our job."

"I'm with you on that, Ron," Beth said. "If there is one thing I have learned in two meetings, it's that we have to focus on all reasonable means of making the fund generate a reasonable return. I know we need to protect the fund and we need to build the fund. I guess I just think there are some large issues that . . ." Beth let her thought trail off.

"What do you mean?" Jerry wasn't trying to impress Beth. He just wanted to get her fully engaged in the discussion so he could figure out what she was all about.

Beth had taken a drink of her martini. Now she scooted her chair back a little and folded her arms into the power position. "Like the guy who wants to build the bridge. I like that kind of progressive thinking. He may be full of hot air, but I doubt it. And that's the kind of thing that will never get done. The State has almost forty billion dollars sitting there, and there will never be a consensus on how or when we should use it. I know we have to use it to make money, but we'll never agree on how to spend it. I can see it having a hundred billion in it in a few years, and there still won't be a consensus on how we should spend it. It'll just sit there and make more money. It's a rainy-day fund, but it will never be raining hard enough for everybody at the same time."

Now, Ron was excited, even though it was for the wrong reason. He was almost breathless as he said, "I agree. There are so many things that money could be used for. Shit, you could make everybody in the state rich if you just handed it out to all the residents."

Beth had a surprised look on her face as she said, "Well Ron, that is not exactly what I was thinking about."

"Well, of course not. You're already rich."

Without it even being said, "snooty bitch" was floating around in Beth's and Jerry's heads as Ron spoke. Sensing the direction Ron was taking the conversation, Jerry headed it off. "And famous. Do you ever hear anything about your heroic exploits in Seattle anymore?"

Jerry noticed that the question made Beth visibly uncomfortable, and he wished he could withdraw it. "No . . . well, my brother likes to tease me about it. It wasn't heroic to me, it was embarrassing. Basically, it all happened because I picked out a man to love who was a nutcase . . . and I didn't have a clue until the very end." Wistfully, Beth added, "I guess I'm not a very good judge of men."

Ron and Jerry both laughed. Ron said, "I think there are a lot of mistakes made on both sides of that one."

Beth smiled, but thought, *I really made a huge mistake with that relationship, and it was the second relationship I made a big mistake with.*

Over the next hour and a half, they all talked and laughed, and got to know each other better. For Beth, it became an unexpected part of her agenda to become one of them. Jerry just wanted to find out what Beth was all about. For Ron, it was the same thing it always was with him and beautiful women. . . . He harbored the thought that he could get in her pants if he played his cards right.

Jerry finally said he had to leave, and, as expected, Ron jumped in with the pronouncement that he would cover the bill. For a moment or two after he left, Beth and Ron sat in an awkward silence, and Beth finally said, "I need to go, too."

Alcohol-fueled bravado led Ron to blurt out, "Why don't I buy you dinner?"

"Oh, thank you Ron, but I have plans." Privately, Beth was unsure how to respond to Ron. He was handsome, he was successful . . . and he was married, even though he didn't act married. She considered him to be a bit of a loose cannon, but there was still something about him she found interesting.

Stay away, Beth, she told herself. *You can't afford another man mistake, and you sure as hell can't have anything to do with a business associate who is married. Ron is one of those bad boys your mother warned you about! The kind who is wicked and fun . . . for a little while.*

Ron was intoxicated and disappointed, but he still had his senses about him. "Okay, but the offer stays open. Maybe we can have dinner after the meeting in Juneau."

"Maybe, Ron. Oh, I took care of the bill while you were in the men's room, so you definitely can buy me a drink in Juneau."

Ron said, "You didn't need to do that . . . and I will buy you a drink in Juneau."

"I know I didn't need to pay. . . . I wanted to. See you at the next meeting." As Beth walked out of the Turnagain Room, she felt womanly . . . and she suddenly felt rejuvenated by her station in life.

Reverend Raymond's long stay in Seattle was wearing on him. Almost two weeks after his meeting with Betsy Brooksher, she hadn't called him. He scoured the papers every day for any news about the disposition of the Brooksher estate, with only occasional small pieces of information coming out. Raymond had no way of knowing that Del Brooksher had astutely organized his affairs in such a way that the probate process of turning his assets over to Betsy and a few of his favorite charities was moving along at a brisk pace without any problems. Even though he boldly predicted success with Mrs. Brooksher to Billy, Raymond was mildly surprised when Betsy finally called him.

"Mr., uh, Reverend, Reverend Raymond. This is Betsy Brooksher."
Betsy's voice sounded distant and meek.

"This is Reverend Raymond. It is very nice to hear from you, Mrs.
Brooksher. What can our God and I do for you today?"

Hesitantly, Betsy began to speak. "Reverend, I . . . I have reached a
point where I think I could use some support from someone . . . like you. I
am alone. I have advisors and accountants and division presidents to help
me, but I don't have anyone personal, you know, just someone to talk to."

"That is what I'm here for, Mrs. Brooksher. I am here to provide
you strength and guidance in your time of need. I am God's messenger,
brought here to protect you from those who would compromise you." *Put
not your trust in princes. Psalms 146:3.*

"I still don't know you, Reverend, but I have the strange feeling that
I want to. Can we meet for lunch this week?"

"I am at your disposal, Mrs. Brooksher. Any day is fine with me, and
any place is fine with me." Raymond was feeling a little glow of victory
in his gut.

"Well then, how about tomorrow? The Rusty Turtle . . . it was my
dear Del's favorite place for lunch. Say, eleven-thirty?"

Reverend Raymond was early for the lunch date with Mrs. Brooksher, early enough for him to order a shot of whiskey at the bar and toss
it down. The young bartender was uncomfortable about how he should
react to the whiskey-drinking preacher.

"Uh, do you want another, sir . . . that is, Fath . . . uh, sir?"

"Yes, my son . . . quickly." Within five minutes, Reverend Raymond
had downed two shots and was sitting in the waiting area of The Rusty
Turtle, sucking on a breath mint.

Raymond saw the white limousine pull up in front of the restaurant,
and watched the driver scurry around to open the rear door for Betsy
Brooksher. She walked briskly to the front door and entered the restaurant.
Raymond was surprised at how she looked. She wore an elegant red business suit, and she appeared to be much younger and more vibrant than
she had when he first met her.

Raymond stood up. "Good morning, Mrs. Brooksher. You look lovely
today. It is nice to see you."

"It is nice to see you as well, Reverend."

The hostess approached them and spoke directly to Mrs. Brooksher,
ignoring Raymond. "Good morning, Mrs. Brooksher." She was a little
uncomfortable as she continued, "Would you like your usual table?"

"No Suzy, I . . . I think I want a different table. Something nice, near
the windows."

As they sat, Betsy explained, "I wanted to come to my husband's favorite restaurant, but I didn't want to sit at *our* table. I think I want to preserve those memories."

"That is understandable, Mrs. Brooksher. *I* certainly understand." Sitting across from her, Raymond began to notice things about Betsy Brooksher that he hadn't noticed before. She was an attractive woman for her age. Noticing that her white blouse was open much more than he would have expected it to be, he continued to evaluate her.

She has nice tits! I can't believe I'm thinking this.

"Reverend, I guess you would like to know what this is all about."

"Well, I—"

"Pardon me, Reverend, but let me explain before you say any more. I've had some of my people trying to check on your background. Needless to say, someone who goes by Reverend Raymond, with no surname, is hard to check on."

"I—"

"Please allow me to finish. I don't particularly care about that. I called *you* back. If your motives were not honorable, I'm sure you wouldn't have been willing to wait two weeks for me to call. I need someone . . . a friend and a confidant, maybe even an advisor. If you are willing to fill that role, we can move slowly while I get to know you. I have tremendous decisions facing me in the next few months, and I need to have someone help me whom I can trust. If I can't trust a man of God, who can I trust?"

Ignoring Betsy's first hint of a weakness, Raymond said, "Mrs. Brooksher, it would be a blessing for me to get to know you, and to help you. It would be a fulfillment of the mission God has given me."

"Fine. Let's have a lovely lunch, and talk. I'm going to have a glass of wine. Are you allowed to . . . I mean, do you ever have wine with your lunch?"

Raymond almost choked before he made a jerky reply. "Well . . . uh, it would be an affront to a lovely woman not to join her in a glass of wine as we break bread."

After the Reverend exited the white limo in front of his extended-stay hotel, he couldn't wait to get to his room so he could call Billy Peet.

"What's up, Preach?"

"You are not going to fucking believe this."

"What, you got an erection today? You didn't piss your pants?"

"Fuck you, Billy. I had lunch with Mrs. Brooksher. She called me yesterday. We had a nice long lunch today, and she told me she wants me to help her . . . to be her confidant, sort of her advisor. She fucking wants me around all the time, Billy. Says she can't trust anyone, but she can trust a man of the cloth." Raymond finished with a chuckle.

With a new, more respectful tone, Billy said, "Man, that's great. That's just what we need. It sounds like you did great. What else did she say?"

Raymond told Billy everything, with one exception. He didn't mention that Betsy wanted to pay him for his help. In fact, she'd told Raymond she wanted to pay him five thousand dollars a month . . . and he had every intention of double-dipping. He would keep the money Billy was sending him, and take Mrs. Brooksher's five grand a month, too. *It's what Billy would do,* he thought, self-righteously.

"Well, keep me posted, Raymond," Billy continued respectfully. "We've talked about it enough, so I know that you know what you have to do . . . what you have to find out. Basically, you just have to earn her total trust first, and if you do that it sounds like she'll give you whatever you want."

Feeling like he could walk on water, Raymond headed to the nearest liquor store and purchased a bottle of Gentlemen Jack Daniel's with money he had been saving to pay for a prostitute. There would be plenty of money for that soon. He passed out in his room late in the afternoon, before his demons could get the best of him.

At his luxurious ranch house in Montana, Billy was feeling very good after the call from Raymond. Raymond had surprised him before, but he was such a loose cannon, he was never sure what to expect. Reluctantly, Billy decided it was time to call Mario. Billy was rich, but Mario was the guy with the truly big money. He was the one who had initiated the Brooksher caper, and he was reimbursing Billy for most of the money he was spending on it. As ruthless as Billy was, he knew better than to cross Mario.

Billy poured a significant amount of expensive single malt scotch over a big tumbler full of ice and walked into his office. He sat down at his desk and took a large drink of the scotch. With a deep and audible sigh, he reached for the phone and dialed.

Billy was surprised when the lilting voice of Mary Delaney answered the phone. *Jesus, Mario is really getting old,* thought Billy. *He would never have allowed Mary to answer the phone in the old days.*

"Delaneys', this is Mary." Billy saw Mary in his mind's eye . . . an impossibly homely woman who was dumber than a candy frog. Neither he nor anyone else could understand why someone as disgustingly rich as Mario married her. Of course, Mario frequently had someone on the side who looked like she'd been in *Playboy* and acted like she'd been in *Hustler*, and that is what comforted all the guys.

"Mary, this is Billy, Billy Peet. Is Mario available?"

"Available for what, Billy Billy Peet?"

Although almost everything she said astounded him, Billy was still in awe for a moment. He knew she was serious. "I just need to speak to him, Mary."

"Okay." Billy heard her yell for Mario. "Mario, Billy Billy Peet wants to talk to you . . . on the telephone."

Billy heard the click as Mario picked up the extension. "I've got it, Mary. What's up, Billy Billy Peet?" He was chuckling as Mary clicked her extension off.

Billy gave Mario all the information Raymond had given him, even embellishing some of it, with comments like, "It's in the bag." Mario was pleased, but as always, he had questions and concerns.

"What's going to happen if the old woman gives the warehouse to Raymond? What the hell do we do then?"

"We'll create a dummy nonprofit corporation, Mario . . . something religious, something gooey, like Northwest Youth For Christ Foundation, or Washington State Children's Trinity School. We will set us up . . . you and me and Raymond, as the directors. We'll tell the old lady . . . that is, Raymond will, that we are going to turn the warehouses into a big school for disadvantaged kids. Then we stall on the construction we promise to do until we can sell it and get the fuck out of Dodge. If Raymond can keep the old broad happy, it will be easy. If Raymond gets cute or too brave, well, there are lots of things that can happen to a guy like that. You and I will still be the named directors. I think it's in our best interest to keep Raymond happy, but we need to watch him closely. As this moves along, I think I need to spend a month or so in the Seattle area."

"It sounds like you've thought this through, Billy."

"Do you think I just sit around this place and play with myself?"

Mario laughed. "No, I think you sit around that place and play with that hot little Commie you imported."

Mario's words cut into Billy, but he controlled himself. "She's not a Commie, Mario. She's a good-looking babe."

"Okay, okay. I repeat, it sounds like you have done your homework. Remember, Benny can come and help if you need him."

The thought of having Mario's obnoxious little assistant around him was more than he could take. "We won't need him, Mario. I'll bring Budge back down for a while if we need somebody. He knows the area really well."

"Okay, keep me posted."

Everybody is in the hands of God . . . and everybody treats that privilege differently. Some people push the envelope for excitement. Some people push it in anger, and some people push it purely out of stupidity. Many people push it out of one type of gluttony or another, and sadly, many people push it by accident. If you just bump up against it for any reason and survive . . . don't push it again!
— From *Fred Longcoor's Book on Life*

Chapter 11

The Unholy Alliance

By the end of March, Ron Minty had played his Ponzi scheme out in his mind dozens of times, and decided it was time to sit back and take a realistic look at it. *You're a lawyer. You're a smart guy. This is fucking stupid. There's only about a thousand ways this could backfire on you,* were Ron's thoughts as he read his PF Investors plan for about the fiftieth time.

As he was reading it again, he marveled at how some things could look so good when one's judgment was clouded by greed. *Fuck, do I want to spend the rest of my life in jail?* he thought. *Still, there has got to be a way for me to take advantage of my position on the board of trustees. So much money . . .*

Thinking about the board brought Beth Saylor into his thoughts again. He had been thinking about her frequently since the last board meeting and the socializing he and Jerry had done with her afterward. He realized how stupid it was to think about her, but he continued to fantasize anyway. She was what his wife had been when he first met her . . . hot, and unattainable. Actually, Beth was more than what his wife had been because she was also rich and powerful. It all made a potent combination, and he knew he had to try to get next to her some way.

Jerry Holter's receptionist buzzed him at his desk in the opulent office he occupied as the vice president of finance for Foraker Investments. "Yes."

"Mr. Minty for you, sir."

"Mr. Minty, what can I do for you today?"

147

"Who came up with that corny motto your receptionist spouts out every time someone calls you? 'We're not the biggest, but we are close to it?'"

"Don't you get it? Mount Foraker is the fourth-biggest mountain in the US, and it sits right next to Mount Denali . . . the *biggest* mountain in the US."

"Yeah, yeah, I get it. Foraker seems to be everywhere . . . Foraker Room, Foraker Investments. I just think it's silly to say that every time someone calls. Never mind that. You got time for lunch? I think I need a silver bullet."

"I work for someone, Ron. I can't go off to lunch and drink martinis anytime I feel like it. I'll go to lunch with you, and watch *you* drink martinis and make an ass of yourself."

"Aw, you're no fun. I think I'll just run down to The Mud Flats."

"Okay. I have a lot to do anyway."

Fifteen minutes later, Ron entered The Mud Flats and headed straight to the bar. He was pleased to see Vicki Lawner behind the bar. He had known her for a couple of years, and he always figured she was going to jump in bed with him someday. Truth was, he had never been close to having that happen. Vicki liked successful men, but she had an ironclad rule about staying away from married men.

"Vicki baby. Good afternoon. How are you?"

Married or not, Vicki knew how to work a good tip. "Hi there, you handsome devil. What brings you in this early in the day?"

That sounds familiar, thought Ron. "Vodka brings me in, you gorgeous woman. I need a martini, up. Belvedere please, and olives."

Ron looked the bar over while Vicki was making his martini. It was quiet in the usual mid-afternoon, midweek way.

Vicki came back with the martini. She set it in front of Ron and leaned heavily on the wide bar in front of him, with her elbows supporting her. Her low-cut blouse allowed a generous portion of her ample breasts to be exposed directly in front of him. She loved the game, even when she knew she wasn't going to play . . . especially on a slow midweek afternoon.

Ron's reaction was immediate and predictable. "God, you're a sexy woman, Vicki. If I told you I have a private jet sitting at the airport, would you fly to Vegas with me?"

"Sure."

"If I told you I have a Super Cub sitting at Merrill Field, would you fly to Palmer with me?"

"No."

"What? You said you'd fly to Vegas with me in my private jet. Now, you won't fly to Palmer with me in my Super Cub. What was that all about?"

Vicki smiled. "I knew we were just negotiating price." Living and working in a state where every other guy owned an airplane, she had heard the come-on a couple of times before, so she enjoyed turning the punch line on Ron.

"You are a hard woman, Vicki."

There are millions of bar alliances made every day. Sometimes it is a temporary alliance between a man and a woman. Rarely, it is a lasting alliance between a man and a woman. Sometimes it is a friendly alliance between two men or two women . . . and sometimes, it is an unholy alliance.

Budge Brown decided to visit the Mud Flats for a drink on the same afternoon Ron Minty made the same decision. He walked into the bar and took a stool directly across the U-shaped bar from Ron. With nobody else at the bar, the two men acknowledged each other with slight nods.

Vicki approached Budge, saying, "Well, one of my favorite guys is here. What brings you in this early?"

Ron was slightly embarrassed as he listened to Budge and Vicki's banter heading down a path he was familiar with. "Hi, you beautiful woman. Whiskey, gorgeous, I need whiskey."

"The usual?"

"You got it."

Ron watched with interest as Vicki returned with a tumbler full of Jack Daniel's on the rocks and a glass of water on the side. He felt a tiny twinge of jealousy as she set it in front of the new customer and assumed the same elbows-on-the-bar position that she had just struck on his side of the bar. *Tip-grubbing bitch,* he thought.

Budge leaned forward and said in a voice just above a whisper, "Vicki, you make my day every time I come in here . . . and that's why I come in here."

"You're full of shit, Budge. I've seen you drag too many lonely women out of here. You come in here to drink whiskey and get laid."

"Whoa. . . . I didn't see that coming."

"What, you think I'm blind and stupid just because I'm a bartender?"

Budge was surprised at Vicki's tone. Over Vicki's shoulder, Budge noticed Ron's facial reaction of mock surprise on the other side of the bar. It seemed like a déjà vu put-down to Budge, and he didn't have time to say anything as Vicki walked to the other end of the bar and began washing glasses. Budge tried to hide his embarrassment by making a comment to the stranger across the bar.

"Bad time of the month, I guess."

"Yeah. I think I'll be careful." Both men chuckled.

"Name's Budge. What's yours?"

"Ron, Ron Minty."

Shit, Budge thought. *That's the fucking guy from the Permanent Fund board. No wonder he looks familiar.* Budge chose to play dumb. "Uh, your name sounds familiar. You a politician or something?"

"No. You may have seen my picture or some little thing in the paper or on TV. I'm on the Alaska Permanent Fund Corporation's Board of Trustees. What about you? It looks like you get to manage your own time."

"That's it. I think I saw you on TV. My name is Budge Brown. I'm, well I'm sort of independent . . . I guess I'm independently financially secure. Rich family. My grandfather passed, and passed a lot of it to me. Mostly, I just watch the market and drink whiskey." They both chuckled again.

"Okay. It's nice to meet you."

Budge and Ron tried to keep the conversation going across the bar, and it became more difficult as a few customers began to gather on the stools around them. They decided to sit together, and Budge moved to the seat next to Ron.

Budge was wrestling with the personal dilemma of whether or not he should be around Ron. He was worried Ron might recognize him, particularly after what he'd done at the last meeting. He convinced himself that Ron wouldn't have seen through his disguise, and the whiskey made him bolder.

"What's it like . . . I mean, being responsible for all that money?"

"Well, fortunately, it's not just my responsibility. The entire board is responsible, and we pay for lots of professional advice. You know, fund managers, market experts, that kind of thing."

Yeah, I know, Budge thought. "It's just the amount of money you have to deal with. Does some of that rub off, like, are you able to make money for yourself because of what you learn from all these experts?"

Ron was surprised at how blindly and how quickly his new friend had veered close to his pet peeve. "No, I can't say that happens. I guess, if I didn't have a regular job, and had the time to sit around and work at it, some of what we learn might help us make personal investments. Candidly, we don't get much out of it for what we do."

"Why, does it feel like you are being taken advantage of?"

"I guess it's because . . . maybe that will change someday." Then, well into his second martini, Ron continued with, "Maybe I'll just have to steal some of it." He laughed, and took another sip of his martini.

Budge was unsure how he should react. *He's kidding...surely. What*

if he's serious? I need to plow this field a little deeper. "Thirty-five billion . . . or whatever it's worth, is a lot of money. I would think there are
lots of people trying to get a piece of that."

"Oh yeah, but there are all kinds of roadblocks and checks and balances to prevent something from happening. It's pretty secure . . . unless
you're an insider."

There he goes again, thought Budge. "And you are."

By this time, both men were becoming intoxicated. Budge kept his
wits about him enough to back off. He decided that what he needed to do
now was work to become friends with Ron. He could find out later if he
really had larceny in his soul.

"We just met, Ron, but I like to visit The Wild Alaska 'Beaver, Damn'
now and then. Are you interested? I know you like to drink, so if you like to
drink and look at pussy, it's a great place. I know some of the girls there."

Ron looked at Budge with eyes that seemed a little wobbly and said,
"Let's go."

On the way to the "Beaver, Damn" in his own car, Budge dialed a
number that was stored in his phone under the name *Cherry*. The sexy
voice that answered was almost drowned out by loud classic rock music.
"This is Cherry."

"Sounds like you must be at work. This is Budge."

Cherry always remembered the big spenders, and she definitely
remembered the big spenders she had slept with. "Hi Budge. Yeah, I'm
working. You coming to see me?"

"I'm on my way, baby . . . and I need a big favor. I'm bringing a
guy with me. He's a bit of a player in Alaska, and this will require some
discretion. I would like for you to make over him while we're there, and
then I would like for you to fuck him. I'll pay for it, and I don't want him
to know it was paid for."

"I love it when you talk dirty, Budge . . . and I love it even more when
it means money for me. I'm more of a stripper than I am a prostitute,
and you know I'm pretty fussy about who I go with. Is this guy alright?"

"He's a big dog, and he's a good-looking guy. A successful lawyer.
I don't want to say more than that. He's also a little drunk. You got any
blue pills?"

"I'm always prepared, Budge. I'm a little disappointed though. I
thought this was going to be me and you."

"Next time, sweetie."

"Okay . . . just for you. This little act will cost you a couple hundred
extra though, and I'll treat him really well. Maybe the lawyer can tutor
me." Cherry was not your typical stripper or lady of the night. She was

doing what she was doing so she could finish her law degree, and she was only a couple of years away from getting that done. Dancing in clubs in Alaska paid big money, and she figured she could return to California in another year and finish her schooling.

"Okay. He's going to have to go to the bathroom at some time. Keep your eyes open, and when he goes, come over and get your money." Only half seriously, Budge added, "I'm jealous. I wish it was me."

Cherry laughed. "You've got my number, Budge."

"Alright, miss schoolgirl. See you in a few minutes."

Budge and Ron arrived at the "Beaver, Damn" at the same time, and they walked through the front door together.

As their eyes adjusted to the low light in the huge room, Ron issued a breathless, "Jesus." There were beautiful mostly naked women everywhere. Like Cherry, they had come to Alaska from all over the US to dance at the "Beaver, Damn" because of the money.

On cue, Cherry emerged from the gaggle to greet them. "Budge, welcome. It's great to see you." She was a pretty, petite blonde with a gymnast's body and a smile that exposed acres of teeth. Her bikini was one of the new barely-there models in flourescent red. She reached up and gave Budge a big hug.

Ron stood in wonder of the greeting as Budge hugged Cherry. When she released him, he turned and said, "This is my new friend, Ron."

Cherry didn't waste any time. She said, "Hi, Ron," as she walked to him and gave him a big hug.

Ron was immediately taken in by the muscular feeling of her little body and the exotic scent of her perfume. "Ah . . . hi. It's nice to meet you."

Over the next hour, Cherry worked her magic on Ron. When he went to the bathroom, she approached Budge, who handed her seven one hundred–dollar bills. Budge was comfortable that he had accomplished his mission, so when Ron returned, he made an excuse about needing to leave. Before he left, they agreed they would get together sometime in the next week. When Budge arrived back at his condo, he immediately called Billy. It was something he probably wouldn't have done if he was totally sober. Right now, he just wanted to brag to Billy about something he considered to be a coup.

"What the fuck do you want at this time of night? I was just getting ready to slip my dick into the missus."

"Shit, Billy, you're married to her. You can do that any time."

"Yeah . . . anytime she's ready."

Wow, thought Budge, *even the ones you buy in Russia?* "Well, this is important. You're going to want to hear this." Budge proceeded to tell

Billy about meeting Ron Minty and their activities that night.

"Fuck, I hope that's not a mistake. I think you know why I've got Stan on the payroll. I plan to get *him* on the board of trustees."

"Think about this. What if you don't need to do that? This Minty guy hinted several times that he'd like to make some money off the fund . . . and he's already a fuckin' director. He's getting his brains fucked out right now, and I paid for it. We're going to meet again this week."

Billy said, "I'll have to think about this. Mario already approved the plan with Stan. I had a gallon of scotch tonight. I'm not thinking too good right now. Let me call you tomorrow. If you don't hear from me, call me." With that, the phone call ended in Billy's typically abrupt way.

Budge sat for a moment thinking about his conversation with Billy. *He'll come around,* he thought. *He's worried about Stan. Fuck, we can just kill him. He's really a nobody.*

Realizing he was hungry and half drunk, Budge decided to go back to The Mud Flats to get something to eat, and he was smart enough to call a taxi.

When Budge walked into The Mud Flats, it was crowded. He was surprised to see Vicki sitting on a stool at one end of the bar. There was a stool open next to her, so he walked over and asked if she minded if he sat down.

A person who was totally different from the one behind the bar earlier in the day answered cheerily, "Sit down, you handsome cowboy."

Handsome cowboy? Budge thought. *What the fuck is this?*

"Whoa, who sprinkled you with happy dust?"

Vicki turned on her stool and faced Budge. "I'm off work. I was just saying something nice to one of my favorite customers."

Budge could swear Vicki had a twinkle in her eye as she talked to him. "Well, thanks to my favorite bartender. Can I buy you a drink?"

"Absolutely. . . . I think I'm in the mood for a little party."

Okay, maybe that's not a twinkle...but it's something. "You got it. I'm good at party."

Several drinks and a couple of shared appetizers later, Vicki turned on her stool and looked Budge in the eye again. "I think I'm ready to go somewhere else."

Budge's gut did a little jump, and he said, "I'm ready too. Where do you want to go?"

Vicki put a seductive look on her face and said in a loud whisper, "I've never been to your place."

Bingo. I've hit the fucking jackpot. "Well, it's close, and I think you should see it . . . and I have a fully stocked bar. Let's go."

When Vicki entered Budge's condo, she immediately took her jacket off and threw it on the couch. "I like this place, Budge," she said as she walked toward the large window that overlooked downtown Anchorage. "And I love the view."

Budge walked up behind Vicki, and she turned around and put her arms around him. "Thanks for inviting me to your place."

"Well, you sort of in . . . I mean, you sort of surprised me tonight. You usually don't give me the time of day, and I've been slobbering all over myself trying to get your attention." Budge was experienced enough to know you don't question a gift, particularly a woman gift, so he held back his *What's this all about?* question.

"I've always liked you, Budge. I have to be careful. I've got lots of guys hitting on me in the bar. I decided you are alright. Besides, I just feel a little bit . . . adventurous tonight. I feel a little dangerous, and . . . I feel a little sexy." With that said, Vicki released Budge and walked toward the window. She turned around and faced him, then slowly unbuttoned her blouse and threw it on the couch with her jacket. With a quick reach behind her back, her bra fell to the floor, releasing two magnificent, magazine-worthy breasts.

Budge stood watching, and all he could mutter was, "Jesus," as Vicki continued her impromptu striptease.

She continued talking as she pulled her black bartender uniform slacks off. "Do you like my tits, Budge?"

"Yes, yes. I love them." Budge felt like a teenager getting his first look at a naked woman. *Nice forty year old body!*

"Well," she said, "I'm about to show you something you'll love even more." With that, Vicki removed her low-cut panties, revealing a neatly trimmed whisper of brown hair.

So much for her being a natural blonde, thought Budge.

As if she read his mind, Vicki said, "Are you disappointed that I'm not a natural blonde?"

Moving toward her, Budge said, "I don't give a shit about that. You are a beautiful, sexy woman."

Putting her arms around Budge's waist, she pulled herself into him. "And you are a beautiful, sexy man." Looking up at him with a wicked look on her face, she asked, "And are you a bad man? I want to be bad tonight. I decided I liked you because I think you are a bad man."

"You said you decided I was alright."

"I did decide that. I decided you were alright because you are a mystery. I decided you might be a bad man. Sometimes, I want to be bad. You seem like a guy who has a past, like maybe you have killed someone, or smuggled drugs, or something like that."

"Whoa, take it easy. That's a little heavy. I'm just a guy who happens to be well off because someone left me a bunch of money. I have a little too much fun sometimes, but I'm not some kind of criminal." Budge almost believed what he was saying, and it made him sound convincing.

"Okay, Mr. Not Bad Man. Let's see what you've got. Where's the bathroom first? I'll meet you in the bedroom."

Vicki was in the bathroom for a few minutes, and then entered the bedroom, where Budge was lying naked on the bed. "Very nice, big man. You look very sexy."

Vicki smothered Budge with her sexuality, her experience, and a surprisingly physical lovemaking session that lasted almost an hour. Towards the end, with Budge on top of her, she moved into a new place, a place that surprised Budge. His performance was enhanced by a whiskey dick and the fact that the Viagra pill he took while Vicki was in the bathroom had kicked in. He felt like Vicki was close to an orgasm when she began her surprising finish.

"Fuck me, Budge, fuck me hard. Pinch my tits."

Budge didn't say anything, and made an effort to be more physical while he gently pinched Vicki's nipples between his thumbs and forefingers.

She almost looked possessed as she continued. "Harder. Fuck me harder. Pinch my tits harder."

Budge responded by thrusting as strongly as he could, and pinching her nipples harder than he was comfortable doing. Vicki responded with a vocal orgasm that lasted until she begged him to stop.

Vicki rolled over on her stomach, and they both lay on the bed in silent exhaustion for a few minutes. Then the most unexpected request of all oozed out of Vicki's mouth. "You've still got an erection, Budge. I want you to put it in my ass." As she talked, she raised her nicely sculpted backside up seductively.

Bad man, killer, man-whore, whatever Budge was, that was something he just didn't do. Vicki had provided him with some fantastic sex and he wanted to make her happy, but he just couldn't bring himself to do what she wanted.

"I . . . I'd really rather not do that, Vicki."

Vicki pushed herself up on her elbows. "What? You've got a hard dick, you're a bad man, I'm offering something lots of men beg for . . . and you don't want it?"

"You're the one who decided I'm a bad man."

Vicki got up and moved to the end of the bed. She got on her hands and knees on the bed and turned so her backside faced Budge. "There. Look at this ass. You mean you don't want to put your dick in it?" For emphasis, she wiggled from side to side again.

Looking at Vicki in the position she was in, Budge was conflicted . . . but not convinced. "Sorry, babe. You've got a lovely ass, but I just don't do that."

With that, Vicki got up from the bed. "Fuck you. You're a wimp. I smothered you in pussy, and now you won't return the favor?" She hurried into the living room, gathering up her clothes as she went, and headed to the front door and walked out naked, carrying an armful of clothes. As she closed the door, she yelled, "Asshole! . . . Oh wait, bad choice of words."

Budge followed her to the door and looked out the peephole. Vicki was dressing herself in the hallway. It was a curiously sexual scene, and Budge felt his slowly fading erection coming back to life. For a few seconds, he considered opening the door.

Early the next morning, Ron Minty was sitting at the small table in the kitchen nook, nursing a hangover and trying to present a believable story to his wife about where he had been until three o'clock in the morning.

"Just met a new guy. He's some kind of guy who is rich . . . just does whatever he wants. I was having a bad day, so I went to The Mud Flats for a drink, and we got talking. The evening got away from us, and . . . well, we went to the 'Beaver, Damn.'"

Ron thought that small admission would give him up a little and assuage some of his guilt over what he had really done.

Karen Minty was working her indignation to a crescendo. "Three in the morning? Is that place even open until three in the morning? Don't you see enough beaver around here? Don't you get laid anytime you want it here?"

"Karen, it was just a little . . . boys' night out. I'm sorry. I'm sorry I didn't call you."

"Maybe I should be strutting around here with my tits hanging out. I could invite some of the guys in the neighborhood over for a little show . . . show them a little of the local beaver. Maybe even make a little grocery money."

As Karen's rant continued, Ron tried to sort out the fuzzy details of the night before. He was amazed at how Cherry had taken to him. She was all over him at the club, and was soon suggesting she could get off early and they could go to her place. When they arrived at her condo, Ron was surprised to see it was well decorated and immaculate. There were several bookshelves packed with law books, and Ron had to ask the obvious. "Are you . . . you're not a lawyer, are you?"

Cherry laughed. "No, but I will be someday. About another year working at the 'Damn' and two more years of school."

"Wow, I'm impressed."

Ron was with Cherry, whose real name turned out to be Alice, for two hours. She was almost clinical in the way she did a private dance for him, performed oral sex on him, and then made love to him, all of it enhanced by the Viagra pill she gave him as soon as they arrived at her condo.

It had been a surreal experience for Ron. He definitely was not the one in charge, and he felt like he had been properly entertained, fucked, and discharged when he left Cherry's condo at 2:45 in the morning. It never occurred to him that the guy he had just met that night had paid for it.

Ron waited for Karen to cool off for a couple of days before he went back into The Mud Flats for a drink late in the afternoon. He was dying to talk to Budge again, but he didn't know how to get hold of him.

Vicki was behind the bar when Ron arrived. "Hi gorgeous," he said, and it somehow had a hollow ring to it.

"Well, my favorite lawyer. How are you," Vicki responded in an equally hollow tone.

Ron ordered a drink, and after a little small talk with Vicki, he worked up the courage to ask about Budge. "Say, that guy I met in here the other day . . . Budge. Do you know how I could get hold of him?"

Vicki stiffened a little, and then replied, "Ah, I'm not sure. He doesn't have a job, and I'm not sure where he lives."

Ron's lawyer instincts told him Vicki wasn't telling the truth, but he couldn't understand why she would lie about it. "Okay, well, has he been in here since then?"

Again, Vicki looked uncomfortable. "Not since the other day."

Budge was anxious to talk with Ron also, and he didn't want to call him at his office. He had looked in the Yellow Pages and found a number for Minty, Anderson, and Rogers, but couldn't bring himself to call. It seemed more appropriate to stumble into Ron again at the Mud Flats, but it took him a couple of days to get himself ready to confront Vicki. The biggest part of their evening together was something he wanted to happen again. He just wasn't sure how to deal with Vicki's surprising demand, or if she would even talk to him again.

Budge walked into The Mud Flats thirty minutes after Ron. When he saw him at the bar, he headed right to him. "Can I join you?"

"You bet. It's nice to see you again."

After a few minutes of small talk and a laughing recap of their evening together, Ron turned and said quietly, "That woman at the 'Beaver, Damn' took me home and fucked my brains out. She was amazing."

Knowing from experience that Ron was right about Cherry, he exclaimed, "Great. Way to go, you lawyer stud, you."

Ron was slightly puffed up and somewhat embarrassed by Budge's reply. "I didn't really feel like a stud. I mean, she did it all, including making the first move. She said she just liked me, and she felt like she wanted some company."

Budge knew the truth, but his manly pride wouldn't allow him to be one-upped. "I sort of had the same thing happen to me. After I left you, I came down here to get something to eat." Budge turned away from where Vicki was doing an admirable job of ignoring him, and whispered to Ron, "Vicki and I went back to my place, and *she* fucked *my* brains out."

"You're shitting me," Ron blurted out loud enough to make Vicki turn around. "I mean, you are shitting me," he continued in a quieter voice. "Jesus, how was it? I've always thought that would be an awesome piece."

Ron and Budge continued the recap of their conquests for an hour, and then exchanged phone numbers and agreed to meet for lunch the following Friday. Vicki waited on them dutifully and maintained her very cool attitude toward Budge. He finally told Ron why she was giving him the cold shoulder, and Ron burst out with, "You're shitting me!" once again.

Nick loved springtime in Maui, and as he sat on his oceanfront deck having his morning coffee, he thought about how amazing it was that he was spending his third full spring there. Nani was quietly sitting with him, reading the morning paper. As he frequently did, Nick glanced at her and thought to himself what a beautiful woman he had found on the beautiful island.

"What does your schedule with the foundation look like, Nani?"

Nani set the newspaper on the table. "Actually, things are pretty much under control right now, and the staff can handle about anything. Why, do you have some wonderful trip you want to take me on?"

"Maybe. I mean, I love spring in Maui, but I love it in Alaska, too. Spring here is not much different than any other time of year. Spring in Alaska is an awakening. I was just thinking we could do some traveling for a few weeks. Maybe we could go to Seattle first, spend a few days there, catch the Mariners' first home series of the season, and then go on to Anchorage. By the middle of April the weather should be pretty good there. You've been working the foundation pretty hard. You've earned a vacation. And, I could do a little business in both places."

"So that's it. Business, not pleasure. You just want to drag me along on a business trip."

The mischievous look on Nani's face told Nick that she was pulling his leg. She wasn't a subservient wife, but she was willing to go along with almost everything Nick wanted.

"No, no. Very little business, lots of fun. I know you don't care about the ball games, but Seattle has great restaurants, shows, gambling on the reservations. And we can head The Bird anyplace we want to from there. Let's just be spontaneous for a while. We've got money to burn, and we don't act like it or use it like we could."

"I'm in, Nick. Let's go." Nani was pleased at how liberating it felt to say that.

The button for Beth's line lit up on Nancy Singletary's telephone console, and she recognized Nick Saylor's Hawaii number on the LED.

"Good morning, Mr. Saylor."

"Aloha, Nancy. How is everything with you?"

"Very good, Mr. Saylor. Would you like to speak to Beth?"

"Please. Thank you."

"Aloha, Nick. This is an early call. What's on your mind?"

"Nani and I have been talking, and I think we're going to take a little vacation. Seattle for a few days and then Alaska for a week or two. We just want—"

Beth couldn't stand it. "Seattle? Anchorage? Nick, you're worth a few hundred million. You could be flying The Bird to Cancun, or Hong Kong, or the Riviera. You could go off to Vegas and piss away a hundred thousand on fancy hotels, fancy meals, and gambling and never even know it was gone."

Nick waited a moment before answering. "Are you done? I know I'm rich. Flying to Seattle and Anchorage is what I want to do. Maybe I'll fly off to some other place later. Nani hasn't spent much time in Alaska, and she is looking forward to it. I can sniff around the real estate scene in Seattle, too. This is what I want to do right now."

"I'm sorry. I know you are your own man, but it just seems to me like you aren't having as much fun as someone as rich as you are should."

"You're rich, too. What are you doing to enjoy your financial position?"

"Touché. But I'm still a working woman, Nick. Remember this little company called Saylor Industries? I'll get my time. Which reminds me. You and I still haven't had that little talk with Chris yet."

"You're right about that. Let's make a plan to do that when we get there. We'll probably leave here in a day or so. That should put us in Anchorage in about ten days. Let's think about it in the meantime, and then talk later. We can't go in half-assed. We're going to have to convince him."

Bad men are not necessarily unconditionally bad.
—From *Fred Longcoor's Book on Life*

Chapter 12

Stepping Back

"Billy for you, Mr. Faro."

"Fuck," Stan muttered, loud enough for Polly to hear him from where he was pouring himself a cup of coffee.

"That's not nice," Polly said matter-of-factly.

"Sorry, Polly. I'm just getting sick of these calls."

In spite of his semiprivate bravado, Stan hurried into his office to take the call. "Hey, Billy. What's up?"

As Billy replied, Stan immediately noticed a different tone to the conversation. "Nothing, just checking in to see what's going on."

No harassment about all of the things I'm not doing?

"Pretty much the same old stuff around here. No new board assignments, nothing new with the bank board."

"Oh, well, that's fine. Just wondering how everything was there. I want to make sure you don't make waves, Stan. Just do a good job for Henry Kuban. If something else comes along, that will be fine. Don't get pushy with anybody."

"Alright. But I'm keeping my eyes and ears open. I'm getting in tighter and tighter with lots of the community high rollers. Everybody is getting to know me better."

"Oh . . . well, don't get too high profile. At least not until we're ready for that."

Stan's sensors were going up. This was not the kind of conversation he normally had with Billy. "You mean you want me to back off?"

"Well, maybe . . . yeah, maybe a little. I just don't want to stir up a lot of interest in what you're doing."

"That's a little surprising coming from you, Billy. You've wanted me to charge hard ever since I got back here from visiting you at your ranch." As Stan made his statement about the ranch, a vision of Anna standing naked in his bedroom flashed through his mind, again.

"I guess I kind of feel like I have been wrong. We've got to take this slow and steady. Hey, slow and steady is good for you. That's more time on your big fat paycheck."

"I guess you're right. Just as long as you're happy, I'm happy. I just wish I knew what this was all about." Stan rarely touched that subject, but he thought it might be the right time to catch Billy in this mellow mood.

"In due time, Stan. Got to go." Just like that, the conversation was over. Stan sat silently at his desk for a long time, trying to figure Billy out.

What the hell is going on? he wondered. *Every time I talk to Billy, I'm not doing enough. . . . I'm not moving fast enough, and now he puts the brakes on.* Stan suddenly had a cold fear in his gut and a quick realization about how nice the money he had been making over the last few months was.

For the first time in months, Johnny Bosco headed right through town without stopping to see Carmen when he came in from the North Slope. After a stop at a south Anchorage liquor store, he headed straight to his cabin. The early April days were getting longer, and he wanted to use the extra daylight to accomplish a mission he had been thinking about while he was working.

Johnny pulled off of the muddy road, into the parking area next to his cabin. It was always comforting when his initial look at his place after being gone indicated everything was the way he'd left it. He jumped out of his pickup and hurried inside. Everything looked normal there as well. After a quick walk around inside, he went back out of the cabin and unlocked his shed.

The four-wheeler fired right up, and Johnny drove it out of the shed. He left it running and went back inside the cabin for his pistol and a warmer coat. Back outside, he took a case of Alaskan Amber beer out of the pickup and bungeed it to the cargo carrier on the four-wheeler. Ten minutes after he had arrived, Johnny was on his way up the path to Marty Stevens' kashim.

Just like the first time he drove the four-wheeler along the path, he was awestruck by the beauty and solitude of the forest. Unlike the first time, he was anxious to get where he was going, but not wary. It struck him that a few hours earlier, he'd been looking out over miles and miles of flat, frozen tundra from high up in the derrick of a drilling rig as he doggedly repeated his job of manhandling heavy ninety-foot stands of drill pipe that were being pulled out of the ground. From freezing weather on a North Slope drilling rig to this beautiful forest in a few hours. The quick change always fascinated him.

Like before, a small amount of smoke spiraled out of the center of the kashim's roof as it came into Johnny's view. *Okay,* he thought, *where is that sneaky devil this time?* Johnny scoured the rustic homesite for a sign of Marty. Then, he whirled around and looked behind him. No Marty.

Johnny turned back around and nearly fell off the four-wheeler when he saw Marty standing ten feet in front of him with his stately huskies, Shesh and Genen, on either side. "Shit. You scared the crap out of me. How'd you do that?"

Marty laughed. "It's easy if you spend your life out here. You live with the animals, you watch the animals, you become one of them. What brings you out here?"

"Well, I brought you something." Johnny jumped off the four-wheeler, unstrapped the case of beer, turned, and handed it to Marty.

"Wow . . . shades of civilization. I, I . . . thank you." Johnny could see that Marty was genuinely grateful.

"Let's go have a seat and drink a couple of these," Marty said. He turned and walked toward the kashim. It was an unusually warm April afternoon, so they sat out front at Marty's handmade picnic table.

Dutifully, Johnny pulled a beer opener out of his pocket and handed it to Marty. "I wasn't sure you'd have one of these."

Laughing, Marty said, "You'd be right, but I'm quite sure I'd have found a way to open the beer."

"I hope I'm not, you know, destroying your commitment to living like you do."

Marty laughed again. "Not hardly. People have been making home brew for many years. I'd probably have figured out a way to do that sooner or later. In fact, I have a book on it in the kashim. I'm going to open these two, and then I'm going to put the rest of it in my root cellar to keep it cool. The cellar is dug into the side of the mountain, and it stays about forty-five degrees down there all the time . . . summer and winter."

Johnny and Marty chatted comfortably for an hour and a half, and Marty made two more trips back to the root cellar for more beer. Marty was as curious about Johnny's job as Johnny was about Marty's lifestyle.

"So what does a derrickman do?"

"Well, if you don't know much about drilling a well, I'll sort of have to give you the big picture." Johnny told Marty the basics of how a rig operated, then gave him a description of what the derrickman, roughnecks, roustabouts, and driller did. Marty asked him to explain his statement that the derrickman also took care of the mud.

"Drilling mud is a necessary part of drilling a well in most places," Johnny said. "In a few places, they drill with air or foam, but not in Alaska. Mud is pumped down the drill pipe and out the drill bit. It is viscous . . . thick, and it brings the cuttings . . . the dirt, rocks, and sand that the drill bit is cutting, to the surface. The mud does a lot of other things, but that is a basic function that most people can grasp."

"I'm not stupid, Johnny," Marty said, feigning indignation.

"I know, okay, so the drilling mud also provides hydraulic horsepower to the bit, which helps it to rotate, and it controls the subsurface formation pressures by being weighted up with barite, which is an inert, high specific-gravity material that is added to the mud. Water weighs a little over eight pounds per gallon, and you can theoretically make it weigh almost twenty pounds per gallon by adding barite for weight. It exerts a pressure against the formation by a factor of .052 psi per foot of depth times the weight of the fluid. It also builds a wall cake on the side of the hole so the mud is not penetrating the formation, and—"

"Stop. Shit, is there more?"

"Lots more."

"Okay, that's enough for this lesson." They both laughed.

"Now, it's my turn. The first time I was here, you said you would tell me how you were able to just appear right behind me. Now today, I look from the front to the back, and then back to the front, and there you are. How in hell do you do that?"

Marty smiled. "I use the trees, the shadows, the animals of the forest, the birds, the wind. All things talk to me."

"Now wait a minute, Marty. I mean, you seem like sort of a mystical guy, but talking trees?"

"Do not make light of what I am telling you. Be very quiet for a moment." Marty was silent for a minute or so, and Johnny was too. Then he said, "Did you hear the trees talking?"

"No, I—"

"Listen. Listen to the trees. They are telling us everything is alright. Sometimes the absence of sound means as much as sound does. Now, listen to the birds and watch the shadows." Again, Marty was silent and Johnny followed suit.

After another minute, Johnny said excitedly, "I hear them. I hear birds. I hear squirrels."

"You are right, Johnny." As if on cue, a lumbering black bear emerged from the alders on the other side of the clearing from Marty's kashim. "Sit still and be quiet," Marty whispered.

The bear glanced in their direction with disinterest, then glided effortlessly on across the clearing and disappeared into the thick alders again.

"Now, be quiet again."

Johnny could hear the bear crunching his way through the dried leaves in the forest, and he heard the sound of the warning squadron of birds and squirrels fading in the distance. "I can hear the bear, and the birds and squirrels."

Marty leaned across the table towards Johnny. "Why didn't you hear them when they were approaching?"

"I . . . I don't know."

"You weren't tuned in, Johnny. You have to tune in to the sounds of the wilderness. I am acutely tuned in. I heard your four-wheeler long before you got here. My eyes are also tuned in. I saw the shadow of the bear in the forest before I heard the critters . . . long before. It is what I do. It is how I live."

"I'm impressed, Marty. How do I get there? How do I get where you are?"

"You can't, not unless you want to live like I do, but you can become way more tuned in than you are. Practice . . . around your cabin. Sit outside in silence. Turn everything off, and take in the sounds, identify the sounds."

It was getting dark, and Johnny knew he needed to head back to his cabin. "I need to get going, Marty. This has been a very enjoyable afternoon."

"I too enjoyed this, Johnny. I am very grateful for the beer. By the way, I checked on your cabin several times while you were gone. I do it every time I walk by."

"Thanks, Marty. If you don't mind the responsibility, I'll give you a key the next time I see you."

In the fading light, Johnny stopped and shut the engine off on his four-wheeler several times. He listened to the sounds and the silence of the forest. He heard wind rustling the trees, and assorted birds as they settled for the night and thought, *I have to learn more.* For a brief moment, he thought about the life he had in Las Vegas, and quickly dismissed it.

In Anchorage, Carmen was beside herself because she knew Johnny was due in from the North Slope that day. Never having been the bashful type, she decided to drive to his cabin. After four weeks working in the cold and isolation of Prudhoe Bay, Johnny was happy to see her, and he apologetically explained his mission of the day. They were naked on the bear rug in front of the fireplace fifteen minutes after she arrived.

Pilot Danny Wilson and his copilot, Greg, were excited about Nick's planned trip to Seattle and Anchorage. They had spent the last two weeks shuttling The Bird back and forth between those two cities on business trips, carrying an assortment of boring passengers, and they were anxious to get back to Maui. As they were making a northeasterly approach into the Kahului Airport, Danny said, "I never get tired of this landing."

"Me neither," said Greg, "but it's not as much fun as it used to be now that the boss is tied down."

"We can't go back, Greg. Remember, you're tied down too. You're not as much fun as you used to be, either. I'm the only single guy left in this crowd. But we'll at least get a night here. We can go downtown and stir things up a little. Maybe we'll run into George."

Greg was silent for a moment as he thought about the night in Lahaina when Nani's father, George, took them to Sugar Cain's for dinner. It was the night when Greg met Sandy, the woman he was married to now. "I don't think George is doing well. Sandy talks to Nani now and then, and she is worried about him."

"That's too bad. George is a great guy. Nick thinks a lot of him, and he thought a lot of him even before he started going out with Nani. They were a couple of rich-guy buddies, and they spent a lot of time together . . . golfing mostly, and drinking." Danny finished with a chuckle, and Greg laughed too.

After they landed and the G550 was secured, Danny and Greg hurried to Executive Air Service's waiting limousine for the complimentary ride to the Saylors' residence in Lahaina.

When the limo driver opened the back door, they climbed in, and were shocked to find Nick and Nani sitting in the front part of the spacious interior. Nani was her usual beautiful self in a colorful Hawaiian dress, and she had a stack of leis around her neck. She was struggling to hold up a large pitcher of iced reddish liquid in one hand and two large stemmed glasses in the other.

"Aloha," she said. "Mai tais, anyone?"

Danny started to speak. "What the—"

"Aloha," chimed in Nick. "We started our vacation a little early."

"Aloha to you two," Danny said as he reached for one of the empty glasses Nani extended.

Greg reached for a glass also. "Ditto. Aloha."

"We thought we could all go out tonight. Have a nice dinner, walk around downtown Lahaina. Just have a good time."

Danny was surprised at how relaxed Nick sounded. Even in retirement, he always seemed like he was wound tight. "Sounds good, boss. How early are we flying?"

"Anytime we want, which means not early."

"Perfect, then pour me some of that island lightning, Nani." The group laughed, and the tone for the rest of the day was set. By seven o'clock, they were being seated at a reserved booth at Sugar Cain's, and Greg knew that Nick had arranged that for his benefit.

The pleasant surprises continued when George Jong came into the restaurant and joined them. Privately, both Danny and Greg were surprised at how frail George seemed. Even though they had seen him many times since the night he first brought them to the restaurant, they had seen him less frequently lately. His appearance had changed dramatically since the last time they were around him.

Appearance aside, George's dynamic personality ruled the night. He was still revered as a kapuna on the island, and his unofficial duties as a spiritual leader had produced many stories over the last few years. Nothing was said about George's warning to Nick and Beth three years earlier that their company was in trouble. It was the silent elephant at the table and George didn't need to be reminded about how important it had been to the Saylor siblings.

Danny spoke up. "Does being a kapuna . . . with so many people counting on you, does it ever wear on you, George?"

George smiled a big happy smile that made him look like the former George. "Never. Helping people has fulfilled my life. Other than the happiness my family has brought me, it is my reason for living." Only Nick and Nani knew that George was secretly including Nani's beautiful Hawaiian mother, Keona, in family circle. They knew that Nani was the result of an out-of-wedlock affair between George and Keona.

Nick came close to a reference to the warning George had given them before when he said, "Okay George, is there anything hanging over me and Nani, or Beth and Saylor Industries right now that I need to know about?" It was a confident and happy question, and George delivered a happy answer.

"No dark clouds, my friend. You and Nani are blessed, and your lovely sister and your company are secure. But maybe I will need to make a trip to Alaska in that fancy airplane of yours again . . . just to make sure." The laughing subsided as their waiter arrived with a big tray of food.

Later that evening, Nick and George stood together on the sidewalk in front of Sugar Cain's while the others climbed into Nick's SUV. "How are you doing, George?"

"My doctors tell me I am in remission, but I am very tired and very weak. I'd like to get back on the golf course, but I'm afraid it will be a while." George had finally shared his secret with Nick, but had not told Nani about his illness, even though he knew she suspected something was wrong.

"Remission. That's great. Well, just take it easy, and if there is anything I can do, let me know. Nani and I are going to take a little vacation trip. We'll probably be gone two or three weeks . . . Seattle and Anchorage. You know how to get in touch with me."

"I am happy for you and Nani. The gods were playing on my beach when you two met. You have made this old kapuna very happy and very proud."

The Bird was wheels up at one-thirty the next afternoon, headed to Seattle with Nani and Nick lounging comfortably in the cabin, and Danny and Greg, both wearing withering leis Nani gave them the previous evening in the cockpit.

In Seattle, Reverend Raymond was amazed by how quickly and thoroughly Betsy was involving him in the Brooksher business empire. In some ways, he was overwhelmed. He was a shyster, not a businessman. He continually had to push questions aside and call Billy for advice.

During one of those calls, he elaborated about the things that were happening at Brooksher. "Shit, Billy, I think she'd have me running the whole fucking thing if I let her."

"Well, let her. What can it hurt?"

"I don't know anything about big business. I can throw a lot of bullshit at her, and a little common sense, and that's it. It's like she forgot what brought me in here in the first place. She seems to trust me."

"Well, you've got to keep playing the game. Have you had any conversations about the Kent warehouse yet?"

"No, but I have had a chance to tell her about my pet project. She wants to have wine almost every night after work, and it is the best time for me to open up to her. We just sit in her office. The old man had a big-ass wine room right off his office. Anyway, I told her I have a dream of building a church school for disadvantaged young children in the area."

"How'd she react to that?"

"Didn't say much. Basically just said it was an admirable idea."

"Well, that's alright. You've planted the seed."

Hesitatingly, Raymond added, "There's sort of more."

"What, what the fuck else is there?"

"I . . . I think she thinks of me in a way I didn't expect."

"Okay. What is that?"

"Romantically . . . I think she likes me. I mean, it's crazy, but I'm getting these strange vibes. And, she says some things."

Billy was really impatient now. "Romantically? Vibes? What kinds of things?"

"She tells me that she and the old man quit having sex a couple of years ago. She says she misses it."

After a moment of silence, Billy said in a stern voice, "Reverend, do not fuck that woman. You do, you'll fuck this whole deal up." As an afterthought, he added, "I'm coming out there. We've got too much at stake for you to be there alone."

"Billy, you don't—"

"Yes I do. I'll make some arrangements, and let you know when I'm coming."

After Billy hung up, Raymond's head was spinning. *Shit, what do I do now?* he thought. *I've got to move things along with Betsy before he gets here.*

The next morning, Reverend Raymond arrived at the Brooksher Building at 8:00, which was an hour earlier than normal. Betsy was always there before he arrived in the morning, and now, even an hour earlier, she was there.

"Good morning, Mary," Raymond said as he approached Betsy's office. "Is she in?"

"Yes, Reverend. She's always here early. Would you like to see her?"

"Please."

Reverend Raymond entered Betsy's big office and approached her desk, where she had her head down as she signed papers. "Good morning, Betsy."

"Good morning, Reverend," Betsy replied without looking up. "Please give me a moment."

Raymond was jumpy inside as he waited for Betsy to finish. He was going to make a bold move today, and he wasn't the slightest bit sure how Betsy would react.

Betsy finished her work and leaned back in her deceased husband's big chair. "How are you today, Reverend?" She seemed cheery and friendly, and Raymond's anxiety level lowered a little.

"I am fine, ma'am. I just hoped we could talk a little this morning. I . . . I guess I'm anxious about how I'm doing here. Am I fulfilling your needs? Am I making your busy life a little better? You are paying me a lot of money, and I'm not sure I'm earning it." Raymond choked out this last statement bravely and hopefully.

Betsy moved forward in her chair. "Reverend, you are helping me tremendously. Your advice has been invaluable. And your company has given me a great deal of comfort. . . . I love our little wine chats in the afternoon. Remember, I am a very wealthy woman, and if you make me happy, that is all that is required. I answer to nobody."

Raymond relaxed for a moment. "Thank you, Betsy. It has been very rewarding to work for you." Raymond thought about what he'd said and quickly added, "With you. I always want to do more. I thought maybe one of these evenings, we could, you know, just you and me . . . go to dinner."

Betsy smiled broadly. "You are a mind reader, Reverend. I have been thinking about inviting you to dinner . . . at the mansion. I have a wonderful chef, and Del has . . . had. I mean, there is a much better selection of wines there than we have here. What do you say?"

Shit, Raymond thought, *this couldn't have gone any better.* "I would be honored to dine with you at your mansion. I have heard fabulous things about the mansion, and even read about it in *Seattle Today.*"

Betsy stood up and put her hand out as a means of politely dismissing Raymond. "Can you make it this evening? I'll call Gerard and have him prepare something wonderful. He loves it when I entertain. Is there anything on your restricted list?"

"Thank you, Mrs. Brooksher. I'll be there, and the only thing I don't eat is liver."

"Yuck, I don't eat it either. I'll have the limo pick you up at six o'clock. And please don't bring wine. I'll be dead before I drink up Mr. Brooksher's collection as it is."

Raymond was glowing inside as he spent the day giving bullshit counseling to troubled Brooksher employees and traipsing in and out of Betsy's office to give her bullshit advice on things he had no understanding of. For all his faults, Raymond had enough common sense to give general advice with a sage sound to it. In reality, all he could think about was how he would handle the evening with Betsy.

Raymond had a bouquet of roses in hand when the limo pulled up in front of his extended-stay hotel. He handed them to Betsy when he was led through the cavernous entry to the Brooksher mansion and into their great room.

"No wine, but roses," she exclaimed. "Very nice, Reverend." She leaned into Raymond and kissed him softly on his cheek. He caught the pleasant scent of an exotic perfume he had never smelled before, and she got a much larger dose of Raymond's favorite cologne.

The obligatory tour of the massive mansion followed, and Raymond became lost in the countless rooms. There were over twenty bedrooms, each with its own elegant bathroom and a master bedroom that was larger than many suburban houses. There were huge bathrooms off the great room, one for women and one for men, complete with a lineup of urinals. There was a massive kitchen, two smaller kitchens, and an outdoor kitchen. One recreation room had a twelve-foot by six-foot snooker table, a segregated dart area, and a full-size bar that would rival many commercial bars.

Raymond had never been so close to so much wealth. Their next stop was the wine cellar. As they stepped into the large temperature- and humidity-controlled room, Raymond couldn't comprehend what he was looking at. There were hundreds of bottles, all racked and identified. In the middle of the room, an elegant oak tasting table and six chairs sat across from a glass-fronted stainless steel refrigerator that was full of dozens of varieties of cheeses and assorted condiments. Betsy stepped toward a rack that was full of a wine identified as Domaine de la Romanee-Conti Le Montrachet and pulled one bottle out. As if on some secret signal, Gerard entered the wine cellar and asked Betsy if she would like for him to open it.

"Yes please, Gerard. This is one of my deceased husband's favorite wines, Raymond. We'll start with the white and then go to the Grands Echezeaux." Betsy winked and said, "Maybe we'll even open the '76 La Tache six liter."

"Okay," was Raymond's humble answer, knowing Betsy was serving fine wine, but having no idea that the bottles were in the four hundred– to three thousand–dollar price range.

After the tour, they settled in on the expansive back deck overlooking a huge manicured flower garden and the Kent Valley below. Raymond's head was spinning at the wonders of the world the very wealthy lived in. He thought about how much larger the Brookshers' library was than the community library in his little hometown.

"This is a wonderful wine, Betsy. I've never tasted a wine like this, and your home . . . mansion . . . is unbelievable." Remembering for a moment who and what he was supposed to be, Raymond said, "I know you are going through a tough time, Betsy, but God has blessed you with all of the things anyone could ask for."

Betsy immediately looked sad. "I would trade all my things, Reverend, to have my Del back. This is a very lonely time for me, incredibly sad and lonely. This is the time in life when you want to share the things you have worked so hard for together."

For a brief moment, Raymond felt some guilt for what he was attempting to do. Betsy brought him out of it. "In spite of what I said, I am a realist, Reverend. I know Del is gone and I have to move on. I need to make the best of the time I have left. I have needs, and I have the resources to do anything I want to."

"Yes. You must move on. I can—"

"You can join me in the dining room for one of Gerard's wonderful meals."

Raymond had the sense that Betsy interrupted him to keep him from saying something she wasn't ready to hear. "Let's go," he said. "I'm looking forward to this."

After a sumptuous meal featuring Gerard's specialty, osso buco, they retired to a cozy quiet room off of the great room with the remains of the DRC Grands Echezeaux he had opened. A small fire burned in the fireplace, and Gerard had soft music playing. He reentered the open door with a tray that held a bottle of 1940 Porto Barros Colheita, an elegant wood-aged port. The tray also had a fine Stilton cheese and a cheese knife on it, along with a small bowl of strawberries. He set it in front of Betsy. "Will there be anything else this evening, Mrs. Brooksher?"

Raymond missed the knowing look on Gerard's face.

"No, Gerard. Thank you. You have outdone yourself. You may go. Have a wonderful evening. I'll see you tomorrow."

After Gerard left, Raymond asked Betsy if she was always alone in the big house. "No, Reverend. Gerard has his own quarters in the mansion, but he requested the evening off. The maids and the gardener only work during the day, and they have their own rooms over the limousine garage. We have a state-of-the-art security service."

They finished the DRC and then enjoyed small portions of port and cheese. It was getting late when Betsy excused herself to use the restroom. She was gone long enough for Raymond to become uncomfortable, and he was ready to go look for her when he heard her approaching the doorway.

With his back toward the doorway, Raymond said, "I was getting worried, I thought—"

Betsy's attire stunned Raymond into speechlessness. She flowed into his view in a long white satin robe that hung open. Under the robe, she was wearing a matching low-cut two-piece teddy that confirmed Raymond's earlier assessment of her bosom. More surprising was the fact that the skimpy garment allowed her to display lovely legs that looked like they belonged to someone twenty years younger.

"My God, Mrs. Brooksher. You are beautiful."

Smiling, she said, "Always the preacher, right Reverend? I thought we might go swimming tonight, but it's a little cool out there. How about joining me in my bedroom?"

Raymond felt like a puppy as he was led on the long walk to the master bedroom. It was a little uncomfortable walking into the bedroom he knew had been occupied by Betsy and Del Brooksher, but his guilt was gone the minute Betsy removed the satin robe and threw it into a chair.

"I know you are a religious man, Reverend. I am hoping you have needs like I do. If this makes you uneasy, we can part company gracefully, and say no more. This will not affect our professional relationship, and I will not think anything less of you as a man of God. Are you alright?"

"Praise the Lord. . . . I'm definitely alright."

Betsy was lying back on the bed as she said, "Well then, come over here and put that wonderful face of yours right here."

She was wriggling out of her thong as she spoke.

Thou shalt love thy benefactor.
—From *Fred Longcoor's Book on Life*

Chapter 13

"She Did What?"

The morning after arriving in Seattle, Nick and Nani were settled into the penthouse suite at the Executive Plaza Hotel in Kent. After a room-service breakfast, Nick excused himself to make a call from the suite's business office.

"Good morning. Brooksher," was the simple greeting from the receptionist when Nick dialed the number to get hold of his old friend, Betsy Brooksher.

"Good morning. This is Nick Saylor. May I speak with Betsy Brooksher, please?"

"Let me see if she is available, Mr. Saylor."

"Nick Saylor, what a pleasant surprise." Betsy sounded genuinely happy to hear from Nick.

"Betsy, I just wanted to call and tell you I am in town, and I wanted to personally express my condolences for your loss. It was very sad to hear about Del. He was a good man."

Betsy's voice now conveyed sadness. "Thank you, Nick. And, I did get the wonderful bouquet of flowers you sent, and your note. Del was a great man. It has been a tough time for me, but I'm coming out of it. I just have to move on. There is so much to do." Her tone moved from sadness to exhaustion.

"I'm sure there is. I'm here with my wife, Nani. We are just taking a little vacation trip, and maybe combining it with some business."

"What business? I thought you left all of that to Beth?"

"Beth *is* running the company, Betsy, but we . . . I'm almost ashamed to say this, but we have a large cash position, and we are looking for some investment property. I like to keep it sort of close to home, so we have been looking in this area."

There was total silence for a moment, and Nick thought he had lost the connection. Then, Betsy spoke. "What kind of investment property, Nick?"

"Ideally, I'd like to find a nice warehouse. Price is really no object right now. The bigger the better."

Happily, Betsy said, "I have one, Nick. A brand-new one . . . never been used. It was Del's pet project. He built it on spec, and finished it just before he died. Would you like to see it?"

Nick and Betsy agreed to meet for lunch and then look over Del's warehouse. Nick emerged from the office in the suite in high spirits.

"I can't believe this, Nani. Betsy Brooksher's company has a brand-new warehouse for sale. She wants to meet for lunch and then go look at it. Do you want to go with us?"

After lunch, Nick and Nani followed Betsy's limousine in their rental SUV to an area near one of Boeing's plants in Kent. Nick was immediately struck by the look of the new building as they approached it. It was massive, and it had a clean modern look that he liked. The area around it was manicured nicely, the huge parking lot was freshly lined with spaces, and a twelve-foot chain-link fence surrounded the entire ten acres of property.

"I'm liking the looks of this, Nani."

The building was as impressive inside as it was outside. Del had designed it to handle one large company's warehousing needs, or to be used by two or three smaller companies. The building was a modified U-shape, with the offices in the middle section of the U. It would allow the offices to be segregated into two or three sections that would be handy to each part of the U.

"Oh, Nick, I can't tell you how proud Del was of this building. He said he had thought of everything to make it a state-of-the-art warehouse building. He said that and the fact that it was so close to the Boeing plant made it a very desirable piece of property."

"That's obvious, Betsy. Beautiful offices, quality construction materials, first-class security system, plenty of yard space, unlimited warehouse space, and a great location . . . it has it all. Why do you want to sell it?"

"Nick, we have so much . . . so many buildings, so many holdings, so much going on, I don't really want to deal with it. Plus . . . it was Del's idea, his baby . . . something that was important to him. I think the best thing I can do is find someone Del would have wanted to own it. Maybe, someone like you."

"What is the price on the building, Betsy?"

"It appraised at one hundred eleven million dollars. It didn't cost that much to build it."

"Wow . . . that's a lot of money. I don't—"

"You didn't let me finish, Nick. I would sell it to you for what we have in it . . . actual cost plus the carrying charges to this point. Just a minute." Betsy pulled her cell phone out of a coat pocket and dialed. "Mary, please get Mr. Frederick for me."

The businesslike voice of Marvin Frederick, Brooksher's controller, came on the phone. "Mrs. Brooksher? What can I help you with?"

"The U Building, Marvin. What do we have in it to date?" Though it hadn't been formally named, everyone, including Marvin, was familiar with the nickname Del had given the building.

"Give me one moment, Mrs. Brooksher. I just updated the file a couple of days ago."

A few moments later, Marvin was back on the phone. "A little over eighty-three million. I can give you an exact—"

"That's good, Marvin. Thank you." Betsy closed the phone and looked at Nick. "Eighty-three million five hundred thousand. I can show you the appraisal . . . done by one of the most prestigious commercial real estate appraisal companies in Washington State."

Nani was standing next to Nick, and the big numbers were taking her breath away. When Nick said, "Betsy, I think we have a deal. I want to talk with Beth first," Nani looked like she was going to faint.

Nick was dialing his cell phone as he walked to the low exterior stairway leading to the U Building's main entrance doors and sat down. "Beth, I have a story to tell you, and we have a decision to make."

The eighty-four million–dollar decision was surprisingly easy to make. Beth liked the sound of everything Nick told her, they had enough cash in the bank to swing the financing easily, and it had the feel of something that was just meant to be. Like Nick, Beth knew Betsy Brooksher, and she knew she was an honorable woman who had been married to an honorable man.

"Let's do it, Nick." Then, as an afterthought she added, "We could even move our own operation into the new building and lease our old building."

Nick smiled to himself. "You know, like I've been telling you, it gets more and more scary."

"What are you talking about?"

"You and I . . . we think alike. A lifetime of being around each other has done that. Tell Wayne that Brooksher's controller . . . his name is Marvin Frederick, will be contacting him." Nick knew that Saylor's controller, Wayne Hudson, would know all the right things to do to prepare Saylor Industries for an investment of this size. "Congratulations, sis . . . we keep moving up."

Nick stood up from the steps of the building that would soon belong to his company and walked deliberately toward Betsy Brooksher, who was chatting with Nani. Without saying anything, he put his arms around Betsy in a big bear hug and said, "We have a deal, Mrs. Brooksher."

When Nick released Betsy, she stood back and smiled. "Your timing has always been impeccable, Nick."

"What do you mean?"

"Del's estate was settled this week. I can sell it to you now without doing any financial maneuvering."

Betsy was in a happy mood when she arrived back at the Brooksher Building at 4:00 that afternoon. She encountered Reverend Raymond as she crossed the foyer, heading toward her office. Raymond had not seen Betsy all day, and he was unsure how he should act around her after the previous evening. Betsy seemed unfazed, and said jauntily, "Reverend, can you join me in my office?"

"Yes, yes, Mrs. Brooksher." Raymond had the little-puppy feeling again as he followed her into her office and sat in one of the big chairs before her desk.

"Wait one minute while I take care of something, Reverend." Betsy called Mary on the office intercom. "Mary, please have someone with a good digital camera go over and take fifteen or twenty pictures inside and outside of the U Building and email them to the name and address I just left on your desk."

I wonder what that's about, thought Raymond.

"Reverend, I have been thinking about something. Mr. Brooksher's estate was just settled this week. I have been thinking about the project you have been dreaming about . . . you know, the children's school. Brooksher just happens to have an empty warehouse right now. It is a building that could be converted into a school, and I would pay for the conversion."

Raymond listened to Betsy, and he was in shock. *That's what it's about*, he thought. *She's going to give me that new fucking warehouse!*

"It's in Tukwila. It's a great central location. I think—"

"Tukwila? I thought it was in Kent."

"Kent. What are you talking about, Reverend? This is a former furniture warehouse close to the Southcenter Mall in Tukwila."

As quickly as Raymond's hopes lifted, they nosedived. "I, I just thought . . . . I know you have a new warehouse in Kent."

"Kent! Are you talking about the U Building, the new building Del just had built? You really didn't think I was going to donate a hundred million–dollar building to your pet cause, did you? Besides, I just sold it. An old friend of mine from Alaska. Nick Saylor. He bought it today. About an hour ago, in fact."

Jesus, Raymond thought, *I'm dead. Billy will kill me . . . especially if he finds out I fucked her last night. Were we stupid? Did we really believe we were going to get her to give us a hundred million–dollar building? But she is ready to give us another warehouse. I wonder how much it's worth.*

As if on cue, Betsy continued, "The other warehouse is older, but we've had it on the market for five million dollars. That's probably a little high, but it's easily worth three and a half or four million dollars. As I said, I will pay for the renovation. It's all tax deductible. I like the idea of helping kids, and I like knowing they are getting God's word along the way. You seem shocked, Reverend. Didn't you think I would help you with your dream?" Betsy leaned forward, and in a lower voice said, "Are you worried about the fact that I let you get into my knickers last night? Did you think that was going to backfire on you in some way? I quite enjoyed myself, so you don't have to worry."

Raymond passed on their usual wine session in the afternoon with an excuse about having some banking business to take care of and hurried back to the hotel. The first thing he did when he got there was open a dresser drawer and take out a bottle of Jack Daniel's. It took several strong pulls on it before he had the courage to call Billy.

"Billy, well, I have some news. Some of it's good and some of it's not so good."

"What the fuck is that supposed to mean?"

"Well, you know it was a stretch to expect Mrs. Brooksher to give us a building . . . but she is going to."

"Wow, great. I mean, how'd this come down?"

"She told me today that she was going to give us a warehouse and she would pay to renovate it."

"That's fantastic, Raymond. You've done an unbelievable job. You mean pay to convert it into a school?"

"Yes, and well, that's the good news. I have some bad news. But, you won't have to come out here now. She . . . she. I mean, it's not, you know, *thee* warehouse. It's an old furniture warehouse in Tukwila."

"What? What the fuck is that about?"

"It's a five million–dollar warehouse, Billy. She's just going to give it to us and pay to renovate it. I mean, five million dollars is a lot of money. If we let her renovate it, and then sell it, it may be twice that much."

With a tone that said, *Get this all out right now,* Billy growled, "What the fuck happened to the other warehouse?"

Raymond blurted it out. "She sold it . . . today. She sold it to Saylor Industries."

In a voice so loud Raymond moved the receiver away from his ear, Billy demanded, "She did what?"

In resignation, Raymond spoke quietly. "She sold it, Billy. Turns out Nick Saylor is an old friend of the Brookshers'. You know the Saylors were looking for a warehouse. I had no way of knowing they were all old friends."

In a sudden revelation, Billy asked, "Did you fuck her Raymond? I told you not to fuck her. Did you fuck her, Raymond?"

Fearing Billy would see through his lie, Raymond made a strong reply. "No, goddamn, no." Liking the sound of that, he continued. "I haven't fucked anybody. I've just sat around this boring, barren hotel and worked my ass off for months. How do you think I feel? And we are going to get something."

Ignoring Raymond's forced reply, Billy continued his rant. "You did, you fucked her. I told you not to fuck her."

Raymond's voice now reeked of guilt as he spoke quietly. "I didn't fuck her, Billy."

"I know you like a fucking book, Reverend. . . . I can tell it in your voice. You literally fucked us out of a hundred million dollars."

Raymond was getting angry, and his voice level increased as he said, "Billy, she asked me if I really thought she was going to give me a brand-new hundred million–dollar building for a children's school. She's not a dummy. She's pretty smart."

"I'm coming out there anyway." The phone connection went dead in Raymond's ear.

Both Billy and Raymond sat in silence and thought about the impact of the day's events. Billy remained pissed at Raymond, although the little shred of common sense he allowed into his thoughts told him Betsy was right on. Had they really believed she was going to give up a hundred million–dollar building? Betsy Brooksher was not your average broken-down weeping billionaire's widow. Billy consoled himself with the thought that they could still get the five million–dollar warehouse. He was not about to let Raymond fuck that up.

Billy reached for the phone to call Budge, and then stopped. *Let's think about this for a while,* he thought.

Raymond was pensive on an entirely different level. *Billy's going to kill me,* he thought. *I've got to get out of town.*

Can I ever get far enough away from Billy to be safe? Can I risk staying here and get the other building from Betsy? That would make it a little easier with Billy. I do like her. What could I get out of this if I just stay close to her?

Driving back to their hotel, Nick was almost giddy. "What do you think about that, you beautiful island girl?"

Nani looked at Nick and said, "The same thing I always think. We could do so much with the foundation with eighty-four million dollars in the bank."

Nick was not happy that Nani had so quickly taken the glow off of his perfect investment. He said, "The foundation is well funded, Nani. And we are not just pouring eighty-four million dollars into this building. Most of it will be financed." Bluntly, he added, "We'll put another million into the foundation. I'll have Beth tell Wayne to do it." Without another word to Nani, he dialed Beth's office number.

When Beth answered, Nick was smiling again. "We pulled it off, sis. It'll take a little while for it to close, but you'll need to get down here and look it over pretty soon. You and Donnie can see if it makes sense to move our operation into it. Wayne will have to figure out if it makes financial sense. It's a beautiful building. I can't believe our good fortune. I mean, you talk about being in the right place at the right time."

Beth laughed. "That's your style, Nick. Always has been, always will be."

"I don't know about that, but I know a great deal when I see one. In one respect, we just saved Saylor Industries almost thirty million dollars. That's thirty million dollars we could put back on the bottom line if we wanted to turn around and resell it." Nick turned thoughtful for a moment and added, "It is too bad a good man had to die though."

"I feel bad for Betsy. I do think we need the building more than we need more cash. That would make our return-on-direct-investment number look great. . . . Then we'd have a bigger cash problem to deal with than we have now."

"Nice problems, sis. Speaking of cash, have Wayne transfer a million dollars into Nani's foundation."

"You got it. What now, I mean, are you going to have some fun now?"

"That was fun for me, but if you mean play, yeah. Some ball games, some shopping, and then whatever we feel like doing. In fact, I just had an idea. Have Donnie talk with one of his contacts and get us a suite for a ball game . . . in fact, get it for a couple of games. Have him pick out a handful of deserving employees . . . including him, and invite them to the games. I know the Mariners are in town against the Angels, so try for tomorrow and the next day. Have him let me know when he's got it done."

"Okay. Sounds like fun. I wish I was there."

"Well, you know how to get here."

Things that happen in Alaska impact the Seattle-Tacoma area in a big way. The Port of Tacoma's third largest trading partner, behind only China and Japan, is Alaska. By the same token, many things that happen in the Seattle-Tacoma area have a huge impact on Alaska. When Saylor Industries purchased the U Building in Kent from Brooksher, the ink wasn't dry on the documents before the minor firestorm started. After talking with Raymond, Billy Peet immediately called Budge.

"Are you ready for this?" Budge hadn't been able to say anything more than hello before Billy began his diatribe.

"What?"

"The fucking Saylors are fucking up everything we are trying to do. Guess who just bought the Brooksher warehouse in Kent?"

"Saylor Industries?"

"How in hell did you know that?"

"I didn't, Billy. You sort of led me to it by telling me the Saylors are fucking up everything we are trying to do."

"Yeah, well, they're fucking it up in Alaska, too. Having Beth Saylor on the board up there is fucking things up. Are they everywhere? We've got two deals working in two fucking states, and somehow the Saylors end up right in the middle of both of them."

Suddenly feeling a need to sound wise and being in the uncustomary position of trying to be the voice of reason, Budge said, "Billy, the Saylors are rich. Betsy Brooksher is rich. Rich people travel in the same circles. It's not surprising they know each other. . . . They both have big businesses in the Seattle area. And it's not surprising that Beth Saylor is favored by the governor. They're both independent, well-known, powerful women who know each other." *And cunts,* Budge added to himself.

"Don't give me all of that rah-rah bullshit. I don't know which way to go now. The Saylors have both of our deals fucked up." Ominously, Billy added, "We may have to do something about that."

Purposely ignoring Billy's final statement, Budge said, "I still think I may be able to help our deal here. I think Ron Minty is a loose cannon. He's pissed because he can't get his hands on some of the Permanent Fund money . . . and he's so close to it. I don't think we need to get someone on the board. I think we may *have* someone on the board."

Billy sounded a little calmer when he replied to Budge. "I hope you're right. Maybe we need to concentrate on him and forget Stan. I hate to dump him, but he's costing me lots of money. I don't know how he'd react if I pulled the plug on him. I guess I really don't give a shit, but I don't want him pissed and running all over Alaska talking about what happened to him."

"Maybe we need to wait a little. Let me see if I can take my relationship with Ron to the next level. Maybe I need to go to the board meeting in Juneau as myself . . . just tell Ron I've never been to Juneau, and that I think it would be fun if he and I could party a little there. I think he'd like for me to be there."

"That's a gamble, but what the fuck . . . everything's changing. All this goddamn time and money for nothing."

"It's not for nothing yet, boss."

Doug heard about the sale of Del Brooksher's U Building quickly through his connections in the Seattle-area commercial real estate network. He sat in his grungy office and had a few shots of cheap courage. It was early evening when he called Billy Peet, who had just finished talking to Budge.

"What the fuck do you want?" Billy knew that Doug was worthless to him now, and he didn't want to chitchat.

"I've got some news. You're not going to like it. I just—"

"The fucking Brooksher building. You're a little late. I heard about that this afternoon."

"How'd you—"

"I got sources . . . lots of sources."

"Nick Saylor bought it."

"I just told you I know about it. Now, what the fuck do you want?"

For the first time ever, Doug realized that he really didn't give a damn about Billy, and he was tired of being insulted by him. Abruptly, he said, "Nothing. That's it," and clicked the off button on the portable telephone receiver, leaving Billy listening to a dead connection, just like he always left everyone else.

Billy shouted into the dead receiver, "Fuck you, you little weasel!"

With the deal on the Brooksher building in the works, Nick and Nani turned their trip into more of a vacation than a business venture. Two long and enjoyable days of shopping and lunches in and around downtown

Seattle, including a couple leisurely passes through Pike Place Market, were followed by baseball games in the evening. Both evenings, Donnie brought a collection of Saylor employees to the suite at the ballpark, and everyone had a great time watching the games while feasting on the special menu Nani had coordinated with the catering manager. Both evenings were also capped by wins over the visiting Los Angeles Angels, and the victories over their division rival put everyone in a celebratory mood.

On the first evening, Nick and Donnie were cloistered at the back of the suite talking. "You know, Donnie, we just piled a little more on you. Even if you and Beth decide that moving into the new building is not the best thing for us, you will have to look after it. And even if you have a good lessee, or a good couple of lessees, it will add to your workload."

"I know that, boss, but I can handle it. I think the ideal situation, no matter which location we are trying to lease, would be to find one big client. The fewer people we have to deal with the better."

"I'm glad to hear you say that. That's the kind of thinking we need. I don't want to be in the middle of it, either. I want you and Beth to make the decisions. That's all part of the transition that needs to be made."

"I don't like the sound of that. You're not getting completely out of the business, are you?"

Nick laughed. "No, but I want to allow the people who are going to be running the company in the future to get used to total responsibility now. This is sort of on the QT, but Beth and I are going to attempt to get Chris more involved . . . maybe roll SayCo completely into Saylor Industries. All of this will be good for you. You've done a great job for us, and you are almost like family to Beth and me."

"That's interesting, Nick, and nice to hear. I love the company, and I've enjoyed every minute . . . well, almost every minute of the time I've worked at Saylor Industries."

Nick grinned when he said, "Does that mean you didn't enjoy the time when Devon was the Alaska manager?"

"No shit. It just seems like a bad dream now."

Nick always felt the need to apologize for what happened. "That was our fault, Donnie. Beth and I made a mistake . . . an emotional mistake. You should have been made the Alaska manager then. It was a mistake with almost-disastrous consequences. We certainly learned our lesson. I can't help but think about it when I get here to the ballpark . . . all of the people who could have . . ." Nick's voice trailed off.

Trying to pick the moment up a little, Donnie said, "Well, that's over, and we've got a ball game to watch . . . and I need another beer."

After the second busy day and the second night at the ballpark, Nick and Nani were lying naked on the giant bed in their hotel suite after making love. Nick rolled himself over on his side, facing Nani. He put his hand on her flat stomach and began gently rubbing her skin.

"I think we need to spread our wings tomorrow."

"What do you mean?"

"I mean, let's fire The Bird up and go somewhere . . . like Canada, or Las Vegas. Danny and Greg would love to do something different, and so would I."

Nani raised herself up on her elbows. "I've never been to Canada *or* Las Vegas."

"Well . . . let's go to both places. We could fly to Vegas tomorrow, spend two or three days, and then stop in Victoria, BC, on the way to Alaska. I think we've done enough here. We can go straight to Anchorage from Victoria."

"Sounds like fun. Let's go, rich guy."

"I'm not a rich guy. But *we* are a rich couple. And, you will have fun in Las Vegas, but you will love Victoria. It's a wonderful old city with lots of great restaurants. And, the Butchart Gardens. It's a little early in the year to visit there, but it is still spectacular."

I'm not going to mention all the young hookers on the street corners after 9:00 p.m., Nick thought. *She'll see them herself soon enough.*

Nick was up early the next morning making arrangements for Las Vegas and Victoria. Danny and Greg happily had The Bird in the air by one o'clock.

In Anchorage, Budge Brown was moving forward with a mission he was now taking personally. After just finding out about losing the Brooksher warehouse in Kent, he wasn't bothered nearly as much as it was bothering Billy and Raymond. He had only been peripherally involved in that deal, and he had already been paid a bonus for getting Raymond set up and for getting rid of Marc Madrid. He really didn't care about Stan Faro, either. His mission now centered on Ron Minty.

Ron Minty's receptionist buzzed him. "Mr. Minty, Budge Brown is on the phone for you."

Ron answered right away. "Good morning, Budge."

"Good morning to you. Are we still on for today?" Budge was confirming their agreed-upon Friday lunch.

"We're on, buddy. I made reservations at Mr. Z's. Is that okay with you?"

"Perfect. I'll see you there."

When Budge entered Mr. Z's, he saw that Ron was already sitting at the bar, and he joined him there, saying, "The bar . . . my favorite spot," as he took a stool next to him.

"Mine too. We can get a table if you prefer it, though."

"No, this is great."

Both men ordered martinis, and as the bartender began to make them, Ron volunteered that he was taking the afternoon off. Budge took that as a message that the social gloves were off, which was what he wanted.

Their conversation in the beginning was a little awkward. Beyond the surprising turn that their first evening hanging out together had taken, they needed time to really get to know each other.

"Have you been back to see Vicki?"

Budge snorted a muted laugh. "No . . . chicken."

Ron laughed and said, "Yeah, I haven't been back to the 'Beaver, Damn' either . . . chicken."

Privately, Budge hoped Ron wouldn't go back there. He didn't want him to find out that if he wanted to sleep with Cherry again, he'd have to pay for it.

"My wife was pissed," Ron said. "I told her I had just met you and we went there. She threatened to treat the men in the neighborhood to some lap dances as payback."

"Oh shit. Never tell."

"I know that, but I got home really late, and I felt like I had to give something up."

"I'm afraid my little adventure with Vicki was a onetime deal. She won't even talk to me when I go into The Mud Flats, and I'm not going to do what she wants even if she wanted to go another round."

With his tongue firmly in his cheek, Ron said, "Yeah, you appear to me to be a bit of a prude."

Budge laughed. "Enough of that. How is the lawyer business?"

"It's a living. I guess it's a pretty good living. Being on the board has given my firm some prestige, too, and it brings in some business we wouldn't have otherwise. I guess I'm like most alpha males . . . it's never enough."

Recognizing a small opening, Budge replied, "Yeah, being close to billions would make anybody itchy."

"I don't know if itchy is the right word, but maybe jealous is. You know, APFC has really started to focus on this infrastructure thing, and we're looking at everything you can imagine . . . pipelines, natural gas–processing facilities, airports, ports, railroads, bridges, water-treatment plants, cable networks, and a jillion other things. Somebody out there, or many people out there, are going to get rich with our help."

Budge's juices were flowing. He couldn't believe how quickly Ron's conversation honed in on the Alaska Permanent Fund Corporation's plans. "Sounds like some big-money projects."

Ron was animated now. "Shit, they are. I can see us investing in some billion-dollar projects. . . . I can see APFC putting a quarter of a billion dollars into something."

Budge was excited, too. *I think I understand what Billy is onto now,* he was thinking. *I think I know why he wants Stan on the board. I'm going to make sure we don't need to have Stan on the board.* "So how do you guys do this? Do you just go out and look for things to buy into?"

"No. Our infrastructure resolution calls for us to enter into partnerships or agreements with investment managers . . . sort of commingle funds with our chosen partners. It falls under alternative investments, but right now the only thing the board is looking at is infrastructure investments."

Both men finished their first martinis, and a nod to the bartender by Budge brought two more. By this time, they had both squared themselves on their stools so they could look at each other as they talked.

"So, how far along in this process are you? You got any hot deals going yet?" Budge steeled himself so he wouldn't sound anxious.

Having no idea what Budge was thinking, Ron said, "No, it's early in this process. We've pretty much got the rules down, though, so we're going to get serious now. But what about you? You interest me. We didn't really talk about anything but pussy the first night we met. You don't become independently wealthy by accident."

Budge was at ease now. "I'm really not wealthy . . . just comfortable. My family is fairly well off, or they were fairly well off. I was favored by my grandfather, and he left me a bunch of money when he died."

"So you ran off to Alaska with it."

"Kind of." Now Budge was lying on the run, and he had to think fast. "My father was an alcoholic, and he and his dad . . . my rich grandfather, were estranged. Granddad didn't leave him anything. My father pissed his money away on bad women, bad deals, and bad whiskey, so he came after me and the money my grandfather gave me. I ran up here to get away from him. He doesn't know where I am, and he's too fucked up to find me."

"And your mother?"

Budge continued the lie. *Forgive me Mom.* "She died years ago. She was always sickly."

"Didn't you ever have to work?"

"Oh, sure. I did some time working on rigs." Realizing he had another opening, he continued. "I did do some work in the Seattle area. I was a sort of do-it-all for a group of big-money guys from the Midwest. They made all kinds of investments, and sold them for big profits. It was fun. I was flying all over the place . . . setting things up, closing things down."

Now Ron was really curious about Budge. "Sounds interesting. Are these guys still doing their thing?"

"Oh yeah . . . they call me now and then. Mostly just old friends chatting."

"You don't ever think about working for them again . . . because you've got money?"

"I guess I'd still help them on the right project. It would have to be big, though."

I fucking don't believe this, Budge thought. *I couldn't have written a script for this conversation that would have been better than this.*

Just before their lunches arrived, and right after their nice bottle of pinot noir was opened, Manny came out of nowhere and walked up behind Ron. He put his arm on his shoulder and said, "Good afternoon, Mr. Minty. It's nice to see you."

Turning, Ron said, "Hi, Manny. Thank you. It's nice to be here. Do you know my friend Budge Brown?"

With the introduction completed and some small talk out of the way, Ron offered Manny a glass of wine. For a fleeting moment, Ron wondered how many thousands of dollars Manny saved his restaurant by drinking his guests' wine. He even wondered if Manny got a signal from the bartender when someone ordered a nice bottle. At the very least, Manny drank enough wine to force Ron and Budge to order another bottle while they ate their lunches.

With two martinis and most of two bottles of wine in them, they were ready to move after they finished eating.

Ron said, "Well, what do you say we wander down the street and check out the action?"

"I'm ready. Let me pay for this, and we'll go."

"You don't have—"

"I insist. You've got the drinks at the next place."

Ron and Budge stopped at a number of bars on Fourth Avenue, having one or two drinks in each. By late in the afternoon, the afterwork crowds were starting to gather, and they were gloriously inebriated . . . so inebriated that a stop at The Mud Flats to finish the day made sense.

Vicki was surprisingly cordial as they stumbled up to the bar. "Well, look what the cat dragged in. If you two aren't a pair to draw to, I've never seen one."

"What the fuck is this, cliché day?" Ron was too drunk to care if he offended Vicki. Surprisingly, she laughed.

"You got me, cowboy . . . and you win the daily prize. You get a choice of a cup of coffee or a free ride home."

Budge stayed silent as Ron continued the banter. "I'll take the free ride . . . if you come with me."

"Well, cowboy, I was making the offer that The Mud Flats would pay for a taxi to take you home."

"Can't go home yet. Me an' Budge got business to talk. Right, Budge?"

Budge was caught slightly off guard, but picked it right up. "Yeah, some business to discuss."

He hadn't fooled Vicki. "Monkey business would be my guess." With that said, she moved to take care of two customers at the other end of the bar.

Ron turned to Budge. His words were slurred as he said, "Do you think those guys you worked with before have anything going on now . . . you know, like infrastructure projects?"

"Well . . . I know they always have something going on. There is one project . . . but , ah, I don't think I'm supposed to talk about it. You know, they always worry about somebody jumping in there and beating them to the punch."

Budge's comment interested Ron. "Well, maybe you need to talk to them and see if they have something going on that they would like to partner with the State of Alaska on. If they do, and if it sounds interesting enough for me to take to the board, and if the board likes it . . . we might be able to make some kind of deal." As a calculated afterthought, Ron added, "I'd just want to be compensated."

Damn, Budge thought, *he just threw that out there.* He decided to take a gamble. "You mean, like a finder's fee?"

"Yeah."

"I don't think that would be a problem. I'll have to call and see what they think. They may be too far into their current deal to make changes." Budge pondered for a moment. Intent on giving Ron the idea that he would be his willing partner in collusion, he finished with, "I'd want to get something out of it, too."

Dirty-deeded miscreants have a way of finding each other much more quickly than honorable men are able to forge a united defense against them . . . but it is inevitable that they will eventually be destroyed by their own dishonorable bond.

— From *Fred Longcoor's Book on Life*

Chapter 14

It Does Run Downhill

I hate bowing to this fucker, Billy thought as he dialed Mario's number. *But, I've got to tell him about this now.*

"Mario. Billy. How are you today?"

"I'm old, I'm grouchy as hell, and I think I just pissed myself. That's how I am. What's up?"

"Well, we've just had a surprise turn of events in Seattle. It's . . . well, there is no easy way to say it. The old lady sold the goddamn warehouse out from under us. She just told Raymond." Billy waited for the explosion.

Following a few moments of dead silence, Mario said, "Now, there's not much you can do about that, is there?"

Billy was so shocked at Mario's response that he was speechless for a moment. "Well . . . no there isn't, but it was a shock to me. I thought Raymond was doing well with the widow."

"Don't be ignorant, Billy. How many times out of ten is a half-assed scheme to get some rich widow to give you a hundred million–dollar building going to work out? I thought all along that this had about a five percent chance of working."

"Really? Maybe I had blinders on. I thought we had a real shot at this. There is some good news. The widow has agreed to give Raymond another building. It's allegedly a five million–dollar warehouse. She told him she would pay for all the renovations to make it into a school for young people. Raymond says he thinks it might be worth ten million after the remodel is done."

"Ten million is a lot of money."

"Yeah, and you know what else?"

"What?"

"I think the Reverend is fucking her . . . the old lady."

"Jesus. The widow? I don't know if I'm disgusted or jealous. I saw a recent picture of her in a magazine, and she looks pretty good."

"Yeah, well I don't care about that. I'm already out a couple hundred grand between this fucking deal and the crapshoot in Anchorage. That one's a worry. The fucking Saylors are in the middle of that, too, and there are more potential problems there than there were in Seattle. I really thought we were going—"

"Get over it, Billy. I'm responsible for getting you into the Seattle deal, so I'm sorry about that, but let the Reverend work on what's left of it, and hopefully you can get your money back and then some. Whatever you get is all yours. I don't want my cut. Let's concentrate on what we are doing in Alaska. That's the big money, and if we handle it right, it's a lot cleaner. Benny's been doing a lot of background work. He's got the new international bank account set up. It's set up for handling accounts receivable and accounts payable, so we avoid having to deal with the Department of Treasury's FBAR reports on foreign financial accounts with balances greater than ten thousand dollars. You know, in and out, no continuing balance. We are even going to move some money in and out of it just to establish it as a legitimate account."

"I guess that's all good, Mario . . . and thanks on the Seattle split. I was going to fly to Seattle, but now I'm thinking I need to fly to Anchorage. I need to get a close-up feel for what's going on. I've got Budge there, but I'm not sure what he's doing half the time. He *has* made a good contact on the board recently. Then there's Stan Faro. Because of the contact Budge made, we may have to dump him. Since I'm his old college buddy, I should probably do that myself. That may take some work."

"Go up there, but be low-key. When this is all done, the shit will hit the fan big time, and you don't want to be connected to it in any way. This is not the good old days, Billy. You can't just start eliminating everyone who gets in your way." Mario laughed. "Even though it's a lot of fun doing it that way."

Billy laughed with Mario. "Ah, for the good old days."

Billy made a call to Stan and told him he was making a trip to Anchorage, which jumped Stan's anxiety level by several notches.

"What for, Billy? Don't you think I'm handling things here?"

"That's not it at all, Stan my boy. I just want to get a feel for the place.

Remember, I'm fronting a lot of money up there . . . more than you even know about, so I have a lot at risk. I just want to feel good about where the money's going."

Stan gritted his teeth, thinking, *There's that Stan-my-boy bullshit again.*

"What do you want to do when you get here?" was Stan's intentionally blunt question.

"I'm going to want to meet with Henry Kuban. I'll let you know about the rest of it when I get there. Get me a nice suite in a nice hotel, and find out where we can park the Lear and get it serviced. Just email the information to me. I'll find a rental car. We'll probably come up in about a week. I'm bringing Anna with me."

Stan felt a blush below his belt at the mention of Anna, but he didn't have a chance to say anything further to Billy, who had already hung up.

I think I'm fucked, and I don't even know why, Stan thought as he sat numbly at his desk.

"Budge, this is Billy. Answer your fucking phone. Budge, Budge."

"Billy. This is Budge. What's going on? I'm right here. I was in the bathroom."

"We need to talk. I'm coming to visit you . . . in Alaska. Next week."

"Oh yeah, well come on down, or up, whatever. You need a place to stay? You can stay here."

"I don't want to stay in your fucking place. Probably cum stains all over everything. Stan's getting me a suite at a hotel. Anna's coming with me. She's never been there. I mean, I guess she landed there when she came from Russia, but she's never been there and actually visited Anchorage."

Showing no intimidation, Budge casually asked, "So, what's up?"

"Mostly, I need to talk to Stan . . . after you convince me that this new friend of yours can help us."

"Great timing, boss. Let me tell you about the lunch meeting me an' Ron had yesterday. In fact, I was just getting ready to call you." Budge relayed the details of his and Ron Minty's conversation the day before.

"Shit," Billy said. "I smell a partner. It sounds like this guy fits us like a glove. You think he's smart enough to be fucking with you, or worse yet, setting you up?"

"I really don't think so, Billy. I don't mean he's not smart. You'd have to have heard how our conversations progressed. You could feel a relationship building. I think he wants something like we want, and as of now, he doesn't have a fucking clue what we are up to. He just knows that I'll listen to him and agree with him. I mean, he actually drew up a plan to make money off of the fund with a sort of goofy Ponzi scheme. He showed it to me."

Budge saved the best part of the drunken afternoon with Ron for last. "And here's the kicker. The board is on this push to find alternative investments in infrastructure, and he wants to know if the guys I know . . . you, have anything in the works that might fit into their plans. And, he wants a kickback from us if the board ends up buying into something of ours."

"Shit . . . double shit. This is too good to be true." Billy was instantly thinking on his feet. "But what about the regional mall? Will that qualify as infrastructure?"

"Billy, I'm just the field guy, the setup guy, I'm really not in the loop on what you are doing. If this is all about a scam involving a regional mall, my answer is no. I read the infrastructure resolution on the APFC website—"

"What the fuck is that?"

"It's the Alaska Permanent Fund Corporation's website, and it's pretty specific about what qualifies. Think of their definition of infrastructure as critical service assets . . . bridges, airports, pipelines, docks, railroads, communication towers, all of that kind of shit. A regional shopping mall just doesn't fit."

"That puts us way behind the eight ball. We put a lot of fucking work into the original plan to use a regional shopping mall in Colorado as the target. It fit their definition of alternative investments perfectly. In fact, they've already invested in shopping malls down here in the states." Wistfully, Billy added, "Shit, what a loss. Whatever we come up with now, it has to be big, and it has to be something we can dummy up easily."

"I don't know about that, but I'm convinced Ron is the right guy to work with us, whatever you're up to."

Untypically, Billy suddenly sounded tired and discouraged. "We'll find something, or figure something out before I get there. We can both meet with your guy. I'll play the money guy from America . . . I mean, I *am* the fucking money guy from America."

I'm actually the front man for the real money guy, Billy thought.

"Good. I told him I thought you guys were working on something big, but I couldn't talk about it. I guess all of this opens the door for your wild-ass imagination to go to work."

"Yeah, it does, but we are going to have to put the façade together quickly. This is going to be a challenge. We've been working on the regional-mall deal for a year, creating a legitimate-looking background."

Budge thought for a moment and said, "You know, there may be something simpler. Ron told me about other infrastructure options that include things like securities, debt, bonds, and some other things I don't understand. He said something about OECD's, and brownfield and greenfield projects too, and I don't know what any of that means. I'll keep working on him and see if I can't open up some talk about all of that. Wouldn't it be great if we could sell the APFC a couple hundred million dollars' worth of phony bonds?"

"Sometimes you surprise me, Budge. Mostly, I thought you just love to fight, fuck, and drink whiskey, but sometimes you come out with some shit that really makes sense. I'm going to call Mario. This kind of thing requires the kind of research that his guy, Benny, is really good at."

Sarcasm oozed from Budge as he said, "Yeah, isn't he the guy who found Betsy Brooksher?"

"That thing could have happened to anybody. It wasn't Raymond's fault, it wasn't Benny's fault. It was the fucking Saylors. I'll see you next week."

A week later, all intentions pointed north. Nick and Nani had spent three days in Las Vegas and three days in Victoria, BC, and The Bird was on its way to Anchorage. Vegas had been a land of wonder for Nani. They saw the Beatles' LOVE show at the Mirage, which she enjoyed, and they dined at several of the city's exclusive restaurants. At casinos and elaborate hotel pools, she was amazed by the eclectic collection of people. Their dress and behavior was unlike anything she had ever seen before. She and Nick ate too much, drank too much, and generally acted like everyone else around them. Danny and Greg went off on their own, touching base with Nick once a day by cell phone.

"I have never been any place like that," Nani said as she sat in her luxurious leather seat on The Bird.

"Are you talking about Victoria or Las Vegas?"

"Las Vegas."

"Las Vegas is . . . well, you know what they say about things that happen in Vegas staying in Vegas."

"I guess I can see why. I was just thinking . . . wondering. We made love every day. One day we made love twice. It was nice, but we don't usually do that."

"It's the atmosphere there, baby. The place is sexy. Sexy people, sexy shows, sexy clothes, money everywhere."

"People wear sexy clothes in Maui. I mean, every other woman is in a bikini. And *we* have lots of money, but we don't . . . you know, every day."

"Yeah, but the clothes in Maui are functional and traditional. In Vegas, moms from the farm can be whoever they want to be . . . you know, let their hair down without anybody knowing about it. It creates a blatantly sexual atmosphere. People are thinking sexy before they even get there. There's some of that in Maui, but it's what Vegas is all about. And we *can*, you know, every day."

Ignoring Nick's last statement, Nani said, "Victoria is sort of sexy, too, don't you think?"

"You're talking about the young hookers on the streets at night?"

Nick had been sure Nani would be surprised by the young women on street corners in the proper old English city of Victoria. She was even more surprised when he explained that they were regulated by the government and had regular medical exams that were controlled and recorded by the government. In keeping with their stately attitude toward sex for pay, they also wouldn't allow the women on the streets until 9:00 at night.

"Yes. They're just not as . . . outrageous as they are in Las Vegas. And, they're all very young."

"Prostitution in Las Vegas is illegal, so it's controlled by a shady element. They can be as outrageous as they want to be. Prostitution in Victoria is controlled by the government, so they can make the world's oldest profession look almost respectable."

Nani took a hard look at Nick. "Men . . . how is it you all know so much about those kinds of things?"

"It's what men do baby, it's what we do."

On the same day Nick and Nani departed Victoria for Anchorage, Billy's Lear lifted off from the runway at his Montana ranch. Their departure from Montana before the Saylors' G550 departed from Victoria International Airport put them on a schedule that would get them to Anchorage at almost exactly the same time the Saylors arrived.

Anna was sound asleep in her reclined seat, and Billy was deep in thought as they jetted toward Alaska.

I really think Budge is onto something with this Ron Minty guy. We're going to have to do something with Stan Faro. Absolutely nobody can be trusted to keep their mouth shut after losing a hundred thousand–dollar-a-year boondoggle job. Maybe I can pay him off, and he'll just go away . . . but I could just pay Budge five grand to kill him!

Anna stirred seductively in her seat, and Billy immediately thought about the mile-high club.

Billy continued to sort things out in his mind. *Forget that, you've done that. Get this thing figured out before we get to Anchorage. The first thing we need to do is make sure Minty is with us. I mean, a finder's fee is one thing, but we need him to be with us. Mario said Benny is onto something. I hope it's good.*

Benny wasn't flying north, but his focus was in that direction. Since Mario had put him on the project of finding an infrastructure investment for the Alaska Permanent Fund Corporation Board of Trustees to look at, he had been poring over the Internet, business magazines, the *Wall Street Journal*, and anything else he could look at. The morning Billy was scheduled to leave for Alaska, Benny barged into Mario's office with a big grin on his face.

"What the fuck are you grinning like a Cheshire Cat for?"

"I thing I've got it, boss . . . the infrastructure investment."

Impatiently, Mario said, "Well, spit it out."

"Historical bonds."

"What the fuck does that mean? Explain it to me."

"There are lots of historical bonds out there, as many as fifteen thousand different ones, and lots of them are from railroads . . . one of your infrastructure industries. They turn up in all kinds of ways. People find them in archives, private collections, estate sales. They are real bond certificates, and people think they are legitimate because they state that they are payable in gold, and they often have United States of America printed on them."

"Okay, go on."

"In truth, they are traded as collectibles because they have no real value, even though many people buy them because they are convinced they are worth their face value due to the fact that the bonds are backed by the government. Actually, an earlier court case made gold clauses in bonds issued before 1977 unenforceable."

"Okay, I get that. But how is a historical bond from a defunct railroad going to fulfill the APFC's requirement to invest in infrastructure?"

"That's the hard part, but it's not impossible. I found a famous scam on the Internet. The Chicago, Saginaw and Canada Railroad issued bonds in 1873. They were thirty-year gold-backed bearer bonds paying seven percent interest to finance construction of a proposed railroad. They went into bankruptcy, and a predecessor of today's CSX Corporation purchased their assets. The bonds remained in court archives until they were discovered a few years ago. They had a one thousand–dollar face value, but were sold as collectibles for about thirty dollars each. Unscrupulous purchasers who bought them as collectibles then sold them for face value."

"This is a long fucking story, and you're losing me."

"If there are really fifteen thousand of these out there, we ought to be able to find one that belonged to a predecessor of one of today's companies . . . preferably a railroad. We buy or steal the bonds from a collector, turn around and sell them to the APFC as gold-backed, government-backed bonds that are being sold to raise money for something like a new high-speed rail line. There are all kinds of things you can throw at buyers . . . in this case, the board. Tell them the Treasury Department backs them and the Treasury Department has a federal sinking fund to retire histori-cal bonds. By the time they try to collect on them, we'll be on the beach in Costa Rica."

Mario was deep in thought. "I don't know. For that kind of investment, somebody is going to check it out. Plus, you'd have to have hundreds of thousands of bonds to raise the kind of money we're looking at. . . . And I don't want to be on the beach in Costa Rica."

"I didn't say it was perfect. I'm still working on that part. And you wouldn't have to have hundreds of thousands of bonds. You sell them at inflated prices based upon third-party valuations. I just found this. Let me work on it a little more."

When Benny left Mario's office, Mario dialed Billy's number, hop-ing to catch him before he left Montana. When Billy answered, Mario explained what Benny told him about historical bonds.

"I don't know. It sounds a little flimsy to me."

"Yeah, me too. I think the bond idea is weak, but let's give Benny a chance to flesh it out a little more. He'll come up with something."

'I have a bad feeling about this, Mario."

"What do you mean?"

"I've spent thousands of dollars getting to the point where we can get Stan on the Permanent Fund Board of Trustees. We had everything set up on the shopping mall in Colorado . . . the phony corporation, the phony land purchase. We even had a model made up—"

"Don't fucking tell me about that. I spent three grand having that thing made."

"I know. That's my point. We honed in on the fund's push for al-ternative investments, and came up with a great plan that we put a lot of time and money into . . . and now we're fucking around looking for infrastructure investments. Add this goofy bond deal to the mix, and it just feels a little . . . disorganized and desperate."

"I agree, but I don't want to give up. I know there's an opportunity there, and if we don't get to it, somebody else will. We knew this was going to take some time."

"We really need to get our shit together, Mario. I hope Benny has some other rabbit in his hat. I'm off to Alaska."

As Billy flew toward Alaska, he thought about his conversation with Mario: *Right now, this whole deal is fucked up. In fact, right now every deal we have going is fucked up. I could live like a king for the rest of my life with the money I have now. Why am I in the middle of this mess?*

An hour later, they were approaching Anchorage by flying east above Turnagain Arm toward Cook Inlet, where they would turn over Fire Island and land west-east toward the Chugach Mountains.

Anna was awake now, and looking out the window. "It's beautiful, Billy. It looks like my home. Look at the snow on the mountains."

"Yeah, Anna, it's beautiful," was Billy's uninterested reply. He looked out his window and was comforted by the fact that there was no snow on the ground in Anchorage.

The Lear landed at Ted Stevens International Airport and taxied to Williams Air Service. Stan had arranged for the jet to be serviced and secured there, and he arranged for a suite for Billy and Anna at the Susitna Hotel. A white limo that Billy reserved sat near the front of the Williams terminal.

"Smell that fresh air, baby," Billy said as they descended the air-stairs to be met by a Williams Air employee.

Anna followed Billy, appropriately decked out in a fashionable red pantsuit, with a short beaver-skin coat on for warmth against the April chill. "I love it, Billy," she said. "It's different from Montana. It reminds me of Russia."

"Yeah, it's nice," was Billy's condescending reply. He headed straight to the limo, leaving the contract pilot and copilot to take care of the airplane and fend for themselves. As he walked, he noticed a man and a woman coming down the air-stairs of a G550. *Now that's flying,* he thought. *When we pull this off, I'm getting one of those.*

A much-too-young driver in an oversized uniform waited patiently at the back door of the limo. "Mr. Peets?"

"Peet. That's me." *This young fucker won't know anything,* thought Billy. "Come on, baby, let's move it."

Anna obligingly climbed into the backseat. "This is exciting, Billy. I've never been here before."

"Yeah you have, baby. Remember? You stopped here on the way from Russia."

"Oh, I forgot about that. I just got off the plane and got right back on another one. I was too excited to remember anything."

"You mean because you were coming to marry me?"

"Of course, you big bear. I was excited about going to America, too."

"Alaska's part of America."

"Oh, that's right, but it is so close to Russia. My home in Kamchatka is very close to Alaska. Do you think we'll see any Eskimos?"

"Yeah, baby, I'm sure they're everywhere," Billy replied, sure that Anna wouldn't know he was being sarcastic.

Forty-five minutes later, they were settled in one of the corner executive suites at the top of the Susitna Hotel, and Anna was swooning over the view of Cook Inlet to the northwest, and the Chugach Mountains to the east. "I love this, Billy. It's, it's, I don't know how to describe it."

"Yeah, it's nice, but we have work to do." Billy had already called Budge and told him to meet him at their suite. "Why don't you walk around downtown for an hour or so while I take care of business. You can check out the shops, and you might even see an Eskimo."

Anna reacted like a schoolgirl. "Yes, yes. I need some money."

Billy reached into his pocket and pulled out a wad of bills. He peeled off five hundred-dollar bills and handed them to Anna. "What if that isn't enough?" she asked, still in her schoolgirl mode.

"It better be," grunted Billy.

Anna left on her shopping trip, and Budge was at Billy's door five minutes later. For all the history they had together, they greeted each other warily, rather than like old friends.

"How was the flight up here?" Budge asked.

"It was great. Real comfortable. Drink? I had them stock the refrigerator. Jack for you if that's what you want?"

"Sounds good. Rocks, with some water on the side."

Billy dutifully opened the bottle of Gentlemen Jack Daniel's and a bottle of eighteen-year-old Chivas Regal, and poured a generous amount out of each bottle into glasses filled with ice. "I wanted Royal Salute, but they didn't have any. I thought this was a first-class hotel."

"This is Alaska, Billy. You can get a little bit of everything someplace in this city, but you can't get everything everywhere."

"This will do. Let's get down to business. Tell me all about this Minty guy, I mean everything, not just what we've talked about on the phone. Help me get the feeling you have about him before I meet him."

Budge told Billy everything he could think of about Ron Minty over the next thirty minutes. He told him about all the nuances of their conversations, and the times Ron was trying to open up to him without incriminating himself.

"I think he's just like us, Billy. I think the promise of some big money and a solid plan crafted by us would bring him onboard in a heartbeat. Do we have a solid plan?"

"We're working on it. You know how this infrastructure thing fucked up our original plan. It's my hope that we can get this guy on board, and that he might be able to give us some inside information that will help us."

"When do you want to meet him? I mean, I think he will be eager to meet you if he knows you are one of the money guys I've been telling him about,"

"The sooner the better. Tonight for dinner, if you can arrange it. I can have Stan take Anna to dinner someplace, and we can meet him. Tell Mr. Minty we'll pick him up. I'll bet he'll enjoy being picked up by a limo."

Budge made a call to Ron, and quickly arranged a dinner meeting at Mr. Z's for 6:00. Budge left, and Anna returned to the suite a half hour later loaded down with several big shopping bags. "I found lots of great stuff, Billy . . . and I saw some Eskimos. Actually, they looked like they were drunk, but I think they were Eskimos. I found a really beautiful fur in a place called David Green's, but I didn't have enough money to buy it." Anna finished with a twist to her lips to emphasize her disappointment.

"How much was it, Anna?"

"It was only four thousand dollars . . . for a full-length mink. It was beautiful."

"Well, I'll tell you what. I need some privacy for a business dinner tonight. If you will go to dinner with Stan Faro while I'm meeting these other guys, we'll buy you that coat before we leave."

Anna looked excited. "Stan is the man who visited the ranch, right? He was a nice man. I'll do it. Thank you, thank you, thank you," gushed Anna as she grabbed Billy and hugged him.

As soon as Anna released him, Billy dialed Stan on his cell phone. Stan had been anxiously awaiting his call. "Stan, this is Billy."

"Great, you made it. I'm looking forward to seeing you."

Billy was already dismissing Stan from his long-range plans, and he rushed into his mission. "I'm looking forward to it too, Stan. I have a little situation tonight that I need some help with though. I need to meet some people, and I have Anna with me. I was hoping you wouldn't mind taking her to dinner while I'm meeting these guys. We're going to be at Mr. Z's, so it would be best if you took her somewhere else."

Conflicting emotions rushed through Stan's mind. *Shit, what is Billy up to?* he thought. *How am I going to face Anna after she took her clothes off in front of me? I can't wait to see her! What was she up to? What is Billy up to?* "Uh . . . sure Billy. I can do that. What kind of food does she like?"

"I'd say she's a meat and potatoes woman, but I think she'll eat anything."

"Okay. When are we going to get together?"

"Well . . . probably tomorrow. I'll call you in the morning. Not real early though. I'm not a morning person. Can you pick Anna up here about six-thirty?"

"Sure."

Promptly at 6:30, Stan nervously knocked at the door of Billy and Anna's hotel suite. Not sure if he would be encountering Billy or Anna first, he prepared himself for either possibility.

After a long wait, the big door opened slowly. Anna was standing there in a short black dress that was low-cut enough to reveal a generous portion of her ample breasts. The light fabric flowed around her lower body as she moved. The sight of her took Stan's breath away. The dress was what he and his buddies used to refer to as a *come-fuck-me dress* in his younger days. "Uh . . . hello Anna," was all he could get out.

"Hello, Mr. Stan. Thank you for coming to pick me up."

"You're welcome. Uh, do you have a jacket? It will be pretty chilly by the time we are done eating."

"I'll get it. I'll be right back."

Stan decided to take Anna to the South End Steakhouse, a favored restaurant of his that was in south Anchorage, and a long way from Mr. Z's. The food was good, and there was always an interesting crowd there.

When they entered the main dining area, Stan felt like a conquering hero, as almost every eye was on the stunning woman at his side. He felt proud, even though he was just the babysitter for the evening. At their table, Stan helped Anna remove her jacket, and the male eyes in the room glued to her hungrily.

"I like this place, Mr. Stan. It smells good."

And this place likes you, Stan thought.

"Yeah, it does." Almost apologetically, Stan added, "It's not Mr. Stan, it's Stan."

A waitress arrived promptly and asked them if they would like drinks. "I'll have a martini, up, with olives. Grey Goose," said Stan.

Unhesitatingly, Anna said, "Me too."

"I don't remember you having vodka when I was at the ranch," Stan said, happy to have something to start a conversation about.

"Billy doesn't like me to drink it. He says I get too . . . wild!"

Stan's antenna went up. *Oh great,* he thought, *returning a drunken wild woman to the hotel is just what I need right now.*

"Okay, well maybe just one will be alright."

Anna laughed. "Or three."

In spite of her thick accent, Anna was surprisingly easy to talk to, and she told Stan things about Russia that he had never known before. There was a great deal of poverty in the small town on the Kamchatka Peninsula where she grew up, and much alcoholism. With oil development and the arrival of Westerners, she learned more about the Untied States and became passionate about getting to America. When Alaska Airlines began flying direct flights to the peninsula in support of oil development, America seemed so close she couldn't stand it.

"How did you meet Billy?" Stan asked.

"Through a service. There are lots of beautiful Russian women who are anxious to get to America, and they will marry anybody to do it. There are more women in Russia than men, and Russian men don't value women. Many Russian men are alcoholics . . . and pigs!"

The conversation flowed and the vodka flowed, and they were well into their second martini when Stan blurted out an alcohol-fueled question. "Do you remember coming into my room and sitting on my bed . . . and then standing up and removing your clothes?"

Anna was silent for a moment. She put a demure look on her face and quietly said, "Yes."

Stan knew he was treading on dangerous ground, but he had to know what Anna had been thinking. "Why did you do that?"

"I . . . I wanted to. I liked you. And Billy fell asleep right after you went to bed, and I was ready . . . you know, ready."

Stan felt his heart beat faster. "Do you mean sex? Do you mean you came into my room to have sex with me? Billy would have killed me . . . maybe both of us."

"No, he wouldn't. He told me he might want me to have sex with you before you got there. If things didn't go right is what he said. I guess I had been thinking about that. I was a little drunk, and I wanted to feel a man."

"Jesus," Stan muttered to himself as he took a big swig of his martini.

They both ordered filet mignon dinners that arrived on huge oval plates accompanied by baked potatoes, vegetables, and fresh bread. They ate leisurely, each of them now comfortable with the other, and washed their dinner down with a nice bottle of wine.

Stan was amazed at Anna's appetite, and he was anxious about the fact that she seemed to be getting fairly tipsy. The big plate of food had arrived a little too late.

"Would you have?"

Not understanding the question, Stan replied, "Would I have what?" As the words came out of his mouth, he realized what Anna was asking him. "You mean, made love to you?"

"Yes, Mr. Stan."

Suddenly, Mr. Stan sounded good to him. "I don't know. I think so. I would have been afraid of being shot in the back by Billy."

A wicked smile crossed Anna's face. "I would have been on top . . . so you could watch the door." Then she added a wicked laugh that completed the mental picture.

Stan laughed too. "You are a very interesting woman, Anna."

Anna now put a very serious look on her face and said, "Would you now?"

Stan's heart felt like it was going to leap out of his chest. "You mean . . . have sex with you?"

"Yes. Fuck me, Mr. Stan. Right after we leave here . . . in your nice car."

Stan was so shocked he was speechless for a moment. "Billy's right."

"About what?"

"You do get a little wild when you drink vodka." Stan fixed his eyes on Anna for a moment, trying to figure her out. "I'm going to pay the bill now. Let's go."

When they got into Stan's Lexus, he was desperately trying to think of a secluded place where he could park. In the next moment, he was telling himself to take the beautiful inebriated woman back to her hotel.

You've never in your life made love to a woman as beautiful as Anna, he thought. *But it's not worth dying for. . . . But, maybe Billy will never find out.*

Anna reclined the seat and was sitting seductively with her dress pulled up well above her knees. Stan turned to her. "Will Billy find out about this . . . I mean, if we do this?"

Anna's demeanor became slightly combative. "Do you think Russian women are stupid?"

"No Anna, I don't. I'm just a little . . . worried."

She slipped from combative to challenging. "Does that mean you wouldn't be able to get it up?"

"No, no. I don't mean that. I work for Billy. If he found out, and decided not to kill me, he would at least fire me. I like working for him . . . at least, I like the money."

Anna turned to Stan. "I won't tell . . . if you do a good job. If you make me scream Mr. Stan, I won't tell." With that, Anna pulled her dress up to her waist, revealing the fact that she had no panties on. Seeing her neatly trimmed silky patch of hair as they passed under a streetlight was all the convincing Stan needed. His decision made, he quickly found a deserted midtown park and pulled into the parking lot.

This may be the end of me, thought Stan, *but if it is, I'm going out in a blaze of glory!* He was excited and frightened at the same time. He thought he was going to throw up as he watched Anna pull the flimsy dress over her head.

"Do you like my body, Mr. Stan? I was a gymnast in Russia . . . until I got too tall."

Breathless, and trying to figure out how to negotiate the center console, he said, "You have a beautiful body." He opened his door and went around the car to the passenger side. He quickly removed his pants and boxer shorts, and opened the door.

Damn, this is like high school . . . but Susie what's-her-name didn't look like Anna!

Anna scooted herself up onto the console. "Here, sit in the seat." She sounded a little breathless as well, and Stan could tell she was excited too. After he was in the passenger seat, she put her left leg over his right leg and squatted on top of him. It was awkward, but neither one of them cared about that. Stan was shocked when she sat on him and his erect penis slid inside her immediately. Anna began to moan right away. *I don't think making her scream is going to be a problem,* Stan thought.

Their lovemaking session lasted no more than ten minutes. Stan was too excited, and he came quickly, but not before Anna screamed with pleasure. They both remained still for a few moments.

"I liked that, Mr. Stan. I could tell you really wanted me. Sometimes . . . for Billy, I think I am just a place for him to put his . . . you know, thing."

"This was very nice, Anna. But what did you expect when you came to America to marry Billy? Did you expect love, or just comfort?"

Anna was not offended by Stan's question. "I wanted a better life. Life in Russia is very hard. I hoped we would fall in love." In a whisper, she continued. "That will not happen." Pausing to let her words sink in, she continued, "You must understand. Billy treats me very well. He is much older than I am. He loves his money. If I left him tomorrow, he would just get another Russian woman to replace me. There are hundreds or even thousands of beautiful Russian women who would do anything to get to America."

"I am sorry to hear you haven't found someone to love. I mean, I am glad for you that you are here. Right now, I guess I'm glad for me, too. I am happy you have a better life than you had in Russia. I . . . I'm jealous of Billy. He has you."

Anna looked sad as she said, "Yes, I belong to Billy. We can't do this again." She moved her body against Stan's body, and felt him inside of her. . . . "Unless we do it again right now."

Their next lovemaking session lasted longer and was more physical . . . and Anna's pleasure-filled screams were louder. Afterwards, they were sullen as they drove back to the Susitna Hotel.

Stan stopped in front of the hotel. Anna opened her door and turned toward him. "Thank you, Mr. Stan . . . for a nice dinner and a nice . . . you know. You are a nice man. You made me feel like a woman tonight. Goodbye."

Stan watched Anna walk away, and felt sure he would not see her again.

Damning the consequences in the heat of passion feels good . . . until the passion cools.
—From *Fred Longcoor's Book on Life*

Chapter 15

Almost Home

Billy's night was much different from Anna's. He and Budge met Ron Minty at Mr. Z's for dinner. As Budge requested, Manny gave them a quiet booth at the back of the dining room. After introductions, they were settled into the booth, and it became obvious right away that Ron was as anxious as Billy to discuss the fund.

After the first order of drinks arrived, Ron began. "Budge tells me that you are part of an investment group."

Billy was prepared for him. "Mmmm . . . yes, I have a group of friends. . . . It's really an informal relationship, not a corporation or anything like that. Just a few guys who have money. We do form legal partnerships on projects where that is required, usually very large projects, but we always disband the partnership after the project is complete. It's cleaner that way. We invest in the development, and then sell it, or sell our share of it. We invest in all kinds of projects . . . shopping malls, oil and gas plays, housing projects, high-rises, those kinds of things."

"That sounds interesting. How long have you been doing this?"

"Quite a few years. I'd have to think . . . I guess around twenty years. We've made a lot of money. I can't say we've never had a deal go bad, but we haven't had one go bad for more years than I can remember."

Budge sat quietly and sipped his Jack on the rocks as Ron continued to quiz Billy. "Do you have anything you are working on now?"

"Well, we're always working on something. I really wouldn't want to comment on anything right now . . . at least not until I've discussed it with my partners. I'm not sure we would want to give a piece of it to anybody. It just sounds too good right now. Are you looking for something for the APFC?"

"You know about the Alaska Permanent Fund Corporation?"

"What big investor doesn't know about one of the largest sovereign wealth funds in the world?"

"Good point. And yes, I am looking for something for the fund."

"We have a couple of people who are constantly looking for opportunities. They are very good at finding them. Tell me what you are looking for."

"The APFC has a whole host of financial advisors who are very good at finding them also."

"Our guys are not afraid to tread in places most investors wouldn't."

"Do you mean investments that are illegal?"

Billy tried to look like he was a little put off, but not offended. "No. Maybe some things that push the envelope a little, but in those cases, we spend a lot more time doing our homework."

Billy and Ron took a breather from the conversation when their waiter took their order. Both of them were carefully thinking of ways to take the conversation to another level when Budge spoke up.

"Ron, forgive my bluntness, but you indicated that you would want some kind of finder's fee if the APFC actually bought into one of Billy's projects."

Ron looked at Budge with steely eyes and winced slightly. "You certainly laid that turd right on the table, Budge."

"We're all friends here, Ron," was Billy's calming reply.

All three took long sips from their drinks, and were quiet for a few moments.

Billy spoke first. "We would not have any problem paying a finder's fee for the right project, if you were able to lead the APFC to us and help put closure to the deal. We've done that before. More than that, if you could help guide us to the most desirable investment for the APFC, we would pay for that. . . . We would even consider making you a partner."

Now, it was really on the table, and Ron was trying to contain his excitement. "I could do that. Right now, infrastructure is the surest bet, because the board is on a mission to make some infrastructure investments. There's a little bit of a growing fear about equity investments. Just some signs that the board is concerned about. There may even be some off-the-wall opportunities in infrastructure there that most people would never think of." Ron paused. "You realize that I could go to jail for doing something like that?"

"I do realize that. And that is why we need to do everything through Budge. He has no real connection to you, other than a friendship. Few people would be able to connect him to me . . . certainly no one in Alaska." Billy continued his lie by adding, "If I am contacted by anybody from the APFC, I will never suggest that I have met you. This could be huge for both of us, Ron. With the financial clout of the APFC behind us, we could take on some investments that were too big for us before."

The three men continued their hushed conversation while they finished their meals. The more they talked, and the more they drank, the more it seemed like they had found the perfect alliance.

They were close to the end of their evening when Ron said, "How do I know if you and your partners are real? I mean, how do I determine how legitimate your group is?"

Billy laughed. "Do you want to go out to the airport and go for a spin in my Learjet? We could have a nightcap in Seattle, and come back. I could even have a couple of my partners come meet us. One of them owns a G550 like the one I saw at Williams Air today."

Ron chuckled. "No, that's not necessary . . . but I'll take a rain check."

"You're on," said Billy.

Shortly after that, they parted and went their separate directions, all promising to do their part to live up to the dark commitment they had made.

Billy was still in the hallway at the Susitna Hotel when he answered Budge's call.

"What?"

"What do you think? Are you satisfied that Ron is our guy?"

"I think so. I didn't get a feeling that we are being set up . . . but it's hard to know for sure. You need to get as close to him as you can, just to make sure. We need to come up with a test."

"What do you mean?"

"Something for him to do that will demonstrate how far he will go. Something not just immoral, because he's already done that. Something illegal. Think about it."

"Gotcha, boss. I'll think about it. What now, you know, with Stan?"

"*I'll* have to think about that one. Talk to you tomorrow."

When Billy entered the suite, he was surprised that Anna was not waiting for him. He went into the bedroom and found her passed out on the bed with her clothes still on. *She got into the vodka,* was Billy's first thought.

"Baby, wake up," Billy said as he grabbed her ankle and shook her.

Startled, Anna lifted her head up and groggily said, "What?" When she let her head flop back down on the bed, she committed the error that would change her life forever when she whispered, "Stan, that was so good."

For a moment, Billy was stunned. He grabbed Anna's leg and shook her hard. "Wake up, you bitch. What the fuck is this Stan shit?"

Anna was trying desperately to come to her senses. "Stop that, Billy. You're hurting me."

"I don't care. What's this Stan shit? Did you let that little nobody fuck you?"

Anna had now come around enough to understand the situation, but she was still inebriated enough to be defiant. "What are you talking about? We had dinner, and some drinks."

"It looks to me like you had lots of drinks. I know how you get when you have lots of drinks. Did you fuck him?"

"Billy, we just—"

"Just what? Did you fuck him in the car? Did you fuck him at his place? Not here. You didn't fuck him right here, did you?"

Fear, resignation, drunkenness . . . all combined in a weakened moment. "The car. You told me I might have to . . . before."

Billy's face turned red. The big man quickly put himself across Anna's body at her waistline with his elbow resting on the other side of her. She was pinned.

"Billy, what are you doing? You're hurting me. Get off of me!"

He reached under her flimsy dress with his right hand. "No fucking panties. How convenient." Billy easily inserted his chubby index finger into Anna and quickly withdrew it. "Pussy pudding! You're sloppy fucking wet! You did fuck him!"

Anna felt violated, and Billy's crude act combined with her growing realization of how bad her situation was finally made her cry. Her sobs were deep and emotional. She was hurt. She was in grave trouble with Billy. Her first thought was that she would be sent back to Russia, but she realized her more immediate problem was that Billy was probably going to hurt her . . . and Stan.

Billy stood up beside the bed without another word. As he turned and walked out of the bedroom, the words were uttered under his breath. "You're dead, you Russian bitch!"

Sobbing violently, Anna got off of the bed and went into the bathroom. As she sat on the toilet seat in panic, she thought, *you have to get out of here*. The adrenaline was clearing her thoughts, and she decided to stay in the bathroom until Billy was sleeping. Then she would sneak out of the suite. *I don't know where to go*, she thought, *but I'll call Stan. I need to warn him.*

Billy was in the living room area of the suite, pacing back and forth. In a brain cluttered with an assortment of acts of retribution he would like to commit on Anna and Stan, he was trying to sort out what to do next.

I can have Budge make her disappear. Nobody will know she's gone. I can have Budge make both of them disappear. I can't believe Stan would have the balls to fuck my wife! Nobody besides Stan even knows she's here, and nobody at the ranch is going to say anything to me if I come back without her.

Moments later, Billy thought, *I like her . . . and she's beautiful, but I can replace her.*

Billy refilled his glass with scotch several times as he paced. Finally, he sat on the couch and fell into a deep sleep.

Now fully awake due to fear and panic, Anna ventured out of the bathroom when she detected silence in the suite. She peeked through the bedroom door and saw Billy sleeping on the couch. Experience told her that a marching band in the room wouldn't wake him, so she gathered her belongings and put them in her suitcase. She wasn't brave enough to try to get to the wallet in his pocket, so she decided she would have to survive on the small amount of money she had left from her earlier shopping trip.

As Anna left the suite, she whispered, "Bye ,Billy," and her eyes were watering as she closed the door.

Most Russian women are used to being tough when they need to be, and Anna was no exception. In the lobby, she got change from the hotel desk clerk, and found a pay phone. After minutes of racking her brain, she remembered that Stan's last name was Faro, and she found his number in the phone book.

Stan's tired voice came through the receiver. "Hello, who's calling?"

Quietly, Anna said, "It's Anna."

"Anna . . . my God, why are you calling at this time of night? Where's Billy?"

"He's in the hotel. He's drunk. He knows about us . . . you know, earlier tonight."

"What? How can he know? Did you tell him?"

Anna began to cry into the receiver. "Sort of. I didn't mean to. I was half asleep, and half drunk." Hoping to add some drama to her case, she added, "He was hurting me."

"Where are you?"

"I'm in the lobby . . . of the hotel."

"You need to get back to the room before he—"

"I can't. I packed my bag. I left him. I can't stay . . . he'll hurt me."

"Shit." There was a long pause. Stan was resigned as he said, "I'll come and get you. Go to the side door, the one next to the entrance to the bar. I'll pick you up in . . . ten minutes."

When Stan pulled his Lexus up to the curb near the side door of the Susitna Hotel, Anna rushed out and climbed into the passenger seat. Without looking at Stan, she put her hands together in her lap and sat with her head down. "I am sorry, Mr. Stan. I have done a bad thing."

"What do you mean? You didn't . . . do something to Billy?"

"No. I mean you, I mean what you and I did tonight. I will have to hide. I have to run, and I don't know where to go."

"We'll have to find a hotel. Billy could find us at my place." Without really thinking about it, Stan headed his Lexus south of Anchorage toward Girdwood, the ski area forty miles away. Anna was silent all the way, and Stan was in no mood to talk either. He was in deep thought as he drove.

I've lost my big fancy job. There's a guy who is not going to be happy until he finds me...and the woman I'm hiding from him. I can't believe the mess I've made.

Stan turned off the main highway, and after four miles, The Girdwood Alaska Hotel appeared suddenly out of an eerie spring fog. Stan arranged for a room and told Anna to come to the room after him. He parked the Lexus at the far end of the parking lot.

Once they were in the room, Stan couldn't believe the situation he was in. He had a beautiful woman with him whom he'd already had sex with twice earlier in the evening, and all he could think about was that he wanted her to be gone. They both undressed and got into the bed . . . and Stan had no physical reaction to the beautiful naked woman when she crawled under the covers. They both wrestled with their mutual dilemma through a short, fitful night's sleep.

Budge's cell phone rang at 7:00 in the morning. He was still sleeping and only slightly hung over. He answered after the third ring.

"Budge. Get your ass out of bed. Meet me in the coffee shop at the hotel. Now." With that, a disheveled and very hungover Billy ended the phone call. Thirty minutes later, Budge walked into the coffee shop, where Billy was impatiently waiting.

"It's about fucking time," he grunted through a clenched jaw as Budge sat down.

"It's early, boss. What's up?"

Billy leaned across the small table and whispered forcefully, "I want them both dead. The sooner the better . . . right after I leave town."

"Jesus . . . who?"

"My cunt of a wife and that fucking little prick Stan."

"What? Are you shitting me? Why?"

"Just do it. Nobody will miss Anna. Nobody here even knows who she is. Stan . . . I don't care, just make them disappear. There'll be a nice fat bonus in it for you."

"How much?"

"Twenty grand."

"Done."

"I'm leaving this morning. Don't do anything until tomorrow. Call me when . . . when it's done. And stay with Ron."

"I'm going to Juneau with him . . . for the next board meeting."

"Good."

"I'll have some expenses . . . an airplane ticket, hotel, rental car, meals, that kind of stuff." Budge knew it was the right time to mention that to Billy.

"Yeah, okay. Email me. I'll deposit in your account electronically." Billy stood up from the table and left. Budge sat there thinking about how bizarre it was to have that brief a conversation about ending two people's lives. Something about it bothered him. He had done it before, but killing people was not something he relished. He did it when he had to, and he did it for money, but there was something about this he just didn't like.

Budge stayed at the table and had breakfast. He drank several cups of coffee and tried to get his thoughts straight.

I have to find them first. I have to make it clean . . . no evidence, no bodies. This is a big state . . . lots of places to dispose of bodies.

Budge had no way of knowing that Stan was already working at a plan to escape the wrath of Billy. He awakened early from his restless night. Anna was tired, hung over, and dejected, but she doggedly followed him as they made their exit from the hotel a little after six in the morning.

In the car on the road to Anchorage, Stan dialed his office, knowing that Polly's voicemail would answer at the early hour. "Polly, this is Stan. I'm sorry, but I've had a family emergency. I've caught a late-night flight out of Anchorage. Please cancel any appointments I have for today and the rest of this week. I'll call you later in the day and we can map out a schedule for you for the next week or so."

As they drove, Anna realized she was seeing a side of Stan that she didn't know about. Through this adversity, he seemed energized and determined, and she began to feel better about her situation. "What are we going to do, Stan?"

"Billy used to be a friend of mine, Anna, but he's changed. I think he's bad. I think he's way badder than I ever thought he was. I think he is capable of just about anything. Men feel defeated when their women cheat on them. It hurts their pride. Normal men scream and holler, and some of them punch somebody or something. . . . Men like Billy . . . I think they find ways to even the score." Quietly, Stan continued. "We shouldn't have done what . . . last night, we shouldn't have."

Anna spoke with conviction when she said, "Billy *is* bad. I've heard him sometimes when he doesn't think I can hear. It scared me, but I didn't know what to do. Budge is bad, too. He does what Billy wants him to do . . . *anything* Billy wants him to do. What are we going to do, Mr. Stan?" Anna began crying quietly.

"I have a house, that is, I have access to a house. It's a client's house. He has me watching over it, and he wants me to sell it if I can find a buyer. He's a snowbird . . . that means he spends the winter someplace warm. He's in California and he's not coming back until next month. I have a key. We can stay there a while . . . until I can figure out what to do. It's in Wasilla, in the woods, by a golf course."

Billy was halfway back to Montana before Budge could get himself going on a mission that he didn't care for. He started by calling Stan's company.

"Faro-Way Properties, this is Polly Hasey. How may I help you?"

"Uh, this is Jim Smith. Is Mr. Faro in?"

"Mr. Smith, Stan is out of the office for a week or so. Is there something I can help you with?"

"Oh . . . ah, nothing. I just needed to talk to him about a piece of property I want to sell. I can check with him later."

"Can I get your number, Mr. Smith? He will be checking in, and I can have him call you."

"No, no thanks. I'll call back." Budge hung up.

Strike one, he thought. *Now where in hell do I go? I'm sure he's not at his condo . . . but I'd better check that.*

Budge's futile effort to find Stan and Anna continued for the next several days. During that time, Nick spent the mornings at Saylor Industries and the afternoons giving Nani a thorough look at the Alaska he wanted her to know. They spent one night at the Girdwood Alaska Hotel visiting Nick's old friend Olaf Hilmer, who was the hotel manager. It was a chance for Nick and Nani to get to know his new wife, Brenda. Nick and Olaf had a wonderful evening filled with many recollections of good times, while the two young wives learned about each other. Nick and Nani had no idea they were enjoying the fine food, fine wine, and great company in close proximity to two people who were being hunted.

Early the next afternoon, Danny and Greg had The Bird warmed up to provide Nani with a special treat. Danny headed the big jet north toward Fairbanks. Thirty minutes into the flight, he announced over the intercom, "Heads up, tourists. We are going to circle the tallest mountain in North America, and it's clear today." The jet floated gracefully above the magnificent snow-covered vistas on Mount Denali as it made a complete circle around it. Danny came over the intercom again. "You are getting a rare treat. The mountain is usually covered with clouds and fog."

"It's beautiful, Nick," was Nani's breathless reaction.

They then continued on toward Fairbanks. After a flyover of the city, they followed the Trans-Alaska Pipeline route over the Brooks Range to the Arctic Plain. They flew over the Arctic National Wildlife Refuge, the oil fields in and around Prudhoe Bay, and then west over Barrow.

As they flew over ANWR, Nani seemed shocked as she commented, "There's nothing there . . . it's barren."

Nick laughed. "You can't believe all the crap you see on TV about ANWR."

Danny headed The Bird south from Barrow out across Kotzebue Sound and down over Nome, the finishing point of the Iditarod Trail sled dog race. From there, he turned out over Norton Sound toward Bethel, and then east over the smoking plumes from the dormant volcanoes in the Katmai National Preserve, toward Anchorage.

They had been flying for more than four hours, and the beauty and the diversity of the mountains, oceans, rivers and lakes they flew over were staggering.

"It' so . . . spectacular, Nick. And so big."

"Think about it, Nani. We've been flying for over four hours, and we haven't even seen half of the state. You haven't seen all of south-central, none of the Aleutian Chain, and none of the southeastern part of the state." Nick let that sink in a minute before adding, "We've got lots of time for the rest . . . and the resources to do it. We are fortunate people."

On the third morning since Nick arrived in Anchorage, he and Beth were sitting in her office having coffee and making business small talk.

"The business looks solid, Beth. You've done a great job."

Beth smiled. "Thank you."

Nick continued. "When are you going to Seattle? You need to look over the U Building while it's still at a place where we can pull the plug."

"Why would we want to pull the plug?"

"You probably won't want to. I just want you to be comfortable with it . . . and I want you to see it. Then, you and Donnie can decide how you want to go forward. I mean, it would make a wonderful building for our operation, but it may be more than we need. You and Donnie need to decide that."

"What are you now . . . the janitor?"

Laughing, Nick said, "No, but I'm no longer very active in the company. And as long as you keep sending me those big fat checks every quarter, I'm a happy guy. My point is, you guys need to make the decisions, and then live with them . . . which reminds me. We need to get Chris in here before I leave."

"Yes, we do. I'll call him. I'd like to get this done. I need to go to Seattle, and then I need to spend a little time preparing for our next meeting of the APFC board. We're meeting in Juneau this time . . . in a couple of weeks."

Beth called Chris, and he was busy as always, but he recognized the urgency in her request to meet with him while Nick was in Anchorage. He made it to the Saylor Building at 2:00 that afternoon.

Chris looked very mature and businesslike as he entered Beth's office. *He's really grown up,* Nick thought. With his Nordic good looks and six foot athletic frame, he had a presence about him that was hard to ignore.

Nick greeted his younger brother with a hug. "It's nice to see you, Chris. You are looking very well. It's been too long."

"Yeah, it has been. Big sister sounded a little tense, so I got here as quickly as I could."

"Well, we have something on our minds. I'll let her explain it to you."

Beth was anxious to tell Chris what she and Nick were thinking about, and more than a little curious about his reaction. "Chris," she said, "we have thought for some time that we would like you to be more involved in Saylor Industries. That is, more involved than just being a passive officer. Along with that, we think it would be a good idea to roll SayCo into Saylor Industries." Beth was measuring Chris's facial reaction to what she was saying.

Chris was quiet and showed no emotion. She continued. "We would like you to come into Saylor Industries as the vice president of the company, and continue to act as the president of SayCo. I know you have fought staffing issues since you started your company, and this would give you and your SayCo operation the benefit of utilizing Saylor's accounting, human resources, HSE, and logistics resources." Again, Beth stopped, hoping for some reaction from Chris.

It was obvious that Chris was in deep thought, so neither Beth nor Nick spoke for a few moments. Finally, Chris began to speak . . . slowly and deliberately. "I have been expecting this . . . or something like this.

Frankly, I expected it long before now." Chris paused again for a moment. "I am flattered that you want me. I have always hoped that we would all work together someday. This makes sense. Saylor Industries already owns part of SayCo. SayCo has grown into a big company, and, candidly, some additional support infrastructure is needed. I've probably thought about this longer than you have. Yes . . . I would love to play a bigger part in Saylor Industries, and yes, I think it would be a wonderful move for SayCo. Thank you for inviting me."

Beth and Nick both jumped to their feet at the same time. "Wow, you have made me very happy, Chris," said Beth as she reached for him and gave him a big hug.

Nick was right behind her. "This calls for a celebration."

That night, Chris, Beth, Nick and Nani enjoyed a sumptuous dinner at the Denali Room at the top of the Susitna Hotel and congratulated each other on their new business arrangement. While they were celebrating, Stan was sneaking into Wasilla to buy groceries and needed supplies to support his and Anna's hideout. It had been a difficult three days for them. When he returned, Anna was looking out the window over the golf course at the fading light on the Chugach Range. "It's very pretty here, Mr. Stan."

"Yeah, it is, but we can't continue this forever, Anna. Even if Billy fires me, I have a business to take care of. Polly can't take care of it by herself. She's getting nervous. I can tell when I talk to her that she knows something is wrong. I've got enough money in the bank to pay her for the next couple of weeks, and then . . ."

"What will I do, Mr. Stan?"

Stan couldn't take it anymore. He felt cooped up and angry. Loudly, he said, "I don't know. I don't give a shit. I have my own problems. Why don't you go back to Russia? I'll buy you a ticket. Shit, you're almost home now."

As usual, Anna began crying. "I . . . I can't. I can't go back there. I'd rather die."

"Yeah, well, that just may be an option, if Billy or one of his goons finds us. Somebody has been calling my cell phone, and I don't answer it when I see that it's anybody other than Polly."

Like a frightened little girl, Anna ignored the reality Stan was trying to make her understand and asked, "Why aren't you nice to me? We're both in trouble."

"You got us into this."

"Me. You stuck your . . . thing in me. You didn't hesitate to do that . . . twice."

Registering his regret, Stan said, "I am sorry I did that. I knew better."

Pouty now, Anna said, "You didn't like it, Mr. Stan?"

"I liked it. . . . It just wasn't worth it. Look at the fucking mess we're in."

Stan would have been somewhat comforted by Budge's frustration at trying to find out where he and Anna were. He had desperately broken into Stan's condo and looked for clues to his whereabouts. He found Stan's cell phone number, and called it repeatedly, only to have his calls go unanswered. Daily calls to Polly were fruitless, and only made her suspicious about who he was.

Stan called Polly every day, too.

"Good morning, Polly. What's going on?"

"Oh, Mr. Faro, good morning. It's really pretty quiet. One guy keeps calling. I don't know who he is, but I have his number from my caller ID. His name doesn't come up."

"Okay. Give me his number and I'll call him."

Polly gave Stan the number, and after he hung up he quickly confirmed that it was the same person who had been calling his cell phone. An Anchorage number. . . . It had to be someone working for Billy.

The next morning, Stan drove into Wasilla and purchased a throwaway cell phone. He stopped along the road on the way back to the house and dialed the suspicious number. A voice growled, "Budge. Who is this?"

The angry answer made Stan's stomach churn, and he was too numb to speak.

"Who the fuck is this? Who's calling me at this time of the fucking day?"

Inexplicably, Stan spoke. "Quit calling me. Quit calling my secretary."

Startled into full consciousness, Budge said, "Stan? Is this Stan the dead man? Do you have Anna the dead woman with you?"

All Stan could come up with was, "Fuck you," before he pushed the End button. He sat for a moment, fear coursing through his body.

He thought, *I have to call the police. What do I tell them? I fucked my boss's wife and he's going to kill me. My boss, who's no doubt a criminal who is paying me a hundred grand a year because he plans to do something illegal in Alaska.* As he finished his thought, the new cell phone rang.

"Shit," he said to himself as he picked it up. It was Budge. Without answering it and without thinking about it, he lowered his window and threw the phone into the grass along the side of the road. When he returned to the house, he was in a panic. Anna was still sleeping when he charged into the bedroom she was using.

"Anna, get the fuck up Anna. We've got to do something. We're in deep shit. Get your ass out of bed."

Groggily, Anna lifted her head up from under the covers. "What, Mr. Stan? What is the matter?"

"Get your ass out of bed, Anna. We've got to make a plan. I just talked to that Budge guy. He threatened to kill me . . . both of us. We have to call the police."

"Budge will do whatever Billy wants."

"Jesus, Anna. What kind of people do this? Is this the kind of people who work for Billy?"

Anna was now sitting up in bed, her gorgeous breasts pointing directly at Stan as she replied. "Yes. I forgot about him. I know he's in Anchorage. I've heard Billy talking about it."

"Fuck . . . I mean, is he a killer? Is he someone who would chase us down and kill us?"

Now with full realization of what they were talking about, Anna's answer conveyed fear. "I know he is a bad man, Mr. Stan. I've never met him, but Billy talks to him a lot. I know he was working for Billy in Seattle, and he sent him to Alaska a few months ago."

Thoughts raced through Stan's mind. *Shit, he's been in Alaska for a few months. He's been watching me! He probably knows everything about me.*

Anna jumped out of bed naked and rushed to hug Stan. "I'm afraid, Mr. Stan."

Feeling compassion for her for the first time in days, Stan hugged her back. "It'll be alright. We'll figure something out. Let me make some coffee, and we'll sit and talk about this like adults."

For a brief moment, Anna's naked body against him stirred something inside him. An overwhelming fear for their future quickly washed it away.

Mind-numbing fear trumps every other emotion. It reduces the things we want badly and the things we cherish greedily to dust in the wind.
—From *Fred Longcoor's Book on Life*

218

Chapter 16

The Brooksher Connection

A week after they arrived in Alaska, Nick and Nani left Anchorage in The Bird. Their trip back to Maui would include a side trip to Seattle, where they would leave the G550 with Beth and take a commercial flight back to their island home.

"I don't know why we didn't think about this before. This is a good way to get The Bird back to work doing something useful for the company." Nick sat at the table in the lounge with Beth across from him. Nani was in her seat reading a book about Alaska.

"Hauling the CEO around is useful." Beth always defended her big brother's position, and it always embarrassed Nick.

"Thank you. I'm anxious to hear what you think about the Brooksher's U Building. We'll have to call it something different than the U Building."

"How about The George Building?"

Nick slammed his hand on the table. "Brilliant. There probably wouldn't be a Saylor Industries without him."

Nani was listening, and she spoke up. "How about The George Walter Building?"

Nick slammed his hand down on the table again. "Even better. Walter was as important to the discovery of the evil things that were happening as George was."

Now it was Beth's turn. "What about the George Walter Trade Winds Building?"

"Yeah," Nick and Nani said in unison, and they all laughed. The reference to the mystical connection between George Jong in Hawaii and

219

Walter Ataneq in Alaska via the trade winds worked perfectly for them.

Later, they were all in their seats and settled into their own thoughts. For Beth, trips to Seattle inevitably brought memories of the near tragedy they avoided years before thanks to George and Walter's warnings. She continued to feel guilt over the incident because her first husband, Devon, whom she had divorced when she discovered his perversions, and her new man, John, were the two madmen who almost destroyed her and the company. It was little comfort that she had been the brave woman who thwarted their deranged plans.

Betsy Brooksher was sitting in the back of the limo when the G550 pulled up near the fence at the King's Row Executive Service terminal at Boeing Field. The Saylors climbed into the limo and headed to the Sea-Tac terminal, where they dropped Nick and Nani off for their flight back to Maui. Betsy and Beth continued on to the U Building, where Donnie Clayton was waiting for them.

Beth and Donnie were as impressed as Nick was after Betsy's guided tour of the building, and the deal that was really already done was validated quickly. "It's perfect, Betsy. I am so happy you and Nick happened upon each other."

Betsy smiled. "It was meant to be, Beth. Now, let's have lunch. We can have a little mini celebration." Betsy directed the limo driver to head to The Rusty Turtle. When they were all inside, the hostess took Betsy and her group to her favorite table. With authority, she said, "Please bring me a bottle of your finest champagne. . . . Surprise me."

After the champagne arrived, Beth beat Betsy to the punch when she said, "I would like to propose a toast to our lovely business arrangement."

"Here, here," said Donnie.

"Thank you, Beth. May we have more business dealings in the future."

A sudden thought entered Beth's mind. "Speaking of that, Betsy, I don't know if you are aware of it, but I am on the Board of Trustees of the Alaska Permanent Fund Corporation, and—"

Betsy interrupted. "My goodness. I didn't know that. How impressive. Congratulations, Beth."

"Thank you. So you know about the fund?"

"Business people in the Pacific Northwest all know about the fund. It has a huge impact on this area."

"Great. Well, we are always looking for good investment opportunities, and I'm sure a huge, successful company like Brooksher is involved in all kinds of ventures. We should explore that. We're on an infrastructure hunt right now."

Betsy thought for a moment. "I will certainly explore that. I would love to be a partner with the State of Alaska." A little wistfully, she continued, "Del and I made several trips to Alaska. He loved it there. He would be proud of me if we did business with your fund. Can you get me some information on what types of infrastructure investments the fund will consider?" Betsy winked at Beth and said, "We may have something going on that is right down your alley."

"Absolutely, as quickly as I can get to a computer."

When Beth and Donnie arrived at Saylor's Kent office, she immediately used his computer to get on the Internet and download the APFC's resolution on infrastructure. She then emailed it to Betsy at her office.

Back at Brooksher headquarters, Raymond was unaware that Betsy was meeting with Beth Saylor. He was too busy. Betsy had drawn him deeper into the daily dealings of the company, and in spite of the fact that he had to bluff his way through the reality that he was in way over his head, he was learning a great deal about Brooksher's business. In the office, everyone just called him Reverend now.

"Reverend, Betsy is concerned about our Aged Trial Balance. She says that a lot of our customers have gotten sloppy since Del died, and they are taking forever to pay us. She wants you to look into it." The young accounting assistant looked at Raymond hopefully as he posed his question.

Sure, Raymond thought, *what the fuck is an Aged Trial Balance?*

"Ah, sure, I'll get to it as quickly as I can." Figuring he needed to add something that showed he cared or that he understood, he added, "The customers probably figure nobody around here cares about getting paid since Del is gone."

He had been given more to do than he wanted, but he was gradually getting sucked into the web of the things that money and privilege brings . . . not to mention the regular sex that Betsy was providing. He was spending two or three nights a week at the mansion now.

Shortly after the accounting assistant wandered off, satisfied that he did all he could do about the Aged Trial Balance, Raymond's cell phone rang.

"What the fuck is going on in Seattle, Reverend?" With the loss of the hundred million–dollar warehouse, Billy's calls were less frequent, but he still wanted to know what was going on with the other warehouse, since he was still fronting Raymond a considerable amount of money, and there was still a possibility for a nice payout.

Raymond headed toward his office, talking quietly as he walked. "Billy, it's a little awkward talking when I'm here at Brooksher."

"Well, shut the fucking door to your office. You still work for me, you know."

"I know, I know. It's closed. What's up?" *Fuck you*, Raymond was thinking, *Betsy's paying me more than you are.*

"I asked you first."

"Oh, okay. Well, things are moving along. Betsy hired an architect to design the school, and he's asking me a lot of questions. I don't know how to build a fucking church school. I'm just sort of bullshitting him and going along with his suggestions. It's really becoming something that I'm not even part of."

"When's she going to deed the building to you?"

"She wants it completed first. I need to come up with some kind of a nonprofit religious organization and name for the school pretty soon. I determined that we will qualify for tax-exempt status simply by pronouncing ourselves a religious school, which is what Betsy is looking for to make her donation legitimate. We will need to apply for tax-exempt status with the IRS, since it would be obvious that a school would have more than five thousand dollars' worth of gross receipts in a year. We'll also have to apply for an Employee Identification Number. That's all I know, and maybe that's all I need to know, but you may need to help me with that. Maybe Benny can help." Raymond quickly added, "From there."

Billy sounded stunned. "Jesus, how'd you learn all of that?"

"The Internet, Billy. Everything's on the Internet. Betsy got me a computer, and one of these youngsters here in the office has been teaching me how to use it."

Billy said, "I'll talk with Benny. Maybe I'll send him out there."

Raymond immediately regretted telling Billy he needed help. *Maybe I don't need help*, he thought. *Maybe I don't need Billy. I was going to ask him about Aged Trial Balances, but I'll bet I can find that on the Internet, too.*

Raymond barely finished his conversation with Billy when Betsy opened his door and barged into his office. "What's the closed door all about, Reverend?"

"Oh, sorry. Sometimes in the afternoon, I shut the door and pray to our God. Just for a few minutes. Sometimes I pray for help with the things I don't understand around here."

Looking slightly offended, Betsy quizzed, "Like what?"

"Oh, like the Aged Trial Balance. I don't understand why good Christians would quit paying their bills because someone died."

Looking relieved, Betsy said, "Human nature. They probably just feel that I'm the only one left, and I'm rich and don't need the money.

They forget that we have dozens of businesses to run and thousands of employees to pay. That's why I thought a letter from Reverend Raymond might help."

Now, Raymond was relieved, and he thought, *Shit, if that's all there is to it, I can write a letter . . . in fact, I can write a tear-jerker that will have money coming in here in truckloads.* "I can take care of that, Mrs. Brooksher."

"Call me Betsy. Are you coming over tonight? I'll have Gerard make something special."

"You're going to make me fat, Betsy."

With a wicked smile on her face, Betsy said, "I feel really good today. We'll work it off you."

By the end of April, the triangle was a bubbling mix of normalcy and trouble. A week after Nick and Nani were back in Maui; Billy was back at the ranch, still very angry and hurt over the loss of Anna; and Stan and Anna were still hiding out in a house on a golf course near Wasilla . . . running out of money and options. Budge was still frustrated in his efforts to find them. The Reverend was happily banging Betsy regularly, drinking her fine wine, and eating fine food while learning more and more about Brooksher's business and how to form a religious nonprofit organization. Beth had returned to Anchorage and was preparing for the meeting in Juneau.

Fate, in an assortment of forms, was about to change everything.

Fourteen-year-old Herman Wilson was riding his bicycle along the bike path next to Old Knik Road, heading home and thinking about how happy he was that his baseball team was able to practice outdoors now. Spring baseball practice in Alaska meant trying to play an outdoor game in an indoor gym, and he was always anxious to get onto a real baseball field when the snow melted and the ground dried up.

Herman was about a quarter of a mile from his house when he passed what sounded like the muted ring of a cell phone. He stopped his bike and laid it down. Waiting quietly for a moment, he identified the direction the sound was coming from and walked toward it. He was surprised to see a cell phone lying in the brown matted weeds.

The phone was still ringing, so Herman picked it up and pushed the green button. "Hello."

After dialing the number dozens of times for a week without an answer, Budge was surprised when Herman answered it. "Who the fu—" He quickly changed his tone, pleasantly saying, "Excuse me, who is this?"

Nervously, Herman replied, "This is Herman."

"Herman . . . well, Herman, I dialed a number I thought belonged to a friend of mine. Is this your phone?"

"No, sir, I just found it alongside the road. It was ringing, and I heard it."

Budge eagerly asked, "Okay, Herman, my friend must have lost it. Where did you find it?"

"Alongside the road."

Impatiently now, Budge said in his best adult voice, "I understand that, Herman. What road did you find it by?"

"Oh, Old Knik Road."

Trying to hide his impatience, Budge said, "Where on Old Knik Road?"

Herman said, "Close to my house."

Budge was about to erupt when he calmed himself enough to say, "What is your address on Old Knik Road?"

"Uh, Mile Six."

Figuring he had all he needed, Budge dismissed Herman with, "Thanks, kid."

"But what do I do with . . ." Herman realized the connection was gone. He put the phone in his pocket, got on his bike, and rode the rest of the way home. When his dad told him that night that the cell phone was disposable, and it was not worth it for someone to come after it, Herman used it as long as it lasted to call his friends.

Within a few minutes, with help from Google, Budge determined that Herman's house was within a mile of the Settler's Bay Golf Course, and that there were homes around the course and in the area. By early evening, he had rented a nondescript sedan and headed toward Old Knik Road near Wasilla.

Budge spent three days driving around Wasilla. He checked shopping centers, gas stations, liquor stores, any place he thought Stan might go, hoping to spot his cream-colored Lexus. He repeatedly circled through Settler's Bay neighborhoods to the point where people noticed his car and started looking at it suspiciously. He had no luck and was tired after spending many hours sitting in his rented car, on top of the two restless nights he spent in a spartan hotel. He knew that knocking on doors was a hopeless option, and he needed to return to Anchorage to prepare for his trip to Juneau. Frustrated, Budge drove back to Anchorage.

The only trouble in Nick and Nani's life was the worsening condition of Nani's father. After telling Nick that his bout with cancer was in remission, he took a turn for the worse. His body was simply reacting to the stress of his battle with cancer combined with his age.

"I'm going to visit my father today, Nick. I probably shouldn't have taken that trip this month and left him."

Nick's response was immediate and sincere. "I'd like to go, too . . . unless you want time alone with him."

Nani moved right in front of Nick to face him and said, "Why did you say it that way? Do you think he's dying?"

Gently putting his hands on her shoulders, Nick replied, "No, Nani, you're his daughter. I just thought you might want some private time with him. And he's not dying."

"No . . . I want you there. I have nothing to hide from you."

"Okay. Let's go. He would probably love some company right now. We can walk over there."

George was temporarily staying in his condo in Lahaina to be close to his doctor. His wife and children were taking care of their farm in the Upcountry of Maui, and making regular visits to check on him. Nani had talked to him early in the day, and he was at the condo by himself.

Nani hollered through the screen door at George, and he hollered back, "Come in, Nani. I'm on the lanai."

Nani led Nick through the living room area of the cozy condo to the lanai. Even though it was midday and warm, George had a light blanket around himself. "Two of my favorite people . . . aloha."

"Aloha, Papa."

"Aloha, George. How are you?"

"Ahh, a little shaky today. The medicine, it is the medicine. I am glad to see you. You have been on my mind."

"You are on our mind too, Papa. I am worried about you." Nani was glad her father had finally confided in her about his illness, but now she worried more.

"Don't worry, my island flower. I will be fine. I am very tough. I am worried about you two." George's solemn words caught Nick off guard.

"Why would you worry about us, George? We've got the world by its shorts right now."

George laughed. "I know you are well. I know you are healthy and wealthy. I know you are in love. I know all the good things." Now George looked directly at Nick, and with a serious tone added, "But I have had visions recently . . . since you returned from your trip. At first, I thought it was the medicine, but it is the same dream . . . vision, over and over."

Not again, thought Nick. "What is it, George?"

"It is a company, a company in Seattle. A very big company. There is a woman there . . . a nice woman, but there is also an evil presence. My dream is very confusing right now."

Nick was puzzled. "We just made a business deal with Brooksher, which is a very large company owned by a widow . . . Betsy Brooksher. She is a good woman, and her company . . . now it's her company, is very successful. We are buying a big warehouse complex from Brooksher. Betsy made us a very nice deal. It's brand-new. It was built by her husband before he died, sort of his pet project. It's never been occupied."

George contemplated for a moment. "I don't want to be an alarmist. As I said, it is very confusing. I can feel the connection you have with this woman. That is probably why I am dreaming about her. I will say no more . . . unless my dreams get more powerful."

Nani was listening quietly. She was well aware of her father's powers. His actions as a kapuna were legendary on the island, and Nani had been close to the mystery of it all of her life. "Enough of that, Papa. Can I get you something?" She was antsy as they sat and talked with her father for another hour, and anxious to talk to Nick privately. She started quizzing him the minute they left George's condo.

"What do you think of that, Nick? I mean the evil thing at Brooksher."

"I don't know, Nani. I do know that I will never again ignore the things your father tells me. I feel strongly that we have no problems at Saylor Industries. I can't imagine a problem with Betsy. I have known her for a long time. She is an honorable woman. I'm afraid I don't understand . . . unless it is a problem at Brooksher that Betsy is not aware of."

"That's the pattern with Papa. He doesn't know Betsy, but the recent connection between you and Betsy brings her into his circle, our circle. His feelings for you . . . and me, are so powerful that everybody we connect with comes into his circle. We can't ignore him."

"I do not ignore him, Nani. I will never ignore him. I'm just not sure what to do with this one."

If there were problems at Brooksher, Betsy was not aware of them. There certainly were challenges, and she missed Del's wisdom and experience every day, but she felt like both she and the company were making progress. She missed Marc Madrid, too, and had not found anyone to replace him. It was nice having the Reverend around, but Betsy recognized his limitations.

Raymond was gradually slipping into a world that was new to him. He was learning a lot about the business, and whenever he had the time, he researched nonprofit religious organizations on the Internet. Although he had yet to clear it with Billy, he intended to call the phony school the Northwest Light of Life School for Children. He decided to call it that even if Billy didn't like the name. He would tell him that Betsy liked it and he had already started to file the paperwork with that name.

Via a friendship he made with the young assistant accountant he helped with the Aged Trial Balance problem, Raymond stumbled onto the system for transferring funds electronically. It came out as the answer to a simple question Raymond asked him.

"Theodore, other than taking care of the Aged Trial Balance here, what exactly are your responsibilities?"

Theodore A. Pemberton was a quiet young man who took his job seriously, and did not want to be called Teddy. Thoughtfully, he answered, "Well, Reverend, I work primarily on Receivables—that's why I have to watch the Aged Trial Balance. I oversee the electronic receipt of funds . . . and occasionally make electronic transfers to other business units or business partners. Beyond that, I do whatever I'm asked to do related to accounting functions."

"Sounds important. Does everyone pay us electronically?"

"No, sir, but the number of companies that do grows every day. It is inevitable. Del . . . Mr. Brooksher, used to take the checks that came in to the bank himself every day. He did that from the time he started the company . . . to the same bank. He needed a hand truck to carry the boxes. Now, if he was still alive he could carry them in a shoe box. Pretty soon, they will fit in an envelope."

"That's fascinating. Someday, I'd like to see how all of that works."

"Sure, I'll show you."

Raymond restrained himself for a week before he asked Theodore to show him how he handled electronic money transfers. "I would like to show you after normal work hours," Theodore said. "I don't know if anyone would be upset if they saw you in the Secure Room, so I'd like to do it after everyone is gone."

"No problem, Theodore. I don't want you to get in trouble. If you're not sure about—"

"No, no. I'm not worried. I trust you."

Raymond was relieved that Theodore didn't bite on his bluff. "Okay." Hopefully, Raymond added, "I can stay late tonight."

"Come on in, Reverend." That evening Theodore was standing with the door open to an office that was always locked. Raymond knew it was called the Secure Room. "As you know, this is the room where we handle money transfers. These are the computers we use, and they are only used for money transfers. There is redundancy so we can handle more than one transaction at a time, or we can handle transfers if one computer malfunctions."

"This is very interesting, Theodore. I'll bet a lot of money passes through here."

"Electronic funds do, you bet. Millions . . . every day."

"How do you make sure everything is secure?"

"Well, for one thing, we pay for a fraud-detection service. Electronically, they check every transaction to make sure the source account details compare to average past activities. If we have an outgoing transaction, the detection system automatically accumulates risk levels for the destination account. It also checks all kinds of other details, like historical user behavior, transaction amounts, frequency of transactions, etc."

"It sounds pretty sophisticated."

"It is. We haven't had a problem of any kind. Of course, we always have the final say."

"What do you mean?"

"Well, we can always override the system. Say we were transferring an unusually large amount of money to a new account, and the warning alarm goes off. I can override it. Also, if there is a transfer for more than ten thousand dollars, I have to have an observer in the Secure Room. Since there are dozens of transactions every day, several staff members here are approved observers . . . by Mrs. Brooksher. It used to be Mr. Brooksher . . ."

Shit, Raymond thought, *this could be just what we've been looking for. It's beautiful, and it's so simple. But I've got to be cool about it. And I've got to figure out the best way to take advantage of it.*

"This is amazing stuff, Theodore. Thanks for showing this to me. Anytime I can help you with this . . . or anything else, let me know."

"You are welcome, Reverend."

That night, Raymond wrestled with the new information he had learned about electronic money transfers at Brooksher.

Should I call Billy and tell him about this? Maybe not yet. I have to think this out. Betsy's going to give the warehouse to me. When she does, we'll have to sell it and skip town. Maybe we could just get the money some way and not have to deal with selling it.

Raymond went to bed without calling Billy.

Beth was preparing to make the trip to Juneau for the APFC Board of Trustees meeting. She was excited. She had been to Juneau several times before, but this was different, and it seemed like an adventure. As she was organizing her office and a travel case a few hours before leaving, Nancy buzzed her on the intercom. "Ms. Saylor."

"Yes, Nancy."

"Betsy Brooksher is on your line."

Beth punched the button. "Betsy, what a surprise. How are you?"

"I'm doing very well, Beth. I wanted to catch you today. Didn't you tell me you had a board meeting in Juneau tomorrow?"

"Yes. I'm heading to the airport in about an hour."

"Good. I caught you just in time. Listen, you told me that the Permanent Fund Corporation was looking for infrastructure investments. I was pretty excited when you told me that, but I wanted to check a few things before I said anything. I have something . . . that is, Brooksher has something that might interest your board. I have to rely on your ability to keep what I am going to tell you confidential . . . you and the board. This is something that has tremendous potential, and fits like a glove with your state."

"I'm intrigued, Betsy, and I'm all ears. You can rely on me."

Beth sat at her desk and listened intently as Betsy talked for forty-five minutes. By the time she left for the airport, she was very excited and grateful for the opportunity to have the board's undivided attention because of an offer she had made. In a move of bravado, unsure if it would be appreciated or if it would appear to be ostentatious, she'd offered to take the entire board to Juneau in The Bird. She was pleased by everyone's positive reaction.

On the Wednesday before the meeting, the board members met at the Williams Air Service hangar at 3:00 in the afternoon. Beth had arranged for Williams' caterer to put a generous selection of appetizers on the plane, and the usual compliment of beverages.

Beth could hardly contain herself, and as quickly as The Bird leveled off, things started to happen. Greg came out of the cockpit and helped Beth organize the appetizers. Not surprisingly, Ron Minty asked where the alcohol was, and Greg made him a martini. Most of the other board members had beer or wine. Beth then stood at the front of the cabin and said, "Ladies and gentlemen, may I have your attention, please? This is not a flight attendant spiel, this is board business, and I am excited enough about it to want to share it now."

Reactions around the cabin were mixed. Some appeared to be anxious to hear what she had to say, some looked at her like she was an upstart, and some displayed looks of boredom. All of that was about to change.

"I am eager to give you some information in this private setting. It is information that came to me today, and has nothing to do with my offer to fly all of you to Juneau in this plane . . . although it is working out great. It has to do with our search for infrastructure investments."

Ever the gentleman, Richard Cally said, "Thank you for the plane ride, Beth. It is very nice." His thank you was followed by a chorus of mumbled words of agreement.

"Thanks to all of you. Now, the information I am about to give you has to be kept confidential. I believe some of you know that I have a relationship with Betsy Brooksher, the widow of Del Brooksher, and the sole owner of one of the largest corporations in the Pacific Northwest . . . maybe in America. And, I guess I should say that my brother and I and our company have a relationship with Brooksher. It is not a relationship that should be considered a conflict with what I am about to tell you. We simply purchased a piece of commercial property from Brooksher recently."

Fred Feck spoke up. "I don't know what you are going to tell us, but that should not constitute a conflict."

"Okay. Brooksher is a highly diversified company, and that diversification includes a division that deals with investments in energy-related projects. It is simply called Brooksher Energy. Recently, Brooksher Energy has been working with a company in British Columbia . . . Vancouver Island Natural Gas. VING is in the final stages of the permitting process to build an LNG plant on Vancouver Island."

"Wait a minute, Beth, BC produces its own natural gas in the northeast part of the province. Why would they want or need an LNG plant?" Jerry Holter was the board's unofficial expert on oil-and-gas issues.

"You're right, Jerry. They can get gas for their own use, but VING has taken a broader look at the market. Vancouver Island is a large island that is lightly populated. As such, there has not been much of a public outcry about building an LNG plant there. Since there are a number of pipelines in place in BC, including one to Vancouver Island, and others that connect to cross border lines into the US, they see an opportunity to supply gas to much of the Pacific Northwest. They think it's something they could do for many years to come. Instead of receiving gas on Vancouver Island, they would be shipping it the other way. That would require some engineering and some equipment changes, but it can be done. Washington, and particularly Oregon, have struggled with natural gas–supply issues for years. Most of their natural gas is imported from countries that are a long way from there. Also, there are existing lines in BC that run into the US Midwest. This would free up gas from the northeast of BC to go to Canadian provinces and other US markets farther east."

Jerry spoke up again. "Beth, I have two questions . . . maybe three. What does this have to do with Brooksher, and the fund? You say they are in the final stages of the permitting process. How much potential is there for a permitting problem? Finally, and most importantly, where is the gas going to come from?"

Ron Minty took himself away from his martini long enough to scoff, "Yeah, that's kind of a big one." He chuckled at his question, but nobody chuckled with him.

Beth looked self-satisfied and confident as she continued. "Good questions, Jerry. I'm going to change the order a little as I answer them. Remember, a large part of this project will be built in Canada. VING has been assured that their permits will be issued there. Their major silent partner took the lead on the required permits where they are sourcing the gas, and they have assured us it will not be a problem. VING and their silent partner have both handled all issues related to their due diligence thoroughly and professionally. They have been working on this for ten years. They need Brooksher . . . and hopefully us, because they simply need some additional financial strength behind them. Now, as for your last question, I'm glad you all are sitting down. They are going to get their gas from Alaska!"

In unison, several cries of "What?" shot through The Bird. When everybody calmed down, Beth continued.

"VING has an agreement in principle with a major North Slope producer. The silent partner I have been referring to will provide LNG to their new plant. This producer . . . which Betsy will not name at this time, will partner with VING to build the gas-to-liquids facility on the North Slope, four 145,000-cubic-meter LNG ships, the receiving LNG plant on Vancouver Island, the assorted transmission lines that are needed to get the gas to the North Slope plant and out of the Vancouver Island plant, and the loading and unloading facilities."

Now Jerry Holter was indignant. "How will they get the gas to the ships from the North Slope? And haven't there been studies done that suggest that LNG using Prudhoe Bay natural gas is not economically viable?"

"The liquefied gas will flow down the existing Trans-Alaska Pipeline with the oil and be separated in Valdez. The pipeline is operating at one-third capacity now. As to the economic studies that have been done, they were not done with a delivery location as close to Alaska as Vancouver Island."

Every board member in the plane was quiet for a moment, so Beth continued.

"You can imagine what all of this costs. It's an amount somewhere north or south of twenty billion dollars. Jerry, I thought your fourth question might have to do with the proposed Alaska natural gas pipeline. The unnamed producer believes it will never happen, or it will happen twenty years from now. They believe the State of Alaska and the North Slope producers have missed their window of opportunity for the near term. While everybody has argued over the best route for a pipeline, LNG suppliers from all around the world have been signing long-term contracts with companies that are building new LNG plants in the Lower Forty-eight and Mexico to supply natural gas to the US."

The board members were silent. For Jerry Holter in particular, Beth had landed right on something he had been saying for years. He finally spoke. "They're right. I hate to say it out loud, but they're right."

A lively debate ensued, and it continued until Danny announced their approach into the Juneau-Douglas airport. The upcoming public board meeting would be followed by a long private meeting. When they were done, they would agree to listen to a presentation from Brooksher Energy as quickly as it could be arranged.

Beth called Betsy after the board had met the first day and told her they were interested in Brooksher Energy's proposal. Betsy was excited, and assured Beth that she would have a contingent from their energy group plan a trip to Alaska as quickly as everyone agreed on a good date for the meeting.

After calling Betsy, Beth headed down to the hotel's lounge for her previously arranged meeting with Ron Minty. She was uncomfortable meeting with him alone, and was privately regretting the commitment she had made. As she passed through the lobby, she noticed a man checking into the hotel who immediately gave her a chill. It wasn't that she sensed anything particularly ominous about him. It was the uncomfortable reality that she had seen him on the commercial plane flight to Seattle . . . and a feeling she had seen him somewhere else she couldn't recall.

Powerful women and power-hungry men are like hot grease and water . . . put them together and somebody's going to get burned.
—From *Fred Longcoor's Book on Life*

Chapter 17

Bloodless Budge

Budge decided not to tell Billy he missed the first day of the APFC Board of Trustees meeting in Juneau, even though he had missed it because he was trying to find Stan and Anna. He had convinced himself, what Billy didn't know wouldn't hurt him.

Budge did not see Beth as she walked through the Capital Hotel lobby. He knew she would be at the two-day meeting, and he knew she would recognize him without his disguise because they had sat across from each other in first class on the flight to Seattle months before. He was confident she had not seen through his disguise when he threw Mickey Muse out of the last board meeting, even though his fake mustache had come loose. He was not aware that Ron Minty had meetings arranged in Juneau with her *and* with him.

Ron was more excited about meeting privately with Beth for drinks and dinner than he was about meeting with Budge. He was disappointed that Beth insisted they meet in the Governor's Table restaurant in the hotel, because he was sure other board members would see them there. He always thought with his penis, and he was sure this was an opportunity to bed the lovely Ms. Saylor.

Ron gave a lame wave to Beth as she walked into the restaurant. Ignoring the wave, she crossed the dining room and extended her hand. "Good evening, Ron."

"Good evening Ms. . . .uh, Beth."

Ron sat there awkwardly as Beth pulled her chair out and seated herself. Taking the lead to clear the uncomfortable feeling, Beth said,

"Well, what did you think about today's meeting? I mean, I thought it was a little on the vanilla side."

Ron perked up. "It's always different here. There's usually not much input from the public, so that part of it goes fast. Today was no different. Somebody always comes in with some project or some recommendation that is small-time . . . you know, something that is a local issue or a local want."

Beth laughed quietly, "You mean, like the guy who wanted the fund to buy his restaurant?"

Ron laughed too. "Yeah. Well, we had a kind of weak agenda, too. Couple that with the fact that everyone on the board is thinking about what you presented on the plane yesterday, and that is what we all wanted to talk about but couldn't, and you've got a boring meeting. Maybe we'll adjourn early tomorrow. Do you want a martini?"

"Sure, I'll take whatever you're having."

Ron signaled the bartender, pointing to his drink and putting two fingers in the air before pointing to Beth. The bartender nodded.

They continued a conversation that never went anywhere interesting for Ron. Every time he tried to interject something suggestive, Beth dismissed it like she totally didn't get his point. Another martini, dinner, and wine passed, and they had reached their conversational limit. Surprisingly, no other board members entered the restaurant.

Abruptly, Beth said, "Well, this has been a nice dinner. I am tired, and I have some phone calls to make in my room. I'd like to buy if you don't mind."

"No . . . uh, you're not leaving already, are you? It's early." With disappointment, he added, "I said I'd buy in Juneau."

"Alright, well then, thank you for dinner."

Ron sat at the table by himself for several minutes, pissed and frustrated. Even through his thick ego, he realized there was nothing about him that interested Beth. He was about to get up and leave when Budge walked into the dining room and approached his table. "Your guest is gone for the evening?"

"Yeah. Cunt. How'd you know I was in here?"

"I've been looking through the window from the sidewalk. I didn't want to barge in. Did you think you were going to get to that? A rich bitch like that?"

"No . . . she is a good-looking rich bitch, though."

"With long legs."

"Don't fucking remind me. When did you get here?"

"This afternoon. I couldn't get out of Anchorage until today. How was your meeting? You got anything left in the tank? I thought we were going to party in Juneau."

Defiantly, Ron said, "My tank is full. Let's go."

Ron and Budge left the Capital Hotel and headed down the street. As Beth stood looking out her second floor hotel window, she was shocked to see the two of them together. They were jabbing each other, laughing, and generally acting like long-lost buddies.

Ron and Mr. first-class big-shot, she thought. *Interesting. Well, Ron, take him and your lame innuendos down the street.*

Ron and Budge went into the Red Dog Saloon, Juneau's most famous bar. They found a table and ordered drinks.

"You mind if I sit in on the board meeting tomorrow?"

"You're here, why not? The public is invited. Probably bore the shit out of you. In fact, we don't have much left on the agenda. We'll probably shut it down early. We're in rich bitch's zillion-dollar jet, so we can leave whenever we get done. You ever wonder what it would be like to fuck somebody that rich? I'll bet she smells rich. Probably wears gold-flecked panties."

Budge squirmed in his chair. "Damn, I'm getting a little excited." They both laughed.

After an hour of drinking, Budge sensed the time was right to pry some information out of Ron. "The board got anything special going on with new investments?"

Ron was drunk. "Why do you care, Budge?"

"Well . . . we talked before. You know, about finding something."

"Well, have you found something?"

"No, but you were going to see if you could come up with some ideas."

"I think the rich bitch beat us to the punch."

"What do you mean?"

"I can't talk about it. It's secret shit. Private board shit."

Budge was losing his patience, even though he knew Ron was drunk. He was feeling no pain himself and said, "That's exactly the shit we need to know about if you want some kind of fucking finder's fee."

"Whoa, tiger. I'm on the fucking Board of Trustees of the Alaska Permanent Fund Corporation. Who in the fuck do you think you are?"

Budge decided to let that pass and give Ron a few moments to calm down. Quietly, he said, "I'm nobody, Ron . . . I'm really nobody." Inside, he wanted to take Ron out in the street and break his neck.

After a long silence, Ron spoke. "Saylor, Beth rich bitch. She has found an investment. It sounds spot-on with what the board's looking for. Natural gas, an LNG play. It's a big deal. Billions of dollars."

Suddenly, Budge was all business. "How . . . where? Is it in the US?"

Ron became as serious as he was capable of at the moment. "Right under our fucking noses. British Columbia and Alaska. You can't tell anyone about this shit."

Ron proceeded to give Budge all the details he could remember from Beth's presentation on the G550 the day before. Early in Ron's exposé, he disclosed the fact that the deal would be made with Brooksher Energy.

"Holy shit," was all Budge could say.

When Ron was done, Budge simply said, "Shit . . . that's monstrous. Shit, Brooksher. I can't fucking believe it. Billy is really going to shit."

Budge tried to figure out if what Ron was telling him was something good or something bad. He knew this blew their plan . . . whatever it was! Now there was no way they were going to be able to use Ron to help direct the board toward any phony investment they would come up with.

After towing Ron up the street to the hotel by his tie, Budge left him in front of his room. He had puked on the sidewalk twice, and now he was looking for his key.

Even though it was late, Budge called Billy when he was back to his room.

After several rings, Budge heard Billy's gruff voice. "Did you get 'em? Are they fucking gone? They better be when you call me this fucking late."

"I'm in Juneau, Billy. The board meeting."

"I don't give a shit about that. Did you do your job?"

"Well . . . uh, no."

Billy exploded. "Fuck! . . . You mean you can't find two people in a hick state like that? Do you want me to send someone up there to help you?"

Now Budge was pissed. "This is a huge fucking state, Billy, and I don't need any help. I had to come down to this meeting. I'll be back in Anchorage tomorrow. I'll find them. I have important information from the meeting."

Billy was silent for a few moments. "What's your goddamn big news?"

Billy was quiet as Budge told him everything Ron Minty told him. When Budge finished, Billy said, "Shit."

"Yeah. I don't know what the hell we do now. We can't use Ron to help guide the board to our infrastructure investment . . . if we have one. Do we have one?"

Billy was fully alert now. "No, we don't. Trying to throw something big together at the last minute is bullshit. We're acting like a bunch of fucking amateurs. Does this Brooksher deal sound legitimate?"

"Yeah. Brooksher Energy is a heavyweight company. It sounds like Betsy Brooksher is a heavyweight, too. I guess a few billion dollars will do that for you. Her and Beth Saylor have a connection."

"There's that fucking name again. I've had about all I can take from the Saylors. They're right in the middle of everything we are trying to do. I need some sleep. We'll talk tomorrow. I need to think about this. Get off your ass and do something about Stan and that sorry Russian cunt."

When Billy hung up, Budge was pissed. *I've had about all I can take from that sorry bastard,* he thought. *He's the one I'd like to kill. But then, I'd be out of a job.*

The next morning, Budge was the first person seated in the public section of the conference room where the APFC held their board meeting. He watched with interest as the board members arrived. Beth Saylor looked crisp and businesslike in a gray two-piece suit. Budge was struck by her confident stride and an elegant hotness that her attire couldn't hide.

Ron Minty looked like death warmed over, and he quickly averted his eyes when he saw Budge sitting there. He had been right when he told Budge the meeting would be boring and over quickly. He was the only person sitting in the public section, and a few furtive looks from board members were shot his way. They adjourned the meeting at the lunch break. Budge checked out of the hotel and headed to the airport. His flight on Alaska Airlines left before The Bird lifted off.

Beth was the only board member who was seriously curious about Budge's presence, but she resisted the urge to ask Ron Minty about him. He had been coldly avoiding contact with her anyway, which suited her just fine.

Another creepy guy who's pissed because he can't get in my pants, and he doesn't realize how far away from that he always was.

Johnny Bosco's life in the Last Frontier was good. In fact, it was the best it had been since the fateful day when he returned to Las Vegas to find out his wife had left him and taken every asset he owned. That was still a bitter memory, but it was fading with the good things that were happening to him.

His rig job was going well. It was a foregone conclusion on the crew that he would have a driller's job before long. His previous experience, his work ethic, and his great attitude were the winning combination that would assure that. Everyone working on the rig also knew he was sent to Alaska by Taylor's drilling manager, Bobby Woods, and that didn't hurt Johnny's prospects with the company, either.

When he was in town, he continued his relationship with Carmen Sandy, and she spent almost every night at his cabin. He occasionally spent the night at her condo in Anchorage, although he preferred having her visit him at his cabin. His friendship with Marty Stevens had grown, and he visited him frequently. One evening, he surprised Marty with an invitation.

"You've been living out here a long time, Marty. How about coming to my cabin for dinner?" he said. "Let Carmen make whatever heathen meal you miss the most. She's a great cook. I'll buy some good wine and we'll have a nice dessert. It won't hurt you, I promise."

Marty laughed. "Okay, I'd love it. Let me think . . . no, I know. I would like to have rack of lamb . . . with mint sauce."

"Easy. Baked potato?"

Marty laughed again, a guilty laugh this time. "Fries . . . I think about fries sometimes. Lots of fries . . . with ketchup. And corn on the cob . . . I love corn on the cob."

Johnny laughed with him. "Okay, lots of fries, corn on the cob, and whatever else we can think of to surprise you."

Johnny and Carmen worked hard to prepare the meal for Marty. The rack of lamb was accompanied by mounds of French fries. Since it was early in the year, Carmen could only find frozen corn on the cob. With that, she served a fresh fruit-and-vegetable salad, using fruits and vegetables she knew Marty wasn't able to grow for himself.

They topped the meal off with vanilla ice cream sundaes topped with chocolate syrup, accompanied by a tawny port.

Marty sat on the bear rug in front of the fireplace with his second glass of port in hand. He was a satisfied man. "I haven't had a meal like that in . . . over ten years. It was wonderful. Thank you. You are a wonderful cook, Carmen."

It was the first time Carmen and Marty had spent much time around each other. "Thank you. You are a very interesting man, Marty. I mean, living clear out where you do. Don't you miss . . . things?"

"I don't dwell on *things*. I love the peace and serenity of my life. I love the physical part of my life. I work hard for everything, and I walk many miles to get the things I eat. I eat a great deal of fish, and lots of berries. I feel healthy. I do get a little lonesome some days . . . in the evening. I love the spirituality of my life. I am connected to the animals and the forest. I am connected with a superior being, although I am sometimes frustrated that I cannot identify him."

"Or her?"

Marty smiled. "Or her." Thoughtfully, he continued, "This will sound like my ego talking, but I am not used to drinking this much wine. I feel powerful. The life I live gives me power. I don't think I would feel this way if I rejoined your world. I guess I do miss . . ."

There was a long pause, and Carmen finally asked, "What, Marty?"

"A woman . . . I miss having a woman in my life."

Later in the evening, after Johnny had given Marty a ride back to his cabin on the four-wheeler, he was lying in bed with Carmen. "What do you think of Marty?"

"He is a fascinating man. If he lived in Anchorage, he'd be gobbled up in a heartbeat by the women I know."

"You kind of like him."

Carmen rolled over on her side and looked at Johnny. "I like him. I *really* like you."

Beth was back in Anchorage when her phone rang Saturday morning. She was surprised to see *Brooksher* on the caller ID display. "Hello, Betsy?"

"Yes, it is, Beth. I'm sorry about bothering you on Saturday, but I am anxious to get some information to you."

"I live a twenty-four–seven life, Betsy. Please don't apologize."

"You and me both. Well, I have talked with the people I would like to make the presentation to your board. I would like to bring Gaylord Tenant, he is the CEO of Brooksher Energy, and Jeremy Nygard, who is the CEO of Vancouver Island Natural Gas . . . and I am coming as well. We are anxious to get this thing moving, so we would like to schedule this within the next two weeks."

"That's great, Betsy. I will contact the board members as quickly as I can, and get back to you. I am very excited that you are coming, and I just thought of something. Would you like for us to send our plane for you? It's a Gulfstream 550, and it's very comfortable."

Betsy's muted laugh was followed by an apologetic answer. "Thank you, Beth. We'll be coming in the Brooksher corporate plane. It's a Boeing 757."

"Oh, well, okay. I guess you'll be alright then."

There's rich, thought Beth, *and then there's disgustingly wealthy.*

Beth handled a mix of reactions as she called each board member Saturday morning. Most of them were congenial. Some were excited and anxious to meet the people who were coming, including the billionaire widow. Ron Minty continued his pout.

"This is Saturday, Beth."

239

"I know that, Mr. Minty. I apologize. This call is about an issue that transcends normal behavior, or I would never call you on Saturday . . . never!"

Ron caught Beth's subliminal message, and it made him more combative. "I have two kids who are still sleeping. There's no school today."

"I can only apologize so much, Mr. Minty. The other board members all agree that they can clear their schedules next Friday. Can you clear your schedule Friday?"

"I'm not sure. I'm going to be very busy this week."

"Fine. I'm going to go ahead and set it up. We won't be making the final approval next Friday anyway, just listening to the presentation. We can go ahead without you."

Grudgingly, Ron said, "I'll try to be there."

"Okay, I'll get an email out with the exact time and place." With that, Beth ended the conversation, and quickly called Betsy back.

"Betsy, we are set for next Friday, if that works for you. I'll find a place to hold the meeting, and let you know exactly what time we will meet, and where."

"That's wonderful, Beth. I'll need a hotel reservation. Any suggestions?"

"The Susitna. I'm going to try to get a meeting room there. They have very nice executive suites."

"Okay, I'll have my secretary call them. Can you have them set up a PowerPoint projector for the meeting?"

Beth hung up and immediately began giving board members their second Saturday morning call.

There was nothing normal about the life Stan and Anna were living. They were holed up in a house at the Settler's Bay Golf Course that didn't belong to them, and the owner didn't know they were using it. A pissed-off gangster of a husband and his henchman were still looking for them, and they were running out of money.

Anna had become zombie-like. Her assumption that her life might end soon, or that her life in America might end soon, had put her in a silent funk. Stan's thoughts were tormented, and Anna complicated them by walking around the house naked most of the time. He was angry, angry at Billy Peet, angry at Budge Brown, angry at Anna, and mostly, angry at himself.

He spent hours pacing, beating himself up for his indiscretion, thinking, *you got yourself into this, you idiot . . . all for a piece of ass! We can't just sit here, we need to do something.*

Stan refused to make advances toward Anna, but her naked presence was finally getting to him. She aroused him, and the only way he could vent his sexual frustration was by going into the bathroom and masturbating.

This is sick, he would think. *You've got a beautiful, naked woman running around here, and you're in the bathroom getting yourself off!*

In repeated angry phone calls, Billy Peet was on Budge's butt constantly. "Haven't you found them yet? If you don't do something soon, I'm going to send someone up there to do your fucking job for you."

"I'm working on it. I have a lead."

Budge finally told Billy about the cell phone Herman had found.

"Get your ass up to Wasilla. Isn't that a little-bitty town? Camp out at the grocery store if you have to. They've got to eat."

"I've al . . ." Budge thought better about telling Billy he had already done that. Now desperate, he had another idea. "I've been planning on doing that. Remember, I just had to make that trip to Juneau. Have you thought about what I told you?"

Maybe I can get Billy off on another tangent, Budge thought.

"Yeah. I'm not sure what good it will do us, but I'm thinking about it. I'm pissing away a lot of money in Seattle *and* in Alaska, and nothing looks really right. The most important thing to me right now is knowing that little Commie bitch is dead . . . and her limp-dick friend, too. The only good thing right now is that I don't have to pay anything for the two of them. That's gonna save me way over a hundred grand a year."

Budge knew he had to do something drastic, but he decided not to tell Billy that he was going to break into Stan's office. He parked his car across from Stan's office building at 7:00 that evening. He saw two cleaning people moving through the offices one by one, turning the lights on and then turning them off after each office was cleaned.

It was after 9:00 when all the lights were turned off, except for the one in the foyer. It looked to Budge like the lights in the first-floor hallway were on, too. He watched one cleaning woman leave through the front door. A few minutes later, the remaining cleaning woman exited the building through the door at one end of the hallway with a large garbage bag in each hand. She dragged them across the parking lot to the Dumpster area at the back of the lot. She had to unlock the gate to the fenced-in area surrounding the Dumpster. Returning to the building she, picked up two more bags, and took them to the Dumpster, and then locked the gate and reentered the building. A few minutes later, the remaining lights went off, and the woman came out the front door, locking it behind her.

If she leaves the hallway door unlocked when she goes to the Dumpster, I can sneak into the building when she is inside the fenced area where the Dumpster sits, Budge thought.

The next night, wearing all black clothes and a tool belt with a small flashlight and tools in it, Budge parked across the street from the building again. He arrived at 8:00 to begin his wait. Right on schedule, a few minutes after 9:00, the same lights that had been on the night before were the only lights on, and one cleaning woman left the building. Budge left his car and sneaked around the opposite end of the building from the Dumpster. He moved along the back of the building, hugging the wall. He stopped at the end. From there he would be able to make a quick run to the door when the cleaning lady was inside the fenced Dumpster area.

Right on cue, the woman came out the door with two large garbage bags in hand. Budge made the instant decision to run to the door while she was dragging the bags across the parking lot. He was relieved to find the door unlocked. He quickly ducked inside and pulled the door closed just as the woman was unlocking the gate. She glanced back toward the building, but Budge was already hidden in the stairway to the second floor.

Hiding quietly in the stairway, he pictured the scraggly-haired woman in his mind as she came back into the building and picked up the two remaining garbage bags. A few minutes later she was back, and he heard her lock the door. She was only ten feet away from him, and through the closed door he could hear her make a cell phone call.

"Hey, baby. I'm done. I've been thinking about you. You still have a fantasy about fucking me on the conference-room table here? This is a good time. I'm all alone in this big building."

Shit, Budge thought, *you've got to be kidding me. Not tonight!* He couldn't avoid the mental picture of the chubby, overly made-up woman naked on the conference room table.

"What? You're too tired? I'm the one working all goddamn day and all goddamn night. . . . All you've done is sit on your ass in that fucking trailer and drink beer."

The woman's tirade faded away as she walked down the hall toward the front door. "I'm going to take all my clothes off and walk outside, and then I'm going to fuck the first guy I see. What? I did not! But I would tonight, I . . ."

A few minutes later, Budge saw the light under the doorway disappear. He quietly ventured into the dark hallway. The light in the foyer was also off, and the building was quiet. Just to be safe, he waited another five minutes before he turned his small flashlight on and continued up the stairs to the second floor.

Budge expertly picked the lock to Stan's office suite. The first thing he looked at was the phone-set on Polly's desk. By playing back the Calls function, he was able to see that Stan was calling in every day from his cell phone . . . information that did him no good. There were lots of other numbers, but no pattern of any particular one appearing on a regular basis.

He went into Stan's office and looked at his calls. Nothing for the last week. He recognized earlier calls from Billy. Budge opened all of the drawers in Stan's desk and clumsily thumbed through an assortment of files with this gloved hands. Most of the files related to real estate transactions.

Frustrated, Budge went through Stan's Rolodex, from A to Z. Nothing stood out. There were scribbled notes on his desk calendar, and nothing stood out there either. He noticed a manila folder lying on the desk that had *Listings* written on it, and he opened it. He looked through the listings, one at a time. Halfway through the folder, he came upon one that grabbed his attention.

Lovely Settler's Bay home overlooks the fifteenth fairway on the golf course. Call listing broker, Stan Faro, to see this property. Excited, Budge skipped the details and found the address: *1223 Bear Run Road, Settler's Bay Golf Course.*

There was a handwritten note in the folder that stated, *Stan buddy, please sell this for me. If we can't get a buyer, I'll take a lease, but I want at least six months. Would consider a lease with an option to buy. I won't be back to Alaska until the end of May. Keep me posted. Sam.*

Out loud, Budge said to himself, "Bingo." He tried to make the offices look undisturbed, and left the building. Unable to lock the door at the end of the hallway from the outside without a key, he left it unlocked. Over her futile protests that she had locked the door, the poor cleaning woman was fired the next day for failing to lock it. It would be the best of the consequences of Budge's visit to the building.

The next morning, Budge rented another nondescript car. His only strange requirement was that it couldn't be white, the color of the car he had rented the week before. The rental-car clerk obliged him with a dark green sedan. By early afternoon, he circled through the Settler's Bay subdivision and located the house that belonged to Sam. It did not look lived in, but there was light smoke coming from the furnace chimney. It was still very cool in early May, and you would need some heat to be comfortable in the house. Budge was sure the two-car garage had a cream-colored Lexus parked inside.

Budge spent the afternoon driving around the area. He stopped long enough to have a couple beers and a hamburger. The reality of what he was going to do that night put him in a solemn mood. He didn't care about Stan, but he didn't like to hurt a woman. He would make it quick. If Sam wasn't going to return until late May, it would be almost a month before they would be discovered. That part of it was perfect.

Budge waited until 10:00 that night. By then it was dark and quiet in the neighborhood. He had picked his parking spot earlier—he would have to walk a couple hundred yards through the woods to get to the house. In the same black clothes he'd worn the night before, he worked his way through the trees and the alder to get to the house. From the back of it, he could see through a window in the rear door. Stan was pacing in the living room, a bottle of bourbon in his right hand.

"Anna, get your ass out here. We've got to talk." Stan was drunk. "Come on. Get your little Russian ass out here."

From outside, Budge was surprised to see Anna walk into the living room naked.

"What? What is it now, Mr. Stan? You're drunk."

"I don't care how drunk I am, we've got to get out of here. Tomorrow, we've got to leave. I've got a friend in the police department. Sergeant Baker, Bob Baker. He works in Missing Persons, but he would help us. We've got to get out of here. I called and left a message for him earlier today. I'm going to try to meet with him tomorrow."

With resignation, Anna said, "I don't care, Mr. Stan. I am going to have to go back to Russia. I don't care about anything."

"Yeah, including clothes."

"You don't like to see me naked?"

"I don't care. You being naked is what got us into this mess. This is all your fault."

"You've said that already, Mr. Stan. It's your fault, too." Hopefully, Anna added, "If I could stay with you, I wouldn't have to go back to Russia."

"No, neither one of us would have to worry, because Billy would kill us. You think I want that fucker after me for the rest of my life? You want to rub salt into the wound?"

"What wound?"

"It's just a saying."

Anna approached Stan and tried to put her arms around him. "Please, Mr. Stan. Please help me stay in America. I can't go back . . . I just can't." Now Anna began to cry softly.

Stan pushed her away, but he did it gently.

"Tomorrow . . . tomorrow we go," he said quietly.

Budge watched the scene playing out in front of him, having to be content to imagine what they were saying. Seeing Anna naked made him realize why Stan was in the mess he was in. *Jesus,* he thought, *I'd be all over that too.*

By midnight, Stan was passed out in a big chair in the living room. Budge decided to take care of Anna first because he was confident Stan would not wake up. He picked the lock to the rear door of the garage. The door that led into the house was behind the Lexus and a black SUV that obviously belonged to Sam. Budge easily picked the simple lock on the door and he walked through a laundry room and into a hallway. He could see the light from the living room at the end of the hall, and heard the television. There was a stream of light coming from a closed door that Budge assumed was a bedroom. He approached the door and listened for a few minutes. There were no sounds coming from the room. He cracked the door open.

Budge could see through the small opening that Anna was sound asleep. She had her covers pulled up around her neck, and there was a small bedside lamp on. Budge eased his way into the room and approached the side of the bed. He stared at Anna for a few moments, and then quickly pulled the covers down far enough to get his big hands around her neck. Anna's eyes flashed open, and she began to struggle violently, but she was helpless under the covers. She wasn't able to make a sound as Budge held her down and applied enough pressure to her neck to prevent her from breathing. In a few moments, she went limp.

Bloodless Budge flashed through Budge's mind as he was killing Anna. It was the name Billy had tagged him with because of his unwillingness to kill anybody with a knife or a gun. He held his grip on Anna's neck for another minute, just to make sure he had done his job. Then, he released her and stood up. He couldn't resist the thought, so he pulled the covers down to get a close look at Anna's naked body.

Jesus, he thought again, *no wonder.*

Budge went into the living room. He circled the inebriated Stan a couple times, thinking . . . *poor simple slob, I have to kill you because you laid the wrong woman.* He quickly disposed of Stan. Getting hold of a drunk from behind and breaking his neck was an easy job that took him just a couple of minutes. He left Stan in the chair. Making sure the shades and drapes in the house were all closed and the lights were off, Budge slipped out the back door and made his way to the rental car. He didn't want to imagine what the house would smell like when Sam opened the door at the end of May.

No matter what the cause, instant and unexpected death brings an overwhelming sense of the loss of promise.
—From *Fred Longcoor's Book on Life*

Chapter 18

Betsy in Alaska

"You're going where?" Raymond couldn't believe it when Betsy told him that she was going to Alaska to meet with the Alaska Permanent Fund Corporation.

"Yes, I and the CEO of Brooksher Energy and the CEO of Vancouver Island Natural Gas . . . this Thursday."

Raymond was curious, but didn't want to appear that way. He tried to sound casually interested as he said, "Oh. What's going on in Alaska?"

Betsy put on her best demure look and said, "Well, Reverend, I can't really say right now."

Uncomfortably, he replied, "Oh, okay," while thinking, *Brooksher Energy and Vancouver Island Natural Gas. I wonder what the hell that's all about.*

"I'd ask you to go with me, Reverend, but this has to be a private business trip. I don't mean that I don't trust you, but it would not be appropriate for you to be along, particularly with the CEO of Vancouver Island Natural Gas going with us. I'll tell you about it when I get back." Then, Betsy winked and said, "If I can."

Raymond called Billy that evening. "What the fuck do you want, Reverend?"

Coolly, Raymond said, "I thought you might like to know that Betsy is going to Alaska this week to meet with the Alaska Permanent Fund Corporation, and she's taking the CEO of Brooksher Energy with her . . . and the CEO of something called Vancouver Island Natural Gas."

Suddenly, Billy became civil. "That's very interesting. What's

247

Brooksher Energy?"

"Mostly oil and gas projects. I mean, they are involved in some wind and solar projects, but it's mostly oil and gas."

"And what about this Vancouver whatever?"

"Vancouver Island Natural Gas, and I don't know anything about them. I can try and find something out."

"Okay, I'll have Benny dig into this, too. Sounds to me like they are presenting some kind of a joint venture to the Permanent Fund boys."

"Boys and girls. Betsy said there are two women on the board of trustees."

"Okay, smart ass."

Raymond's line went dead. Billy was his old self again.

Billy started to become his old self again after Budge called and told him not to worry about Stan and Anna anymore. He didn't really care about Stan, but privately, he was grieving over Anna. It was part of a complicated love-hate process he needed to go through. When it got him down, he would think, *come on, you're a fucking tough guy. Get over it. She was just flesh and bones. Get another one.*

For Budge, it was just a job. In fact, once he found them, it was an easy job. It was not personal. He just looked at it as an easy way to make twenty thousand dollars.

Three days after Budge killed Stan and Anna, Sergeant Bob Baker called Faro-Way Properties looking for Stan. Polly answered the phone. "Faro-Way Properties, this is Polly."

"Polly, this is Sergeant Bob Baker, APD. Stan tried to get hold of me a few days ago. He left me a message. Could I talk to him, please?"

"Well sir, Mr. Faro is not available right now. Could I take a message?"

"Polly, this is not police business, at least I don't think it is. Stan is an old friend of mine. We did some Little League umpiring together."

Polly was relieved. "Then I'm really glad you called. I was afraid . . . something bad had happened. Stan left here early last week. Said he had a family emergency. I don't know where he went. He was calling me every day from his cell phone, but now he hasn't called me in almost four days. I'm worried."

Sergeant Baker's policeman antenna went up. "Do you know where his ex-wife is, Polly?"

"No, I'm sorry. I haven't worked for him long enough to know a lot about his personal life."

"Well, Polly, it's probably nothing, but I happen to work for our Missing Persons Department. I can do some checking. For one thing, I can find out where the cell phone calls are coming from. I have the number. If I find anything out, I will call you."

"I'm scared, Sergeant Baker. The company account is almost out of money, and I have bills to pay."

"I'll try to help you, Polly."

Sergeant Baker knew Stan Faro well enough to know that this was not typical behavior for him. When he arrived at his office, he immediately ordered one of his detectives to check cell phone records, and it was not long before the young detective returned with some information.

"Settler's Bay, boss. They've pinpointed a house with some GPS help. It's twelve twenty-three Bear Run Road. Most of the calls are coming from there. A few are scattered around Wasilla. That house is right on the golf course. Want me to go out there, or do you want me to call the Wasilla PD?"

"No, I'll go . . . but I want you to go with me."

Excitedly, Detective Tim Parks hurried to get his coat.

When the policemen arrived at the Settler's Bay housing development, Sergeant Baker parked his car about two blocks from the address they had confirmed as they drove by it. "Okay Tim, let's approach carefully, then take a position where we can observe the house for a little while without being seen."

"Gotcha, boss."

They found a spot about fifty yards from the house where they were out of sight in the woods. There were still patches of snow on the ground, and it was chilly, but both of them were warmed by their adrenaline rush.

"I have a feeling, Tim . . . and it's not a good one." Even though there were no obvious signs of any kind of disturbance around the property, Sergeant Baker's years of experience in Homicide and Missing Persons had given him an extra sense for trouble.

Sergeant Baker's words put a tingle in Tim's gut. All he could say was, "Yeah."

After thirty agonizing minutes, Sergeant Baker said, "Let's go. I'll ring the front doorbell. You wait at the corner of the house . . . with your piece ready."

Nervously now, Tim mumbled, "Okay, boss."

"Sergeant . . . Bob, or even Officer Baker . . . but not boss. You make me sound like a goddamn construction foreman."

"Okay b . . . .Sergeant! Sorry."

Sergeant Baker rang the doorbell several times. It was quiet. There was no indication anybody was moving around in the house. He moved away from the front door and signaled for Tim to follow him around to the back of the house. At the back door, he looked through the same glass Budge had looked through. "Shit!"

"What?" Tim said anxiously.

Bob saw Stan Faro's body slumped over in the chair. He knew the look of someone who was not just sleeping or passed out. "It's Stan . . . he's dead."

"Shit!" echoed Tim.

"Go get the car, Tim. Call this in. Get Wasilla PD out here pronto, and tell them we need the coroner, too. We've got at least one dead body. Anybody has questions, give them my cell number."

Sergeant Baker was sitting on a large decorative rock in the front yard when Wasilla PD arrived fifteen minutes later. Detective Parks was pacing around the yard like a caged tiger. "Shouldn't we break in, Sergeant?"

"This isn't our case, young gun. This is Wasilla's case. I can see one dead body." Quietly, Sergeant Baker added, "A friend of mine . . . Stan Faro."

Two policemen got out of the car and identified themselves.

"What do we have here?"

"I'm Sergeant Baker, APD Missing Persons. This is Detective Parks. I'm on a case, and I found my MP. I saw him through the back window . . . in the chair. He's very dead. We did not enter the house."

"Good. Let's take a look." The middle-aged police officer led the group around to the back of the house and looked through the window.

"He's dead alright." Looking at his young officer companion, he said, "Get it open . . . and be prepared."

"For someone in the house?"

"No . . . for the smell."

The young officer forced the door open with his shoulder, and then jumped back, yelling, "Jesus!" He quickly pulled the door closed.

The older officer laughed and said, "Let's wait for the coroner. He'll have some masks." Right on cue, the coroner pulled in the driveway.

Tim Parks had seen dead people before, but they were usually victims of recent accidents. He had never seen the discolored, bloated bodies of people who had been dead for days. And he had never smelled anything like it. He ran around to the side of the house so nobody would see him puke.

Sergeant Baker listened to the coroner's clinical description of what he believed was the cause of death for both people. "The girl was asphyxiated . . . strangled . . . right where she is lying. Young and pretty . . . before. Whoever did it is probably very strong. Your friend's neck was snapped like a twig. Probably the same muscle guy. I'd say your vic' was drunk.

That's not forensics, it's because of the almost empty bottle of hooch on the floor next to the chair. Probably smell it if it wasn't for the other smell. My guess is that they both died about the same time. Your guy was probably passed out, and the girl was probably killed first."

The case was out of Sergeant Baker's jurisdiction, so he and Detective Parks were on their way back to Anchorage within a couple of hours of giving the Wasilla PD the information they had. As they were driving, he turned to Detective Parks and asked, "Did you get it all out?"

Tim knew what the sergeant meant, but he sheepishly asked, "What?"

Bob laughed at the young detective, and said, "You know what. Don't be embarrassed. Happened to me too . . . the first time."

When they were back in Anchorage, Sergeant Baker called Polly Hasey.

"Polly? This is Sergeant Baker. I'm afraid I have some bad news. I want you to hear it from me before you see it on the news tonight."

"Oh no . . . what is it?"

When Polly calmed down after hearing that Stan was dead, Sergeant Baker told her that she needed to collect herself and notify their clients. "I know Stan was on the board at Arctic North Bank. I know Henry Kuban. I'll call him for you. I know about the ex-wife, did he have other relatives?"

"No . . . well, I don't think so. And there's some guy who calls all the time, too. Billy Peet. I think he's like, a business partner . . . from outside of Alaska."

"Someone from APD or from Wasilla PD will call the ex-wife if you call them and give them a number. Give me the business partner's number. I'll call him for you, too. One more thing. Did Stan have a girlfriend . . . real pretty blonde?"

"Mr. Faro? No, I don't ever recall him even talking about having a date. I think he was . . . kinda lonely."

The staff at Executive Air Service had seen many notables come in and out of their air-service center in Anchorage . . . actors, athletes, musicians, politicians, and people who were just rich enough to own private airplanes. They were excited about the arrival of Betsy Brooksher, not because she was one of the wealthiest people in America, but because of her airplane. They had never serviced a privately owned Boeing 757 at their facility.

Vince Martin arranged to park the Saylors' limousine inside the fenced area at Executive Air Service. They would be near Betsy's plane when it was parked. Beth climbed out the back door before Vince could get around to open it for her.

"Are you a little anxious, Ms. Saylor?" Vince said with a mischievous grin on his face.

"You are about to meet one of the nicest and richest women in the world, Vince. Be a good boy."

VInce kept the grin on his face as he snapped his heels together and saluted.

"Yes ma'am."

Beth waited alongside the limo while the pilots shut the engines down on the huge jet. Once the door was open and the air-stairs were in place, Betsy's party began to exit. A steward in a white Nero jacket and navy blue pants led two men down the stairs, followed by Betsy. Both men wore expensive-looking topcoats that were not buttoned, revealing dark three-piece suits underneath. Betsy followed in a stunning full-length black cashmere coat that had a hint of her bright red dress showing.

Beth moved toward the stairway to greet them. The first big man in line put a hand out and said, "Ms. Saylor, I presume. I am Gaylord Tenant, Brooksher Energy's CEO." He turned to the man behind him and said, "This is Jeremy Nygard, the CEO of Vancouver Island Natural Gas."

"I am very happy to meet you, Mr. Tenant, and you, Mr. Nygard. Welcome to the Last Frontier."

Betsy was right behind Jeremy, and she rushed to Beth with her arms out. "Beth, it is so wonderful to see you . . . and so wonderful to be in Alaska. The scenery when we flew over Prince William Sound was spectacular. Glaciers, islands, snowcapped mountains . . . beautiful."

"It's wonderful to see you too, Betsy. And you're right about Alaska. Sometimes we are blasé because we see it all the time . . . and we shouldn't be. Come on, Vince will take us to the hotel."

On the way to the Susitna Hotel, Beth told the group their meeting with the Alaska Permanent Fund Corporation's Board of Trustees was set up in the Foraker Room at the Susitna, where the board normally met. It was scheduled for 9:00 the next morning.

Beth felt like a tour guide as they drove through Anchorage. She answered an assortment of personal and business questions from her three guests, particularly from Jeremy Nygard. Beth speculated that he wanted to get a good feel for the people his company was thinking about partnering with.

The group checked into the hotel, and they met at 6:00 for dinner in the Denali Room. With its spectacular view of the area surrounding Anchorage, the top-floor restaurant at the hotel was the perfect place for a great dinner that impressed their out-of-town guests. It also gave them an informal opportunity to get to know each other better before the business presentation the next day.

When everyone was settled in the conference room the next morning, Executive Director Richard Cally turned to Beth and said, "Beth, you are the only one here who knows everyone. Would you please introduce our guests?"

"Yes, Mr. Cally." Betsy and her two traveling companions stood as they were introduced. Each board member in turn introduced themselves.

Richard Cally looked at Betsy and spoke. "Mrs. Brooksher, we are honored to have you and your guests here. Thank you for coming to Alaska. We are anxious to hear your proposal. Please proceed."

Betsy did not look or act like an overwhelmed widow of a business tycoon as she addressed the room. She was stately and confident as she spoke. "Thank you, Mr. Cally, and I want to thank your board members for being here as well. And, a special thanks to you, Beth, for helping to facilitate this meeting. Mr. Tenant will take you through the introductory part of this presentation, and then Mr. Nygard will present the details of the proposal. All this information is on the PowerPoint presentation, and you all have a copy of that in front of you. Please feel free to ask questions at any time during the presentation."

Gaylord Tenant presented general information about Brooksher Energy, including the obligatory statement about Brooksher's commitment to alternative forms of energy.

"We are a green company. We are involved in numerous recycling projects and we are constantly evaluating new ways to use wind and solar power. In fact, we have existing wind-energy and solar-energy projects that are active in six western states. We are also exploring exciting opportunities to use the power of the oceans and the ocean tides . . . including the tremendous tidal currents in the Cook Inlet in Alaska. As you know, those tidal currents are the second largest in the world. I might add that we are well aware of the fact that Alaska holds one-sixth of the world's coal reserves. We have even done some research on underground coal gasification."

That comment created a murmur in the room.

"While we try to react to the realities of today's energy demands and the fact that oil and gas are nonrenewable resources, we can't ignore the realistic demands for fossil fuels that will exist for many years to come. Internal-combustion engines will be around for a long time. Try to imagine a Boeing 757 like the one we flew to Alaska in yesterday flying on solar power. Oil appears to be a more finite resource than natural gas, and there are about four thousand byproducts that come from oil, not just gasoline, diesel, and jet fuel. Natural gas is the only resource that can become a reasonable replacement for gasoline, diesel, and jet fuel. Obviously, using alternative sources of energy as a replacement for the three petroleum-based fuels frees up more oil to be used for plastics, medicines, and the other four thousand byproducts of oil that are part of our everyday lives."

Jerry Holter spoke first. "So, Mr. Tenant, if I can speculate on where you are heading, you are proposing to replace a finite, nonrenewable resource with another finite, nonrenewable resource?"

"That is basically true, Mr. Holter. We feel like the world needs to face our energy future with honesty. As I said, we will need petroleum products for many years to come, and we feel that we need to manage that resource. We are not suggesting that the world abandon the drive to find alternative forms of energy. Recently, the industry has come to recognize the tremendous quantities of natural gas this planet holds, and it is available in many places. For example, non-associated reserves of natural gas on the North Slope of Alaska are estimated to be close to fifty trillion cubic feet. That's trillion. And there are many trillion more cubic feet of natural gas that are associated with oil reserves." Gaylord stopped for a moment to let his words sink in. "Are there any other questions?"

The room was quiet. "Alright, if there are no more questions, I'd like to turn this over to Jeremy Nygard, CEO of Vancouver Island Natural Gas."

Jeremy Nygard stood up deliberately. He was an imposing presence at the front of the room, and Beth was sure he wanted the board members to feel his power. "Good morning, ladies and gentlemen. Thank you for inviting us to your wonderful city in this amazing state. I have worked in the oil and gas industry for over thirty years. I retired from US Oil and Gas five years ago and joined Vancouver Island Natural Gas. I did that because I was presented with a tremendous opportunity, and because I believe in the future of natural gas as an alternative source of energy. Yes, I said alternative source of energy . . . an alternative to oil."

Mr. Nygard spent the next hour defining the history and scope of his company's LNG project. His presentation included slide after slide of information on oil reserves, gas reserves, and existing long-term supply contracts for natural gas use in the Lower Forty-eight. He also had art-ists' renderings of the liquefaction plant on the North Slope and the LNG plants in Valdez and on Vancouver Island.

"Simply put, ladies and gentlemen, we believe your state has missed the boat in terms of getting North Slope gas to market. It is too expensive, and competing companies have outmuscled your state. Foreign suppliers and forward-thinking distributors have made the financial commitments necessary to build LNG plants, LNG ships, and the related distribution infrastructure to support long-term contracts . . . while your State government and the North Slope producers have haggled over which pipeline to build and when to build it. Most of the contracts already signed by the companies your state is competing with are for thirty years."

Ron Minty spoke up. "I have two questions. If all that business is in place, why will your proposal work? And, will you name the North Slope producer who is supplying the gas?"

"Good questions, Mr. Minty. Two reasons on your first question. Transportation cost, including the estimated thirty to forty billion–dollar cost of a pipeline, is a huge obstacle for delivery of North Slope gas. In our case, in relative terms, it is a short distance from Valdez to Vancouver Island, and we will be using the existing Trans-Alaska Pipeline to get the liquefied gas down from Prudhoe Bay. Secondly, there is not an adequate supply of natural gas available for the future in the Pacific Northwest. Therein lies the strength of our position. Importantly, we are almost through the planning and permitting process, with no other competing company anywhere else on the horizon."

Jeremy was quiet for several moments.

Ron said, "And my second question?"

"I'm sorry, Ron, I was trying to analyze the ramifications of revealing the name of our heretofore silent supplier partner now. I guess the time is right. It is GB Petroleum. They are also a part owner of the project, and not just the supplier of the gas."

Now, the room buzzed again. Mary Brunser spoke up. "You have a heavyweight player involved in this project. What about the other end of the supply chain? Do you have commitments from customers?"

"I'm glad you asked that, Mary. Yes we do. We have contingency agreements with two major distributers in Washington and Oregon. We also are in discussions with two others, another one in Oregon, and one in Idaho. We'll name them all and produce supporting documents when we move to the next phase of this relationship."

Richard Cally then asked, "With GB Petroleum in this with you, why do you need Brooksher now, and why would you need us?"

"More good questions, Mr. Cally. First of all, Brooksher has been part of this from the beginning. They are a major participant, a major owner if you will, in this project. Del Brooksher was a visionary businessman, and now Betsy is happily carrying the ball after him. We simply would like to strengthen our cash position. Our primary lender would like to see us put some additional cash into the project, even if it means we have to give up some percentage of our ownership. The amount of cash we are talking about would be unencumbered seed money we could begin to distribute to our assorted major contractors right away without having to go through the process of making draws from our lenders. Simply stated, it is money that would enable us to get going right away."

Now, Executive Director Cally asked the question that was on everyone's mind. "How much cash are you looking for, and what percentage of the overall project would that give us?"

Jeremy laughed. "You can count on the executive director to ask the money question."

Everyone laughed with Jeremy, and the tension in the room eased a little.

"Well, Mr. Cally, we are proposing to give up one percent of the project . . . for one hundred million dollars. We wouldn't require the money until we receive all the permits and we are ready to move forward. Brooksher Energy is represented here because we would want you to make your investment through their company. The reason for that is so we don't compromise or complicate the permitting process at this late stage of the game. Brooksher's ownership position would be increased by one percent, and they would simply transfer the money to VING, or to the contractors and suppliers we designate."

Each board member was running all of the ramifications of what they had heard through their heads. Nobody spoke for a few moments, and then Richard Cally said, "Thank you for your very thorough presentation. You have given us a lot to think about. My immediate reaction is positive. However, we have lawyers and financial advisors who will need to get involved in this. Do you have a formal proposal?"

"Yes sir, we do. Gaylord, could you give that packet to Mr. Cally?"

The group stayed in the room for another hour. Dozens of questions were asked and answered, and it was a satisfied group that broke for lunch. In the dining area of the Turnagain Room downstairs, Betsy signaled for Beth to sit next to her.

"What do you think, Beth?"

"I'm very impressed, Betsy. It's huge, but it all makes sense. Sort of the right idea at the right time. Thank you for telling me about it."

"We owe *you* and your board thanks if this all goes the way I think it will. The timing was right. We would have been out there looking for an investor, and nobody would have ever thought of the Alaska Permanent Fund Corporation."

"We'll meet next week and dig into your proposal. We'll get all the financial and legal guys involved. A hundred million dollars is a lot of money, but it's not unprecedented for the fund to make that kind of investment. It just seems so right, I mean, Alaska natural gas, a major producer in Alaska as a partner, your company as a partner. I like it."

"I agree, Beth. If we get this done, we will really celebrate."

"Sounds great to me."

The phone-set buzzed in the small tidy office. Robert was barely able to hear it over the hum of the server and the half dozen PCs that were on in the room. It was his direct line, and he picked up the receiver.

"Hello, this is Robert."

A silky voice answered, "How is my handsome little computer nerd today?"

"I'm fine, I guess."

"What do you mean, you guess?"

"I mean I'm tired of being stuck in this fucking little cave of an office. I'm horny. I miss you. I need to see you."

"Baby, you know we can't do that right now. Be patient. It won't be long. I can call you at home tonight and give you phone sex."

"That just makes it worse. I'm getting tired of whacking off. I may have to go out . . . find somebody, anybody."

"Don't piss me off, Robert. You know what happens when you piss me off."

"Oh. You going to put some big bad curse on me?"

"No, actually, what I would do is get someone to come over and break one of your legs."

"You would do that to me?"

"You would cheat on me?"

"Okay, we've been here before. I'm just fucking bored."

"Hang in there, baby. I'll call you tonight."

In Seattle, Reverend Raymond was enjoying a day when he didn't have to answer to Betsy, and looking forward to an evening when he could go out by himself and have a couple drinks and some dinner. Thanks to Betsy's generosity, he could afford to go anywhere he wanted to.

Raymond was about ready to leave the Brooksher Building when Theodore came to his open door. "Are you leaving, Reverend?"

"I was thinking about it, Theodore. What's up?"

"Well, we have a large electronic cash transfer coming in tonight. About an hour after everyone leaves. I need to be here to transfer it to one of our subsidiaries right away. Remember what I told you about the security rule? If there is a transfer for more than ten thousand dollars coming in or going out, I need to have an observer in the Secure Room? Last week,

I asked Mrs. Brooksher if it would be alright to use you as an observer, and she said she trusted you so it was okay. I thought it would be better if we didn't have to sneak around. You were interested, so I thought you might not mind doing that."

Suddenly, Raymond's freedom getaway was not important. "I'd be more than happy to do that, Theodore. I'll stick around. Thank you."

Raymond anxiously puttered around his office until almost 6:00. Most of the building was dark, and all of the employees were gone . . . with the exception of Theodore, who stuck his head in Raymond's door and said, "Ready, Reverend?"

Raymond followed Theodore to the Secure Room. When they were inside, they waited for a few moments, and then one of the computers signaled that there was a new message for Theodore:

J.B., sender United Industries, ID # 4041UI, is ready to transmit. Are you ready?

Theodore quickly typed out a reply:

Theodore A. Pemberton, Brooksher, ID # 1217BA, is ready to receive.

Raymond was excited as the electronic transfer started to take place. Theodore explained what was happening. "In this case, we are coordinating the transfer of money from United Industries' bank through our system and into the bank of our subsidiary, Brooksher International Holdings, which happens to be an offshore bank."

Raymond watched an assortment of acronyms, numbers and letters scroll across the screen. "What is EFT?"

"That means electronic funds transfer. All the rest of that crap is the financial cryptography. United Industries security numbers, our security numbers, all of that. Bank information, too." Theodore laughed and said, "Here is the main number."

Raymond's eyes got big as he saw, *26,000,000.00 US* scroll across the screen, followed by, *Transmission complete.*

"Holy sh . . . shucks! Is that twenty-six million dollars?"

Theodore laughed again. "Yup. I've seen way bigger ones. Now, we've got to move it to our subsidiary's bank." With that, Theodore turned to work on the computer keyboard. Very quickly, a large warning message came across the screen. *Unknown Receiver!*

"What is that?"

"That's the warning system I told you about the first night I showed this to you. This bank is relatively new to us, and that's a bug we haven't removed yet." Proudly, he continued, "As I said, I can override it."

Raymond decided to push his luck. "How do you do that?"

"I just put an override code in."

Raymond pushed his luck further. "How'd you come up with an override code."

"Simple stuff. You need letters and numbers, at least four of each, and today's date. I used my birthday . . . and . . . and."

Raymond decided to use his bluff again. "Oh, that's alright, you don't have to tell me."

Embarrassed, Theodore continued, "No, it's alright. It's my birthday, and BRIT. I'm a little embarrassed to admit it, but I love Britney Spears . . . even though she gets a little strange now and then. "

Got it, thought Raymond. *It should be easy to find out his birth date.* Silently, he watched Theodore complete the transfer, mentally cataloging each function he performed on the computer.

After the transfer was complete, Raymond thanked Theodore, and decided he now owed himself a night out more than he did before. Familiarity pushed him to The Rusty Turtle, and he called for a cab to pick him up and drop him off there after he went to his room and changed his clothes.

Raymond did not want to go out as Reverend Raymond, so he went home and changed into his black pants and black shirt. He took his black sport coat out of the clothes bag in his closet and put it on. The only part of his black identity he left in his room was his black Stetson.

Raymond walked into The Rusty Turtle and headed straight to the bar. Occasionally, he felt like having a martini night, and this was one of those times. When he sat down, the bartender turned, looked at him, and smiled. *Shit,* thought Raymond, *it's the same bartender who was here when I met Betsy for lunch.*

"Back again . . . uh, sir."

"Yeah, I'm off duty tonight. I'd like a martini, up. Your best vodka. Rub a little vermouth on the glass."

"Gotcha." Reaching across the bar, he added, "I'm Wade."

Surprised, Raymond took his hand and said, "Oh, uh, nice to meet you. I'm, uh, Ray."

"Alright Ray, I'll fix you right up."

I never worry about the big guy with the big mouth who comes into the place and tells everybody how tough he is. It's the quiet little cowboy sitting in the booth that I don't want to piss off.

(Bar owner in a small South Dakota town)
—From *Fred Longcoor's Book on Life*

Chapter 19

Let's Make a Deal

Betsy and her traveling contingent returned to Seattle the morning after making their presentation to the Alaska Permanent Fund Corporation, confident that their meeting had gone well. They also left with a level of comfort after rubbing against the financial power of the APFC.

Betsy moved around the luxurious lounge in the big jet with a cup of coffee in her hand, playing the role of lead cheerleader for the merger of Brooksher Energy, Vancouver Island Natural Gas, and APFC. "What do you think, Jeremy? I think this is a marriage made in heaven. Alaska has more money than most small countries, and I trust Beth Saylor . . . I have known her family for a long time."

Jeremy Nygard was always measured in his responses, and his deliberate reply to Betsy fit him perfectly. "Mrs. Brooksher, I believe the people we met with are very professional, very aware of their responsibility to the people of the State of Alaska, and maybe most importantly, I believe they are not afraid to visit new frontiers." Jeremy hesitated for a moment and then added, "I guess that sounds a little ironic when I'm talking about people who refer to their state as the Last Frontier, but there is no question about their financial viability."

"Good, Jeremy. I am glad to hear that you feel that way." Turning toward Gaylord Tenant, she continued, "What do you think, Gaylord?"

Knowing the company line would be expected, but not being the kind of executive who felt a need to suck up to Mrs. Brooksher, he said, "I agree with Jeremy. We do have to make sure this is the best thing for us, but we definitely don't have to worry about having a business partner like the State of Alaska. What do you think it will take to move this forward?"

"Beth told me this is on their front burner. It just takes a consensus approval of the board of trustees. She said she would push for a meeting with their lawyers and advisors on Monday or Tuesday, and hope to get full board approval by Wednesday . . . Thursday or Friday at the latest."

By late afternoon on Monday, Beth had successfully spearheaded a drive to get all the necessary players into a meeting on Tuesday morning. She also provided a copy of the proposal Gaylord Tenant gave her for the APFC legal department and their primary financial advisors on Monday morning. When everything was in place, she called Richard Cally.

"Richard. Beth. We're all set for tomorrow morning. Nine o'clock . . . in the large conference room. We're going to have a big group."

"Great, Beth. I really appreciate the way you've taken the lead on this . . . all of this. This could be the beginning of something really special. I *am* concerned about how the governor is going to handle it, though. You know she's been pushing for a pipeline."

"I think she is a very sensible person, Richard. If this makes sense for the state, I think she'll get behind it. This *is* going to stir the pot, though . . . if we approve it."

"You may have to take the lead on that too, Beth."

"What do you mean?"

"With the governor. I know you get along with her. You may have to sell her on what we are doing if we go ahead with this. I mean, we can approve this without her, but it would be nice if she took a public stance supporting this investment."

Sergeant Baker had been busy, too. By Monday afternoon, he had called Billy's cell phone a dozen times without an answer. It wasn't particularly alarming to him because he didn't feel Billy was someone close enough to Stan to require personal notification about his death. He had no way of knowing Billy was intentionally ignoring any calls from numbers in Alaska he didn't recognize.

Bob managed to get hold of Henry Kuban Saturday morning, before the news about Stan and Anna became public information.

"Henry, this is Sergeant Bob Baker, APD. I apologize for bothering you at home on the weekend, but I need to talk with you."

Henry's insides went into an instant churn. *Oh fuck*, he thought.

261

Something from my past just caught up to me. "Hey Bob, no problem. What's up?"

Bob recognized the strain in Henry's voice and thought, *Don't worry, Henry. I know more about your past than you realize, and that isn't what this is about.*

"Something has happened to one of your board members. It's Stan Faro. I'm afraid he has been murdered."

The instant relief made the shock Henry blurted out sound legitimate. "Jesus. What happened?"

"I can't talk about it too much. The investigation is ongoing. He was killed in a house in Wasilla. There was someone with him, but I can't talk about that right now, either. I just wanted you to know. You're not on the official notification list."

"Oh . . . well, thank you, Bob."

Sergeant Baker made a follow-up call to Polly Hasey and updated her on what he had done. After telling her about being unable to contact Billy Peet, he asked her to have Billy call him if he called the office. Now, the case was really out of his hands. APD was not involved, and that meant that APD Missing Persons was definitely not involved. In spite of that, with his mind free of any other responsibilities, he was becoming more curious about the mysterious Billy Peet.

In Montana, Billy Peet continued to ignore calls from Alaska and finally had one of his men go into town to get a new cell phone with a new number for him. He was also eliminating everything that would connect Anna to him or the ranch. He emptied the closets and drawers and watched as everything that belonged to her was burned. His old cell phone was burned with Anna's belongings. He even had the carpets professionally cleaned and hired a cleaning crew to go over the house thoroughly.

The men who had worked for Billy for a long time had whispered conversations about Anna, but they were smart enough not to quiz him about her. Jeremiah Standing Tall didn't know Billy as well as the others did.

Billy was standing in the middle of the garage with a big glass of scotch in his hand as he admired his car collection. It was an escape from everything that was going on for him. Jeremiah walked up next to him and innocently asked, "Where is Anna, Mr. Peet?"

Billy turned to Jeremiah with fire in his eyes. "It's none of your fucking business."

Shocked, Jeremiah stepped back. "I . . . I'm sorry, Mr. Peet. I just haven't seen her since . . . since you came back."

Realizing that Jeremiah was simply asking a question, and that he really had no idea what happened to Anna, Billy became contrite. "I'm sorry, Jeremiah. I'm sorry I jumped on you. I'm just a little sensitive right now."

I might as well practice this now, thought Billy.

"When we got to Alaska and Anna realized how close she was to her home . . . she decided that she wanted to return to Russia. I put her on a plane in Anchorage. I . . . I miss her. She said she may come back, but I don't think she will."

Jeremiah was sincere when he said, "I'm sorry, boss. I liked her. I hope she comes back."

As soon as Jeremiah walked away, Billy called Budge. "What's going on, Budge? Someone from Alaska was calling my cell phone, so I got rid of it."

"Now I understand why I can't get hold of you. I've been trying since early this morning. We've got a problem, Billy. The police have already found the bodies . . . Stan and Anna. It was on the news today. They found them yesterday."

"Shit . . . I'll bet that's why someone from Alaska was calling my cell phone. They probably got my number from Stan's telephone records. I asked you to make it clean, no bodies. What the fuck did you do? You just left them in a house?"

"I thought it was perfect. The house belonged to some guy who wasn't going to be back in Alaska for a month or so."

Billy exploded. "A month or so! A fucking month or so? We needed several more months there. How in hell did they find them already? Now, I've not only pissed a lot of money away, the cops are going to figure out that I was in Alaska right before Anna and Stan died. You're more in the clear than I am. I'm fucked."

"Look boss . . . I'm sorry. I guess I didn't think very well. I'm trying to do this Permanent Fund thing, and then you wanted me to get rid of those two and you were jumping all over my ass about that. I don't know how they found them so fast. I did what I thought was . . ." Budge let his thought trail off. He knew it sounded weak.

Billy allowed Budge to get his defensive rant out and then was quiet for a moment. "I've got to think about all of this. Lay low. Don't do anything stupid. Don't talk to anyone. I'll call you. Do you have caller ID? Do you have this new number, in case you need to call me?"

When Billy finished talking to Budge, he went into his man-room and poured another full glass of scotch. Sitting in one of his oversized leather chairs, he tried to sort out the realities of his current situation. He began to add up all the things that could tie him to Anna. Executive Air Service and the FAA would have the Lear's airplane identification number, and that would put him in Anchorage shortly before her death. When they became curious about him, they would be able to connect the cell phone calls from Stan to his old number. Then they would go after Budge when they found out he had been calling him, too. Not to mention the paper trail that was created when Anna came to America and married him. If they actually came to the ranch looking for him, nobody would admit to anything . . . except Jeremiah Standing Tall. Billy decided to call Mario.

"What's up, Billy?" It was mid-afternoon, and Mario was still in his silk lounging pajamas.

"I . . . I think I have a problem, Mario. I need to talk about it." Mario grunted and emitted several expletives as Billy told him his story.

"What the fuck were you thinking, Billy?"

"He fucked her, Mario. Stan fucked my wife. What could I do? I just sort of went crazy . . . and I told Budge to get rid of her."

"Jesus, Billy. You've created a world of shit over pussy . . . pussy!"

"What could I do, Mario? What would you do if Mary . . . you know, did the same thing?"

Mario laughed a sadistic laugh. "I'd probably ask her to do it again so I could watch. Then I'd kill her. But I wouldn't leave the body someplace where it could be found in a few days."

"I think I'm going to have to get out of here, Mario . . . at least for a while. I love this place. I don't want to lose it, but they can track me down here. I can't believe all of this. I'm really fucked. I have enough money . . . that is, I had enough money. I could have just lived here comfortably until . . ."

"Calm down, Billy. Get your head on straight. Think everything over before you do anything stupid. I may end up having to explain why you have been calling me, too."

In Anchorage, Nancy buzzed Beth's office phone and said, "Somebody very important on your line."

Nancy put the call through, and Beth recognized Nick's Maui number. "Aloha, Mr. Saylor. How are things in the land of sunshine?"

"Wonderful, as usual. I do have some news for you."

"Nani's pregnant!"

"No, not that. I just found out I got elected to the Maui County Council . . . by a landslide."

"Wow, congratulations . . . Mr. Councilman. Next thing I know, you'll be the governor."

"No, this is the apex of my political career. This is very low-key. You make much bigger business decisions every day than we will make all year."

"Well, if this is something that makes you happy, then I'm happy. And, I haven't really kept you up to speed on what's going on with my political job."

"No, you haven't. What's up?"

Beth gave Nick all the details about the proposed project merger of the APFC, Brooksher, and VING, and he was almost speechless. "That's amazing, Beth. You've done an amazing job. I hope the APFC realizes how lucky they are to have you. I'm almost . . . jealous. You are going to have fun with this. I mean, it all sounds just too perfect."

"Thanks Nick. I always count on your support."

"You know you have that. And speaking of big deals, I received notice from Betsy's attorney that our deal on the U Building is about to close. Wayne needs to get ready to spend a lot of our money. I'll go to Seattle for the closing. If you can make it, you should be there, too."

"Yeah, that will be exciting. I want to be there for the closing. Lots of things going on."

"Speaking of . . . has Chris moved in yet?"

Suddenly, Beth was quiet.

"Beth?"

"Yes, he moved in over the weekend. Kind of an exciting time for Saylor Industries. The employees like him. It's just that . . . .."

"Yes."

"Well, we sort of had to put him in my old office."

"And what's wrong with that?"

"It's just that it leaves . . . no office for you."

Nick laughed loudly. "'No soup for you!' Beth, I'm hardly ever there. Why would you worry about that?"

"You're still the CEO, Nick."

"Yeah . . . no matter where I'm sitting. I'll just sit in your office when I'm there, or use whatever office happens to be open at the time. End of story. I'm happy to know that Chris is jumping into it. I hope to see you in Seattle."

Budge had been hunkered down in his condo since he first saw the information about Stan and Anna on the evening news. He knew there was nothing to connect him to the murders yet. . . . Like Billy, he replayed everything that could eventually come back to haunt him in his mind. The only potential connection he could come up with was through telephone records. He had called Stan and Stan's office many times. When someone eventually connected Billy to Stan, and then connected him and Billy, he would have some explaining to do.

He saw a television interview with a Settler's Bay resident who said she had seen a suspicious-looking white car in the neighborhood a week or two before the bodies were discovered, but she had no idea what type of car it was, and she said she couldn't see the driver.

Budge knew he had to begin to cover himself. He went to an electronics store near his condo and bought a disposable phone that he could purchase minutes for when he needed them. He bought nine hundred minutes. He also bought three plug-in timers. When he was back at his condo, he put two timers on lights and one on the TV, and set them to go on and off at random times. Then, he packed a small bag of essentials and called for a taxi. He asked the driver to take him to an extended-stay motel in midtown, where he checked in under an alias, using an old phony ID. To avoid any appearance of suspicious behavior, he told the landlord at his condo building that he intended to leave at the end of the month.

"Billy, this is Budge."

"What the fuck now?"

"I want to give you a new number. I bought a disposable phone. I felt like I needed to get rid of the other one."

"Good choice. As you know, I got rid of my old phone, too. In fact, I think I'm going to have to leave the ranch."

"I've already done that."

"Left the ranch?"

Don't be stupid or cute right now, Billy, Budge thought. "My condo, Billy. My perfectly lovely condo. I'm in an extended-stay motel. I'm keeping the condo until the end of the month, just so it doesn't look like I'm pulling up stakes and running for some reason."

"Okay, that's a good way to handle it. We're running out of time. We've either got to put something together, or we've got to give it up. I mean, I may have to sell this fucking ranch. This is my dream place. I've already lost my dream wo . . ."

Billy became so quiet that Budge thought he was gone. "Billy?"

"Yeah."

"Let's not give up yet."

Suddenly, Billy sounded upbeat. "Yeah, Raymond said that the APFC was getting ready to do something with Brooksher. I don't know if that means anything right now, but we've got the Reverend on the inside at

Brooksher. Get with Minty. See if you can find out what's going on. I'm waiting to see if Raymond or Benny can come up with something on this Vancouver Island Natural Gas company."

"I can meet with Ron. I've got to give him my new phone number anyway. I'm not going to tell him I've moved yet. I'll call him today."

Business was brisk at Minty, Anderson, and Rogers, so Ron was not overly excited when his receptionist announced that Budge Brown was calling. His weaknesses didn't allow him to duck the call. Budge's calls usually led to something adventurous. "This is Ron Minty."

"Aren't we formal today? You not only sound formal, you sound busy. I guess you can't come out and play today?"

"I'm really busy, Budge. We're loaded here, and then we've got all this APFC board shit going on. I've got a meeting tomorrow morning, and then probably another one later in the week."

"Well, let's just meet for a drink or two after work, and then you can go study or whatever you have to do. We can meet early or late . . . whatever works for you."

"Shit . . . I shouldn't. Aw, what the fuck. Okay, The Mud Flats. Six o'clock."

"See you there."

Budge was sitting at the bar when Ron walked into The Mud Flats a few minutes after 6:00. He already had a drink in front of him, and Vicki was being surprisingly pleasant to him again. He turned on his stool to face Ron.

"Welcome, hard-working guy."

"Must be nice to be a nonworking guy. Looks like you got a head start on me."

"Yeah, and Vicki is talking to me."

"There you go. You'd better jump back into that." Ron got a cheesy grin on his face and added, "Or jump into that back."

"Not going to happen. The front . . . maybe. Not the other side. Sit, have a drink. You're working too hard. Relax a little."

"I've got to make a short night of it. Tomorrow's APFC meeting is going to be intense. I need to have a clear head."

An hour later, both men were on their fourth drink, and Ron's head was not clear, although he kept insisting he needed to leave so he would be clear-headed in the morning. He was ripe for Budge to quiz him.

"So Ron, what's going on with the board's big investment?"

"I'm not supposed to discuss it, Budge. It's just an investment."

"So what do you think, that I'm going to go out with my thousands and beat you to it?"

Ron laughed. "You might. You never seem to have to worry about money."

"I have canned soup for lunch, wash my own clothes, and I don't own a car. I'm just a little saver."

"Right."

"I guess that means you won't tell me what the latest is. Remember, if there is a way for us to make a deal, you get a cut out of it."

"I remember. I don't know how this could work for us. It's a big deal. Big money."

The suggestion that Ron could make some money off of a deal worked through Billy, Budge, and his "money people" was all that was needed to loosen his tongue. Over the next thirty minutes, he spilled all the latest details about the proposed joint venture with Brooksher and Vancouver Island Natural Gas.

"It sounds really good. I think the board will approve it. All of the lawyers and money guys are evaluating it right now. I told you who put it together when we were in Juneau, right?"

"Yeah."

"Beth . . . the long-legged cunt I'd love to get my hands on."

"And I'd love to get my hands on her, too. You didn't tell me how much money we are talking about?"

"One hundred big ones."

Budge was instantly disappointed. "A hundred thousand dollars?"

"Think big, Budge. One . . . hundred . . . million . . . dollars."

"Fuck. That's a lot of coin. When's all of this supposed to happen?"

"Well, if we come out with a good result tomorrow, the lawyers and the money guys will work it a couple more days, and then we'll meet Thursday or Friday and vote on it. If we approve it, the only holdup will be the gas company getting the permits. We don't send any money until the permits are approved."

"How long will that take?"

Ron turned toward Budge. "You're a nosy fucker."

"Remember, I'm looking for a way for both of us to make some money . . . some big money."

"Don't know. They say it's a done deal. Shouldn't be long."

Budge suddenly realized that he had all the information he needed from Ron right now, and that it really would be a good thing if he had a clear head in the morning. "You know what. I need to get out of here, and you need to be fresh tomorrow. Let's shut this party down."

Ron argued, and they had one more drink before Budge convinced him to go home.

The minute Budge arrived at his midtown hotel room, he dialed Billy. Unlike most of the other late night calls he made to the ranch, Billy seemed uncharacteristically eager to talk with him.

"What's up, my Eskimo friend?"

"I ain't no fucking Eskimo. You shipped me here, remember?"

Laughing, Billy replied, "Oh . . . yeah, I forgot that. Okay, what's up?"

"I met with Ron tonight . . . got him drunk. He gave me the latest about the APFC and Brooksher deal with Vancouver Island Natural Gas."

Budge repeated everything Ron Minty told him earlier that evening. Every few minutes, Billy would say something like "Holy shit" or "Wow," but he mostly listened. When Budge was done, Billy said, "That's a big fucking deal. I mean, that's a monstrous fucking deal."

Both men were quiet for a few seconds. Then Billy said, "I've got to get hold of Raymond. I don't know what he can do, but he is on the inside at Brooksher. It seems like the old lady trusts him more each day. In fact, I actually think he's fucking her."

"No . . . not Raymond. Can't be."

"Wanna place a little wager?"

"Sure. A hundred bucks says that Raymond is not fucking old lady Brooksher."

"You're on. I say he is. And thanks for the information from Ron. I'm going to hang up and call Raymond right now."

The Reverend was into his second martini at The Rusty Turtle when his cell phone rang. Thinking it might be Betsy, he got it out of his pocket quickly and looked at the caller ID.

Billy, shit. What does he want at this time of night?

"This is Raymond."

"Midnight mass?"

"Midnight martini."

"I thought religious men didn't drink . . . or fuck. Where are you?"

"Is that what you called me for . . . to ask me about my personal habits? And I'm in The Rusty Turtle. I started coming in here when Betsy was in Alaska, and I kind of like it."

"Don't blow your cover . . . *Reverend*. I don't think most religious men sit around in bars and drink martinis."

"As I said, did you just call me to get on my ass?"

"No, I called you to tell you about a very interesting conversation I just had with Budge." Raymond listened intently as Billy gave him the latest information.

"That is interesting. That's a lot of money. I don't know what it means to us, but it is interesting. It seems like Beth Saylor has her toes in everything."

"Yeah, she's really pissing me off. . . . And I don't even know her."

It was then that Raymond decided it was time to tell Billy about the electronic cash transfers. As he left his stool and walked out the front door to get some privacy, he quietly said, "I . . . I probably should tell you about something. I didn't know if it was important, but it may be."

When Raymond finished, Billy shouted into the phone. "You didn't know if it was important? How fucking stupid can you be? Why have you been fucking keeping this from me? Do you know what this means? Do you remember what I just told you? The APFC is going to make their investment in the project *through* Brooksher. Do you know what that means? They'll be transferring their money to Brooksher . . . one hundred million dollars. Right under your little observer nose! This is fucking huge!"

Raymond hated it when Billy talked to him like this . . . but he suddenly saw the big picture. "If I could get rid of Theodore, or trick him, I could transfer the money on to our . . . your offshore account."

"No shit!"

Raymond's mind was racing. "My cut still the same? Same as it was going to be on the new warehouse?"

"Slow down, cowboy. Let's not get ahead of ourselves." Quickly remembering how important Raymond was, Billy added, "Yeah, the same. A cool ten million."

"What about the other warehouse?"

"Forget that. You can't do both. And, you'll be on a plane to Costa Rica."

"I don't want to go to Costa Rica . . . maybe Thailand. Over there, you can get a six-pack of beer and a six-pack of young hookers and go to your room for a hundred bucks."

"Nice talk for a man of the cloth."

"When the ten million actually comes my way, my preaching days are over."

"You need to think about how you are going to use this young accountant. I don't think it's a good idea to have anybody else in on this. Could you handle a money transfer without him?"

"Yeah, especially after I observe a few more times. I'll have to find a way to incapacitate him. Maybe I need to take him to The Rusty Turtle for a drink one of these nights. See if I can figure out what he's all about.

270

I know he has weaknesses, I just don't know what they are . . . except one. He has the hots for Britney Spears."

"That's weird . . . but I wouldn't hesitate on him. From what Budge says, this could all come down fairly quickly." Billy was hesitant, and then he said, "You know, I need to get away from the ranch for a while. I think I may come to Seattle . . . sort of be close to the action."

Oh fuck, thought Raymond, *just what I don't need.*

"Well, that's pretty much up to you . . . but I can handle things here."

"Yeah, but you're too close to 'things' there. I mean, like, I wonder if you've got your dick in them."

"I don't know what you mean. I'm taking care of business here. You, Budge, nobody else could have gotten as close to Betsy as I have. I get buried deeper into Brooksher's business every day—"

"You're right, you're buried in Betsy Brooksher's business . . . right up to your nuts."

"I've heard enough of this. You do what you want to. I have to go."

Billy answered abruptly, "I will," and hung up. Sitting by himself in the man-room he loved, he realized it was time for action. He would put the ranch up for sale right away, and head to Seattle.

On Tuesday morning in Anchorage, the APFC Board of Trustees met with their circle of legal and financial advisors to discuss the proposed investment in Vancouver Island Natural Gas. Everyone agreed the investment met all the established criteria for an infrastructure investment. The financial advisors had quickly thrown together facts and figures about the future of natural gas development as measured against the stagnating progress the State was making toward getting gas production from the North Slope to a market. All agreed that VING had a viable proposal.

Daniel Oaken, in his dual role as a board member and the Commissioner of Revenue for the State, brought up the question that was in the back of everyone's mind. "What about the politics of all of this? You know the governor has backed a proposal for a trans-Canada pipeline."

Mary Brunser quickly pointed out, "We don't need the governor's approval to make investments."

A slightly hungover Ron Minty chimed in, mostly because he didn't like Mary and he didn't want her to be the only one contributing. "We've all talked this to death. We have to make a decision, and the governor is just going to have to like it."

Executive Director Cally spoke up. "That's the hard line, Mr. Minty. We don't need her approval to make the investment, but I would like to have her blessing. I really don't want to offend her. Remember, we are all political appointees, and she is a popular governor. And remember, the governor can help push GB Petroleum's permit applications along. We are going to talk with her . . . that is, Beth is going to talk with her. Right, Beth?"

Beth was deep in thought over everything that was being discussed, and Richard Cally's comment shocked her. They had loosely discussed her talking with the governor, but he hadn't formally asked her to do that. "Uh, sure. . . . I mean, yes, I'm going to talk with her."

The executive director continued to blindside her. "When are you going to meet with her, Beth?"

"She's . . . she's going to get back to me. I'll press the fact that we need to talk soon." Beth quietly wondered if she looked as flustered as she felt.

After two hours of debate, Chairman Feck called for an informal vote to see how the members felt. It was approved without dissent. "Well, it seems that we all feel strongly that this is a good move for the APFC. I am hereby calling for a closed meeting of the board of trustees for this coming Friday, at nine in the morning. I would like for all of you here who are financial and legal advisors to continue to explore as many facets of this investment as your experience and your imagination can develop. Pending your continuing positive findings, we will take a formal vote on Friday."

Chairman Feck looked at Beth and said, "Beth, since we arrived at this point fairly quickly, please make an attempt to meet with the governor tomorrow or Thursday. If you have difficulty getting that scheduled, call me or Mr. Cally. I'm not going to tell you what you need to say to the governor. . . . I am sure you know how to present this."

Ron Minty puffed up privately, since he knew that a public display of disdain for Beth was futile. She had rocketed into a favored position on the board way too quickly for him.

"I'll take care of it, Mr. Chairman," Beth answered confidently.

Beth called the governor's office immediately after the meeting.

"Governor Powers' office. How may I help you?"

"Good afternoon. It's Susan, right? This is Beth Saylor. May I speak with the governor?"

"This *is* Susan. Thank you for remembering my name. The governor is in, Ms. Saylor . . . and you are on her approved list, so I'm allowed to tell you that. Let me see if I can get her."

Governor Powers' voice came on quickly. "Beth, how nice to hear from you. What can I do for you today?"

"I would like to be able to meet with you . . . soon, like tomorrow or

Thursday. It's about APFC business."

Stacey laughed quietly, like she had her mouth closed, and said, "The Vancouver Island Natural Gas deal, I'm guessing."

Beth was taken aback by Stacey's comment. "How'd you . . . I mean, I didn't know if you knew about it. But yes, that is what I want to talk to you about."

At 11:00 the next morning, Beth was sitting in the waiting area outside the governor's office. She had only been waiting a few minutes when Stacey came out of her office. She walked to Beth as she was getting up, and hugged her warmly. "I am so glad to see you. Please come in. Susan, please hold my calls . . . unless the president calls." She had a big grin on her face when she said that, and Beth didn't know if she was pulling her leg or really expecting a call from the president.

"Thank you so much for seeing me on such short notice, Madam Governor."

"Stacey. Please call me Stacey . . . remember? And I am very happy to see you. Now tell me about this big natural gas deal the APFC is playing with."

Beth had practiced her approach to the governor, but she was not sure what to expect. She knew the governor was aware that she didn't have to approve the board's actions. She didn't want their meeting to touch on that subject. "Stacey, you apparently know that the APFC Board is considering an investment in a company called Vancouver Island Natural Gas. I would like to give you some details about that and how it fits perfectly into our criteria for an investment in infrastructure."

Beth spent twenty minutes giving the governor an abbreviated version of what the investment was all about. "We . . . the APFC Board of Trustees and our advisors, all feel strongly that this is a great investment for the Permanent Fund, and for Alaska. We also know about your position on building a trans-Canada natural gas pipeline. We hope that you would be willing to support this decision by the board, even though you have supported a competing proposal in the past."

Suddenly looking like a wise-warrior governor, Stacey leaned back in her big leather chair and said, "Beth, I respect the APFC board. I respect the decisions that have made our Permanent Fund the financial juggernaut that it is. I don't give a shit what you invest in . . . if it works. I pushed for the trans-Canada line to try and make something happen. Candidly, your proposal sounds like the most promising opportunity for us to produce North Slope natural gas."

Stacey paused, then continued with a smile. "Is that relief I see on your pretty face?"

Beth blushed. "I guess it might be. Maybe we have all worried about this for nothing."

"Paranoia is a necessary ingredient in the formula for success, Beth. You have certainly been successful in your life, so I know you understand that."

"Thank you, Gov . . . Stacey. It is really nice to know we have your blessing on this, even though we don't—"

"Need it?"

"Yeah, I guess."

"Okay, we got that bullshit out of the way. When are we going to have a girls' night out? I need to get away from all the formalities around here for a little bit."

Not sure how to react to the governor's surprise invitation, Beth said, "Well, I don't imagine you can just cruise into any place in town. I am a member of the Petroleum Club. It's private, and you wouldn't get mobbed there. Everyone would be respectful."

"That's a great idea. I've been there a few times. Let's meet there. We can have drinks and dinner. I'm sure I'll run into old friends . . . and adversaries."

"Wonderful. I don't want to be presumptuous, but we can pick you up in our company limousine."

"Great. When? How about this Friday night?"

"Perfect. We'll pick you up at, say, seven o'clock?"

"You're on. And thank you, Beth. This will be fun!"

"You are welcome, and the board of the APFC thanks you. I can't wait to take the word to the board members that you are blessing this investment."

"Yes, and I will now get prepared for the media attack on my credibility."

The only place where hit-and-run is appropriate is in a baseball game.
—From *Fred Longcoor's Book on Life*

Chapter 20

Girls' Night Out

In Montana, Billy was melancholy as he made plans to sell the ranch. He talked to everyone who worked at the ranch individually in his man-room, and telling them he was selling it was emotionally tough, even for a tough guy. Jeremiah Standing Tall took it very hard.

"Why are you leaving now, Mr. Peet? Is it because Anna left? I'm really going to miss this ranch. I don't have anywhere to go. I have some friends left on the reservation. . . . I just don't want to go back there."

"It's hard to explain, Jeremiah. Part of it is because Anna is gone . . .." *Maybe even most of it*, he thought.

"I just need a change of scenery. I need a place closer to a large city. You know, more action."

"I am sorry you are going, Mr. Peet. This is the best job I've ever had."

"I'm sorry too, Jeremiah. But you'll have at least another few months here. The broker told me it would probably take six months to a year to sell a property like this, and I'll need a caretaker until then. You can live in the house, and keep it tidy for the broker when he wants to show it. Keep a shine on the cars, too. I haven't decided if I'm going to sell them, or just move them when I find a new place."

"Thanks, Mr. Peet. That'll give me some time to find a new job."

"And another thing. I'm not sure where I'm going to end up. I'll probably just take some vacation first, and then look for a new place. Hell, I may fly around the world. If anyone calls or comes around asking about me, just tell them I'm on vacation, and you don't know where I went. I'll check with you regularly. You'll be the only one here. Can you handle

275

this big place by yourself?"

"My great-grandfather was a warrior. My grandfather and my father had the hearts of warriors. I have the heart of a warrior. I can handle it. I think it will be very peaceful."

"I can take care of the bills and deposit your pay in your bank account electronically, so you won't have anything to worry about that way."

"Thank you, Mr. Peet." Jeremiah turned and walked away like the proud warrior he was. Billy couldn't see the tiny tear under his right eye.

Billy wandered around the vehicle building. He went back into the man-room and poured himself a glass of scotch. It was his favorite place for meditation. He went back into the main part of the building and reflected on the story behind the purchase of each car as he slowly walked past them. *I love these cars*, he thought. *I don't want to give them up.*

Billy had spent many hours thinking about his current situation. In down moments, he pined for what he had lost and what he may be losing—Anna, the ranch, his precious car collection, and, very possibly, his freedom.

At other times, usually when he was fortified with a generous amount of fine scotch, he speculated about what his grand future would look like after they took the APFC for one hundred million dollars . . . a much bigger ranch, a Gulfstream jet, fine-looking women companions, and a car collection that was twice as big as the one he had now. Realizing that he would probably have to leave the US to have all of those things always put a damper on his happy thoughts.

For now, Billy's future was going to be in Seattle. He had packed his traveling belongings in the Learjet. He waved goodbye to Jeremiah from the doorway as he boarded the plane. After directing the pilot to circle the ranch one time, he saw Jeremiah standing stoically in the same spot. Billy wondered if he would ever see him again.

Billy had contacted a vacation rental company and put money on a nice condo near Sea-Tac airport on a month-by-month agreement under the alias Ben Parker. The new name allowed him to continue wearing his monogrammed shirts with BP on the cuffs. It was a small, vain attempt to hang onto who he really was.

Since his talk with Billy about the electronic cash transfer between the APFC and Brooksher, Raymond concentrated on getting closer to Theodore. When he invited him out for drinks and dinner at The Rusty Turtle, he learned about Theodore's fondness for good tequila. He knew immediately how he could put him out of commission so *he* could manage the cash transfer from Alaska. Among the small collection of nasty things the Reverend Raymond kept with his miniscule cache of belongings was a supply of Rohypnol.

Rophy, ruffies, roofies, forget-it, Mexican Valium . . . were just a few of the street names for Rohypnol. Raymond had obtained it in its original form, before the manufacturer modified it to make it change color when it came in contact with a liquid. It was a tasteless, colorless, odorless substance that could be added to any drink without detection. The quick-acting "date rape" drug was virtually undetectable, leaving no traces in the body after seventy-two hours. The beauty of it for Raymond was that it would render Theodore unconscious with little or no memory of what had happened. It also would make him uninhibited. That was an effect that would not aid him in temporarily incapacitating Theodore, but it had come in handy before with unsuspecting women he had encountered.

Timing would be the critical factor. Getting Theodore to drink some drugged tequila right before they were supposed to handle a hundred million–dollar electronic cash transfer would not be easy. Making sure he was the only observer would be difficult as well. He had a feeling Betsy and Gaylord would want to witness that significant event. He would need a diversion.

On Friday morning, the Foraker Room at the Susitna Hotel was abuzz with excited conversations. All of the APFC Board of Trustees members were there, talking excitedly about what they were about to undertake. Chairman Feck stood up at the head of the large conference table.

"Good morning to all of you." He had a satisfied smile on his face as he continued. "It's no secret what we are here about, and accordingly, I call this special meeting of the Alaska Permanent Fund Corporation Board of Trustees to order, and turn the meeting over to Executive Director Richard Cally."

"Thank you, Mr. Chairman. Like Fred, I feel very good about what we are about to do . . . at least what I think we are about to do."

There were muted laughs around the room, and Richard continued. "The financial and legal folks have all reported in to me . . . actually, many times, over the last two days. There are no apparent glitches, particularly in light of the fact that no APFC money goes into the project until VING has received all the permits that are required. As with any investment in oil or natural gas, there is a market-driven risk related to market prices. Our oil and gas guys think it is minimal in this case. That is due to the unique market niche that VING is already tied into, and the totally unique supply chain."

Daniel Oaken spoke up, one of the rare times when anyone heard from him. "Mr. Cally, have we gotten any feedback on how Governor Powers feels about this?"

"You took the words right out of my mouth, Mr. Oaken. Beth met with the governor Wednesday morning. To paraphrase Beth's recap, the governor is on board with anything that appears to be right for the state. She knew what we were up to before Beth met with her."

"I think we have beat this thing to death," Mary Brunser interjected. "I also think it is a brilliant move on our part . . . sort of kills two birds with one stone. We make a great investment, and we help the state and the oil and gas industry by getting North Slope natural gas to market."

"You are right, Mary. Unless there is something we have missed, or any further debate required by anyone here, I would like to put this to a vote. Anybody?"

Nobody said a word, and the executive director became very formal as he said, "In accordance with the bylaws of the Alaska Permanent Fund Corporation, I hereby call for a vote by show of hands of the members of the board of trustees for approval of a motion to invest one hundred million dollars in the Vancouver Island Natural Gas project. Said investment will be contingent upon the receipt of all permits required for the project by Vancouver Island Natural Gas, hereafter referred to as VING. Said investment will be made through Brooksher Energy, a wholly owned subsidiary of Brooksher, of Kent, Washington. Brooksher has an ownership position in VING. This investment will be categorized as an infrastructure investment under Infrastructure Resolution 07-05."

The executive director finished his wordy proposal and looked around the room. "All in favor, raise your right hand and say aye."

Without hesitation, every right hand in the room went up accompanied by an "Aye," with the exception of the stenographer's. When she saw the unanimous vote, she shyly raised her right hand a little and quietly added her "Aye." Everyone laughed.

"This resolution is passed unanimously . . . and I do mean unanimously," Richard said with a big smile on his face. Everyone laughed, and it was a happy, victorious, relieved laugh.

"One final thing. I would like to commend Beth Saylor, and thank her for utilizing her connection with Betsy Brooksher to facilitate this unprecedented investment for APFC." Richard began to clap his hands lightly, and the rest of the board members issued their assorted agreements and clapped as well.

Beth blushed, and thanked the board members. Her thoughts quickly turned to her upcoming night out with the governor, and she was the first board member to leave the Foraker Room. She hurried back to the Saylor Building to take care of a few urgent business matters that had been ignored during the last two busy weeks. In the middle of the afternoon, she rushed to her appointment for hair, nails, and makeup, and then she hurried back to the penthouse.

Beth wanted everything to be perfect. She had an almost giddy thought. *I'm going out for a night on the town with the governor!* As she often did, Beth privately thanked the ethereal being who had given her such a blessed life. Her faith was solid, but she had never come to grips with a definitive identification of who her prayers were directed to. She prayed to God, without really knowing who God was:

Thank you, I am a truly lucky woman.

Modestly, she never gave herself proper credit for being the dynamic woman she was.

Vince was standing by the limo when Beth came out of the front doors at the Saylor Building. "Good evening, Vince. This is a big night. . . . We're going to be squiring the governor around."

Vince smiled. "Yes ma'am. I've brushed my teeth, used my deodorant, and I have clean underwear on."

"Good God, Vince. This is me, Beth . . . we're going to pick up the governor. This is not boys' night out with Nick."

"Sorry, Ms. Saylor. It was just a little humor to help unwind you a bit. You're wound up like an eight-day clock."

"You're right, Vince . . . and it was funny. I'll try to relax a little on the way to the governor's mansion."

As per their previous arrangements, Beth called the governor's private cell number when they were five minutes from the mansion. "Madam Governor, we are five minutes away."

"Great Beth, I'll meet you at your limousine."

Vince barely had time to get out and open the door for the governor when he stopped the limo. She had exited the front entrance to the mansion as they pulled up.

"Good evening, Madame Governor."

"Good evening to you too. You look familiar to me. And your name is?"

"Vince, ma'am."

"Well, Vince, we are going to have a good time tonight. Remember, what happens in the limo stays in the limo."

"That *is* part of the limo driver's code, ma'am."

"Good. If I do something bad tonight, I don't want to read about it in the newspaper tomorrow morning."

"You have nothing to worry about. I was Nick Saylor's driver for years. Did you ever hear any limo stories about him?"

Stacey smiled. "Come to think about it . . . no. And he did have a bit of a reputation . . . I'm told. Anyway, it is nice to see you . . . meet you, Vince."

"My pleasure, Governor."

Vince had a moment of déjà vu, and found himself wondering if she had been in the limo before.

"Good evening, Governor," Beth said as Stacey climbed into the back of the limo.

"Good evening, Beth. I like your limo driver. How long have you had him?"

"Vince? Years. He worked for Nick for a long time."

Thoughtfully, Stacey said, "Yeah."

Thinking that this was kind of an odd reaction, Beth ignored it and said, "Welcome. We have a fully stocked bar in the limo. Would you like a glass of wine or something?"

"I thought you'd never ask. Can you make a vodka martini?"

Irreverently and inexplicably, Beth replied, "Does the governor of Alaska pee sitting down?"

Beth blushed at her own question, and Stacey laughed out loud. "I knew I liked you, and now I know why."

At Stacey's request, Beth asked Vince to drive around the city for a while. The limo drew curious looks from one end of Anchorage to the other as Beth and Stacy ignored the passing sights and engaged in girl talk while consuming two martinis each. By the time they pulled up in front of the Petroleum Club, they were giggling friends.

As a courtesy, Beth had called ahead earlier in the day to let the club manager know that she would be bringing the governor in that evening. Selfishly, Beth knew that her call would also assure the head chef would be working that evening.

When Beth and the governor entered the club, they were taken to a small private room off of the main dining room. Wisely, they both requested wine when the waiter approached them, rather than another martini. The club manager came by their table and welcomed them, followed by the head chef.

Stacey raised her wine glass to Beth and said, "Thank you, Beth. So far, this is lovely. I don't get out like this very often."

Beth raised her glass and touched the governor's. "You are welcome, Madam Governor. It is my pleasure."

Stacey laughed. "We've each had two martinis. Don't you think it's time you get back to to calling me Stacey?"

Beth laughed too. "Yes . . . Stacey."

They spent an hour eating a meal dominated by fresh Alaska seafood and good wine. When they were done, Stacey said, "Let's go into the bar. That's where all the men hang out."

"Are you sure? You'll be surrounded by admirers."

"What's wrong with that? There may be a keeper in there."

Realizing that she had already seen more of the private side of a very public person than she'd ever thought she would, Beth said, "Let's go."

Because of her frequent dealings with oilmen and businessmen of all types, Beth's prophecy about Stacey being surrounded was right on. Stacey introduced Beth to many men she had heard of and never met, and Beth introduced the governor to several people she didn't know. After thirty minutes in the bar, Stacey said, "Let's go."

When they were back in the limo, Stacey said, "It's a good thing they hadn't heard the news yet, or I'd never have gotten out of there."

Beth knew what she meant, even though they hadn't discussed it. "So you know . . . that we approved the VING investment today?"

"Yes, my lovely new friend. I know . . . and I think it is a good thing, even though I will be doing a lot of explaining. I don't want to think about it tonight. I want to have fun. Let's go to a sleazy bar . . . you know, have some fun."

"Stacey . . . Governor. Are you sure you want to be seen in a sleazy bar? How about a semisleazy bar?"

"Okay, whatever. Let's just go someplace where there is some action. There are a lot of really nice men in the Petroleum Club, but it's a little . . . quiet."

"It's supposed to be quiet. It's a private club, a club for businessmen."

"Okay. It's nice, but I want some rock-and-roll music and a broad cross section of my constituents. Like I said, I don't get to do this very often . . . or ever! I've got you, Vince, and your lovely limousine. What can go wrong?"

When they walked into The Mud Flats, there was a lively Friday-night crowd there to greet them. Surprise was quickly overtaken by appreciation, and a few people began to clap for the governor. When they did, two men who were sitting side by side at the bar with their backs to the door turned around on their stools to see what was causing the commotion. That's when Ron Minty and Budge Brown saw Beth looking right at them.

"Shit," was all Budge could say under his breath as he caught Beth's eye. Ron quickly flushed and wore a pained look as he saw Beth. He acknowledged her with an embarrassed nod. His meeting with Budge to give him the details about the board's final approval of the APFC investment had backfired on him.

Beth was equally surprised, and turned away from the two men. They both turned toward the bar. "Fuck, that was not good," said Budge.

"She doesn't know you."

"She's seen me around, like on a flight I took to Seattle a while back. We were both in first class."

"That doesn't mean shit."

"Yeah, unless she saw us together in Juneau."

"Oh shit. You're right . . . but she still doesn't know anything. Shit, we haven't done anything."

"Yet."

Beth was trying to follow Stacey around and share in the great time she was having, but the curious relationship between Ron Minty and the man she had seen with him in Juneau and on the flight to Seattle wouldn't leave her thoughts.

There's something about that man that is just not right, she thought. *I've got to find out who he is from Ron.*

Stacey was working the room. It was almost like a campaign stop. She was greeting everyone, shaking hands, and laughing and joking like she was among old friends. With a few exceptions, she was. Beth hoped the crowd didn't realize she was at least halfway intoxicated. As she moved around the bar, Beth realized she was headed toward Ron and his companion.

"Mr. Minty, are you trying to hide from me?"

Ron turned on his stool. "Of course not, Madam Governor. I could see you were busy. Good evening." Turning toward Beth, he said, "Good evening to you, too, Ms. Saylor. What are you ladies doing this evening—girls' night out?"

"Yes . . . girls' night out. We're celebrating the APFC's latest investment. And who is your friend, Ron?"

It was obvious to Beth that Ron was flustered as he said, "Oh . . . uh, this is Budge. Budge Brown."

Oblivious to Beth's concern about how strange it was to find these two men together, Stacey said, "It's nice to meet you, Mr. Brown. Did you vote for me?"

"Well, it's a pleasure to meet you, Madam Governor. Of course I voted for you." Budge was quick on his feet with his lie.

"Great. Thank you." Turning to Beth, she said, "Let's find a place to sit."

Glancing back and forth at both men and looking them in their eyes while ignoring the fact that Ron had not introduced her to "Budge," Beth said, "Good evening, gentlemen."

An alert waitress had cleared a table at a booth near a quiet area in the bar, and waved for them to follow her. After the waitress took their order, Stacey leaned across the table and said quietly, "I have decided something tonight. I have been thinking about it for a while. You would be a great successor to me. You have everything it takes . . . and you are beautiful to boot."

"I don't know what to say."

"You don't have to say anything. You don't have to do anything . . . at least not yet."

"Stacey, that is very flattering, but why are you telling me this?"

"I am telling you this now, because . . . you have to keep this to yourself. I know we've had a lot to drink tonight, but we haven't had that much to drink over the last hour or so, and I know exactly what I'm telling you. I have some issues . . . medical issues. I don't want to talk about that, other than to tell you that I may have to step down."

"My God, Stacey. Now I really don't know what to say. I mean, is this something that can be fixed . . . you know, cured?"

"I don't know yet."

"They can fix almost everything these days. You're the governor. Go to the best specialists, go to the Mayo Clinic."

"I'm exploring all options right now, Beth. I don't want to go any farther on the health issue tonight. As far as what would happen if I stepped down, the Alaska Succession Law is rather unique and very specific. The lieutenant governor will take my job until the next election. It is his responsibility to appoint *his* successor . . . and I already have that worked out."

"What does that mean?"

"It means you would become the lieutenant governor. In the next election, you would run for governor as the incumbent lieutenant governor, and easily win the election."

"What makes you think I would win?"

"Because the governor would be running for the seat in the US Congress that will be open, and he will win it. You are also the best-known, most-respected, and most-admired woman in Alaska . . . aside from me."

"I'm . . . I'm shocked. It is too much to absorb." Beth was thoughtful for a moment, and continued apologetically. "I'm not sure I want to be governor."

"You will. Once you become lieutenant governor, you'll get a taste of it, and you will love it."

For a little while, thought Stacey.

"Now, I've had a great time. I'd like to get laid tonight."

"Governor!"

"Don't worry, Beth. I'm not going to pick somebody up in a bar. I have a friend, you know, a special friend. A friend with privileges." Stacey put a wicked smile on her face and added, "A fuck buddy. I'll bet you have a fuck buddy."

Beth had consumed too many drinks to be embarrassed, but the question caught her off guard. "I, well . . . no, I don't have a friend with privileges. Maybe I should have one. . . . I mean, if the governor can have a fuck buddy, I should be able to have one."

Both women laughed.

Vince was very anxious about dropping the governor off at a condo complex, even though it was in a very respectable part of Anchorage. Beth made him wait until they saw Stacey disappear inside the front door. Neither one of them noticed the dark sedan that was now parked a block behind the limo, the same dark sedan that had been following them around town all night.

Five minutes after Stacey entered the condo, the doorbell rang. She opened the door wearing only her jacket, and welcomed her "friend with privileges."

"Good evening, you beautiful man. I am so ready for you."

Once Beth was back at her penthouse, she couldn't go to sleep. She lay by herself on her king-sized bed and thought about her night with the governor.

Lieutenant governor, governor . . . how bizarre. And the governor has a . . . a . . . fuck buddy! And I don't!

Beth got up from the bed and walked into her bathroom. She stood there looking at herself in her skimpy white lace bra and panties. She could view her tall sculpted body from all angles in the floor-to-ceiling mirrors.

"I'd do you," she said to herself out loud, and then laughed quietly as she went back into the bedroom. Her last thought before falling asleep was, *I'm going to call Ron Minty about this Budge guy tomorrow morning.*

Ron and Budge were still in The Mud Flats when they heard the crowd reacting as the governor and Beth were leaving. "Thank God they're leaving," Ron said.

Budge was defiant. "It don't mean shit, Ron. They're not going to bother us. As far as they know, we just met in here . . . which we did."

"What about Juneau? What if the big redhead saw us together there?"

"That don't mean shit, either. We're just friends."

"I hope you're right. She could blow this whole thing."

"You're really getting paranoid. She can't blow what she doesn't know about. You know, if we can pull something off, you're going to have to cover your ass."

"Well, we probably never will, so don't worry about it."

Budge decided it was time to let Ron in on the things he had talked to Billy about. He leaned toward Ron and said, "We just might. We have a plan." Ron was all ears as Budge spilled the cash-transfer plan.

"Fuck. One hundred million dollars! By just fucking with the electronic cash transfer? You've got to be kidding me."

"Shhh. Calm down, and turn it down a little, please. It can work. We've got our guy on the inside at Brooksher. Billy thinks he's fucking old Betsy Brooksher. The only thing we'll need out of you is information on when the transfer is being made. Other than that, we don't have to do anything on this end."

"What do I get out of this? I mean, it's got to be enough to set me up for life on some fucking South Sea island."

"I don't know. I'll talk to Billy. I think, five mil."

"I want ten."

"Ten million dollars for doing nothing? You are fucking crazy. Billy will never go for that."

Now Ron had an evil, greedy look on his face. "Ten," he said, "or I'll fuck the whole deal up."

Anger boiled inside of Budge, but he held it back. "As I said, I'll talk to Billy."

With that, he got off the stool and turned to leave The Mud Flats, telling Ron before he left, "I'll call you tomorrow," and thinking, *I hope your wife has a life insurance policy on you.*

When Budge was back in his hotel room, he called Billy.

"Yeah."

"Billy, Budge. You still at the ranch?"

"No, I'm in Seattle. Rented a condo for a month. I'm going to sell the ranch. I hope I can sell it before this Anna-Stan thing catches up to me. I still can't believe how you fucked that up."

Budge felt the frustration and anger he felt almost every time he talked to Billy, but pushed it aside for a more important issue. "I didn't fuck it up. I want to tell you about the meeting I had with Ron tonight. I told him . . . about the cash-transfer scheme. I told him the only thing we needed him for was to bird-dog the day and time when the transfer would be made. He's on board with that. Now, you won't like this . . . he wants ten million dollars."

"What?! Ten million dollars, for doing nothing? Is he fucking crazy? Five, maybe. No more."

"I'm on your side, Billy, but I think we need to tell him he's going to get ten . . . and then get rid of him right after we pull this off. If he disappears, he'll be the first suspect when the money disappears."

"That's solid thinking, Budge. But you can't fuck that one up. He has to disappear in a way that will guarantee he will never be found. I could send someone up there for that."

"You keep saying that. I can handle it, Billy. One more goon in the middle of this is not a good thing."

"I guess you're right."

Budge hesitated. "I . . . have one more little problem. Beth Saylor saw me and Ron together tonight. She was with the fucking governor."

"So?"

"Well, she saw me when I went to Seattle for, you know, the Madrid thing. We were both in first class."

Impatiently, Billy mumbled, "Still don't get it."

"She may have seen us together in Juneau, and the day I threw the guy out of the board meeting, my fake mustache came loose. I don't think anybody noticed it . . . but she was looking at me kind of funny."

"I guess I'm getting the picture, but I'm still not sure what it means."

"I'm really not sure, either, but she could raise some questions with the trustees. It just makes me nervous."

"Maybe she needs to take a hike . . . into a very deep lake."

APFC's investment hit the media the day after the board approved it.

Last Frontier News
Saturday, June 2, 2007
APFC TO INVEST $100 MILLION
The Alaska Permanent Fund Corporation (APFC) announced late yesterday afternoon that its board of trustees approved an investment of $100 million in Vancouver Island Natural Gas (VING) in a new project that will deliver liquefied North Slope natural gas to a new LNG plant on Vancouver Island in British Columbia. The unique project calls for a gas-to-liquids plant to be built in Prudhoe Bay, allowing the liquefied natural gas to be shipped to Valdez in the existing Trans-Alaska Pipeline, which is now operating at less than half its capacity.

VING will also build a facility in Valdez to handle the LNG and trans-

fer it onto company-owned ships. VING's ambitious project will include the construction and purchase of new LNG ships and the construction of a receiving facility on Vancouver Island.

In a statement from APFC's executive director, Richard Cally, he explained that VING has an existing pipeline system in place to deliver the natural gas to various locations in British Columbia and the Pacific Northwest, and several purchase agreements are imminent with customers. He also stated that this investment was contingent upon VING receiving its necessary permits, and that they had been assured by government sources that the permits would be forthcoming shortly.

Mr. Cally also stated that the APFC financial commitment would be made through a Washington company, Brooksher Energy, a wholly owned subsidiary of Brooksher, a part owner of the VING project. He also stated that this was the first major investment in infrastructure under the APFC's Resolution 07-05, and that North Slope producer, GB Petroleum, was also a partner with VING.

Governor Stacey Powers, who has been a vocal promoter of a trans-Canada pipeline project, was unavailable for comment.

Stacey was in the governor's office late Saturday morning dealing with a hangover and questions from dozens of media personnel. Staying with the theme that she was in favor of anything that appeared to be good for the state, she and her press secretary made a coordinated and diplomatic effort to fend off all questions.

Stacey took the angry calls from representatives of the other North Slope natural gas producers herself. She steadfastly stood her ground on the position that this new opportunity was one that would get gas moving quickly, and that it was an investment by the APFC, which she didn't control.

Beth's Saturday morning was not as busy as Stacey's, but she had a little hangover, too. She nervously waited until 10:00 to call Ron Minty, assuming he would be sleeping late.

"This is Ron."

"Good morning, Ron. This is Beth . . . Saylor."

Ron's insides went cold. "Uh, good morning."

"Ron, I want to discuss something with you. It's about that man you were with last night . . . Budge."

"Oh, uh sure. What about him?"

"Well, it may not be my business, I mean your relationship with him, but I am curious about him. I have seen him before, on a flight to Seattle.

We were both in first class. That doesn't really mean anything, but then I saw you and him together in Juneau. It was after you and I had dinner. Then, seeing you with him last night, it just gave me a strange feeling about him."

Shit, Juneau. "Well, we're just friends. Bar friends. We actually met in The Mud Flats. He's kind of an interesting guy. He has money left to him by his grandfather. He's just fun to be around."

And he's going to make me ten million dollars, and I don't want you to fuck it up, Ron thought.

"Well, there's one other thing. Remember when one of the public members at the board meeting in Anchorage threw the loudmouth out of the meeting?"

Ron knew what was coming. "Yeah."

"He had a fake mustache. I didn't know it was fake until I thought I saw it come loose when he grabbed the troublemaker. Just that little glimpse of his face with the mustache coming loose made me think there was something familiar about him. I didn't figure it out until last night. I'm sure it was Budge."

Ron scrambled. "Huh, I didn't see that. I mean, he was out in the open at the board meeting in Juneau. I don't know why he would have come into the meeting in Anchorage in a disguise. He's just a guy who's well off, and because he met me, he likes to see what the board is doing. Just like Juneau. He'd never been there, so he just wanted to see it . . . and take in the board meeting."

"Oh, well, it all just seems strange to me. Do you trust him?"

"Trust him? With what? We aren't business partners, we're just friends." Ron was trying to sound a little indignant now.

"Okay. I'm sorry to bother you. I guess I'm developing a little paranoia in my middle age."

But I don't believe you, Beth thought as she said, "Goodbye, Ron."

When you do something you really regret, you can't make it go away. Contrition helps, but only time heals . . . and it never heals completely.
—From *Fred Longcoor's Book on Life*

Chapter 21

A Time Of Change

Billy was comfortably settled into his rented condo in Seattle when he finally called Raymond.

"This is Raymond."

"So, you're not the Reverend anymore?"

"I recognized your new number, Billy. Otherwise, I'm the Reverend."

"Okay, Reverend. I'm in Seattle, so I want you to come and visit me."

"What? When did you get here?"

"A couple of days ago. I've just been getting settled in, renting a car, buying some supplies, like your favorite whiskey."

As much as Raymond hated knowing that Billy was in his part of the world, he knew he couldn't duck him. And he knew he had to sit down with him and discuss what they were going to do. He'd just thought he would be doing it long distance.

"What's the address? I'll have to take a taxi. I don't have a car."

An hour later, Raymond rang the doorbell of Billy's condo in full Reverend-Raymond regalia. It seemed strange when Billy answered the door himself. In spite of his girth, he seemed less significant than Raymond remembered him. A running man in a rented condo.

"Welcome, Raymond, to my humble abode." Billy had his arms out like he expected Raymond to hug him. Raymond brushed past him with a mumbled, "Hullo."

Billy's furnished condo was luxurious. Raymond eased his big body into a large chair in the living room. "Nice place."

"Yeah, for a condo. It's not like the ranch. I already miss that fucking

289

place. Can I get you a Gentleman Jack?"

"You bought the good stuff . . . sure. Make it a double . . . rocks."

"You fucking preachers certainly can drink." Billy laughed, and for a moment he sounded like the king of the ranch again, not the master of a rented condo.

Billy brought the big glass of whiskey to Raymond and sat on the end of the couch that was close to his chair. He had a large glass of scotch in his other hand, which he set on the table in front of them. "What's the latest, Raymond?"

"Not much. I've been waiting to hear from you or Budge or somebody about the date of the transfer. I guess we have some time. I've been thinking about it, and I believe we'll need some kind of diversion. I can take care of the kid, but I'm betting that Betsy and some of the Brooksher big shots are planning on watching that huge fucking amount of money come in."

Suddenly, Billy realized he could play a part in the transfer. "I can help," he said. "I'm staying here until this thing is done. I could help to create the diversion."

Ignoring Billy, Raymond continued. "I've been thinking about this. It has to be something that would get everyone away from the Secure Room. Maybe a fire, or an explosion somewhere. It has to be someplace important enough for Betsy and everyone else to feel like they need to go there. One of the other Brooksher businesses, something like that. Not in the Brooksher Building, because they would shut the transfer down."

Billy had an idea. "How about the school?"

"My school? Wouldn't work. Betsy wouldn't understand it if something happened there and I didn't want to be there."

"Are there other Brooksher businesses around here? Anything that is Betsy's pet business?"

"There are Brooksher businesses every fucking place. Nothing I can think of that she particularly favors. Her only passion is some church she . . ."

Raymond stopped cold. "Bingo! She'd be over there in a shot if she thought something was wrong. She gives it money like she owns it." Now Raymond had a stir in his gut at the thought of burning that big fancy church.

"Perfect. Where is it? I can set a fire. Shit, I can blow it up. Boom, no church." Billy was excited at the idea of contributing, and he laughed.

Raymond recoiled. "No. I'd have to do it."

"You can't fix the transfer and fuck up the church all at the same time."

"Maybe the church isn't the right thing. Maybe we need something else. If we don't want her at the office, maybe you need to kidnap her."

Billy began to get it as he thought about Raymond's past. "You church-burning son-of-a-bitch . . . you *want* to set that fire so you can get off on it. What do you do, whack off while you watch them burn? You are a sick fuck, Raymond."

Raymond was embarrassed by what Billy said, and more than a little pissed. "I'm just saying we need a surefire way to get everybody away from the Secure Room, or make sure they don't go there in the first place." Raymond wanted to change the subject so he could have time to think. "What about the other end? What's happening there?"

"Nothing to sweat there. Budge's guy is on the APFC board, and all he has to do is tell us when the transfer is going to happen."

"Can we trust him?"

"Yeah, he's getting a cut."

"How much?"

"That's none of your fucking business."

"More than me?" Indignantly, Raymond added, "I mean, I've been at this for months."

"Relax, Rev. It's not near as big as your share."

Like nothing, Billy thought, *and then he's dead!*

An hour later, the two men were talking about past ventures and laughing it up like old buddies. Both new bottles of whiskey were one-third empty when Billy's phone rang. He pulled it out of his shirt pocket and answered in his typical fashion.

"Yeah."

"Billy, it's Budge."

"Well, speak to me, Budge. I'm just sitting here with the nastiest preacher man on the planet, trying to out-drink him." Billy laughed at his own wit.

"I can call back . . . but I think you want to hear this."

"Go."

"Ron just called me. Beth Saylor called him Saturday morning and quizzed him about me. Said she saw me on the plane going to Seattle, said she saw him and me together in Juneau, and she said she thought I was the man who threw the bum out of the APFC meeting. All of this after seeing us together at The Mud Flats Friday night."

Billy sat upright. "Shit. That's not good. That is, I don't think that's good. But what can she do? What did he tell her?"

"He said we were just friends. Just met in a bar. He told her it was no big deal." Budge hesitated. "She wasn't buying it."

"That's it. She's got to go." The anger and resolve in Billy's voice were palpable as he casually delivered Beth's death sentence.

291

Budge was surprised by what he heard, and wanted to make sure he understood. "Go . . . as in gone . . . forever?"

"She's poked her nose into our business for the last time . . . Seattle, Anchorage, Tim-fucking-buktu, everywhere we are trying to do something. We've got to get rid of her now. The longer we wait, the bigger mess she'll make out of our business."

Prophetically, Budge said, "We may regret this."

"Just don't fuck it up. This has to be very clean."

For the next two weeks, events moved forward quietly in the Alaska-Hawaii-Seattle triangle. Ron Minty laid low and tried to keep up with what was happening with VING. VING's permit applications were steadily churning their way through the bureaucratic system in British Columbia and the State of Alaska. Beth settled into her work as the president of Saylor Industries, trying to make up for the time she had lost working on APFC business. Billy and Raymond spent many boozy hours trying to conjure up a plan to assure that Raymond would be alone with a drugged Theodore in the Secure Room when the hundred million–dollar electronic cash transfer came through. Billy also handled repeated calls from Mario, who was now sniffing a big payday and getting very anxious.

Oblivious to the nefarious plan to use her company to steal one hundred million dollars from the Alaska Permanent Fund, Betsy Brooksher continued to smother Raymond with sumptuous meals and sex that was becoming more adventurous by the week. She really liked the Reverend, and she had a feeling that he was tiring of her because he seemed to have frequent excuses for not being able to visit her at the mansion. She was not desperate, but she was trying to please him.

Budge kept in touch with Ron regularly to make sure he wasn't coming apart. He had to force himself to care about what Ron was doing because his every thought now was about planning to eliminate Beth Saylor. He realized how much of a public figure she was, and he understood Billy's demand that he make her disappearance clean. He would have to make it a clueless mystery that frustrated authorities would agonize over for years.

Budge rented a car and spent several hours a day patiently waiting for Beth to leave the Saylor Building. Then, he followed her. Since her private penthouse was right above her office, she rarely left the building . . . trips to the beauty salon, the grocery store, Nordstrom, a restaurant now and then, and one other place that intrigued Budge. Two evenings a week, she drove to south Anchorage to take an exercise class in a small strip mall. The unlikely location for a downtown dweller to go to for exercise was due to the fact that Beth's favorite instructor had leased the space and started her own business there.

As Budge conducted his clandestine surveillance, he realized that the quiet area the tiny mall was in, near the southern edge of town, would be the perfect place for him to grab his high-profile target.

Budge purchased a small backpack, three rolls of duct tape, and twenty-five feet of sturdy rope. He put the tape and the rope into the backpack with his .38, the silencer, and a Slim Jim. On the day of the abduction, he planned to have a taxi drop him off at the grocery store a few blocks from the mall. He would walk to the mall parking lot while Beth was in her class, use the Slim Jim to break into her SUV, and then hide in the backseat until she got into her vehicle. His only enemy would be the Alaska summer with its nineteen hours of daylight, so he checked the long-range forecast every morning, looking for a cloudy, rainy day . . . one that fell on a Tuesday or a Friday.

As Budge made his plans to abduct Beth, he couldn't help but think about what a beautiful woman she was. He couldn't get his mind past that to actually imagine killing her . . . even when he became angry thinking about how she'd ignored him on the flight to Seattle.

"Nani," Nick said, "I'm going to call Beth. We need to meet in Seattle to close on the new building next week. Do you want to go with me?"

Nani was standing in the doorway of Nick's home office in a bright floral-print bikini. She had a flower behind her ear in her long black hair, making the perfect Hawaii Department of Tourism postcard picture. "I don't think so, Nick. I'm worried about Papa. I want to stay close to him for a while."

"I understand. Have I told you lately how beautiful you are?"

Nani smiled. "You tell me that all the time . . . but I love to hear it."

"I tell you that because I mean it. I really think George is going to be alright, but I would do the same thing if he was my father."

Hesitantly, Nani said, "He's talking about it again."

"What?"

"Some unidentified danger . . . in Seattle and Anchorage. He asked me again yesterday to remind you to be careful if you go there."

"No details?"

"No. He said it's not like before, but he senses some danger for both you and Beth. Please tell Beth to be careful when you talk to her."

"I will. As I have said many times, I will not ignore your father's warnings. I am a believer in the power of the kapuna." Nick was thoughtful for a moment, then continued. "You know, he could be just thinking about the danger of being in a big city, or maybe he thinks of flying across the ocean as being dangerous."

Nani didn't look convinced as she turned and left the doorway. Nick returned to his desk to call Beth.

"Aloha from Maui."

"Aloha to you. I'm glad you called. I've been stewing on something for a couple weeks that I need to talk to you about."

Beth told Nick about her night out with the governor, and what the governor had told her. When she finished talking, Nick was silent for a moment.

"Are you still there?"

"I'm blown away, Beth. My sister . . . governor of Alaska."

"Slow down, island boy. I haven't agreed to it yet, Stacey hasn't stepped down yet . . . and I hope she doesn't, and I would have to get elected if it did happen. I don't know if I want it, Nick. I'm not a political animal."

"You may not be a political animal, but you are a wonderful businesswoman, you're loaded with common sense, you're full of fight, and everyone in Alaska loves you."

"I'm just not sure it's what I want to do. Everybody else who runs for governor has a burning desire to be the governor. I have a burning desire to be who and what I am right now . . . and then I want to be you."

"Me?"

"Yeah, sitting on my ass on a beautiful tropical island drinking Chi-Chi's."

Laughing, Nick said, "You can't take my job. You need to take the lieutenant governor job. I don't want to be the only politician in the family."

Now Beth laughed. "And how is that going, Mr. County Councilman?"

"It's fun. We've had a couple meetings. It's more involved than I expected. We have budget shortfalls, legal battles, long-range planning, all that stuff. I'm glad I did it. But enough of that. We need to close on the Seattle building next week. Can you make it?"

"I've been expecting that to happen soon. I'm really snowed here, Nick. Not just Saylor business, but all of this APFC stuff. Can we just do a power of attorney for me and Chris? I can get it done and send it overnight to Betsy right away."

"Sure . . . I would love for you to be there, but I understand. We're scheduled to close Monday . . . June eighteenth. Go ahead and do the power of attorney, and give Wayne a heads-up about the date we have to transfer the down payment. If he hasn't done it already, he'll need to get information from their guy . . . what's his name, Marvin, about the details of the electronic transfer of the funds."

"He's already done that. We're set up. Have a good trip, and tell Nani and George hello. I'll take care of the power of attorney right now."

"Oh, about George. He's having his visions again. They're pretty vague this time. He just says for both of us to be careful."

"I'm always careful these days, Nick. That's probably why I don't have a man friend."

"You've got to get back on that horse one of these days, Beth."

Tiredly, Beth said, "I know. Goodbye, Nick."

It was a quiet two weeks for Sergeant Bob Baker, too. It was one of those rare times when he didn't have missing-persons cases piled high on his desk. That allowed his mind to wander, and it kept wandering to Billy Peet. He knew the murder of Stan and the unidentified woman was not his jurisdiction, but he couldn't help but think about it. Occasional conversations with law-enforcement personnel in Wasilla made him aware that their homicide case was hitting nothing but dead ends.

"I've got it, Bob."

Sergeant Baker looked up at his young assistant, Jill, as she came into his office. He always marveled at the way she bounced into the room like the diminutive blonde former cheerleader she was. She seemed too cutesy to be taken seriously, but was actually very good at her job.

"A phone number for the Peet Ranch in Montana."

"Thank you, Jill. Let me have it. I'll call it right now."

Bob dialed the Montana number, and it rang a dozen times. There was no answer and no answering machine picking up the call. He was about to hang up when a deep voice answered. "Hello . . . Peet Ranch."

"Uh, hello. May I speak to Billy Peet, please? This is Sergeant Baker with the Anchorage Police department."

It was quiet on the other end for a few seconds, and then the deep voice of Jeremiah Standing Tall said hesitantly, "Mr. Peet is . . . is not at the ranch."

"Do you expect him back soon?"

Still hesitant, Jeremiah said, "Well . . . I don't think so. Not soon."

"Can you tell me where he is? Do you have some way I can contact him . . . a cell phone maybe?"

"No, I don't know where he is . . . maybe going around the world. He calls *me*. I don't know his number."

Jeremiah found himself in an unexpected position, and he wasn't astute enough to ask the caller what business he had with Billy.

Frustrated, Bob asked, "Do you have caller ID? Could you look at that and get his number?"

"I don't know. I don't think so." Jeremiah hesitated for a moment, and then he asked, "You're in Anchorage? Is this about Anna?"

Sergeant Baker's detective instincts jumped into action. "Yes . . . yes. What can you tell me about her?"

Dutifully, Jeremiah said, "Mr. Peet said she left from there. He said she flew back to Russia from there. That's why she didn't come back with him. They were married. I think he was very upset about her leaving."

"That's very interesting. What's your name? What do you do at the ranch?"

"My name is Jeremiah Standing Tall. I am the caretaker while Mr. Peet is gone . . . until the ranch is sold."

"Mr. Peet is selling the ranch? Well, Jeremiah, when did Mr. Peet and Anna come to Anchorage?"

"That was about two months ago . . . April, I think."

Bob knew he was onto something.

I'll bet the woman who was killed with Stan was Anna, he thought. *Something went wrong, and she was killed with Stan. Stan had regular contact with Billy. She was Billy's wife, and she was killed in a home on a golf course in Wasilla with Stan Faro. Must have caught Stan fucking her.*

"Thank you Mister . . . Standing Tall. If I have any further questions, I'll call you."

Bob hung up and immediately called the homicide unit of the Wasilla Police Department. Within twenty-four hours, four Montana State Police cars swarmed the Peet Ranch. After questioning Jeremiah for two hours, they came to the conclusion that he was nothing more than an innocent employee. Jeremiah was set free to spend the rest of his life on a reservation he hated.

A search of Billy's office turned up identifying information about his Learjet, and with the help of the FAA, authorities in Seattle quietly impounded the plane in a hangar next to King's Row Executive Service at Boeing Field the following morning. They assigned a team of officers to keep surveillance on it twenty-four hours a day. Billy's ranch was gone, and his plane was gone. His big life had become very small, and he didn't know it. The only things the authorities didn't find at Billy's ranch were his financial records. . . . He had those files with him.

Most damning of all was the information Jeremiah gave them about Anna's immigration into the US and her marriage to Billy. After searching through several months of passenger records on flights to Russia from

Alaska turned up nothing, a warrant was issued for the arrest of Billy Peet for questioning in the disappearance of his wife. Billy was nowhere to be found, but authorities were sure he was in the Seattle area.

Sergeant Bob Baker was a happy man. He was grudgingly recognized by the captain, who didn't like him, and praised highly and publicly by the Wasilla Police Department. An official request by the Wasilla Police Department to have Sergeant Baker assist them in the continuing investigation of the murders was met with disdain by Bob's captain, but he reluctantly agreed to it for the sake of cooperation between the two departments.

After Bob became part of the official investigation team, Wasilla PD gave him access to all the information they had gathered related to the murders. That included a recap of their investigation of Stan's phone records. They were checking every call that Stan made over the last few months, and every call that came in to Faro-Way Properties during that time. They were doing the right things, but Bob was way ahead of them in his suspicions about Billy Peet.

Bob decided to visit Polly Hasey at the Faro-Way office. She looked stressed.

"I know this has been very tough for you, Polly. How are you holding up?"

"I guess I'm doing alright. I liked Stan. He was good to me, even though I didn't work for him very long. Every time I feel sorry for myself for what happened, and for losing my job, I think about Stan. I don't know why this happened, but he didn't deserve what happened to him . . . at least I don't think he did."

"Polly, you know we are on the trail of Billy Peet as a result of the connection telephone records established between him and Stan. I can't give you the details right now, but it was a very strong lead. One other phone contact of Stan's looks strange to me. Do you remember him talking with a Budge Brown? Our telephone-record search indicated he was someone who called the office several times . . . including several calls after Stan disappeared. The strange thing is that number is no longer in service . . . at least it's no longer being used."

"Sure, I remember him calling for Stan. You're right, he called several times after Stan took his emergency leave from the office. I didn't know for sure who he was, but I checked Stan's Rolodex, and the number that came up on our caller ID was listed in it as 'Budge.'"

Okay, Bob thought, *Budge Brown is definitely someone of interest. Now we just have to figure out where he is.*

297

Governor Powers spent a restless Thursday night. She had decided to announce that she was stepping down as the governor on Monday morning.

Nancy buzzed Beth just before 10:00, Friday morning. "Ms. Saylor, the governor is holding on your line."

"Madam Governor. It's nice to hear from you."

"You may not say that after I finish saying what I have to say."

Beth's heart fluttered—*Oh shit!*

"I hope it's not what I think it may be."

"It is, Beth. I'm going to announce that I am stepping down Monday morning. Then I'm going to announce that Lieutenant Governor Peter Harris will be stepping into my job right away. He will be there with me, and he will announce that Beth Saylor...you, will be the new lieutenant governor . . . if you will agree to it."

"My God, Stacey . . . I don't think I'm ready for this. I mean . . . don't be upset, but I'm still not sure I want this."

"Beth, you've got to want this. You are the right person for the job. Everybody in this state loves you. This is a job you can do, and you can do wonderful things for the state . . . because you are . . ." Stacey hesitated for a moment, like she was struggling to get the next word out: "honorable."

"I have to have some time, Stacey."

"You've got two days, Beth. Then I will have to go to plan B, and it's not a plan I'm comfortable with. Call me by early Sunday afternoon at the latest."

Beth hung up the phone and sat at her desk for several minutes. In spite of Stacey's warning, she was stunned. Finally, she walked deliberately to Chris's office. Chris was on the phone when she walked in and shut the door behind her.

Chris read the look on Beth's face and immediately spoke to the caller. "Forgive me, but I have to go. I'll call you later." He hung up, and, afraid that someone had died, said, "What is it, Beth?"

Beth told Chris the entire story, and he sat silently, taking it all in. When she finished, they both stared at each other in silence for a few seconds.

Finally, Beth said, "Well?"

A big grin spread across Chris's face, and he said, "Congratulations, Governor."

"Damn, Chris. I'm not governor yet. I haven't even agreed to become lieutenant governor. Wipe that goofy grin off of your face and talk to me. This is serious."

"You're damn right it's serious, and I seriously think you'd make one hell of a governor. Let's get Nick on the phone." Chris put his desk-set on speaker and speed-dialed Nick's number in Maui.

"Aloha, little brother."

"Aloha to you. You are on the speaker with Beth and me. Beth has news."

"Oh . . . I think I can guess. What is it, Beth?"

"You know, the lieutenant governor thing. Stacey is going to announce her resignation Monday. She wants an answer from me by early Sunday afternoon."

"You know how I feel, Beth. How about you, Chris? What do you think?"

"Easy. She needs to go for it."

"That would leave you alone on the bridge of the Saylor Industries ship."

"I can handle that, Nick. I'm feeling pretty comfortable here now. I'll be able to talk to both of you when I need to. I've got good people around me. What happens here shouldn't be a factor in her decision."

Beth jumped into the conversation. "I'm right here, guys. You're talking about me like I'm not here."

Chris and Nick laughed. Nick said, "Well, you're looking to us to help you make a decision. We need to talk."

The discussion went on for another thirty minutes. Beth realized that both of her brothers were strongly in favor of her taking the position Stacey was offering. Finally she said, "Alright, I need to sit on this for a while by myself. I don't want to be pushed into something for the wrong reason. I mean, it's a big ego boost, but that can't be the reason for doing this."

When the discussion was over, Beth left Chris's office and went to her penthouse. She took a bottle of water out of the refrigerator and sat near the huge living room window. As she looked over the city, she reflected on where her life had taken her and where she wanted to go:

I have a good life now . . . a life I enjoy. Sometimes, I am lonely, but at the end of the day, I would be even more isolated and lonely as the governor. Everyone would want a little part of me, but they would not be my friends. I love this magnificent state, and there is so much potential here. I would have at least four years to head the state in a direction that I believe would be best for the people of Alaska. Maybe I could do something that would help secure the future of the state. What if my vision for the state is wrong? What did Dad say . . . everything happens for a reason? Could this be a calling?

"Yes, Ms. Saylor," the governor answered. It was now late Friday afternoon.

"I'm on board, Stacey. I may be crazy, but I think I'm ready."

"Are you sure, Beth?"

"I'm a commitment person, Stacey. When I make a commitment, I fulfill it. But, if you have some time, I have a few questions."

"Sure . . . fire away."

Beth spent almost an hour quizzing Stacey about the status of education, subsistence, the budget, resource development, environmental issues, pending legal issues, Peter Harris, and a broad range of other issues the state was facing.

At a point when Beth hesitated for a moment, Stacey said, "Wow, is that it? You've been studying. You are very thorough."

"Yeah, for now. I've made my decision, but there will be more questions on Monday."

"That's fine. This is wonderful. You will make a hell of a governor. I'm happy you made your decision this quickly. It makes it easier for me. Get yourself fluffed up and be here at the governor's office by nine o'clock Monday morning. I want some additional time with you before we make the big announcement at eleven. I want you to get to know Peter Harris. He'll be here, too. . . . I think you'll like him."

Beth had to ask the question that was in the back of her mind. "Are you going to tell me what got you to this point so quickly?"

"No. It's . . . uh, medical, and it's very private."

The same afternoon Beth was agreeing to become the new lieutenant governor of the State of Alaska, Betsy Brooksher notified APFC Executive Director Richard Cally that Vancouver Island Natural Gas received final approval on their permits to begin construction, including the permits GB Petroleum had applied for in Alaska. Cally immediately had his secretary notify all the board members that their deal with Brooksher Energy and VING was ready to be funded, and that the electronic funding would take place the following Wednesday.

Ron Minty called Budge the minute he ended his short phone conversation with Richard Cally's secretary.

"Budge here."

"VING received their permits. We're going to make the transfer to Brooksher Energy next Wednesday."

"What time?"

"I don't know that yet. I just heard about it. I'll nose around until I find out. Then I'll call you. Keep your phone handy."

Budge quickly called Billy in Seattle.

"Yeah."

"Billy, they're going to make the transfer next Wednesday."

"Shit . . . already? I thought we'd have more time. Does he know exactly when the transfer will take place?"

"Ron doesn't know the exact time yet. He'll find out as soon as he can and call me."

"Call me the minute you know. We've got a little scrambling to do here."

"You mean you guys aren't ready for this . . . after all this time?"

Billy went ballistic immediately. "You take care of your fucking business and I'll take care of mine! Have you done *your* job yet?"

"Tonight!"

"Good. I'll talk to you later."

By the time Beth's busy day was almost over, she was anxious to get to her Friday workout. It was one thing that brought her stress level down quickly. It wasn't the only thing, but it seemed to be the only thing that was available to her right now. Her final bit of business in the afternoon was to get the power of attorney that their company lawyer had drawn up signed and notarized, so it could be over-nighted to Seattle for the closing on the U Building on Monday.

Beth hurried to the penthouse to change into her workout clothes. As she pulled her tights on over her long legs, she looked out at the steady rain that was falling. Anchorage looked dark and dreary.

Budge was nervous as he thought about what was ahead of him. It was Beth's normal workout day, and it was dark and rainy . . . everything he needed to complete his morbid assignment. He was also strangely excited. The idea of having a beautiful and powerful woman like Beth under his control kept his insides churning all day. If she followed her normal pattern, she would be leaving her workout between 7:00 and 7:30.

Budge called for a cab to pick him up at 6:00. By 6:15, he was walking south on the sidewalk next to the Old Seward Highway, toward the parking lot where Beth parked her SUV. His backpack held the supplies he would need to silence her, immobilize her, and kill her before he threw her into the fast-moving tide in Turnagain Arm. Budge had been in Alaska long enough to know that two hundred–foot workboats that supplied the oil platforms in Cook Inlet sunk and had never been recovered because of the tides. One lifeless six-foot redhead would be crab bait in the Gulf of Alaska before anyone even knew she was gone.

Budge approached the lot, and he was relieved to see Beth's Black Navigator at the back part of the parking area. *She must have gotten here late,* he thought. *Perfect.* Circling the back of the lot and staying out of sight behind parked cars, he made his way to her vehicle. He was flushed with anxiety as he pulled the Slim Jim out of his backpack. In spite of his anxious state, he had the door open in less than a minute. He hit the Unlock button and closed the front door. Then he opened the back passenger-side door and wriggled his way into the floor area behind the front seat.

Budge lay quietly for a few moments. As experienced as he was at this type of thing, his heart was beating rapidly. "Calm down, big boy," he whispered to himself. He had already considered plan B. If Beth spotted him in her vehicle, he would simply kill her right there as quietly as he could, and drive her SUV out of there.

As Budge waited in Beth's vehicle, he drifted into a kind of slow-motion world. He felt out-of-body as he thought about what he was going to do. Sometimes, in these moments, he felt sick to his stomach. Whether it was his body punishing him for his willingness to take another person's life or just his nerves building to a crescendo, he knew it would go away the minute he took control of Beth.

It's frequently said that when your time is up, it's up, and there is nothing you can do about it . . . but your time really isn't up until you give up.
—From *Fred Longcoor's Book on Life*

Chapter 22

Dying in the Backwoods

Beth was refreshed after her Friday-night workout. It always sent her mind to a good place. Suddenly during her workouts, at a point when she figured the endorphins must be fully charged, she relaxed and went with the moment. It put stresses of the day into the right perspective. She was preoccupied and thinking about how good she felt as she walked to her SUV.

Beth had intentionally left her keys inside the Navigator, so she entered the code on the keyless entry pad on the door. Surprisingly, the dull click told her the doors were not locked. She stood for a moment, trying to remember locking the doors. Shrugging it off, she opened the door and eased into the driver's seat. The instant she was settled in the seat, she knew something wasn't right. The inside of the SUV didn't feel right . . . and it didn't smell right! That's when she heard the ominous voice from the backseat.

"I have a gun with a silencer on it pointed at the middle of your back."

Beth screamed. "Who are you? What do you want? I . . . I have money, a couple hundred dollars . . . in my purse."

"I don't want your fucking money. Start your vehicle and get out of this parking lot. Turn south on Old Seward Highway. Don't do anything stupid. I can shoot you through the seat . . . you may not die, but you'll probably be paralyzed for life. If you do something really stupid, I'll shoot you in the back of the head." Bloodless Budge had no intention to shoot Beth, but she didn't know that.

Beth's mind raced. *What is this? What can I do? I'll have to go along with this . . . this maniac.*

303

It seemed to Budge that Beth took forever to get the SUV started and back out of her parking spot. "Let's go, let's get the fuck out of here." He saw the tops of the doors and windows in the other mall businesses pass by from his place on the floor, and had no way of knowing that Beth was quietly flashing her lights on and off as she drove by them.

Beth tried to think clearly. *I've got to make someone notice me. Is this a robbery . . . a rape? I've got to do something quick.* She reached for the radio button and turned it on. Music from her favorite classic rock station blared out. She tried to reach her cell phone and dial one of her stored numbers . . . any one, using the music to cover the sounds.

"Shut that fucking radio off." They had reached the end of the mall next to the highway, and Budge felt he could get up now and not be seen. As he struggled to sit up in the backseat, he added, "Do you want to see how serious I am? I'll blow one of your fucking ears off."

Beth could see Budge's face in her rearview mirror. "You! It's you! I knew there was something wrong with you." She was very afraid now. This wasn't a random attack. "What do you want?"

"I said to shut that fucking music off. What I want is for you to turn south on the highway. Head out of town."

"I know you. I saw you on the airplane . . . on the way to Seattle. I saw you in Juneau . . . with Ron Minty, and at The Mud Flats. Budge, isn't that it? Budge. You're the man who threw the street person out of the board meeting. What do you want?"

"I told you, get on the highway."

Defiantly and angrily, Beth said, "No. I'm not going out of town with you in my car. I'm going to stop, and I want you to get the fuck out of here."

Budge laughed a sinister laugh. "You're a tough-talking bitch. But, you're not in charge here." He lifted the .38 and leveled it over the center console. Then, he fired a silenced round into the front floorboard on the passenger-side.

At the sound, Beth screamed and jumped sideways in her seat. "Jesus, you're fucking crazy."

"So the ice queen has a potty mouth?"

"You associate with pigs, you act like a pig."

"Maybe that should be, if you sleep with pigs, you act like a pig."

Beth was quiet. *So that's it. This is about rape . . . at least partly.*

"Are you planning to rape me . . . is that what this is about?"

Budge laughed. "Oh, I'd love to get my hands on that cute little thing you have under your britches, but this is more serious than that."

Beth turned and tried to look Budge in the face. Using her best angry voice, she said, "You're going to kill me? You are actually thinking about killing me? Why? What did I ever do to you? Do you really even know anything about me?"

Beth slowed the SUV to a crawl as they approached the onramp to the New Seward Highway at the very southern edge of the populated area of Anchorage.

"Get this fucking thing on the highway or the next one blows your ear off."

Not knowing how to avoid it, Beth turned onto the onramp. Rush hour for the commuters who lived south in Girdwood was over, and there were few cars on the darkening highway. Anxiously, Beth asked, "Where are we going?"

"Just a pleasant little joyride. Keep driving, and I'll tell you where to turn off. And I see you blinking and flashing your lights. If you keep doing that I'll keep my promise about that ear. Put your lights on dim and leave them there."

A thousand thoughts went through Beth's mind as she drove along the rainy highway. The rain was heavy, and, she could barely see the highway. She knew the churning waters of Turnagain Arm were at the side of the winding road, but she couldn't see past the guard railing.

Why would someone want to kill me? she thought. *This is like a nightmare . . . just when my life is taking an upturn. You can't kill the governor . . . or, the future governor. I am not ready to die!*

They had been on the highway for twenty minutes . . . twenty silent minutes, when Budge said, "Slow down." They almost reached the sign that said Indian Valley Road before he could read it. "There," he said excitedly. "Turn onto that road."

Beth stopped the vehicle in the highway and said angrily, "I'm not going on that road."

His own anger flaring instantly, Budge lifted the .38 and fired a shot into the dashboard. Tiny plastic and metal pieces flew everywhere, some striking Beth in her face. She screamed and covered her face with her hands.

"Now, turn this fucking thing onto that road. I *will* put the next one through your ear."

Reluctantly, Beth turned onto Indian Valley Road and continued to drive slowly along the bumpy gravel road. She reached her hand up and wiped small amounts of blood from her stinging face. Now more afraid than angry, she began to cry softly.

"Don't start that shit. Rich bitches aren't supposed to cry."

Beth didn't answer her tormentor, and they continued along the road. She was hopeful as they approached each house with lights on and disappointed when no savior jumped out to help her. She thought about honking the horn and realized that would only anger Budge. The road narrowed, and as she noticed an open area to the right, Budge shouted in her ear. "There, pull in there."

Beth was unwilling to challenge Budge again, so she pulled the SUV into the small clearing next to the road. "Get as far in here as you can get," Budge said breathlessly.

Beth sensed the excitement in Budge's voice, and she knew something very bad was imminent.

Shit, she thought, *is this the place where I'm going to die?*

She stopped and quickly put the SUV in Park. Just as quickly, she opened her door and jumped out. She had only taken a few running steps when she heard Budge behind her.

"You're quick, but you're not that quick. Keep running, and I'll shoot you right in your tracks."

Beth stopped running and put her head down with her back to her kidnapper. Anger and resolve filled her, and a curious strength began to build. It was a strength she had used only one time before. She slowly turned around to face Budge.

"What's the big man and his gun going to do now? Do you want to kill me . . . or do you want to fuck me?

Budge was shocked by Beth's words. He'd known all along that he was going to take advantage of her before he killed her. He was a bad man who had done lots of bad things, but he had never consciously thought about the taboo connection between death and sex.

"Do you want to fuck me here on the ground in the rain or in my car?"

"What's this all about?"

"I'm betting."

"Betting on what?"

"I'm betting you won't kill me once you've fucked me."

Weakly, Budge said, "I've got a job to do."

"We'll see."

Beth had hit on Budge's biggest weakness. Now, her willingness to make a sexual gamble to save her life excited him in a way he had never experienced. In a voice that sounded almost childlike, he said, "In . . . in the car . . . in the back."

Beth knew her life depended upon playing this deadly game out as far as she needed to. She walked boldly to the rear passenger-side door and opened it. With deliberation, she lowered the seat back, extending the rear area of the SUV. While Budge stood looking dumfounded, she went to the back of the vehicle. After opening the rear door she lowered the tailgate.

Okay, Beth thought, *you've got to do this.* Turning to look at Budge, she took her coat off and threw it in the spacious rear area of the SUV.

"I hope you're not one of those pencil-dick guys. This better be good." With that, she pulled her exercise top and sports bra off over her head in one motion.

"Jesus . . . those are beautiful tits," Budge whispered. It was at that moment that Beth felt the life-or-death pendulum swing slightly in her favor. She crawled into the back of the Navigator and spread herself out provocatively on her coat.

"If you think you can handle this, get in here. If you're not man enough, shoot me and get it over with." Beth couldn't believe what she was saying and doing, but she knew this was now a battle for survival.

Budge was silent as he approached the back of the SUV. He took his jacket off and threw it in beside Beth. Awkwardly, he crawled in and lay down on his side next to her. "Let me see you . . . all of you."

Boldly, Beth said, "Let me see you. Let's see what *you've* got."

Beth instantly knew she had touched the wrong button. "What I've got is a fucking gun. Get those goddamn things, whatever they are, off."

"Okay, okay." Thinking quickly, she continued, "I just want you to lay back. I like it when I'm on top . . . deeper penetration. I'll be able to feel you better."

Beth's words and actions had turned the big man into mush. He allowed her to get up onto her knees facing him and obligingly rolled onto his back. He still had the gun in his right hand, but now his arm was lying limply next to her left knee. She put her thumbs into the sides of her tights and began to pull them down. Budge was becoming increasingly mesmerized as he got a glimpse of soft auburn hair coming into view.

Beth thought about Nick's words to her when she first took delivery of her new Lincoln Navigator: *Be safe, Beth. Make sure you buy a good all-purpose fire extinguisher and put it in your vehicle.* In one athletic motion, Beth reached and pulled the two-and-a-half-pound fire extinguisher out of the pouch at the side of the SUV with her right hand and put her left knee on Budge's gun hand.

Budge looked shocked as the fire extinguisher hit him across his left temple. He was too stunned to move before it hit him again, this time squarely across his left eye and his nose. Blood gushed out of his nose.

It took Beth a few seconds to realize that she had knocked him nearly senseless. She was regaining her wits, and quickly crawled out of the SUV, grabbing her coat and her exercise top as she did.

Shit, what do I do now? she thought. *He still has the gun. I've got to run.*

Budge moaned and made a weak motion to raise the gun. When Beth saw that, she started to run, not realizing she was running deeper into the backwoods. In a moment of clarity, she realized how thankful she was that she had her workout shoes on. Clasping her coat and top to her half-naked body, she continued to run on the gravel road as fast as her legs would allow. She covered about a quarter of a mile before she allowed herself to look backwards. The light was dim, but she couldn't see any shadowy figure following her. There certainly wasn't a vehicle following her.

Then, it hit her . . . *my cell phone!*

She stuck her hand in her right pocket, and there was no phone there. She jammed her left hand in her other pocket . . . no phone. Then she remembered.

I left it on the console when I tried to dial someone from the mall. Shit, shit!

Beth would have felt better if she knew that Budge was still lying in the back of her SUV. He would lie there for over an hour before he was able to pull himself up. His head was throbbing, his left eye swollen closed, and it hurt badly. He didn't know it, but Beth had crushed his eye socket.

Beth stopped and put her workout top and coat on, then continued to run. She was well aware that she was running farther away from the highway, but she knew she couldn't turn back.

There has to be someone living out here, she thought. *There has to be someone who can help me.*

She calmed enough to analyze her situation, and turned and looked behind her. Her footprints were clearly visible in the mud. She quickly moved off of the gravel road and forced herself to fight her way through the brush.

Johnny Bosco had spent a good day in Anchorage after coming home from the North Slope on Thursday. He spent the night in town with Carmen because he had been summoned to the Taylor Drilling Company office for a meeting Friday morning. At the meeting, he was told the company was very happy with his performance, and they were going to dispatch him out as a driller with a pay raise when he went back to work in two weeks.

After the meeting, Johnny stopped by Carmen's office to tell her the good news.

"Congratulations, Johnny," she said. "One more promotion, and you'll be in the office. I'll be able to get my hands on you every day." She gave him a big hug.

"I'm afraid not. Two more. Driller and then toolpusher. I've got several more years in the field before I can think about a town job."

Carmen put an animated pout on her face. "Darn . . . well, at least the money's better. And speaking of money, I have to fly out to show a home-site across the inlet to a customer after work tonight. I hate flying over there in the rain, but he is insistent because he's leaving town in the morning. I won't be able to come down to the cabin tonight."

"That's okay. I think last night will carry me for a day, and we've got two weeks before I go back to work. I think we need to celebrate tomorrow night. I'll drive back into town and take you out for a nice dinner. You decide where you want to go. We can fluff up like real city folks."

Carmen laughed. "Sounds like a date. I want to go to Mr. Z's. It's my favorite place."

"Mr. Z's it is. If you can make a reservation for eight tomorrow night, I'll pick you up at seven-thirty."

Johnny left Carmen's office by one o'clock, and after stopping at the grocery store and the liquor store in south Anchorage, he drove to his cabin. He was tired after a particularly tough week on the rig and a long night in bed with Carmen. After putting the supplies away, he built a fire in the fireplace and lay down on the bearskin rug. Warmed by the fire and listening to the rain beating a soft rhythm on the roof, he fell asleep. He woke up at eight o'clock, moved from the bearskin run to his bed, and quickly fell back asleep. He slept peacefully and had no way of knowing a beautiful woman was running for her life on the road to his cabin.

Beth ran through the brush until she was exhausted. She finally spotted a small partially collapsed log cabin about fifty yards off the road. She stumbled through the thick undergrowth and into the old cabin. When she was inside, she crawled under the part of the roof that had collapsed, thinking there was no way Budge would find her there. Wet and cold, she drifted in and out of a fitful sleep. She heard real and imagined sounds and had an ongoing dream that Budge found her in the old cabin and was attempting to rape her.

When he finally sat upright, Budge was too dizzy to stand on his feet. He scooted toward the back of the SUV and sat on the tailgate. After sitting for a few minutes, he was able to crawl out of the back and make it around to the driver's side by bracing himself against the vehicle. He struggled into the driver's seat, where he sat for a long time, his brain addled by the concussive blows from the fire extinguisher. He was aware that Beth had escaped, but his body couldn't respond enough to do anything about it. He was partially in shock—cold, and shivering violently. He started the Navigator to warm it up and continued to do that every hour or so throughout the night. Sleep was an on-and-off nightmare of pain, cold . . . and blind anger.

Repeatedly, he thought, *I am going to kill that bitch. I'll find her!*

Billy was up early Saturday morning. He and Raymond agreed they would meet to make a plan for the Wednesday money transfer.

"No whiskey, Reverend. Just coffee and serious talk. Be at my place at nine o'clock."

"I'll be there," Raymond replied impatiently." He knew Billy needed him, and he hated the way he was being ordered around. He arrived at Billy's condo promptly at 9:00.

"So, Reverend, I have been thinking, and I . . .

Raymond decided it was time to assert himself. "I think all this planning is bullshit . . . kidnapping, fires at the church, all bullshit. We need to keep it simple. A smoke bomb someplace in the Brooksher Building. I'll hide and go into the Secure Room when everyone is out of the building."

Billy allowed a tiny, knowing smile to show. "That's pretty good, Reverend. Who's going to plant the smoke bomb? Where are you going to get a smoke bomb? Where should we plant it? Who's going to light it? Who's going to sign you out of the building at the front door when everyone is evacuating the building?"

Raymond thought for a moment. Confidently, he said, "Well, I can make it using simple materials I can buy at the store, and I can plant it . . . probably in the utility room so it will blow smoke through the air ducts in the building. You can come in to visit me an hour or so before. I'll show you around the building, and we can plant the bomb in the utility room then. You can hide there, and you can light it. You'll have enough time to sign out and get out of the building before anybody smells the smoke. The only hard part is to figure out a way to distract the guard so I can run my electronic badge through the reader to sign myself out early. I'll check into that on Monday."

"Shit, Reverend. . . . That's simple and, dare I say it, brilliant. What will you do after the money is transferred?"

"I'll get the fuck out of there through the back entry, and you better be waiting for me."

Billy almost choked on that. "Uh . . . yeah, of course." Recovering his composure, he added, "We'll get out of here in the Lear. Straight to Mexico."

"Okay," Raymond said, "we've got three days to work out the details."

It was still cloudy on Saturday morning in Indian Valley, but the rain had stopped. The midsummer sun was up very early, and even with the heavy cloud cover, daylight lit the cramped spot Beth had crawled into by four o'clock in the morning. She was stiff from the cold and the forced run in the rain the night before. Like some wary newborn creature emerging slowly from a cocoon, she ventured out of her hiding place. Staying behind the weathered log walls, she peeked out the window opening and tried to see the road through the thick forest. After a long period of watching and listening and deciding there was nobody around, she left the cabin and made her way to the road.

I've got to keep going this way, she thought as she continued to head farther into the backwoods. A chilling thought hit her . . . . *What if nobody lives out here?*

Beth stayed in the brush at the side of the road and kept up an animal-like pace running and run-walking through the wet foliage. She didn't know it, but she had covered four miles since she left Budge in the Navigator.

Budge was up early too, and by five o'clock in the morning, he came around enough to start the SUV again. When he was warmed up, he looked around for signs that would indicate which direction she headed. The unmistakably female footprints in the mud at the edge of the road were partially washed away, but they were the only footprints there. Beth had headed deeper into the woods. *Dumb move, bitch,* he thought.

Budge drove the Navigator slowly along the road, keeping his eyes on the footprints in the mud. Suddenly, they were gone. He stopped quickly. When he was outside the SUV he could see she had turned into the bushes at the side of the road. *Maybe not as dumb as I thought . . . bitch.* Knowing it was now a new game, he carefully scoured everything in sight.

"Shit," Budge said out loud. "You could hide a fucking elephant in this thick shit." He got back into the SUV and continued at a much slower pace, stopping every fifty yards to get out and look and listen. He heard birds and occasional sounds he couldn't identify . . . *could be someone walking, could be a moose or a bear . . . could be a cunt of a woman.*

Ron Minty woke up early Saturday with pre-larceny jitters. He didn't know what time the money transfer was going to take place on Wednesday, and he only had Monday and Tuesday to find out about it. Having no idea where Beth was, he worried about the way she had connected him with

Budge. He decided to call him.

Budge was standing on the side of the gravel road, looking and listening, when his phone rang. "Shit . . . shit," he said as he tried to get it out of his pocket. He finally succeeded, then tried to decide if he should answer it. *Who the fuck is trying to call me at this time of day?*

Quietly, he said, "This is Budge."

"Budge, this is Ron. I'm sorry for calling you so early. I . . . I'm worried about the fucking redhead. I'm afraid of what she might do, I mean, about seeing us together."

In spite of the ridiculous situation he was in, Budge laughed into the phone. "That is so fucking funny . . . you have no idea how funny that is. Guess what, I'm worried about the fucking redhead too, but not for the same reason you are." Budge paused, then said deliberately, "Don't worry about her. I'm taking care of it."

Ron felt a sudden chill. "What do you mean?"

"I said not to worry about it. Now, I'm busy. Goodbye."

Ron stared at his cell phone. *Oh shit,* he thought.

Back in the Navigator, Budge continued his slow hunt along the road. He had no way of knowing Beth was miles ahead of him. He also didn't realize his cell phone had fallen under the seat as he tried to put it back in his coat pocket.

Shivering with fear and cold, Beth was thinking about what dying in the backwoods would be like. Not only was a crazy man trying to kill her, but she knew that nocturnal creatures used the early-morning hours to forage for food.

Suddenly, Beth stopped. She smelled smoke. She climbed up onto the road and began to run. She ran for a hundred yards, and then she rounded a bend in the road and saw the source of the smoke . . . a small tidy cabin with a faded red pickup sitting next to it. She sprinted to the cabin and climbed the short stairway to the front door. Through the glass, she could see a man at the kitchen stove. Her desperation emerged as she knocked frantically and screamed, "Help . . . help me! Please help me."

After fourteen hours of sleep, Johnny Bosco was up very early making coffee when he heard someone run up the front steps. He hadn't had time to turn around before he heard Beth's pleas for help. Suspicious of a woman beating on his door at six o'clock in the morning out in the middle of nowhere, he eased up to the door and looked out. Beth looked haggard and genuinely frightened. He slowly opened the door, warily checking for an accomplice in some nefarious scheme.

Beth was so relieved when she saw Johnny, she collapsed against him. "Please . . . please help me, mister."

Holding Beth firmly as she lay limply against him, Johnny took her to one of the cozy chairs near the fireplace and sat her down.

Johnny stepped back. "What the hell are you doing clear out here at this time of the morning? You look exhausted."

Groggily, Beth said, "He's after me. He wants to kill me. He tried to rape me. He's crazy."

"Who?"

"Budge, Budge Brown. He's been stalking me . . . I think."

Johnny went to the bedroom and found a blanket to wrap around Beth. Then he poured her a cup of hot coffee. All the while, she was rambling.

"He kidnapped me . . . at the mall. He was in my car with a gun. He said he would shoot me. I know him . . . I mean . . . I've seen him before. I think he targeted me."

Johnny sat in a chair beside her and talked to her in the most soothing voice he could conjure up. "Don't worry. Calm down. I'll protect you. I've got a gun of my own. Now, slowly, tell me your story . . . starting with who you are."

Beth was still very afraid that Budge would come busting through Johnny's front door at any moment, but she calmed down enough to tell him her story.

"Wow," Johnny said, "I thought you looked familiar. I think I've seen your picture in the newspaper or on television."

Almost apologetically, Beth continued. "Yeah, well, there's more." She told Johnny about the appointment that was going to be announced on Monday.

"Holy shit," he said. "I've got the lieutenant governor in my cabin?"

"Not quite yet," Beth said, and for the first time, she had a slight smile on her face.

"We've got to get you to Anchorage," Johnny said.

Beth became panicky. "We can't go back down the road. . . . He's there. He's got my Navigator. Do you have a cell phone?"

"I've got one, but it's useless here. You have to go back down the road about three or four miles before you get any service. It picks up a repeater on the mountain above Hope."

Beth's eyes showed her fear. "He's down there. He's probably trying to follow me."

"You're probably right. Unless you hit him hard enough on the head to cause brain damage, he's probably getting his senses back this morning." Johnny walked over to pick up his coat off of one of the dining room chairs.

"What are you doing? Where are you going?"

"I'm just going outside . . . out the back door. I want to look and listen for a couple of minutes. I won't be far, and I'll be right back."

"Please be careful. I'm afraid of him. He's crazy."

Slowly and quietly, Johnny eased out the back of the cabin through the rear door. He remembered Marty's words as he moved silently around the cabin, toward the outhouse. He stood quietly behind the outhouse and listened to the forest sounds for several minutes. There didn't seem to be any unusual sounds or anything ominous in the quietness, and he went back into the cabin, where Beth was waiting anxiously.

"I can't see or hear anything unusual."

"Does anybody else live out here?"

Johnny didn't want to give Marty up, but decided this was not a time to keep anything from Beth. "A Native man, an Athabascan. He lives a few miles past my cabin. He is a fine man. We have become good friends."

Now Beth was curious. "Both of you, you live out here by yourselves? There must be a story there . . . or two stories."

Johnny smiled. "Oh yeah, we both have stories." He became serious again. "But we don't have time for stories. We need to figure out how to get you out of here. You know, he wouldn't know my pickup. If we just had you keep your head down, we could probably just drive out of here."

"He'd stop us . . . I know it. He's crazy."

Impatiently, Johnny said, "We can't just sit here. If he's still out there, I don't want to go through tonight waiting for him to knock on my door. We need to get you out of here today and get the authorities on his butt."

"Please just let me rest a little. I need to think. I'm sorry for putting you in this position. I already owe you a lot . . . just for a warm place with some hot coffee . . . and . . . and for protecting me."

"No problem. I need to think, too. I know if I could just get far enough down the road for my cell phone to get a signal, I could call the authorities. Maybe I can try that."

Beth was panicky again. "Please don't leave me here alone."

"Okay, okay, let me think. Can I make you a sandwich? You've got to be hungry."

"That would be wonderful."

Johnny convinced Beth that he would look like he was doing normal chores if he went outside and chopped some wood and worked around the cabin. It would give him an opportunity to watch and listen for Beth's kidnapper, so he went outside while she ate her sandwich.

Now, the forest seemed very quiet, and there were no unusual sounds. Johnny puttered around outside for a half hour and didn't see or hear anything that concerned him.

She'll be getting scared, he thought. *I'd better go back inside.*

Johnny entered the back door quietly. Beth was sleeping on the bear-skin rug. She had the blanket over her, and it was the first time he saw her face without fear on it.

He thought, *she is a beautiful woman. She's apparently an important woman. I've got to get her back to Anchorage safely.*

Johnny was getting angry. Being held hostage in his own cabin by some crazy man he didn't know and couldn't see was beginning to piss him off. He wasn't used to hiding from trouble . . . that was certainly not part of the roughneck mentality.

It was afternoon when Beth woke up with a start. As soon as she saw Johnny sitting at the small dining table, she relaxed. He left the table and walked over and sat down on the warm rug as she sat up. "It's alright, Beth. I'm right here."

"I . . . I was warm and comfortable . . . and not afraid. Thank you. Last night was really bad. I was exhausted, but I didn't think there was any way I could sleep . . . considering the circumstances."

"I'm glad you were able to rest. Now, we need to make a plan. I can't sit here and wait for some phantom to come flying through my door."

"I know. I'm afraid. I'm afraid to drive down that road."

"It's the only way out. As quick as we get into cell range, we'll call for help."

"What about the other way . . . toward your friend?"

Johnny hesitated for a moment. "I don't want to drag him into this situation. Going toward his place just puts us farther away from help. We've got to try to get out of here."

"Okay. May I use your bathroom?"

Beth was in the bathroom for several minutes. Johnny heard the toilet flush, and then he heard the water running in the sink.

Johnny needed to use the bathroom himself, so he decided to go outside. He said in a voice loud enough for Beth to hear, "I need to use the bathroom. I'm going to the outhouse." Before Beth could answer, he went out the back door.

As Johnny came out of the outhouse, an angry voice behind him said, "Get your fucking hands in the air. I have a gun pointed at your head. Don't turn around. Walk to the front door."

Johnny fought the urge to turn on the voice and suffer the consequences. Wisely, he began to walk steadily toward the front door of his cabin, thinking, W*hy didn't I take my* .357 *to the outhouse with me instead of leaving it on the kitchen table?*

When they reached the steps, the voice said, "One step at a time . . .

slowly. One fucking stupid move, and I'll shoot you. Then I'll go in there and make that pretty redhead pay for what she did to me."

Johnny climbed the short stairway slowly and reached for the door handle . . . which he knew was locked. "It's locked."

Budge moved over to the side of the doorway. He was still holding the gun on Johnny, and Johnny could see his face now. The big man's left eye was swollen completely closed, and streaks of dried blood ran down his face in several places. *Looks like she got your ass pretty good,* thought Johnny.

"Yell at her. Tell her to open the fucking door."

"She's in the bathroom."

"Well, I guess we'll just wait until she gets out, then. I've got lots of time. And you two aren't going anywhere."

Johnny's anger was getting the better of his common sense. "What do you want? Why is a big ugly son-of-a-bitch like you picking on a woman?"

"You got a big mouth, son. You want to die right here, right now?"

Through the small window in the door, Johnny could see Beth coming out of the bathroom. She saw him and started to walk toward the door. "Beth, don't—"

Beth pulled the door open at the same time Johnny was hitting the front deck after a blow from the butt of Budge's gun. She screamed and turned back toward the bathroom. Before Budge could get over Johnny's body and make it across the room to grab her, she locked the bathroom door with the heavy bolt on the inside.

"Open that fucking door, you cunt. I owe you. I'm blind in one eye and I'm going to poke one of your eyes out." Budge was like a wild man as he pounded on the heavy wooden bathroom door. He was so frantic about exacting revenge on Beth, he failed to notice Johnny groggily picking himself up off the front deck.

Johnny started across the room toward the kitchen table just as Budge turned away from the bathroom door. Budge raised his gun and pointed it at Johnny's forehead. "Stop, fucker. I'll put a bullet right into your thick skull."

Turning his head to the side to keep his good eye on Johnny, Budge yelled to Beth, "I'm going to blow a hole in your boyfriend's head if you don't come out of that bathroom."

Budge could hear Beth crying. "Don't . . . don't hurt him. I'm coming out."

"Stay in there, Beth. He's bluffing."

Still sobbing, Beth yelled, "No he isn't, Johnny. I told you . . . he's crazy." Both men heard the sound of the bolt sliding on the door. It opened slowly. Beth walked out of the bathroom with tears streaming down her face.

"Well, good morning . . . bitch. You're looking pretty good today, except for the phony tears. How do I look to you? You did a nice number of my face." Budge was slowly backing to the side so he could see both of them easily with his one good eye. He turned to Johnny. "Okay hero . . . get over beside your new girlfriend so I can keep an eye . . . the only eye I have left, on both of you."

Johnny moved slowly toward Beth's side and turned to face Budge. Defiantly, he said, "What do you want now?"

Budge had moved between Beth and Johnny and the front door so he could face them. "I want the pretty lady to watch me blow a few fucking holes in you."

Having no idea that Budge really wouldn't kill them with a gun, Beth pleaded, "No . . . please, no. Don't shoot him. I'll . . . I'll do anything."

"Oh, you mean you'll fuck me like you promised last night? I mean, you *did* fuck me last night . . . you just fucked me with a fire extinguisher."

"No . . . I mean, yes. I'll do whatever you want."

Johnny couldn't take any more. "You're not going to do anything for this scumbag, Beth. He's not man enough for you."

Furious that Johnny had questioned his manhood in front of Beth, Budge said, "That's it for you, fucker." He raised his gun and pointed it at Johnny's head. Beth screamed.

At that instant, glass exploded into the cabin and flew everywhere. Budge's eyes widened and he had a startled looked on his face. Beth and Johnny stood in shock and surprise, trying to figure out what had happened.

Budge made a gurgling sound and slowly fell to his knees, and that's when Johnny noticed the spear point exiting the middle of his chest. He looked up to the broken window in the front door, and at that moment, Marty Stevens burst through the door. As Budge fell over, the remaining five feet of Marty's hand-crafted spear was visible, sticking out of his back.

"Are you two alright?" Marty's warrior-like look of confidence gave him away. He knew they were alright.

"Shit, Marty. . . . I've never been so happy to see anyone in my life." Johnny rushed over to the big Athabascan and hugged him. When he released him, he turned toward Beth and said, "Marty, this is Beth Saylor . . . Alaska's new lieutenant governor."

Beth rushed toward Marty and hugged him, too. "Marty, I agree with Johnny . . . I've never been so glad to meet someone as I am right now. Thank you. And it looks like you have supporters with you." Beth had spotted Shesh and Genen standing anxiously on the front deck, peering through the open door.

Marty laughed. "I've certainly never met anybody in these circumstances before, especially a lieutenant governor. And those are my scouts. They alerted me that there was trouble here . . . them and the forest."

Beth put a puzzled look on her face, but decided not to ask Marty what he was talking about.

Beth turned and looked at Budge lying on the floor. The reality of what had just taken place hit her, and she began to cry.

Johnny put his arms around her and said, "You're alright, Beth. It's over. You're safe."

Johnny's strong arms were comforting, and she replied, "I know . . . but he's . . . dead, and he was going to kill us, both of us."

Johnny pulled away from Beth and looked at her. "He can't hurt anyone now, and we've got a little business to take care of. We'll need to get in cell range and call the State Troopers first. Then we can see what kind of shape your Navigator is in, and we've got to get you to Anchorage. You've got a big day coming."

Johnny turned to Marty. "Beth and I will need a bunch of time to thank you properly."

Ethereal *adj,* **1 :** celestial, unworldly, spiritual
The things that happen in the backwoods in Alaska stay in Alaska.
—From *Fred Longcoor's Book on Life*

Chapter 23

Do You Swear . . .

"Okay, baby, the Executive Jet Service car is here. I'm off to Seattle."

Nani came running in from the patio to say goodbye to Nick. They had enjoyed a pleasant Sunday morning having breakfast in the sun, and Nani was still sitting outside when it was time for him to leave.

"I'll miss you. Be careful . . . remember Papa's words."

"Don't worry about me. *You* be careful. A beautiful woman in Hawaii by herself can get into a lot of trouble."

"Only if she wants to. Papa will look out for me . . . and you."

On the way to the airport, Nick tried Beth's number again, and it went right to her voicemail just like it had done three times before.

C'mon Beth, he thought, *pick that thing up.*

Five minutes later, Nick's cell phone rang. "It's about time," he answered without looking at the caller ID.

"Nick, it's Chris."

"Oh, I'm sorry. I thought Beth was returning my call. I've called her several times."

"Well, she's right here. We're in my office."

"What are you both doing in the office on Sunday?"

"I'm going to put you on the speaker. Beth has a little story to tell you."

Nick listened in stunned silence while Beth recounted her near-death experience with Budge and her rescue by Johnny and Marty. With the exception of a few brief interruptions to utter, "Shit," "No Shit," or "You're shitting me," Nick sat with his mouth open and said nothing until she was finished.

"Jesus, Beth . . . that's incredible. Thank God you're alright. We really owe those two guys who helped you. But . . . what is this about? Why did he want to kill you?"

"I don't know, Nick. One of the guys on the board, Ron Minty, knows him. I've seen them together. I'm going to talk to Ron."

"Do not do that by yourself. Take Chris with you. Do you want me to come to Anchorage? We can reschedule this closing."

"No, Nick. You go ahead and take care of business. I'm fine now. Chris wants to hire some extra security for a while . . . until we know what this is all about. We're going to do that."

"Okay. Be careful. Jesus . . . I just can't believe this. I mean, is this what money gets us? That crap in Seattle three years ago and now this?"

"We're in the public eye, Nick. We're very visible. We own a very big company. Dare I say it . . . we're rich? And now, I'm about to become more visible. I hope this isn't a mistake. I just decided to go ahead with it . . . and now this."

Chris and Nick tried to talk at the same time. "Don't let this stop you, Beth." "You've got to go ahead with this, Beth."

"Yeah, yeah. It's a higher calling. I know. I'm . . . I'm still committed. I'm just a little afraid."

Nick beat Chris this time. "A little fear is healthy, Beth. But don't let it consume you. I think you've already come through the worst thing that can happen. Shit, kidnapped, running through the backwoods, spears. It's bizarre."

Chris laughed. "I'm not sure you're helping, Nick."

"Okay. I'm done. We're at the airport. Be careful . . . both of you, and keep me posted. I'll do the same." Nick had already decided The Bird was going to head right to Anchorage as quickly as the papers were signed in Seattle on Monday.

Chris hung up and looked at Beth sitting across the desk from him. There was concern on his handsome young face. "You look a little forlorn, Beth."

"It's a lot, Chris. A lot to absorb. Almost dying. Bashing him in the head with a fire extinguisher. Running through the dark woods half-naked in the rain. Thinking he was going to kill me and Johnny, and then watching that amazing mystery man throw a spear that went clear through him. And now, I'm supposed to just calmly go off and become the lieutenant governor of the state?"

"It's all ordained, Beth. It all makes you special . . . a survivor. It makes you more powerful than everybody else."

"But I don't know why, Chris. I just don't know why."

"Go with it. My big sister is going to be the governor! Wow."

"Lieutenant governor, Chris. I would still need to run for governor, and then I need to get elected. It's a couple years away."

"Yeah, and by then you'll be so ready for it."

Right then, the main number for the Saylor Building rang on Chris's desk-set. "Who in hell would be calling here today? I'll let the answering service get it."

"No, Chris . . . there's been a lot going on. Please answer that."

"Okay. Saylor Industries, this is Chris Saylor."

"Mr. Saylor, this is Governor Powers. Is Beth there by some chance? I've been trying her cell phone without any luck."

"Madam Governor. Hello. Uh, she's right here. I don't know if she's found her cell phone yet. She had quite a weekend."

"So I heard. May I speak to her?"

"Good morning, Madam Governor. This is Beth."

"Sounds like you've had lots of excitement this weekend . . . Ms. Lieutenant Governor. I heard the news this morning."

"Yeah, I've had an adventure of sorts. I don't care for another weekend like this one."

"Are you alright?"

"I'm alright . . . I am tired. After everything I went through, I spent hours with the state troopers and the police department. They want to know why I was targeted, and *I* really want to know why I was targeted. Nobody . . . me included, believes it was random. After that, I went back to my place and slept like a baby . . . with a security guard outside my building."

"I can't imagine what you've been through, and I can't imagine why anyone would want to hurt you. Do you have any feelings about why you were picked out? Do you think it had anything to do with your company, or your position on the APFC board? I doubt that it has anything to do with your new job. Very few people know about your appointment tomorrow."

"I honestly don't know, Stacey. I do know that there is a connection between the guy and . . . Ron Minty. I've seen them together several times."

"Our Ron Minty . . . on the board Ron Minty?"

"The very same. And I think this Budge guy was in our board meeting in a disguise. I think he's the one who threw the street person out of our meeting."

"I can't believe that. Have you told the authorities about this?"

"Not yet. I want to confront Ron first. Not by myself. I'm going to take my brother, Chris, with me."

"Be careful. Now remember, tomorrow is our big day. I don't remember what time I told you to be here, but let's get together at nine in the morning. I want to hear all the details of what happened, and we have a lot of transition details to discuss."

Beth called Ron Minty from her office at 1:00 Sunday afternoon.

A sleepy voice said, "This is Ron."

Very formally, Beth said, "This is Beth Saylor, Mr. Minty. I would like to meet with you as soon as possible."

Ron, who had played poker with some buddies until almost five o'clock in the morning and then slept until Beth called, had not heard any news or read a newspaper since Saturday morning. "Uh, what's up?"

"Have you seen the news today, Ron? Budge Brown was killed yesterday in a cabin south of Anchorage. He kidnapped me with the intention of killing me. He is your friend, and I want to know what your connection to him is."

Ron was wide awake now. "What? I . . . I . . . I can't believe this." Budge's words, *Don't worry about her. I'm taking care of it,* flashed through his mind. "We're just friends . . . really, just bar friends. Just like I said before, I met him in a bar . . . The Mud Flats. I fucking can't believe this."

"I'd like to meet with you to talk about it. I need to know more. The police need to know more. I think you can see how important this is."

Ron was scared, and more than willing to cooperate with Beth. "I do. This afternoon. . . . How about this afternoon?"

"Three o'clock. My office. My brother Chris will be with me."

"Okay, I'll be there."

Ron closed his cell phone and sat on his bed, stunned. His wife walked into the room and asked, "Who was that?"

"Oh . . . uh, surprise board business. We're transferring the money for the VING project this week. I need to go to a meeting at the Saylor Building for a couple of hours this afternoon."

Ron arrived at the Saylor Building a few minutes before three. A uniformed off-duty policeman was sitting in a police cruiser in front of the building. APD's policy of allowing policemen to take their cruisers home with them gave an added police presence around town, and many officers worked special security jobs for extra pay. The regular Saylor guard was at the front door. He greeted Ron and took him from the entry to Beth's office. Beth was sitting behind her desk, and Chris was sitting in a chair to the right of her. He rose out of the chair and walked to Ron.

"Good afternoon, Mr. Minty. I am Chris Saylor. Thank you for coming."

Ron was obviously very uncomfortable. "Nice to meet you, Chris." Acknowledging Beth, he said, "Good afternoon, Ms. Saylor."

"Good afternoon. If you don't mind, I'd like to get right to business."

"That's fine," Ron said as he sat in a chair directly across the desk from Beth.

"Budge Brown kidnapped me with the intention of killing me Friday night. You've admitted to me that you are a friend of his . . . apparently you are a good friend of his, since I have seen you together several times. What do you know about him?"

Ron moved forward in his seat. "Beth, I can't believe this. I mean, like I said, I know . . . I knew Budge, but just casually. We just kind of hit it off."

Beth was firm as she continued. "You didn't tell me why was he in Juneau when I told you I saw him there with you. Why were two casual friends together in Juneau?"

"I told him I had a meeting in Juneau. He said he'd never been there. He asked me if I would mind if he went down there and sat in on the meeting. I told him I didn't mind, the meeting was open to the public, and we agreed we could party a little."

"Why do you think he was in our meeting in Anchorage . . . in a disguise?

"I have no idea why."

Disappointed with the information she was getting from Ron, Beth pressed on. "He was also on the same flight to Seattle I was on . . . in the first-class section."

Finally getting to project confidence as he answered something he could respond to easily, Ron said, "You told me that before. That could just be a coincidence. I see people I know all the time on airplanes."

"That may be, but you add everything together, and throw in the night Stacey . . . the governor, and I saw both of you at The Mud Flats, and it looks pretty strange."

Trying not to show guilt, Ron said, "None of it means anything. It may mean that I spend too much time hanging out in bars, but that's it."

Beth wasn't finished. "Where did he come from? What does he do?"

"I thought I told you about all of that. He was independently well off. Grandaddy or someone left him a bunch of money. He came from Seattle. I think he just played the market."

"It all sounds very vague and very suspicious to me. Did he ever ask you for information about the APFC?"

Ron tried not to react with surprise. "No . . . I mean, general questions, like what I did and what the board did. The same questions everybody asks."

"Did he ever ask questions about me?"

Ron sensed an opportunity to lighten the conversation a little. "Just wanted to know what the story was on the hot redhead."

Beth ignored Ron's answer and continued, "Did he have any other friends?"

"Probably. I really don't know. I just didn't know him that well."

Beth felt the dead end approaching. She glanced at Chris, who had sat quietly while she questioned Ron, and sensed that he didn't have anything to add or ask.

Trying to be civil, Beth concluded the meeting with a small fib. "I guess that's all I have to ask you. I need to warn you that I told Richard Cally and the authorities about your connection to Budge Brown. I'm sure they will be contacting you." She thought she detected a slight reaction from Ron.

"I expected that. If you're done, I'll be leaving." Ron left Beth's office, whispering under his breath to himself when he reached the hallway, "Too bad Budge fucked that up."

Beth and Chris sat in silence as Ron left. Finally, Beth said, "I guess I better tell Richard Cally and the police about Ron Minty."

Ron was in distress as he left the Saylor Building.

What do I do now? Do I run, do I just forget about the money-transfer scheme? Do I go through with the money transfer and get ready to run?

He drove around Anchorage for a few minutes, and then decided he needed a drink. He knew it would be quiet on a Sunday afternoon at The Mud Flats. He was surprised to see Vicki standing behind the bar.

Vicki looked at Ron, and the look told him she knew about Budge.

Ron said, "I'm surprised to see you here today. You don't normally work on Sunday, do you?"

"No, Tina called in sick. They called old reliable . . . me. I didn't expect to see you here, either. I heard about your buddy on the news. Too bad."

Ron replied, "We weren't buddies. We knew each other . . . that's it."

"Oh, *yeah.* Budge told me about paying that stripper to jump your bones. Only good buddies do that for each other."

"What? What are you talking about?" Ron was seething inside.

He paid her? And then he bragged about it to Vicki?

Vicki leaned over the bar and whispered, "Cherry. . . . Budge told me he paid her to fuck you. Now, do want to keep chatting about old times, or do you want your usual?"

Flustered, Ron blurted out, "The usual."

Vicki delivered Ron's martini, and headed over to take orders from two men who had just sat down on the other side of the bar. He was relieved. He needed to think.

Okay, let's organize this. Beth and her brother know about Budge and me. Richard Cally and the cops know about Budge and me . . . or they will soon. Vicki knows about Budge and me. Nobody knows about my connection to Billy Peet . . . that I'm aware of.

Then it hit him: *Shit, I don't know how to get hold of Billy! I don't know how to tell him when the money transfer is happening!*

Ron took another big drink of the martini.

Okay, calm down, he thought. *One thing at a time. You're going to have to answer questions from the board, or at least Richard Cally, and from the police. Answer them just like you answered Beth.*

The vodka was calming Ron down. He finished his martini and ordered another one.

Find out about the money transfer. . . . Billy will call me. He'll panic because he can't get hold of Budge, and he'll call me. He may even see the news about Budge and call me. It's all going to work out.

Robert's cell phone rang late Sunday evening. Gingerly, he picked it up and looked at the caller ID. "Hello."

"Hi. How's my sweetie tonight?"

"Anxious. I can't wait to get this thing going."

"I know you've been working hard. Are you still loading supplies?"

"Yeah, I've made two round-trips from Anchorage today with this poor old pickup. If I put any more stuff on the boat, it'll sink. It's *sooo* ready . . . just like me."

"I'm anxious, too. This will be fun. It may be stressful at first, but then it'll be fun. How far do we have to go before . . . .?

"Before what?"

"Before we can stop so I can climb all over you?"

Robert laughed. "I don't know . . . maybe a quickie when we get out into the sound. And I do mean quickie. I think it'll take me about thirty seconds and I'll blow like a whale."

"Okay, baby. Here we go."

Raymond was at work at Brooksher early Monday morning. One of the first things he did was engage the receptionist at the main desk in small talk while he paid close attention to the people passing their badges through the electronic reader before they entered the main lobby. She never focused on what he was doing, and the guard at the front door was busy greeting dozens of workers who were arriving. Raymond soon realized that watching the morning arrivals didn't help. He decided to come back down midmorning to check what was happening as people were leaving.

Raymond had gathered the supplies he needed to make a smoke bomb on Sunday. He started bringing the ingredients in piecemeal under his jacket and hiding them in his office Monday morning. *We're really going to do this,* he was thinking as he unloaded his first stash into a desk drawer.

Around ten o'clock in the morning, Raymond went down to the lobby and sat on one of the benches, pretending to make a call on his cell phone. He watched as several people left the building and ran their security badges through the electronic reader. There was nothing unusual about what was happening until the phone rang in a small kiosk about fifteen feet from where the guard was standing. He left his post near the reader and answered the phone. In the meantime, two people left the building and ran their badges through the reader. The guard didn't pay any attention to them.

That's it, Raymond thought. *I can have Billy dial the front kiosk from the utility room, and I'll run my badge through the reader as the guard is walking to the phone.*

Billy was busy, too. He called his pilots and put them on paid standby beginning on Tuesday, telling them they would need to be ready to leave on a moment's notice Wednesday, and that they would not be coming back to Seattle. They had flown for him for several years, and they were well aware that Billy's business was not aboveboard. They didn't care. They had both lost their licenses years ago, and flying for Billy was not only lucrative, it was just about the only flying job they could get.

The authorities had hoped to identify the pilots. Their anonymity frustrated the leaders of the team that had Billy's plane staked out.

Billy had been trying to get hold of Budge since early Monday morning. He realized that Ron Minty probably hadn't been able to find out when the money transfer was going to take place yet. . . . He just wanted to impress upon him again how important it was to find out about it soon. He also wanted to know if Budge had completed his mission to get rid of Beth Saylor.

"Answer the fucking phone, Budge, call me!" he yelled into the phone at the completion of Budge's voicemail message. Little did he know that Budge's phone had ended up under the front seat of Beth's Navigator, which was sitting in the back of the yard at TIG Collision Repair. Beth's limo driver, Vince, had taken the SUV to TIG early Monday morning after Beth cleared her personal things out of it. The owner, Tig, told him, "I'll tell you man, it looks like that bullet fucked up a lot of stuff in that dash. I'd guess it's going to take two weeks just to gather all the parts." Vince had just walked far enough away from the SUV that he couldn't hear it when Budge's cell phone rang the first time.

In Anchorage, Beth had gone to bed early Sunday night and was up early Monday morning. She felt good. She was refreshed, and for the first time, she really thought about how glad she was to be alive. Throwing a long coat on over her silk pajamas, she took the elevator down to the parking garage to get her personal things out of the Navigator. She was pleasantly surprised to find her cell phone in one of the cup holders in the center console.

When she returned to the penthouse, she took a long hot bath and put her favorite red business suit on. She had decided to have Vince drive her to the Capitol building in the limo. He was waiting by the limo in front of the Saylor Building at 8:30.

"Good morning, Ms. Saylor. You look lovely this morning . . . Madam Lieutenant Governor. Those little cuts on your face barely show."

"Good morning and thank you, Vince." Beth reached up and lightly touched her cheek. "The marvels of makeup. Did you get the Navigator to the body shop?"

"Yes ma'am, I just got back. I think it's going to be there awhile. The dash is a mess. I told the owner to check it over really good. Are you ready for your big day?"

The shot being fired and the pieces from the dash striking her face flashed through Beth's mind. "As ready as I can be. I'm not sure what I'm getting myself into, Vince. I hope I can handle all of this."

Vince started to close the rear door of the limo when he stopped to lean in and say, "You can handle it. I think you can handle anything."

"Thank you, sometimes I feel like I can . . . and sometimes I feel vulnerable." To herself, Beth thought, *without someone to help me.* By the time Vince dropped her off at the Capitol building, she had a plan.

"Vince, I want you to go on a very important mission for me, and you'll have to go fast. Here's what I want you to do. . . ."

"Good morning, Madam Governor," Beth said as Stacey greeted her

327

outside her office door."

"Good morning, Madam Lieutenant Governor," Stacey replied, and they both giggled like little girls. "Come on in, let's talk. You don't look worse for wear."

"Just some small battle wounds. Wait until you hear this story."

Stacey leaned back in her chair. "Wow," was all she could say when Beth finished telling her about the ordeal with Budge Brown.

"Yeah . . . wow."

"You're a brave girl. I mean, taking your top off and lying back in the car and basically saying, 'Come and get me.'"

"I had to do something to change the dynamics. I don't want this to come out wrong, but the minute he saw my tits . . . I was in charge."

Stacey laughed. "Some things never change. No matter what the situation is."

For the next hour, Stacey talked to Beth about what she should expect to face as she took over as the lieutenant governor, and Beth asked questions. When it was almost 11:00, Stacey said, "That's it. That's all we have time for right now."

Beth looked overwhelmed. "Well, I'm assuming I can talk to you if I need help."

A strange look crept across Stacey's face. "I . . . I'm not going to be around here, Beth. I'm leaving tonight. I don't know when I'll be back."

"You're kidding. Where are you going? To the Mayo, or something like that?"

"Something like that."

"I'm sorry, Stacey. I don't know what you have . . . I mean, what your condition is, but I'll be thinking about you."

"Thanks. Don't worry. And Peter Harris is a good man. He can tell you everything you need to know about your new position, and he knows a hell of a lot about mine." Stacey stood up and took a brief nostalgic look around her office. "So, it's time. . . . Let's go do this."

Nick had a quiet night at the Executive Plaza Hotel after arriving in Seattle Sunday afternoon. He awoke refreshed and ready to tackle the day Monday morning.

"Good morning, Betsy. This is Nick."

"Good morning, Nick. I hope you had a nice trip. Are you excited about getting this done?"

"I am. Donnie Clayton is chomping at the bit to take over the building. Are we still set for three o'clock this afternoon?"

"Yes. Marvin and Wayne have been talking regularly, and everything seems to be in order. We received the power of attorney from Alaska by FedEx first thing this morning. I'm sorry Beth couldn't make it . . . and Chris. I've never met him."

"I hope we have more dealings in the future, Betsy. With Beth moving into her new job with the State, Chris will become the president of Saylor Industries, and I'm sure you will meet him. You know, the governor is going to make the announcement about Beth's new position in Anchorage in four hours. I don't know if it has made the news here or not, but there is another story about Beth I will have to tell you."

"Alright, come to the office an hour before the closing. The lawyers, the title people, and the bankers have all agreed to do the closing here. Sometimes, being a rich old broad is a good thing. You know, this will be fairly simple, and then maybe we can have a couple drinks and an early dinner."

Nick thought about his plan to head right to Anchorage after the closing. He started to say something about that to Betsy, and then thought better of it.

I'll talk to Beth right after her press conference and see how she's doing, Nick thought.

"Sounds good, Betsy. I'll see you about two o'clock."

At noon in Anchorage, all three local television stations broke into their regular programming to announce the shocking news. Bursting on-screen with the headline, *Powers Resigns,* they all documented the startling news conference that Governor Stacey Powers held an hour earlier at the State Capitol. She was stepping down for undisclosed personal reasons, and, by state statute, Peter Harris would succeed her as governor. Peter Harris in turn announced that Beth Saylor would succeed him as lieutenant governor. Both Peter and Beth made short statements about how sad they were to see Stacey step down, and confident-sounding statements about how the State government would move forward without her.

In a separate statement at the conclusion of the news conference, Beth introduced Johnny Bosco and Marty Stevens, the two men who had rescued her from a kidnapper over the weekend, killing the man who kidnapped her.

Beth and Peter were inundated by the media, state legislators, and friends for the rest of the day. Most of the focus was on Beth because of her involvement with two major news events in four shocking days. Johnny and Marty became instant cult heroes, and Beth's heroics in Seattle three years before were quickly dragged out of the archives.

When Beth spotted Vince in the crowd, she walked over to him and said, "Thank you, Vince. I wasn't sure you could pull that off in time."

Laughing, Vince said, "It wasn't easy. Johnny had to jump on his four-wheeler to go get Marty. Then he had to convince him to come with him. When he got him back to the cabin, he loaned him some clothes, and then it took me ten minutes to get that damn limo turned around in that little space in the woods."

Nick waited for a half hour after the news conference and then called Beth.

"Madam Lieutenant Governor. How does it feel?"

"It's crazy right now, Nick. I had to excuse myself and hide in an empty office just to be able to answer your call. It's . . . I've got to admit, it's exciting. But it's also scary, and I know the reality of it all will hit me later today. Unfortunately, there's more interest in my wild weekend than the fact that I'm the new lieutenant governor . . . or will be when I'm confirmed."

"You are up to it, Beth. I am very proud of you. You are one hell of a woman."

"Thanks, Nick. Coming from you, that means more than anything else I've heard today . . . and I've heard a lot."

"I can only imagine, and I don't want to hold you up. I'm heading to meet Betsy in a few minutes. I wanted to get there early so I could tell her about what happened to you on the weekend. I wanted her to hear it from me. Mostly, I want to find out if you are alright. I was planning on heading The Bird your way today . . . just to support you, but Betsy wants to celebrate this deal of ours. I wanted to—"

"Nick, don't worry about me. I'm fine, and I've got Chris here for support. I actually thought you would stay there a day or two and help Donnie get organized. Taking over a property like that is a big deal. We haven't made the definitive decision on what we're going to do with it yet."

"Well, if you're doing alright, I'll do just as you suggest. That *was* my plan before I heard about your little weekend adventure."

"Okay. It's a done deal. We'll talk later today or tomorrow."

"Great. Congratulations, Beth. I love you."

"I love you too, big brother."

Wow, thought Beth, *this is a big deal when I get an I-love-you out of Mr. Conservative.*

Forty-five minutes later, Nick was sitting in Betsy's office. "Are you ready to hear an amazing story?"

"Yes. I've already seen a snippet of something on CNN about the governor stepping down in Alaska, somebody taking her place, and Beth becoming lieutenant governor. Can you top that?"

"I think I can." Nick then told Betsy the story about Beth's kidnapping and rescue over the weekend.

"Holy shit."

Nick laughed. "My words exactly."

"What an amazing week for Beth. She's pretty tough. I admire her. Is she doing okay?"

"Yes. I just talked to her. She's covered up with media people. Chris is there for support, so she'll be okay. I'll head to Anchorage after we get some things settled with your . . . excuse me, our building in the next day or so."

"Well, then we are about ready to get this sale done. Let's head to the conference room."

Nick and Betsy entered the conference room, and introductions were made all around. Betsy stood at the head of the conference table.

"Brooksher is a huge company, and we make business deals every business day. We sell property, we buy property . . . we sell businesses and we buy businesses. Since the passing of Mr. Brooksher, I have been part of many of these transactions. None of them have touched me more personally than this one between Brooksher and Saylor Industries. It is up to all of you to cross the t's and dot the i's, but I want everybody to know how happy I am about this sale. The U Building was a personal dream of Del's, and it is very gratifying for me to be able to sell it to my dear friends, the Saylors. Their use of the building will make Del proud . . . wherever he is."

All the related paperwork was blessed by a fleet of lawyers and accountants representing both companies, and the formal signing was accomplished quickly.

Betsy turned to Nick and said, "With your approval, you may have your bank make the transfer of the twenty-six million–dollar down payment to our bank."

Nick picked up his cell phone and called Wayne Hudson, who was waiting for the call. "Wayne. Nick. Please notify our bank that they may make the transfer to Brooksher's bank now. Thank you."

The conference room buzzed with small talk for a few minutes, and then Brooksher's bank representative's cell phone rang. "Thank you," he said, and closed it. With a small grin on his face, he looked around the table and said, "Done. Congratulations, Mr. Saylor . . . you own a new building . . . that is, you and your bank own a new building."

Everyone laughed, and sporadic clapping circled the big table.

After everyone had cleared out, Betsy said, "Let's go celebrate. If you don't mind, I'll ride with you. The limo is in the shop today for routine maintenance."

Betsy directed Nick to The Rusty Turtle, and they were seated at Betsy's table. "I'd love some champagne, but I feel like something with a little more kick today. I'm going to have a Manhattan."

Nick burst out laughing.

With a hurt look on her face, Betsy asked, "What's so funny?"

"A friend of mine," Nick said. "I ordered a Manhattan once, and when the waiter walked away, he said, 'That'll make you puke straight up.'"

Betsy laughed, and she laughed even harder when the waiter showed up and Nick ordered a Manhattan.

By Monday afternoon, Billy had worked himself into a lather. He had called Budge's cell phone a dozen times and left angry messages every time. He finally decided to call Ron Minty.

"Hello . . . this is Ron."

"Minty, this is Billy."

Ron instantly gushed. "Jesus, am I glad you called. Just a minute." Ron rushed over and closed his office door. "I've got something to tell you."

"Well, I've got something to tell you. I've been trying to talk to Budge all day, and the fucker won't answer his phone."

Ron hesitated for a moment, and then pronounced solemnly, "Billy . . . this probably hasn't made the news in Seattle yet. Budge is dead."

"What. What the fuck do you mean, he's dead?"

"Dead, dead. With a spear . . . in the back."

"With a fucking spear? What is this, Nanook of the North?"

Ron told Billy the whole story, tolerating dozens of interruptions and a litany of profanity. When he was done, all Billy could say was, "Fuck . . . I can't believe this."

"I'm afraid it's true, and I was scared to death I wouldn't be able to get hold of you. I'm glad you called."

Billy had an assortment of thoughts running through his head: *Well, now I won't have to give Budge a cut . . . but I'll have to give this fucker a cut. I guess that's a push, unless I hire someone to kill him afterword.*

"The time for the transfer. Do you know it yet?"

Ron was ready for the question. "No, but I'm meeting one of the board members tonight for drinks. The vice chairman. I think he'll be able to tell me. I can get it out of him. We're buddies."

"Jesus, man, we've only got two more days . . . really only today and tomorrow to find out. Don't fuck this up."

Or what, Ron thought, *you'll send Budge after me?*

"I know. I'll get it. At least now I have a number to get hold of you. And . . . I . . . I have some questions."

"What?"

"The money, where is it going?"

"To an offshore bank account . . . in the Cayman Islands."

"When do I get my cut? I mean, how do I get my cut?"

"You're going to have to be patient. After it goes into our offshore account, it will be transferred immediately to an offshore security fund . . . almost literally across the street in the Caymans. We can't just have a hundred million dollars sitting around in our account. After we transfer it to the offshore security fund, we will immediately close our account. Nobody, not the US Government, not anybody, has access to these security funds."

"*When* will I get my money?"

Ron's tone was beginning to irritate Billy, but he knew he had to be careful until he got the information he needed from him about the money transfer. "It will be a while. Maybe six months to a year."

Ron erupted. "Six months, a year? I can't wait that long. What'll I do?"

"Get the fuck out of Anchorage. Go to Mexico . . . that's what I'm going to do, or go farther. Get yourself a bartending job if you have to. I'll tell you what. That ten million you were begging for? Now that Budge is dead, ten million it is. Lay low. Eat shit if you have to. You'll have ten million *or more* in six months or a year."

Ron calmed down. "Why so long, and what do you mean about more?"

"Because it goes into a fund. We can't run around spending money like crazy right after a hundred mil disappears. These funds—this one is with a major Wall Street company—will make a lot more money during the year. They're like insurance funds . . . credit default, they call them. All tied to the housing market. As soon as this is done, I'll tell you the name of the company . . . a big, famous financial company. You'll feel good when you hear it. In the meantime, you'd better make some plans to get out of town . . . quickly."

Hesitantly, Ron said, "I will. What guarantee do I have . . . that I'll get the money?"

Billy laughed. "You think I want some pissed-off guy running around who knows who took a hundred million dollars from the State of Alaska?"

Ron was quiet, and Billy continued. "Okay. Call me the minute you know about the timing. I don't care what time of day it is. If I haven't heard from you by noon tomorrow, I'm calling you."

Finally, Ron spoke up. "Have you ever thought about how ridiculous this is? I mean, a few guys with a half-assed plan stealing a hundred million dollars . . . electronically? And I don't think you even had a plan a month ago."

"You know Ron, you're supposed to be a smart lawyer. You're supposed to know a little bit about everything. Do you know what half the criminals in the world are thinking right now?"

"What?"

"Technology baby . . . ain't it beautiful?"

Hundreds of millions of phone calls taking place simultaneously; teenagers passing explicit images of themselves back and forth by the millions; movies, videos, songs, sporting events, stock market information, and news being downloaded to millions of handheld phones every day . . . would Alexander Graham Bell be very proud . . . or very frightened?

—From *Fred Longcoor's Book on Life*

Chapter 24

It's Not Here!

"Jerry, this is Ron. I know this is late notice, but do you feel like having a drink tonight? We haven't done that in a while."

Jerry Holter had put in a very busy Monday. He was so busy, he hadn't attended the news conference announcing that the governor was stepping down. He had swallowed that surprise in the privacy of his office. "Hi. You know, it's been a really crazy day. I think I'd like an opportunity to talk with somebody about all of these bizarre things that are going on. The Turnagain Room? Say, five o'clock?"

"Perfect. I'll see you there." Ron breathed a sigh of relief after hanging up.

Buffy Lantry saw Ron Minty come in the door to the Turnagain Room a few minutes before five o'clock and head to a table toward the back of the room. Remembering the outrageous tip he left her before, she decided to push it.

"Good afternoon, you handsome devil. Are your friends joining you?"

"Hi. Friend, just one friend." Ron had too much on his mind to be flattered by the waitress's greeting.

"Okay. Can I get you a drink?"

"Big tip if you can remember what I drink."

Buffy thought for a moment. "I think, Belvedere, up, olives."

Ron smiled. "Close enough. Belvedere, dry, up, three olives."

Moments later, Jerry walked in. Buffy returned with Ron's martini, and Jerry ordered the same thing. Ron was anxious to get down to business, but he knew he needed to talk about something other than the money transfer first.

335

"Pretty wild day. Did you see any of this coming?"

"Hell, no. How could anybody predict this? And the thing with Beth over the weekend. That's incredible."

Ron really wanted to avoid a conversation about Beth and Budge because it made him uncomfortable. He knew he had to suck it up. "Yeah. I mean, why would someone want to kill Beth?"

"Do you think that was it? Or do you think he just wanted to fuck her?"

Now Ron was really uncomfortable. "Who would go to all that trouble for a piece of ass? You'd have to know you'd get caught . . . so you'd have to plan to kill her anyway."

"Yeah, all that and then boom . . . she's the new lieutenant governor. What an amazing few days. Every tabloid in the world is going to be hounding her."

That's all we need, thought Ron, *lots of publicity before the fact.*

Sensing an opening, Ron said, "That's for sure. Then the world will hear about us investing a hundred million bucks in a natural gas project."

"I think that's positive, don't you?"

"Yes, yes I do." Ron eased into his fishing expedition. "I don't understand why the transfer is being made directly to Brooksher. Why isn't it going to their bank?"

"VING wants to use this hundred million to get the projects going, and they want to get the money to several different companies . . . the ship builder, the primary contractor, GB Petroleum. It's just easier for them to do it rather than send it to their bank and then have them transfer it all over the place. It's money that is easy for VING to use, rather than making a draw against their primary lender."

"Makes sense. It will be out there Wednesday. I wonder what time of day that will happen . . . like if it will be on the national evening news?"

Casually, Jerry said, "It's in the morning. Ten in the morning . . . and that's ten in the morning Alaska time, but still, I guarantee you it will be on the national news."

Ron almost jumped out of his chair. He wanted to call Billy, but he knew he had to remain calm. He was patient for another hour while they discussed an assortment of mundane subjects that were privately driving Ron crazy. Abruptly, Jerry said he had to leave. He wanted to pay the bill, and did so, adding a very modest tip. Neither one of them noticed Buffy standing in the corner looking highly indignant as they left.

Ron told Jerry he had to use the bathroom. Jerry said goodbye and left. When Ron came out of the bathroom, he moved over to a quiet waiting area in the hotel where he could make a call.

"Billy, this is Ron."

"Speak to me."

"I've got it. Ten o'clock Wednesday morning."

"Shit . . . that's early. Afternoon would be better."

"Yeah, well I can't change it."

"Don't be a smart ass."

"Sorry. I'm not being a smart ass. I'm just nervous. And . . . it's ten in the morning Alaska time. That's eleven for you."

"Well, that's better. And what the hell do you have to be nervous about? You've got the easy part. In fact, your part is done. All you've got to do now is wait . . . and then spend a shit-pot full of money."

"About that, Billy, I—"

"I'm not going there again. You can call me every week if you want. Use this number. Remember, I'm Ben Parker from now on. You need to get yourself a new ID, too."

Somehow, the fact that Billy gave him his new alias reassured Ron. "Okay. I'll come up with something and let you know what it is . . . and, good luck."

"Okay, rich guy. Goodbye."

When Billy finished the call with Ron, he immediately called Raymond.

"Reverend . . . we need to get together. First thing tomorrow morning. Ron just called me. The transfer is at ten o'clock . . . actually, eleven o'clock Seattle time, Wednesday morning."

"Shit, that's early. I was sure it would happen in the afternoon."

"Yeah, that's what I said, but it shouldn't make any difference. We just need to have a plan. I mean, we need to plan this down to the minute. Be here tomorrow morning early . . . say, eight-thirty."

"Okay. I'll be there." Raymond had it planned out in his mind. He had decided that since it was taking place on his turf, he would make the rules.

As planned, Raymond was at Billy's condo at exactly 8:30 Tuesday morning.

Billy started. "I've got some ideas of how—"

"Billy, this all happens in my building . . . a building I know every square foot of now. Here's the way I see it. You come to visit me at nine-thirty. Come in through the reception desk. Sign into the guest log and tell the receptionist you are there to see me. She'll call me, and I'll tell her that I'll come down and get you. When I meet you, I'll take you on a tour of the building. We'll finish up in my office. I'll put the supplies for the smoke bomb in a briefcase, and we'll go together to the utility room. When we get there, we'll hide you in a small room in the back. Okay so far?"

Billy had been listening intently. "Yeah, sure. Go on."

"We'll synchronize our watches in my office. I'm going to get Pemberton up to my office for a drink to celebrate the big money transfer at about ten-fifteen. The ruffie will put him out quickly. I'll leave him in my office and lock it up. At exactly ten-thirty, you use the in-house phone in the utility room and dial the guard's kiosk at the front door. Just pick up the phone and dial zero-zero-one. When he answers, apologize for dialing the wrong number and hang up. I'm going to be down there, and I'll swipe my security badge while he's walking away from me to the phone. That's why our watches need to be synched exactly . . . and why you need to call at exactly ten-thirty. Got it?"

"Of course. Don't be a smart ass like Minty was."

Raymond ignored Billy and continued. "Now, it gets really critical. At exactly ten-forty, you need to light the smoke bomb. I'll show you where to set it when we go into the utility room. Then, you leave the utility room and break the first fire-alarm glass you see in the hallway. Make sure nobody sees you do it. Walk calmly down to the main lobby, sign out, and leave. I am sure there will be mass confusion with the fire alarm going off, and you should be able to sign out and exit without a problem."

"Jesus . . . there's a lot to think about."

"There's not that much for you to do. Then I'll hurry to the Secure Room. There shouldn't be anybody around there by then, with the smoke filling the building and the alarms ringing. I'll go in and lock the door. I should be in the Secure Room by ten minutes to eleven easily. When the transfer comes in, I'll forward it to the Caymans using the account information you gave me. Then, I'll get the hell out of the building using one of the emergency backdoor exits. The alarm going off for one of the emergency exits shouldn't surprise anybody with the chaos that will be going on in the building."

"Wow . . . you *have* been thinking about this. I think all of that can work, but it just takes one hiccup to blow it."

"Yeah . . . and if that happens, we will need to get the fuck out of Dodge. You need to park around the back of the building. There's a small parking lot there not more than fifty yards from the building."

"I got it. We've got a lot at stake. If anything gets fuzzy in your mind before tomorrow morning, call me."

When Raymond left, Billy reluctantly called Mario.

"Mario."

"Mario, it's Billy. Wednesday at eleven in the morning. Seattle time."

"Good. I'm anxious to get this done. This is it for me. No more deals. I'm going to enjoy life."

Privately, Billy was pissed. Mario had fronted the money, but he really hadn't done anything else. "Yeah, me too. Right after the funds hit our Cayman account, I'll move them into the Goldman Sachs fund using the information you gave me. You're sure the money will be secure there, right?"

"Goldman Sachs is one of the giants in the financial world, Billy. These offshore funds in the Caymans are completely secure and private. The government can't touch them. The funds are all tied to real estate. Real estate is booming. What could go wrong?"

"I hope nothing. I'm sure you know what you're doing."

"I do. Call me tomorrow after it's done. I'll be waiting."

In Anchorage, Beth was having a whirlwind Tuesday. Nancy Singletary was fending off calls from every local media company and dozens of national ones. "Nancy, I'll talk to my brother, representatives from the local television and radio stations, and the local newspapers, and that's it. Take names and numbers, and I'll return as many of the other calls as possible. Just tell everyone I'm in meetings all day."

Chris was sitting in Beth's office with a wry smile on his face. "So, Madam Lieutenant Governor, when does it become official?"

"Well, it is official. I do have to be sworn in, and that will happen next week."

"You know every rag and every major network in America is trying to get a story out of you. Nancy is about to tear her hair out trying to keep them at bay."

"I know. Actually, I think she's enjoying it. I'm not ready to bare my soul yet. It's all too fresh . . . especially my weekend in Indian Valley. The only good part of that was meeting those two great men. Johnny is a great guy . . . handsome, strong, level-headed. Marty is an enigma. Handsome, educated, and living like some hermit Indian warrior."

"Sounds like you made a connection of some kind."

"Chris, when someone saves your life, you develop an instant bond. I owe both those guys, and I need to find a way to reward them."

"I don't think they are the kinds of guys who want something. Take them out to dinner . . . they'd probably be tickled to death."

"I'll at least do that. Right now, I've got loads of work to do. You and I have loads of work to do, too. Saylor Industries is going to pretty much be your baby now."

"I'm comfortable with that, Beth, and you're going to be right back in this building every night."

"Speaking of that, I guess I should be thinking about giving up the penthouse."

"No way. I have a great place . . . with a real backyard. I want to get out of this building at night, be able to barbeque in the summer and chase the moose out of my yard. You stay right where you are."

Beth laughed lightly. "Okay. Well, if you change your mind, let me know. We have never drawn up an official line of succession for the penthouse."

Now Chris smiled. "Let's not think about it until you move into that big white building."

"That's a long way off, Chris . . . maybe never."

"It's your destiny, Beth."

"We'll see. Right now, I've got a mystery to work on. I really want to know why Ron Minty and Budge Brown were hanging out together, and why Budge seemed so interested in the APFC. I think I'll call Nick's old friend at APD . . . Sergeant Baker."

It hadn't hit Ron until his last conversation with Billy. *I've got to get out of town. I've got to just drop everything I've worked for and leave. I've got to leave my wife . . . I did love her once...I still like her. I hate to leave her like that. She doesn't even have a job. I've got to just walk out on my law firm...... and for what? For ten million dollars, you dumb shit!*

Ron didn't have a clue how to come up with a new identity, particularly on short notice.

I'll just buy a plane ticket to Seattle using my real name, he thought. *When the hundred million is gone tomorrow and I'm gone, they're going to know I had something to do with it anyway. When I get to Seattle, I'll take a bus or a train to Southern California and find someone who can forge some documents for me so I can go to Mexico.*

As he drove to his bank, Ron felt like he was having a surreal experience. He checked his balance and confirmed that he had over fifteen thousand dollars in his account. Feeling more empathy for Karen than he'd thought he would, he withdrew ten thousand dollars and left five thousand in the account for her. Ron then drove home and told her that he had to make an unexpected trip to Seattle on business. He packed more than anyone would need for a short business trip and snuck the two big suitcases into his car.

Karen may have suspected something when he gave her a long hug and a big kiss before he left the house, but she didn't say anything. He did see a quizzical look on her face when he said, "You're a good woman, Karen." He drove to the airport with tears streaming down his cheeks, thinking, *what the fuck have I done?*

Nick called Donnie Clayton Monday after the closing on the U Building, and they agreed they would meet at their new building at 9:00 Tuesday morning. Donnie was waiting outside the fenced complex when Nick drove up and opened the gate with Betsy's electronic gate-opener. She had given it to Nick when he dropped her off at her mansion the night before. She'd been slightly inebriated and very upbeat, saying, "I am so happy you bought the building, Nick."

Donnie followed Nick and parked his car next to his, in front of the building. They were like the proud owners of a new toy as they greeted each other.

"Good morning, Donnie. There she is. Isn't it beautiful?"

"It is beautiful, Nick, and I can't wait to see what we can do with it."

"Me too. Let's give it the once-over . . . two or three times."

Donnie laughed. "I'm ready."

Nick and Donnie spent the next six hours in their new building, only taking a thirty-minute break to drive to a nearby McDonald's for a quick lunch. As they surveyed the building and thought about their company's needs, it became apparent that they were both leaning toward using if for their own business.

"You know, Nick, we could expand our operations here in the Pacific Northwest and easily support it with this building. Then, we could lease the building we're in now. We could spread our business units into Idaho, get more established in Oregon. Hell, eventually, we could move into California. This building might be a little big for us right now, but we could grow into it quickly."

Nick listened to Donnie and smiled. "Donnie, are you sure you don't have some Saylor blood in you somewhere? You are just like family. You're just like Beth and Chris . . . shit, you're just like me."

Donnie had a man-blush as he said, "Thank you, Nick. That is a very high compliment to me. You all feel like family to me. You've treated me like family."

Nick became serious. "I've just had a thought, Donnie. It's something

I've had in the back of my mind for a long time. How would you like to become a part owner of Saylor Industries?"

Donnie had a shocked look on his face. "I . . . I don't know what to say. I would love it. I'd be very proud, no, honored . . . both."

"I'll talk with Beth and Chris."

When Beth finally caught her breath late Tuesday afternoon, she put a call in to Sergeant Bob Baker.

"Sergeant Baker."

"Sergeant Baker, this is Beth Saylor."

"Well, our new lieutenant governor. Congratulations. Is this official business?"

"Sort of, but nothing related to my new job. It's more about some old business. I'm sure you know about my weekend adventure."

"I know. Lot of talk about that around here."

"Well, there's more to it than what's out there for the public . . . and even the police department. There is a guy on the APFC board. Ron Minty, you've probably heard of him."

"I have."

"Okay, well he and Budge Brown were very tight. I saw them together several times . . . even once when we had an APFC meeting in Juneau. I don't know what their connection was. . . . Ron told me they were just casual friends who met at The Mud Flats, but I think there's more to it. I think Budge was at one of our board meetings in a disguise. Anyway, it's strange to me that a guy who was stalking me and who tried to kill me is good friends with Ron Minty, who is on the same board I am."

"Your call is timely, Beth. I was going to call you in regard to an investigation we have been doing. I know about Budge Brown. I knew about him before last weekend. He is connected to a guy who I believe is responsible for two murders. In fact, now that I know what he is capable of, he may have been the actual killer."

Beth instantly went cold. "Shit . . . I'm sorry, but you've just told me that Budge Brown really intended to kill me last Friday night."

Hesitantly, Bob said, "I believe that's very likely."

"I . . . somehow, in spite of everything that happened, I just didn't want to . . ."

"I understand, Beth. It's very sobering when you realize someone wanted you dead. And the fact that this Minty guy is still running around Anchorage doesn't help you."

"No, it doesn't. Can you help me . . . I mean, can you check him out?"

"I can. I'm in Missing Persons, but I've been officially asked to help in the murder case . . . someone named Anna and a guy named Stan Faro. The Wasilla Police Department asked me to help, and my boss approved it . . . grudgingly. It's a stretch, but I can make enough of a connection with Budge Brown to check into what Ron Minty is up to."

"Thank you, Sergeant Baker . . . and my brother thanks you. I'm a little scared. Someone tried to kill me and didn't get the job done."

"I understand . . . please tell your brother hello for me. And by the way, it's Bob."

When Betsy woke up early Tuesday morning, she was happy and a little hungover. She had thoroughly enjoyed her evening with Nick and was genuinely happy that Saylor Industries now owned Del's building. Enjoyable as last night was, spending an evening with a handsome man's man made her feel a little randy.

She thought, *I'm going to get the Reverend here for dinner tonight if I have to drag him here myself.*

Betsy stopped at Mary's desk on the way into her office. "Mary, please talk to Reverend Raymond as soon as he comes in. Tell him I need to see him in my office."

Thirty minutes later, Reverend Raymond walked through Betsy's office door. "Were you looking for me, ma'am?"

Betsy came from behind her desk and walked toward Raymond. "Yes, you big hunk of a man . . . I was." Betsy walked past Raymond and closed her office door. "Have a seat, Reverend."

Betsy returned to her chair. "Do you think everything is set for tomorrow, Reverend? Have you been watching over Theodore? Do you think he is ready? One hundred million dollars. I don't want any hiccups. You'll be there too, right?"

"Of course I'll be there, Betsy. And I'm sure Theodore is fine. He even said that the guy at APFC requested a test transfer just before the actual transfer . . . just to make sure everything is a go. You know, this is really a routine procedure. This just happens to involve a lot of money, and it's a high-profile transaction for the State of Alaska . . . and for us."

"Good. I'm glad to see you feel like you belong at Brooksher enough to call the company us."

"I am blessed, Betsy. Blessed to know you and blessed to be able to work here. My life will be complete when we open the Northwest Light of Life School for Children."

Or rather, Raymond thought, *when I blow out of here with my ten million–dollar share.*

"That will be soon, Reverend. In the meantime, I want you to come to the mansion for dinner tonight. Sort of a pre-celebration. I'll tell Gerard to go all out. I bought something special I want to wear tonight, too." Betsy finished her request with a wicked look on her face that somehow looked angry to Raymond, and not sexy as she intended it.

Shit, thought Raymond, *not tonight.* "I . . . I'm not sure—"

The rich and powerful Betsy emerged. "I will not take no for an answer. I insist. The limo will be at your place at seven o'clock."

Sheepishly, Raymond said, "Okay. I'll see you tonight."

Raymond was tense when he arrived at the mansion that night. He felt sure he was creating the tension himself, but still, he was uneasy.

I haven't seen her much lately. I'll bet she's just lonely, he thought.

After Gerard led him into the small room off of the great room and poured him a glass of wine, Betsy whirled into the room in a beautiful evening gown. *So that's it,* he thought, more than a little disappointed that it wasn't something risqué.

"Good evening, Reverend. I see Gerard fixed you up with wine. I'm going to have some, too."

"Good evening, ma'am. You look lovely tonight. I'll pour your wine for you."

"Thank you, but lay off the ma'am stuff, Reverend. Betsy, I'm just Betsy when you and I are together alone. You know that by now."

"I'm sorry. Good evening, Betsy, and you still look lovely."

Never one to be coy, Betsy said, "You seem to be avoiding me lately. Are you getting tired of being with an old broad?"

"Don't say that, Betsy. You are a lovely, sexy woman. I've just been . . . busy. Lots of things on my mind."

Betsy sat down in a big leather chair close to Raymond. "Is there anything I can help with? You know I have a pretty big arsenal of resources." Betsy laughed at herself. "Listen to me. Before Del died, I doubt that I ever said arsenal."

"You do have a big arsenal. You are a powerful woman. You are also a kind and generous woman. Many men would be grateful to have you in their life."

"But not you?"

"I didn't say that. Where is this coming from? I have enjoyed our relationship. *I* am grateful for it."

Betsy sat up straight in the big chair. "Are you really hungry, Reverend? I mean, this-instant hungry. I want to make love to you . . . now.

Hold me and make love to me."

Raymond sensed some desperation he didn't understand, but he suddenly wanted to please Betsy . . . to pay her back for everything she had done for him. It was especially important on this night . . . the night before he was going to use her company and her goodwill toward him to steal a hundred million dollars.

"I would love that, Betsy."

Their lovemaking was gentle and passionate. Raymond knew it was the last time . . . and maybe Betsy somehow sensed it was the last time. Raymond couldn't help but think of the possibilities with Betsy:

She might even want to marry me. I would be married to one of the richest women in the world . . . so why am I trying to steal money and risking going to prison?

When Raymond left Betsy Tuesday night, he was more uneasy about what he was going to do the next morning than he had ever been.

After his telephone conversation with Beth Saylor, Sergeant Baker pulled out Stan Faro's phone records and looked them over again. There were no calls from Ron Minty to Stan. There were calls from Stan to Budge, and Stan to Billy Peet, and he knew there were lots of calls between Budge and Billy Peet . . . but no calls to Ron from anybody other than Budge. He felt it was more than reasonable that there was a connection between Billy and Ron, but he couldn't prove it. He decided to go straight to the source, and called Ron's office Tuesday afternoon. When the receptionist at Minty, Anderson, and Rogers informed Sergeant Baker that Ron had left the office for the day, he called Ron's home.

"Hello, Mintys'."

"This is Sergeant Baker with APD. Are you Ron Minty's wife?"

"I am. This is Karen Minty. Is there something wrong? Has something happened to Ron?"

"No, Mrs. Minty. I take it he is not there."

"No sir. He left on a business trip to Seattle earlier today."

"Oh. The receptionist at his office told me he was just gone for the afternoon. When will he be back?"

Sounding embarrassed, Karen said, "I . . . I just realized that I didn't ask him when he would be back."

"Does he do this often, just leave and not tell you when he will be back?"

"No, no he doesn't. He does make lots of business trips."

"I'm sure he does, being a lawyer and on the board of the Alaska

Permanent Fund Corporation. Forgive this question, but has he been acting strangely lately?"

Karen was now very concerned. "No. What is this all about?"

"Maybe nothing, ma'am. I apologize for bothering you, but if you hear from him, please have him call Sergeant Bob Baker at APD."

Within the hour, APD determined which flight Ron Minty was on, and he was detained for questioning at the airport in Seattle by the King County Sheriff's Department when his plane landed at 6:00 that evening. He was unable to tell them where his meeting was, where he was staying, or why he had ten thousand dollars in cash on his person.

Sergeant Baker tracked Beth down that evening to tell her what had happened.

"I knew it. I just knew there was something strange about him," Beth exclaimed.

Like a scattered team of players on the day of a big game, everyone was up early Wednesday morning.

In Seattle, Nick gave Donnie the go-ahead to implement his plans for the new building, and he was ready to fly to Anchorage. He woke Danny Wilson up early and told him to have The Bird ready to leave for Anchorage at noon.

Not far from where Nick was, Billy cleaned his belongings out of the condo and loaded them into his rented vehicle. He planned to be at the Brooksher Building promptly at 9:30.

With an uncomfortable guilt haunting him, Raymond arrived at the Brooksher Building at 8:00. Betsy was in the building before Raymond arrived, and he acknowledged her as cordially as his guilt would allow as he walked by her office. He then spent a nervous hour and a half poring over the details of their plan.

Betsy felt the strain between her and the Reverend, but she was too excited about the money transfer from Alaska and the feeling that it signaled the real beginning of the Vancouver Island Natural Gas project to be concerned. She planned to be in the Secure Room when the transfer came in.

In Alaska, Beth Saylor decided that she wanted to be at the Administrative Office at the Capitol when the money was transferred from APFC to Brooksher . . . she was quietly proud of the part she had played in this investment by APFC. She was also more than a little anxious for it to be a success, and she was still dealing with a nagging curiosity about what Ron Minty was up to.

Beth arrived at the Administrative Office at the Capitol at 9:30 in the morning. Newly appointed governor Peter Harris and Executive Director Richard Cally, Chairman Fred Feck, and Vice Chairman Jerry Holter of APFC were milling around in the hallway outside the room where the electronic transfer to Brooksher was to be made.

"Good morning, gentlemen. Okay, who's going to ask me about it first?"

The men laughed. Governor Harris said, "I guess I will. I know you've heard about Minty."

"I have. I'm sort of responsible for his current situation."

Beth spent the next few minutes explaining what had happened, and she could see anxiety growing on everyone's face.

"Do you think APFC is compromised in some way?" asked Richard.

"I don't know, Richard. My hope is that it is not, but I think it might have been if Ron hadn't been stopped. He was obviously running from something."

In a deliberate tone, Jerry said, "If you're running, it means you've already done something."

"That's a great point," Governor Harris interjected.

"You know what? I'm going to spend a few minutes with our man who is handling the transfer. Excuse me," said Chairman Feck, and he walked down the hall.

Fred was back in ten minutes and said, "Everything looks to be in order. It's a lot of money, but handling the transfer is pretty routine. Just to be sure, Richard, why don't you call Betsy Brooksher."

"Another good idea. I'll do that."

Richard went into an empty office and dialed Brooksher. The receptionist quickly transferred the call to Betsy. "Good morning, Mr. Cally. Pre-transfer jitters?"

Richard laughed. "Maybe a little. Is everything alright on your end? This is a pretty big deal, and we want to make sure it all goes well."

"Everything is fine. I'm going to be in our Secure Room myself when the transfer comes in. I'll call you."

"Thanks, Betsy. Talk to you soon."

Richard went back to the group and reported in. "Betsy said all is well, and she'll be there to watch the transfer come in. She's going to call me when they receive it."

As planned, Billy Peet entered the Brooksher Building at 9:30 and told the receptionist he had an appointment with Reverend Raymond.

347

Raymond headed downstairs right away and greeted Billy warmly in front of the receptionist.

"Welcome, my old friend. Come on, let me show you around the building. Are you signed in?"

Bravely, Billy said, "Thank you for inviting me, and I am signed in. It's good to see you."

Raymond gave Billy a tour around the building, and then they headed to his office. He closed the door, and they both sighed nervously.

"Big fucking day today, Reverend," Billy said.

"No shit. I've got the briefcase loaded up. Let's synchronize our watches and wait a few minutes. Then we'll head to the utility room."

At 10:00, they walked to the utility room. Raymond showed Billy to his hiding spot in a small room at the back. He showed him where to place the smoke bomb for maximum effect. Pointing to the wall phone he said, "Phone, there . . . zero-zero-one . . . ten-thirty exactly."

"Yeah, I've got it."

As Raymond started to leave, he turned to Billy and said, "Out back, you better be there. Good luck."

"Good luck. I'll be there."

Raymond hurried back to his office and called Theodore Pemberton in the Secure Room. "Theodore, this is the Reverend."

"Reverend, when are you coming down here?"

"I want you to come up here first. I've got a little surprise."

"Uh . . . we don't have much time."

"It won't take you five minutes to run up here and then go back. You've got almost forty-five minutes."

Curious, Theodore said, "Okay, I'll be right there."

Raymond had two double shot glasses full of Grand Patron Platinum on his desk, with the bottle sitting next to them. Theodore's was laced with Rohypnol. Theodore rushed into Raymond's office. "What's up, Reverend? I've got to get back down there."

"Close the door, Theodore. I have a little surprise celebration drink here for us." Raymond pointed at the two glasses of tequila.

Theodore's eyes lit up. "Wow . . . Grand Platinum. I shouldn't . . . but I will." He laughed, and it was the last thing he remembered when he was questioned by authorities hours later.

Theodore was giggly and accommodating as Raymond dragged him over to his closet. He managed to get him into the closet, and closed and locked the door.

"So far so good," Raymond said to himself.

Raymond took a last look around his office and left, locking the door as he went out. He looked at his watch and hurried to make sure he was in the lobby at exactly 10:30. He made it with two minutes to spare.

The telephone in the kiosk rang at exactly 10:30. When Raymond saw the guard turn his back and head toward the kiosk, he calmly walked to the electronic security-badge reader at the exit. Looking around to make sure nobody was watching him, he swiped his badge and walked back toward the elevators.

Raymond exited the elevator on the second floor where the Secure Room was and let himself in with his key. He locked the door and sat in the chair at the console in front of the electronic equipment in relief. *Whew. Nothing can go wrong now,* he thought to himself.

He had been sitting no more than a two minutes when there was a light knock at the door. Startled, Raymond turned around in his chair. For a moment, he considered not opening the door, and then he heard Betsy's voice.

"Theodore, are you in there?"

In a slight panic, Raymond opened the door. Betsy was surprised to see him.

"Reverend . . . where's Theodore?"

"Uh . . . he had to go to the bathroom. He'll be right back."

"Oh, okay. We have a few minutes."

Raymond looked at his watch. It was 10:42.

Light the goddamn smoke bomb, he thought, *and hit the alarm, Billy . . . now!*

Raymond made lame small talk with Betsy, and one minute later, the fire alarm went off.

"Oh my God!" shouted Betsy. "A fire alarm. What do we do, Reverend?"

Raymond put his hands on both of Betsy's shoulders and guided her out of the Secure Room. "Get downstairs, Betsy. See what's going on. I'll stay here and guard this room until I find out what's happening. This may be a false alarm."

Betsy turned to Raymond and said, "You need to get out of here, too. Lock this room up and go."

"Not yet, Betsy. I'll wait for Theodore. Now go. Use the stairway, not the elevators."

Reluctantly, Betsy headed for the stairway. Halfway there, she turned to Raymond and shouted, "I smell smoke!"

"Go, Betsy. This is a big building. I can get out of here easily."

Betsy said no more and continued toward the stairway.

Raymond went back into the Secure Room and locked the door again.

As he was about to sit down, the communication equipment began to hum with an incoming transmission. He looked at his watch. It was thirteen minutes to eleven.

R.A., sender Alaska Permanent Fund Corporation, ID #9930PF requests permission to send test transmission. Please reply, Transmission Received.

Raymond had forgotten about the test transmission after Betsy knocked on the door to the Secure Room. He knew he had to comply. Hitting the Reply key, he typed: *Theodore A. Pemberton, Brooksher, ID # 1217BA. Proceed with test transmission.*

Two minutes later, the test transmission came in.

06/20/2007, EFT APFC, # 492007SOA, to Brooksher, # 036007WA, SUM 100,000,000.00 US. Under the transmission information were the words, *TEST, TEST, TEST.*

Raymond looked at the huge number, *100,000,000.00 US,* and became bloated with anxiety.

OK, he thought, *let's do the real thing . . . now!*

He quickly hit the Reply key again and typed out the words, *Theodore A. Pemberton, Brooksher, ID # 1217BA. Transmission Received.*

Raymond looked at his watch again. It was seven minutes to eleven. *Shit, I've got to wait seven minutes,* he thought. He tried to focus on what was happening in the building. The alarms were still ringing, and he figured that Billy was safely out of the building. He was worried that Betsy would send someone back to get him, and he decided that if she did, he would stay in the locked Secure Room and hope they went away.

In Anchorage, everyone had gathered around the doorway of the small room where the transfer to Brooksher would be initiated. They all heard the equipment whirring and watched the operator busily tending to it. At 10:00, he announced that the transfer had been made, which sparked a moderate celebration in the hallway.

Two minutes later, the APFC operator produced a piece of paper with the words, *Theodore A. Pemberton, Brooksher, ID # 1217BA, Transmission Received.* All the people in the hallway clapped and congratulated each other.

Everyone was so excited that nobody noticed the small amount of Wite-Out correction fluid on the operator's hands. They were all celebrating in the hallway five minutes later, not paying attention as he closed and locked the small room with the electronic equipment in it and quickly left the Administrative Building.

Raymond had the small piece of paper with the account information from Billy in his hands as he waited nervously for the electronic funds transfer. It was now five minutes after eleven. At ten minutes after eleven, he called Billy.

"It's not here!"

"What's not there?"

"The hundred million. I can't stay here. They'll find me in here."

Deep inside, Raymond always thought it was a fantasy to expect to steal a hundred million dollars. Now, he wasn't ready to go jail for it.

"You can't leave now. You've got to be there to make the transfer to our bank."

"The fire alarms are off. They'll find the smoke bomb. I've got to leave here. This is the hiccup we talked about. I've got to get the fuck out of here."

Billy didn't care what happened to Raymond. He was going to be a collateral loss, no matter what happened. Billy would be a rich man if Raymond stayed there and made the transfer. He shouted into his cell phone. "Do not leave yet! I'll fucking cut your throat if you leave before you make the transfer."

There was silence, and Billy realized he was talking to a dead phone. "Fuck," he said, "I can't believe this."

He also knew he couldn't get his hands on Raymond because he was ten miles from the parking lot in the back of the Brooksher Building where he'd promised to wait for him.

Since it was five minutes after ten in Anchorage, and Betsy had not called him, Richard Cally decided to call her. Betsy was in the lobby when the call came into the switchboard.

"Mrs. Brooksher, I have a call for you," the receptionist shouted over the turmoil in the lobby.

"It's not a good time!" Betsy shouted back.

"A Mr. Cally from Alaska, Mrs. Brooksher. He says it's important."

Betsy walked to the reception desk and took the phone from the receptionist. "Mr. Cally, this is Betsy. I apologize for not calling you. It has been total chaos here, and I left my cell phone in my office. We have fire alarms going off."

"I'm sorry to hear that, Betsy, but it didn't hamper our electronic transfer. Since I didn't hear from you, I thought I would call."

"You made the transfer?" There was alarm in Betsy's voice.

"Yes, right at ten o'clock our time. We have a confirmation receipt from a Mr. Pemberton."

"Oh, well, in all this confusion, I wasn't in the room. Theodore, bless his heart, must have stayed there and taken care of it. I . . . I guess congratulations to both of us are in order. It's a little confusing here. Let me get this fire thing taken care of and I'll call you back."

As Betsy was putting the phone down, a fireman with a smoke-blackened face carrying a wet bag approached her. "Mrs. Brooksher?"

"Yes."

"We found the source of the smoke. It's in this bag. It's a smoke bomb. There is no fire."

Betsy turned ashen. She rushed to the guard and grabbed him by the arm. "Come with me right now."

When they reached the Secure Room, it was locked. They banged on the door and nobody answered. Betsy turned to the guard. "Do you have your master key?"

"Yes, ma'am, but it won't open the door to the Secure Room."

"I know, come with me." When they arrived at Raymond's locked office, the guard opened the door with his master key. Betsy walked in and looked around. The office looked strangely empty. She walked around Raymond's desk and saw the bottle of tequila and the two empty shot glasses sitting on it. That's when she heard a slight sound from the closet. She turned to the guard. "Open it."

Theodore was in a fetal position on the floor, looking like he was totally content being where he was.

"My God . . . I believe we've lost a hundred million dollars," Betsy said as she fell back into one of the chairs in front of Raymond's desk.

The best laid plans of . . . nah, sometimes you stumble around bare-foot in the dark and step on a Lego, and sometimes you stumble around in life and hit the jackpot.
—From *Fred Longcoor's Book on Life*

Chapter 25

The Fallout

When the computer operator left the Administrative Building after the electronic transfer was completed, he drove his beat-up old pickup straight to the middle of Anchorage and turned on to the New Seward Highway heading south. In less than an hour, he was at the Whittier tunnel. He waited impatiently for thirty minutes before he was allowed his turn to go through the one-way access to Whittier. Arriving on the Whittier side of the tunnel, he drove to the parking lot near the small boat harbor where fishermen parked their vehicles while they were fishing in Prince William Sound. After parking the pickup, he walked straight to his forty-foot fishing boat, the E Biz, which was tied up at the guest dock. There was a light on in the cabin, and the engines were running. He quickly untied the lines fore and aft, went straight to the wheelhouse, and carefully guided the boat away from the dock.

Fifteen minutes later, a small voice called out from the cabin below.

"Are we far enough out yet? Can I come up?"

"Sure. It's pretty quiet out here, but put that old baseball cap of mine on just in case."

The attractive woman who came up the stairs from the cabin below was wearing blue jeans with a plaid man's shirt over a tee shirt. The dirty Mariners baseball cap she was wearing made her look like a child. She immediately moved to his side as he was piloting the boat and gave him a warm hug. "It's done?"

The handsome dark-skinned man turned toward her. "It's done, baby. We are rich . . . or we will be when we can start taking funds out of our account in Switzerland."

"When?"

"Not for a while. We'll stick with our plan and run the E Biz all the way to Puerto Pen˝asco. When we get there, we can sell this baby . . . which I hate to do, but we need to separate ourselves from anything that will connect us to Alaska. Then we can head down into Sonora. I'll use my connections there, and we can do whatever we want, buy whatever we want, or go anywhere we want from there."

"This is crazy, Robert . . . sorry, Rodolfo, but I love it . . . and I love you."

"This isn't crazy, it's brilliant . . . and I love you too, Stacey. We're going to have the kind of life people only dream about. No one can recover the money, and thanks to the Swiss government, nobody can trace it."

"You know, they're going to suspect us right away. It probably won't take long for them to connect us. I mean, the money disappears, and we both disappear."

"You're right, but it's going to take them a few days to figure out what happened. The transfer I made is all encrypted. First, they're going to blame Brooksher, then, they'll have computer guys scratching their heads for days. When they decide we had something to do with it, they'll have a hell of a time finding us. Nobody is going to be checking a fishing boat . . . especially one owned by Rodolfo Alverez. We'll probably be off the coast of Vancouver Island before they seriously start looking for us. Then they'll be looking at airline records and border crossings. Once we're in Mexico, we can drop off the planet. I'm going to take care of you, Madam Governor."

Stacey smiled, thinking, *I can't believe I'm part of this, but I've never loved any man as much as I love Rodolfo. I'd follow him anywhere. Besides, we took the money from a state with thirty-five billion dollars in the bank. Before long, it won't even be missed. We'll live like a king and a queen. . . . I just don't know how much time I'll have to enjoy that.*

Beth and the small APFC gang were in a celebratory mood, and they all decided to head to the Turnagain Room for drinks. They were still in the Capitol building lobby when Betsy called Richard Cally on his cell phone. Her tone was solemn.

"Mr. Cally . . . this is Betsy Brooksher."

"Hello Betsy. I'll bet you are a happy woman today."

"I am not, Mr. Cally. Are you absolutely sure the money was trans-ferred to Brooksher?"

"Of course. What kind of question is that?"

"It never made it here. The transfer. It never happened."

"What? I . . . don't know what to say. I saw the confirmation receipt myself. From a Theodore somebody."

"Theodore A. Pemberton. Well, he was locked in a closet in one of the offices . . . knocked out on drugs. He couldn't have handled anything. I think the man who had something to do with this was . . . this will sound strange, but I think it was Reverend Raymond."

"A reverend? Is this a prank call? Who is this?"

"Mr. Cally, this *is* Betsy. This is no joke, and it's not a prank call. Can you go back to your computer operator and see if you can find out what happened? I've notified the police department and the FBI. They are on their way here now."

"Yes . . . yes, right away. I'll call you right back."

Everyone around Richard could hear enough of the conversation to become completely quiet. When he closed his phone, he said, "We've got to get back up and talk to Robert."

When the group approached the computer room, they were surprised to see that it was locked.

"Robert must have taken an early lunch." Richard's assessment had an uneasy tone to it.

Governor Harris spoke up. "I've got a bunch of keys here. I don't know what they all are yet, but I think one is a master." After trying a half-dozen keys, Governor Harris opened the door.

Everyone squeezed into the small room. The computer screen was lit up, but all of the key functions were different from those of a normal PC. Governor Harris said, "I don't understand any of this. We've got to find Robert." He used his cell phone to call his aide. "Find Robert Anderson for me. Quickly."

Beth happened to look into the wastebasket near the door. She picked up the top piece of paper and looked at it. It was the confirmation of the transfer being received at Brooksher that Robert had shown everyone. She saw another piece of paper in the trash and picked it up. It looked exactly like the transfer confirmation Robert had shown them, except that it was obvious that three words on it had been covered up with Wite-Out. Beth turned the paper over and looked at the back side of it. Through the back of the paper, she read the covered words, *Test, Test, Test,* and realized that Robert had shown them a copy of the doctored transmission receipt. "Shit," she exclaimed, "I don't think you're going to find Robert."

Everyone turned to look at her, and she held the paper out where they all could see it. Then she turned it over slowly.

Reverend Raymond knew Billy had stiffed him the minute he went out the back door at Brooksher and saw that Billy's vehicle wasn't in the parking lot. He was pissed, but not surprised. He began walking away from the Brooksher Building and didn't stop until he had walked a dozen blocks to a small shopping center. He used a pay phone to call a taxi and had it take him to the closest branch of his bank, where he withdrew the balance of his funds and closed his account. Thanks primarily to Betsy's generosity, he had over twenty thousand dollars in the account.

After the taxi driver took him to his hotel room, he packed his meager belongings and called another taxi to take him to the bus station. He picked out San Francisco as a destination. There was a bus leaving for The City by the Bay earlier than any other place that interested him.

Raymond had been screwed over before, and he had fled before. This time, it was different. He knew he had blown an opportunity for a good life . . . maybe a boring life for a wandering preacher, but good. Now he would go back on the road . . . and there were all those churches out there. . . .

Billy raced to Boeing Field after getting the call from Raymond, cursing him all the way. He knew he was screwed. He figured he had lost his ranch, he would probably lose his other houses, and he had lost several hundred thousand dollars paying his share of the expenses for Budge, Stan, and Raymond.

"You should have stayed and transferred the money, Raymond . . . fucking Reverend Raymond," Billy said to himself. "If I ever find you, I'm going to take you up in the Lear and drop you out from twenty thousand feet . . . onto a church."

Billy called the pilots and told them to be ready. To be safe, he asked them to meet him a block away from the hangar.

Nick was ready to leave the hotel when his cell phone rang. He could see it was Nani. "Hi baby . . . how are things in paradise?"

Nani was sobbing, and couldn't speak. "Nani, what's the matter? Talk to me, baby. Nani."

"Nick . . . I . . . I need you. Papa . . . Papa died." That was all she could get out before she began sobbing even louder.

"Oh no, Nani. Oh no. What happened, when did it happen?" Nick had an instant remembrance of his good friend on the golf course at a happy time, and couldn't imagine him any other way.

Nani calmed down a little. "This morning. Suddenly. He had more medical problems than we realized. His heart just quit. Please come home, Nick."

"I'm on my way, Nani. The boys already have The Bird warmed up . . . we were going to Anchorage today. We'll just head your way. I'll see you in about six hours. I'm very sorry, Nani. I loved your father."

Weakly, Nani said, "I know, Nick . . . and he knew. He loved you, too."

Nick sat for a brief moment of silence, then dialed Danny's cell phone. "Change of plans, Danny. Make a flight plan for Maui. I'll explain when we get there."

"The Bird is fueled up and loaded up, boss. We'll go into the office and change the flight plan," said Danny.

As directed, Billy's pilots were waiting for him on a street corner a block from Boeing Field. He picked them up and drove to the guard gate. He dug his temporary-access badge out of his pocket and showed it to the very young guard. Being the wary lifetime criminal he was, Billy noticed the panicky look that instantly crossed the young man's face.

Calmly, Billy said, "One of you guys please look back at that guard and tell me what he is doing after we go through the gate."

The copilot sitting in the backseat turned around and looked at the guard shack as they passed it.

"He grabbed the phone, Billy. He looks like he's seen a ghost."

"Something's wrong," Billy said. "I've got a bad feeling they made the Lear." Billy started to turn around when he spotted The Bird sitting fifty yards from the front door of the King's Row Executive Service terminal.

"Can either one of you fuckers fly that thing?"

"Shit, that's a G550," said the pilot. "I've never flown one. I could probably fly it if we could get it started."

"I've been in one," said the copilot. "I think I could get it started."

"Let's go. I've got a feeling we're going to jail if we try to get the Lear out of the hangar."

Billy stepped on the gas and squealed rubber, pulling up next to The Bird. They all jumped out and headed up the air-stairs, leaving Billy's bags in the rented vehicle. The copilot quickly closed the doorway.

"Fuck, Billy," the pilot said as he hurried into the cockpit. "Stealing a forty million–dollar airplane will land us all in jail. We'll have the Air Force after us."

Billy had reached a point that was beyond reason. He knew he had lost everything. He didn't care what the consequences were now. "Get it started. Get it off the ground. Get out of the Seattle area and keep it low. Try to think of someplace we can land it and leave it . . . an abandoned runway, a deserted highway, anything."

Both pilots were cursing and yelling instructions back and forth to each other. Suddenly, Billy heard one of the huge engines on the big jet begin to turn over slowly and then reach a high pitch, indicating it had started. The next engine followed suit.

"Shit, shit. Way to go, boys," Billy cheered from his position standing in the open cockpit door.

At that moment, Nick was pulling up to the guard gate, having arrived at Boeing Field fifteen minutes earlier than he intended to before Nani called him about George. He saw The Bird with its doorway closed, and he heard the engines running. *That's strange,* he thought. *Why would Danny be doing that?*

At that moment, he saw Danny and Greg hurrying out of the King's Row Executive Service lobby. They started running toward The Bird, yelling and waving their arms.

Nick turned to the young guard, who still had a look on his face like he had just seen the devil. "I own that plane. Those are my pilots running to it. It looks like someone is trying to steal it. Do you have a gun?"

The flustered guard said hesitantly, "I . . . I have a gun."

"Give it to me . . . now!"

"I can't do that."

Angrily, Nick said, "That is a forty million–dollar airplane. Would you like for King's Row Executive Service to be responsible for losing a forty million–dollar airplane without doing something about it?"

"I don't think . . . I mean, no." The baby-faced guard was slowly unbuckling the holster strap over the handle of his pistol.

Now in a rage, Nick said, "You've got to move faster than that. Give me your fucking pistol now or it will be too late."

The guard figured it was going to be the last act of his employment with King's Row Executive Service, but he decided he wasn't going to stand by and let someone steal a forty million–dollar jet. He hurriedly pulled the gun out of his holster and handed it to Nick. The guard barely heard the thank you from Nick as the SUV squealed away from the guard gate.

Nick honked the horn as he drove toward Danny and Greg. He pressed the button to open the passenger-side window as he was driving and yelled at the two pilots to get in the vehicle.

As Danny dived into the front seat, Nick said, "What the fuck is going on?"

Danny said, "I don't know! We were changing the flight plan and heard the engines."

"Can they get it off the ground?"

"If they know anything about a G550, they can."

"Can they get it off the ground if the tires are flat?"

"No."

"Okay. Hang on."

The big jet started to roll slowly, and Nick pulled the SUV alongside it as close as he could get. "Grab the wheel, Danny."

All Nick heard from Greg in the backseat was, "Oh fuck," as he opened his window and began firing the pistol at The Bird's tires. Something from his past told him he would be more likely to hit the tires by ricocheting the bullets off the pavement next to them. He fired three times before he hit one of the tires closest to him.. Nick estimated he had three bullets left when he tried the same tactic on the tire on the left side of the plane. The first bullet hit it.

"Will that stop them, Danny . . . or do I need to get the tire on the nose?"

"That'll do it."

Nick stopped the SUV, and they all sat watching in fascination as the wounded Bird struggled along the Tarmac for another fifty yards and came to a stop.

"I guess we'll need some new tires," Greg commented calmly from the backseat.

"Yeah, now what?" said Danny.

Nick heard the sirens and replied as three Boeing Field airport security police vehicles raced up and surrounded The Bird, "I think we just sit and watch now."

Within the hour, Nick learned about Billy Peet and his alleged connection to two murders in Alaska. It would be several days before he would find out about his connection to the attempted theft of a hundred million dollars from the Alaska Permanent Fund. With the exception of his time in courtrooms, Billy never spent another day outside of a jail or prison. Committed to life in prison for complicity in a litany of murders, attempted murders, and financial scams, he would die in prison ten years after he was captured.

Because of Billy's courtroom rants about Reverend Raymond and Ron Minty, Ron was indicted for his alleged part in the attempt to steal money from the APFC. He was acquitted for lack of evidence and because of the questionable character of his accuser. APFC released him from service on their board, and his wife divorced him. He left Alaska, broke and broken, immediately after his trial.

Authorities made a weak attempt to find Reverend Raymond and gave up. *Watch and pray so that you will not fall into temptation. The spirit is willing, but the body is weak. Matthew 26:41*

When all the excitement ended, Nick remembered that Nani would be expecting him in Maui in a couple of hours, and he wouldn't be there. Her voice was quiet and emotional as she answered his call. "This is Nani. Where are you, Nick?"

"Nani, I've had an unbelievable day. I'm not going to be there until late tonight. Let me explain." Nick told Nani about the attempted theft of The Bird, and she listened quietly, whispering only muted utterances of disbelief.

"It was George, Nani. It was George's last act to protect me . . . to protect us. If I wasn't rushing to get home, I wouldn't have been at the airport when they were attempting to steal The Bird. I know The Bird's only an airplane, and an airplane can be replaced, but that was George's message all along. There was danger here, but he didn't feel like it was going to hurt me physically. His marvelous soul reached out one last time."

"I don't know about that. . . . I just know he's gone," Nani said quietly.

"I am very sad that he's gone, Nani, but he was very sick . . . probably much sicker than we knew. It was his time, and I think he felt that."

Nick heard Nani crying softly. "Be strong, baby. I'll be home tonight. We'll leave as soon as The Bird is repaired."

Both Beth and Betsy felt violated by the theft of the money from the Alaska Permanent Fund. Beth because she had been one of the primary movers in getting the APFC to make the huge investment, and Betsy because of the way she was duped by Reverend Raymond.

Amid the confusion that resulted from the bizarre things that happened in the Brooksher Building Wednesday, Betsy felt sure that Reverend Raymond was responsible for stealing the money from the APFC before he fled. She was somewhat relieved when she received a follow-up call from Richard Cally telling her about the actions of the APFC's operator, but then she believed Reverend Raymond had been working in collusion with him.

A special investigator from the FBI was brought in to work on the Brooksher computer. Working with Theodore, he determined that no large electronic cash transmissions had been received or sent during the period when the money disappeared. It gradually became evident that it was Reverend Raymond's intention to steal the money . . . but that he was outmaneuvered by someone working in the APFC office. Betsy felt an added sense of relief at that news, but she would carry the sting of how gullible she had been in allowing the Reverend to bed her and betray her.

Beth's anguish was in the fact that she had come to the APFC board with the investment opportunity, although she knew she couldn't take the blame for the theft. Investigators on the Alaska end of the electronic theft speculated that Robert had been planning to steal funds from a cash transmission for many months and had stumbled onto the huge transaction between APFC and Brooksher. While there was some speculation that Robert and former governor Stacey Powers were connected, there was no proof. Cell phone records indicated Stacey made periodic calls to many constituents, but there were no calls to a Robert Anderson.

The APFC hired a team of specialists to track their one hundred million dollars down. Because of the anonymity of the transfer and Robert's knowledge of how to circumvent their safeguards, the investigators faced a daunting task. Everyone was aware that every passing day gave Robert additional time to move the funds and bury them deeper in a protected foreign account.

"I'm afraid I doubt that we will ever be able to track your funds down," were the searing words from the head of the investigative team to the APFC Board of Trustees.

As the dust settled, the APFC decided it would not be politically wise to make another attempt to become part of the VING project. After Mary Brunser made a strong appeal to the board in the wake of Zed Smith's compelling presentation to the board, and after a great deal of research and debate, the APFC agreed to fund the construction of a bridge across Cook Inlet to the Matanuska Valley. The investment fit perfectly into the APFC's mandate for infrastructure investment and represented a commitment to Alaska's future by APFC.

In Seattle, Betsy and her management team decided Brooksher Energy would step up to the still-critical need for another one hundred million dollars for the VING project. They received an additional one percent ownership position in the project, and their investment allowed preliminary design work and ground preparation to begin a month after the APFC's electronic funds were stolen.

Sandwiched into Betsy's considerable workload at Brooksher was her devotion to the newly named Del Brooksher Christian School for

Children, which opened the following August.

Nick and Nani spent a month getting through the hard details of dealing with the death of George Jong. In spite of his written wishes for a low-key funeral, Nani arranged a joyous traditional Hawaiian funeral attended by dozens of George's friends. It became obvious to Nick that many of George's friends looked to him to fill the shoes of their kapuna. Nick knew he couldn't. He was neither an American Native nor a spiritual person. He did have a big heart, and he tried to counsel as many of George's friends and family as he could.

As Nick sat on his front patio reading the morning paper a month after George's funeral, a small article on the third page grabbed his attention.

Maui News

July 25, 2007

Alaska Fishing Boat and Bodies Discovered

Authorities in San Carlos, Baja California, reported an unmanned fishing boat was discovered floating in Bahía Magdalena, commonly referred to as Mag Bay, yesterday. The discovery follows three days of early-season storms with hurricane-force winds in the Pacific Ocean on the western side of the Baja Peninsula. The large fishing boat, the E Biz, with a home port identified as Valdez, Alaska, appeared to have been subjected to heavy winds and seas. Papers and personal items found on the fishing boat indicated that at least two people, identified as Rodolfo Alverez and Stacey Powers, were on board.

Two bodies that washed up in a remote area of the jagged coastline north of Mag Bay two days earlier appear likely to be Alverez and Powers. Autopsies on both bodies indicated they died from drowning. The local coroner also stated that the female had severe cancer impacting most of her major organs and would not have lived much longer anyway.

Nick jumped up and ran to get his cell phone. "Beth, listen to this." He read her the article.

"Nick," Beth said, "this is huge. Maybe the papers they found will give us some idea where the money was transferred." Beth was quiet as she added, "Stacey . . . I can't believe it. But, she was dying, Nick. Maybe that's why she did it."

Now Nick spoke in a low tone. "I don't know about that. I . . . I didn't know her . . . as well as you did."

There are some things a sister just knows . . . and Beth knew her brother was not telling her the truth.

"I'll notify Richard Cally. He can have the authorities here contact the authorities down there. Maybe we can find our money. Nice catch, Nick." Using information gathered from the E Biz, the FBI attempted to track down the APFC's one hundred million dollars. The US State Department intervened, and the APFC board was told there was a reasonable chance they would be able to get the fund's money back.

Nick was so excited by the news about the fishing boat, he never finished reading the newspaper. On page seven was an insignificant article about a barely newsworthy happening that wouldn't have meant anything to him anyway.

July 25, 2007
Death of a Mobster
Denver, Colorado. A police department spokesman in Denver announced yesterday that the badly burned body discovered in the remains of a fire that destroyed the Rocky Mountain High Church last week has been identified. Infamous reputed mobster Mario Delaney was identified by dental records. Regular church members were mystified by the death of the man, who had never been seen in the church before. Investigators confirmed that the church was burned by a blatant act of arson, citing the discovery of a five-gallon gas can at the rear of the building's remains.

Beth was relieved at the possibility the APFC's money would be recovered. Nobody was blaming her, but guilt had been eating at her. She was now able to settle into a peaceful, yet busy time of her life. A month after becoming the lieutenant governor of the state, she was getting comfortable in her new job. Her personal life had taken a new turn as well. She finally met a man who had no pretensions and no unhealthy agendas or habits. It helped that he was handsome, hardworking, made her feel safe, and made her feel weak in the knees every time he held her.

Nancy Singletary loved her new job in the Capitol as the lieutenant governor's private secretary.

On a quiet Friday afternoon, a call came into Beth's private line from a caller Nancy recognized.

"Good afternoon. You're in luck. She's not in a meeting. She's winding down from the week. I'll tell her you are holding."

"Madam Lieutenant Governor, you have a special caller on your line."

"Thanks, Nancy. Hello Johnny, how are things out in the woods?"

Johnny laughed. "Well, there are no more bad guys out here. I can come and get you. Carmen is coming out to visit Marty tonight. Maybe we can all get together for a glass of wine."

He that endureth to the end shall be saved . . .
(Plagiarized From the Bible, Matthew 10:22)
—From *Fred Longcoor's Book on Life*

LaVergne, TN USA
04 November 2010
203532LV00001B/2/P